Alex Keegan has worked for the RAF, in direct selling and as a computer consultant. He gave up a sixty-thousand-pound salary to take a degree in psychology and sociobiology. He took up writing seriously after being involved in the Clapham Rail Disaster and now lives in Southampton with his wife and their two young children. A committed runner, he is a UK top-thirty veteran sprinter.

Alex Keegan's previous Caz Flood mysteries, *Cuckoo*, *Vulture* and *Kingfisher*, are also available from Headline.

Razorbill

Alex Keegan

HEADLINE

First published in Great Britain in 1996
by HEADLINE BOOK PUBLISHING

First published in paperback in 1996
by HEADLINE BOOK PUBLISHING

10 9 8 7 6 5 4 3 2 1

ISBN 0 7472 5277 7

Printed and bound in Great Britain by
Cox & Wyman Ltd, Reading, Berks

HEADLINE BOOK PUBLISHING
A division of Hodder Headline PLC
338 Euston Road
London NW1 3BH

For Ray Pearson
fond memories

Author's Note

Much of this book is set at Club la Santa, Tinajo, Lanzarote, a large hotel and sports complex on the north-west side of that island. Over the last few years, I have spent a number of wonderful weeks training there in the company of many friendly people, most, but by no means all of them, sportsmen and women.

La Santa Sport is an important character in the book. It goes without saying that, to my knowledge, there are no murderers roaming the corridors of the hotel and that the place is as safe as any well-run resort can be. I would like to express my thanks to those who gave me their time and knowledge, particularly Kenneth Gasque, Arne Nielsen and Monique Collado, who not only was kind and informative but also gave me a neat plot-idea for a future Caz Flood Mystery.

Young people from all over Europe – but particularly from Denmark, from Germany and from England – spend time at la Santa, running the children's nursery, organising just about every sport under the sun, coaching and just generally being friendly. These, the la Santa 'Green Team' are a grand bunch, sickeningly fit, far, far too good-looking and, most of them far too blonde. The 'Greenies' work hard and play hard. Many of them inspired me to write this book and feature the 'Team' but no individual, none of them features. Any similarity is coincidence, an accident.

Lastly, the bird, *Alimoché*, locally *Guirre* (Neophron Percnopterus), is real, and, on Lanzarote, very, very, rare. There is a single nest in the Fire Mountains but it is kept secret, and, hopefully, free of interference.

Alex Keegan, August 1995

I

I

Caz Flood was pissed off, in pain, bored, still on light duties.

She was sat at her desk – she always said sat and her DI MacInnes would tell her the word was sitting – she was sat at her desk, pushing paper, trying desperately to find a sitting position that didn't ache. She had a headache in the grand-daddy league and was not a happy bunny. The phone rang.

'John Street. DC Flood.'

'CID?'

'Yes, madam.'

Older voice, forty minimum, more like late fifties, educated.

'Razorbill,' the woman said. 'I've been traced. I need to make contact.'

'Razorbill?'

'How old are you, girl?'

'Twenty-eight, why?'

'Get one of your superiors, someone with more experience.'

'If you would just—'

'You're a child! Get me at least a DCI! Is Norman Blackside there?'

There was something in the voice. 'One moment please . . .' Caz picked up another phone. When the desk answered she asked George Brown who was in.

'Just me and you, Caz, coupla PCs in the canteen. It *is* Sunday.'

3

'Tom's off?'

'Tom's off.'

Caz put the phone down and up again, buttoned an outside line, Tom MacInnes' number. One long ring, then a steady echo in emptiness.

She spoke to the woman. 'I'm still trying to get someone. Can I have your name, your number? In case we get cut off . . .'

'I'll ring you. Five minutes.' The line went dead.

Caz decided to ring Norman Blackside. *DCS* Blackside. Just the sort of thing to win a bit of grace and favour, drag out a Detective Chief Superintendent half-way through the Sunday match.

A woman answered, a girl's voice, the politeness of middle years.

'Mrs Blackside. I'm sorry to ring on a Sunday, but . . .'

'It's all right. One moment.'

Caz heard heels clipping on a parquet floor. Sunday, metal on wood. It felt cold.

'Blackside!' Even on the phone he was big.

'DC Flood, sir. Just had a strange phone call.'

'Was?'

'Woman, fifty plus, sir. She asked for you. Said she'd been traced, needed to make contact. Razorbill?'

Caz finished on a query, feeling slightly foolish. The DCS ignored it. 'I'll be twenty minutes. If she rings before I get there, say, "Norman's on his way" – nothing else.'

'Norman's on his way.'

'Just that.'

He put down the phone.

II

Blackside lived out in the Downs. He took twenty-five minutes. He crashed into the nick and went straight to his desk, pausing only to bellow, 'Flood!' down the passage from his office doorway. Caz creaked upright and went to see him.

He was in casual clothes, heavy cord trousers, brown shoes, a check shirt collar lipped outside a thick dark green jumper. He looked like a vet.

'She ring, Flood?'

'Not yet, sir.'

'Take a seat.'

He waved at her then picked up the phone. 'George? Any outside calls come to my office, two-four-oh-one or two-five-forty.' He listened a moment. 'Everything, George.'

With a thick finger he cut the call, glanced at his DC and punched an outside number. Caz looked at the wall, him briefly, the wall again, while he waited for an answer. His tan was fading, enough for Caz to see the red of tension in his cheeks, the extra set in his neck, something maybe major going on. He lifted his hand to slicked black hair but stopped himself, leaving it immaculate. Finally, an answer. He was abrupt, loud. 'Blackside, Brighton.'

He listened, nodded, said OK, put down the phone.

Caz looked up, ready.

'OK, Flood,' he said. 'Tell me again, what did the lady say?'

III

Four weeks, four days now, and Caz still hadn't been running. Not even a gentle jog from Inkerman Terrace and along Brighton front. The consultant had said, 'No specific injury but generalised trauma'. He'd also said that if she ran before he gave her the all-clear, she might end up in a wheelchair. Caz was so frightened that, for the first time in her life, she did what she was told.

Now she was climbing the walls.

'You spoke to the wife?' Blackside said.

Caz sat up.

'She tell you I'm not going to the Yard?'

'No, sir.'

'How's your back now?'

'OK, sir. It aches if I sit around, but otherwise it's fine.'

'The girl you saved, she made a statement, said you knew it was the only thing you could do.'

'I wouldn't do it again, sir.'

'No, Flood?'

'Not without a parachute.'

The phone rang. Blackside picked it up second ring. 'Tom? She's in with me . . . Yeah . . . Razorbill . . . That's right . . . OK. See you in ten.'

He looked at Caz. 'Your DI can't keep away.'

IV

Tom MacInnes lived five minutes from John Street. If he could have lived in the back of the nick he would have moved in tomorrow. But then, where would he put his dark books, his leather furniture, his green-glassed Victorian lamps? When Caz had stopped there, she had felt enclosed and safe, like a child wrapped up, swaddled. She didn't know anyone she liked more.

The phone hadn't rung again. She had watched anxiety build slowly in the DCS, the breathiness in his movements, tightness in his face; but now the muscles were beginning to loosen again. Then in a quiet moment they heard Tom's foot-fall in the corridor, tipper-tapper, tip-tap, a lightweight signal, the direct opposite of his worth.

He rapped the glass once, came in.

'Norman. Caz.'

'Thanks for coming in, Tom.'

Caz made a guess, speaking to Blackside. 'Coffees, sir?'

'Thanks, Flood. Put yours on a separate tray.'

She left. When she got back to her office she rang Sergeant Brown on the front desk. George had never heard of Razorbill, but then, as he said, he'd only been at Brighton eight years.

'You checked the card-index, Flood?'

'Under what?' Caz said. 'R for Razor or B for Bill?'

'Search me,' George said, 'I only work 'ere.'

7

V

Caz went down to the canteen for the drinks, running the woman's phone call through her head again. She'd sounded sharp, on-top, assertive, but there was an edge. She'd asked for *Norman* Blackside. Did she think he was still a DCI? How far back did that take her?

'Three coffees.' *A copper, ex-copper.*

She went back upstairs, still thinking, walking stiffly. Stairs hurt. Near the top she had a shooting pain in her back and she thought of some John Wayne film where he'd had a bullet lodged too close to his spine. When she got to Blackside's office she knocked and went in.

'Coffees, sir.'

She was still thinking. George Brown had been at John Street eight years – 'Razor what, Flood?' – and Blackside was a fairly new DCS. Before that a Super. How long had he been a DCI? When?

'Give us ten, Flood, come back. We'll be going out.'

'Sir?'

'DI MacInnes will stay in the fort. You and me are going out.'

She hesitated. 'Sir . . .' Blackside looked at his wrist, at Tom MacInnes. 'This woman, sir, a copper? Here maybe ten, eleven years ago?'

'First time, Flood. DS, drug squad, 1980. Went to Special Branch.'

8

'She thought you were a DCI, sir.'
'I was a DI. She made a guess and marked me up one.'

VI

Blackside came for Caz fifteen minutes later.

She was standing beside her desk, one long leg stretched out across the desktop, her forehead close to her shin. She was wearing 501s, a white Tee, a pair of Asics cross-trainers. Even though the jeans were baggy-fit, she was finding it hard to stretch properly. She heard the door.

'You all right, Flood?'

She held the stretch. 'Yes, sir. Just trying to loosen up a bit.'

'We're out of here!'

Caz swung her leg to the floor, grabbed her Hard Rock Café jacket off the back of her chair.

'Where to, sir?'

'My car. You c'n drive.'

Caz smiled. She loved communicative men.

VII

Caz was as tall as DI MacInnes and as slim as he was underweight. When she walked alongside him she felt his physical equal. But now, walking with the long-striding DCS Blackside, she felt like a little girl. As they went towards the back stairs she had a sudden image of the first time she'd seen him, striding into a room full of battle-weary bickering detectives and taking absolute control. He'd been nicknamed 'Chisel' and 'Garth' in his day – both caps fitted. Even now at, what, forty, forty-five he was a big, simmering, hormonal bull.

'Her name is Veronica Goddard,' he said over the top of his Scorpio as Caz unlocked the doors, then he ducked away inside. Caz got in. She was adjusting the mirrors and pulling the driving seat forward when he continued. 'We know each other from way back. Tom MacInnes too. And she's not fifty-plus, she's forty-four, same as me.'

Caz was backing out.

'She's had a hard life, Flood. You thought she sounded older, that's because she does. She looks it too, at least she did the last time I saw her.'

Caz straightened up the car, rolled it forward, then waited for the security doors to roll up and away. As they did, bright yellow light wedged down the ramp straight into their faces. Blinded, Caz eased out into Williams Street.

'She was a good copper, Flood, ambitious, like you. A good

11

thief-taker. Uniform, CID, then on to region same time as me. After that she joined the drug squad. They still had a separate unit then. Went undercover three-four times, ended up moving up to Special Branch and a few other things.'

'A few other things?'

'Drive down towards the Aquarium, go left, up along the cliff road.'

'I wasn't prying, sir.'

'No one said you were, Flood. Drive towards Roedean.'

There was about a minute's silence, the smooth car's hum, the faint *furrr* of the tyres on the road. Blackside seemed to be thinking. Then he spoke.

'Ireland, animal rights activists, cruise missile protests, drug stings – you do so much, Flood, then you get out. But not Veronica. Not Von. Von liked it. In and out of different roles, she should've been an actress. She didn't get promoted because she was too good out there. She *liked* it on the edge. She liked being other people.'

'It went wrong?'

'It went wrong. You ever been undercover, Flood?'

'A couple of little things, sir. Nothing much.'

'You know then. You have to *be* your role, nothing less. The places Von went it was even more so. She lived almost all the time as other people, under all sorts of stresses. It fucked up her relationships; in the end it fucked up *her*.' He paused, remembering. 'But she had to keep doing it. As soon as she was brought out, she would ask to go back in again. Finally, she lost control of who she was. She'd put so much into sublimating herself that her old assumed personalities were stronger than her real one and they started popping out.'

'She went native?'

'No. If she was on a job, she'd do it, come out. If she took on a new identity it was strong enough to take over. It was when she was out that the problems started. Her other personalities were stronger than the original. She had to be hospitalised. But for Thatcher's "Care in the Community" she'd be inside now.'

They were at Roedean. Blackside told Caz to turn off the road and go up to the old school. The DC's head was ringing. She had been trying to work out exactly why she was out with the DCS and why he had bothered to tell her about Veronica Goddard. She was desperate to ask but was still overawed by the man. Finally she made it, went to speak, but as they bounced through the gates all that came out was a timid, 'Sir . . .?'

Blackside must have been waiting. He cut in sharply. 'To see Von's sister,' he said, pre-empting question one. 'And you being out with me was Tom MacInnes' idea. He said you felt things. Said you ought to meet Veronica.'

She drove up to the main house, thinking of the British Empire, privilege, money . . . 'Nice place; great view,' she grunted, only half sarcastically – the view *was* great. Then she said, 'I think maybe I should send my daughters here.'

Blackside pointed past her face. 'The office is over there.'

Veronica's sister was marking term papers and came crisply through to a waiting room after a phone call from the school office. She was dressed by cliché in tweeds and sensible shoes, and her dark hair was pulled back tightly from a long, politely smiling face. A hand drooped from her offered arm.

'Superintendent? I am Verity Stallwood. Is it Von?'

Blackside had stood up. His handshake was little more than a touch. 'Mrs Stallwood.'

The teacher dropped her hand, clicked her eyes from the DCS to Caz and back again. There was a flicker of concern there. 'Has something happened to Von?'

'We need to speak to her,' Blackside said, 'but we have no reason—'

'She hasn't contacted me.'

13

'But if she does . . .?'

'I will ring you straight away.'

'That's all we ask, Mrs Stallwood.'

'And if she comes here, I'll persuade her to stay.'

Blackside smiled, exchanged wet rags with the teacher and turned to leave the room. The interview had been so brief and so seemingly pointless that Caz had been caught off guard. She executed a little nod and a tiny dip of the knees, which, if she hadn't stopped herself, might have approached a curtsy. She scurried out after the DCS. She had no idea where the deferent gesture had come from. All she knew was that she felt like a complete prat. She decided it was something from school, some sort of long-submerged conditioning, a Pavlovian response to the tweed suit and the bunned hair.

Outside, Blackside said, 'Well?'

'Well what, sir?'

'Verity Stallwood, telling the truth?'

'She didn't sound like she was lying, sir.'

'That's what I thought.'

VIII

They got into Blackside's Scorpio. Caz went to start up. Her
back was hurting but she tried to sound bright. 'Where to, sir?'

'Nowhere.'

Caz waited.

'I'm thinking, Flood.'

She took her hand away from the ignition and sat back.

'Sorry, sir.'

The keys hung, swung, the faintest tick, metal and plastic.

Blackside had raised his fists in front of his face and he
brought them together slowly, as if he was demonstrating a
slow hand-clap. Then he rested his square jaw on his fingers,
still thinking. Under his breath, he muttered something that to
Caz sounded like, 'Fuck!' Then, after a deep breath, he said
clearly, 'OK, Flood, start her up.'

They came out of the school's grounds, and the DCS told
Caz to swing the car left, away from Brighton and towards
Newhaven. Caz glanced to their right. Beyond the hidden
drop of the white cliffs was a filthy sea. It looked almost men-
acing. Caz grunted. It matched her mood.

They skirted Saltdean and came out on the little bit of open
road just before Telscombe Cliffs. The DCS seemed to be
looking for something.

Then he said, 'Next left.'

Caz slowed to turn into a small Wimpey-style estate.

'Not *there*, Flood!' Blackside snapped. 'The *main* road, fer fuck's sake!'

Caz bit her tongue, 'Sorry, sir.'

'We're heading for Butlock's Down.'

'Oh, right!' Caz said.

'And I should've said, Flood. Not your fault.'

They were heading in the general direction of the Sussex Downs now. The roads were up and down but generally climbing, the houses bog-standard dormitories for citizens and commuters. Caz felt depressed. At night, here, people slept but only the kids dreamed.

'Verity Stallwood's got a place out here, edge've the Downs.'

'Sorry, sir?'

'Mrs Stallwood. She lives out here.'

'But . . .'

'We were just passing.'

'Of course, sir. So there's a Mister Stallwood, sir?'

'Whatever gave you that idea, Flood? No. Verity never married.'

'So why, if Mrs Stallwood . . .'

'Why not?' Blackside said. Then he pointed. 'It's that bungalow.'

Caz turned off the road on to a gravelled path, sprinkled with the green of weeds, a couple of potholes filled with dark water. They had spun through a gap that once upon a time would have contained a six-bar gate, but all that remained now were two rotting gate-posts and a sense of something missing.

'Great decor!' Caz said, almost to herself.

'It was Von's,' Blackside said. There was an ache in his voice. 'When she went off-cock, so did the house. It's in Verity's name now, but she spends most of her time at the school.'

'So we're here why, exactly?'

'To let Von know we care,' Blackside said.

16

IX

Caz sat in frustration as well as pain while the DCS got out of the car, walked to the house, then round it, peering through windows. Blackside had already asked her to keep her head down. He'd told her, 'Von knows me, Flood. I'm OK.' But Von *didn't* know Caz and Blackside didn't want to risk spooking her.

Caz watched as he went round one side of the house, stepping in mud and then looking distastefully down as if he'd trodden in something nasty. As soon as he had disappeared, she opened the car door and rolled out. She just *had* to work through some relieving stretches. As she got out she camped it, nervously overplaying her need to stretch – not because she was disobeying Blackside's instructions, but because there was that small chance she was being watched. The DCS was somewhere round the back playing burglars. She was twisting her spine, stretching her hams and the muscles in her back. She twitched with pain and thought that maybe it was time for a holiday.

'Flood!'

She heard him shout, no urgency in it. She stretched another inch.

'Flood!'

As she came upright, she heard the crash, furniture, a body, glass breaking.

17

She waited five more seconds.
'*Flood!*'
This time she went. Running.

X

Caz rounded the bungalow, slowing, faintly limping, her right leg suddenly refusing to bend as much as her left. She was following Blackside's huge shoe-prints in the dark soil between the weeds. There was another crash, china. Shit!

As she reached the back of the house she stopped, a flash of common sense arriving at the same time as the pain that ran down the outside of her leg. Blackside was twice her size. If he was in trouble, what the fuck was she supposed to do? And her leg hurt. 'I've radioed for back-up, sir!' she shouted. 'Three cars, couple've minutes, sir!' She thought she heard a groan.

There was a metal dustbin near the back door and the mark of Blackside's size twelves on the silver lid and on the window-sill just above. The casement swung open, broken wood, slightly rotten, splinters.

'That you, Flood?'

The DCS sounded odd.

'Yes, sir!'

'Get in here!'

Caz clambered up on to the bin and looked into the room. 'Sir?'

'I'm down here, Flood.'

She looked down, paused.

'Well, don't just perch there like a fuckin' parrot, Flood! This thing weighs a bleedin' ton!'

Caz climbed in and down, crunching on glass and china like a detective following up on a pub brawl. She could still only see half of Blackside, his upper left shoulder and arm, most of his left leg. The rest of him was beneath a huge dark dresser. There was glass everywhere. Caz couldn't see any blood.

'You OK, sir?'

'What do *you* think, Flood?'

'What happened?'

'I'm gonna fucking *chat*, Flood?'

'Sorry, sir.'

'You're going to need something long 'n' strong.'

'Sir?'

'To take some of this weight, get me out.'

'You want me to radio in, sir?'

'No, Flood! Just get something to shift this.'

'Yessir. Back as quick as I can.'

Caz stood up. Blackside grunted, 'Try the kitchen way.'

She crunched across the room. The DCS was groaning and muttering. The words were muted but the gist was something like, 'Jesus! If this gets out . . .'

The handle to the bedroom door was old, old-fashioned, circular, with ribs the full circle of the dark brown knob, the door itself painted with the oily mix of browns once fashionable that created an illusion of wood-grain. Caz escaped into a linoed hallway, no more glass.

She went through the door on her right into a simple kitchen, light blue and faded white, the original cupboards, enamels. To one side was a formica-topped table, a china bread bin at its centre, a large bread-knife by its side. Almost automatically, Caz picked up the knife. She hadn't checked the house, but she wasn't about to leave a weapon behind her back.

She unlatched the rear door and stepped out into the garden.

XI

Caz found a garden shed, spades, garden forks, watering cans, rope, wire fencing in a roll. Briefly she considered the strongest spade, but no way was it going to be strong enough. Maybe two together might just do it.

She came out into the day with the two spades, stepped under the clothes line, stopped, looked. The line drooped from the house to a tall steel pole thirty feet away. The pole drooped too. It looked like once upon a time it had been upright, but lately . . .

It took Caz nearly five minutes to get the pole loose, using the spades to start with, then moving the pole backwards and forwards to loosen it. By the time she had freed it, with a final *kkrrummmpp!* of earth, she saw it was about twelve feet long. She had the sudden worry that maybe she wouldn't be able to get it into the room. Then she thought, the window . . .

The pole was long, awkward and heavy, and it hurt Caz's back. *Everything* hurt her back. She tottered towards the house like a trainee wire-walker with lousy gear, shouting a warning to the DCS, then crashing its full weight through the open window. There were vague sounds from within as she shuffled the steel inside, then she shouted, 'Thirty seconds!' before she scampered back towards the kitchen.

'Christ that thing's fucking heavy!' she said as she came back into the room.

'It should be,' a woman's voice said. 'It was made to last.'

XII

Veronica Goddard smiled as Caz walked in, but it was a smile with just the lips, cold, cruel, the kind of smile you might make before you pull a trigger, throw the switch on an electric chair. 'Come just inside the door,' she said.

Caz couldn't think of a good reason not to do as the woman asked but the good reason *to* do it was the fat gun pointed in her general direction.

'You're Von?' she said stupidly as she walked in.

'Sit down,' the woman said.

'I was ... trying to explain ...' Blackside said from the floor. Von's gun clicked towards his voice. 'I've been telling Von that you work with Tom at John Street.'

'I haven't decided who *you* are yet!' the woman said.

'Von?'

'Quiet, man!'

Caz sat down.

'Jesus!' Blackside hissed. His head dropped to the carpet.

The woman waved the gun at Caz. 'Name?'

'DC Kathryn Flood. People call me Caz.'

'What are you doing here?'

'I'm with my DCS, under the furniture there. It was me you spoke to this morning. You called yourself Razorbill and you told me I was a child. You asked me to get hold of DCS

23

Blackside. DI MacInnes is at John Street now, in case you call in.'

'But why are you *here*?'

'That was the DCS's idea. He thought you might have come here. He wants to help, Von.'

'Why do you keep calling me Von?'

'You and Norman go back a long way, Tom MacInnes too.' She paused. 'And you and Norman had a thing going once.'

Blackside groaned, 'Oh, fer fuck's sake, Flood!' But there was a flicker of recognition in Von's face.

Caz went for it, shit or bust.

'And I think if we don't get Norman out from underneath that cupboard pretty soon, he's going to suffocate.'

Veronica's eyes flashed. 'Sit still, girl!'

Caz got up. She was scared, but not *that* scared.

'I'd like to, Von, I'd like to, but if I do, my DCS is going to get very poorly or maybe even dead. You shoot me, he's not going to be any worse off, but if I get him out from under there, he owes me.'

She moved slowly towards the pole.

'Now, where're you gonna stand?'

XIII

Veronica Goddard moved to the window. Caz moved to the pole and grabbed it. She was maybe five feet from the gun.

'Look, I'm gonna put one end of this under the furniture, OK? Try to take some of the weight, so the DCS can wriggle out.'

She did not like the switched-off look in Veronica Goddard's eyes.

'I won't do anything too quick, OK? So you shouldn't have to shoot me.'

'Just do it,' Von said.

It was awkward, wielding a fifty-pound, twelve-foot pole in a confined space, trying not to take off Blackside's head, trying to get one end underneath the dresser in such a way that Caz could get under the other end and apply some upward force, and, incidentally, trying *not* to get blown away by Citizen X. When Caz realised that to manage it she was going to have to step into the hallway, she gestured and did so without waiting for Goddard's nod. She had the vague awareness of pleasure, as if getting really close to being dead was somehow a good thing. Then she was in position.

'OK, sir? I'll grunt, you push, right?'

Blackside nodded.

'And go!' Caz said. She pushed, her back against the pole, her feet against a wall. She felt the weight, then the pain, then movement. Then she heard Blackside's 'Yes!' and there was more weight. Then the world went black. She didn't hear a shot or feel any pain but the world went black anyway, a circle closing over her.

It was nice.

II

One

MacInnes was adamant. 'I am not *giving* you the fucking choice. What is the fucking *matter* with you, you *want* to be a cripple?'

'No.'

'Then go *away*, Caz, take the leave. Jesus! What would *I* give for four weeks off.'

'It's *five* weeks . . .'

'Send me a fuckin' postcard.'

Caz hadn't felt any pain for two weeks. Not a tweak, not a twinge, not even a repeat of the deadness or the pins and needles in her right leg. The blackout had been a one-off, a combination of things: stress, the bad back, trying too hard. She was *better*, for Christ's sake! She opened her mouth to speak again, but Tom MacInnes raised his menu as if he was about to hit her.

'Enough! Don't even *think* about it, lass!'

'Grilled turbot,' she said.

He softened. 'An' one o' they *Il Grigios*?'

'Aye,' she said.

Armando's gorgeous grandson stood by, looking at the wall and sweetly deaf. MacInnes managed a wee smile as he touched his arm.

'OK, we're ready. We'll have two turbots ay summa that garlic bread.'

'And to drink, sir?'

'Gissa coupla Bells an' young Flood here's Chianti.'

'Thank you, sir.'

'Nay lad, thank yew fer waitin'. An' Ah'm sorry about the lassie.'

The waiter winked at Caz as, nearby someone coughed and waved an arm.

'*Uno momento, signor,*' he said quietly, nodding at the other table, then to Caz, handsomely, 'Armando has already opened your bottle, miss, and it's on the house. It's really good to have you back.'

Caz smiled, a little twinkle in her eye. Sexy bastard.

'He's coming out later?'

'Sure.'

'I'll thank him then.'

Anton smiled politely. 'I'm sure he will look forward to it.' Then he nodded again and strode to the kitchens, ignoring the other table.

'God!' Caz said. 'I *love* this place!'

The restaurant was lover-dark, friends-lively, rich and noisy, laced with garlic and mediterranean shouts. The *Il Grigio* was murderously easy to slide down and the fish was white-fleshed, fluffing from the fork.

At some point Caz had finally given in, even under her breath. Now the prospect of thirty-six days of Canaries sunshine, softened by that famous Lanzarote breeze, lifted her spirits. That, the Chianti, and the company of Tom MacInnes. She raised her glass.

'To you, boss!'

'An' you, Flood!'

'And old Norman Tallboy, Veronica Goddard!'

'To Von,' MacInnes said. 'T''keeping your head.'

Two

That was Tuesday. This was Thursday. And Moira Dibben had called round to Caz's flat to grab the suitcases and ferry her mate to Gatwick Airport. She bounced in, brown and happy, dark eyes shining bright.

Caz was immediately annoyed. 'You're supposed to be sick, Dibben!'

'Sick that me mate's got five weeks away? Right in one, Flood!'

'I mean sick as in morning-sick, as in the smell of bacon makes you throw up.'

'Not me, Caz. The Dibbens were made for motherhood.'

'How 'bout Billy Tingle?'

'Hips're too narrow.'

'How's he contemplating *father*hood?'

'Great!' Moira said. 'He's just frustrated he can't tell his mates, yet.'

'Keep it that way, Mo. You know the force. Tell 'em you've missed a period and they put you in the back office. You don't want that.'

'Billy wouldn't mind.'

'Billy's not having the baby!'

'But he's the daddy.'

'You had a blood test?'

'Very funny, Flood.'

Caz sat in the passenger seat of Moira's Fiesta as her friend drove and talked. Mo was managing to maintain an almost perfect monologue, countered by only the occasional 'uh-huh' thrown in from Caz – a steady stream of absurdly optimistic career and family moves for the Dibben-Tingles.

Caz was daydreaming. *That was then and this is now* – letting her mental control go as Moira's Ford thrummed away from the coast. She was thinking about Valerie, on paper still her fella, thinking that he'd been in the States two days now, trying out a month of a new job. Then she thought, Moira Tingle? Billy Dibben? Timothy Tingle-Dibben? If Mo did call the boy that he was doomed, *doomed*!

Moira's voice broke in. 'So what *will* you do, Caz?'

'What?'

'If Valerie takes the job over there?'

'Write once a month.'

'You wouldn't go out there?'

'Mo? This is DC Caz Flood you're talking to. I'm a copper. I'm not following some bloke half-way round the world just because I love him.'

'But you do?'

'What?'

'Love Val.'

'Yes.'

'But not enough?'

'Bollocks *enough*, Mo. What's enough? Does Valerie love me *enough* to stay here? Does he love me *enough* to take the shit hours, the let-downs, the broken dates? D'you think he cares enough *not* to have kids? D'you think he loves me enough to deal with the fear?'

'He loved you enough to ask you to marry him.'

'And I didn't say yes. Why d'you think that means love?'

'You're a sick woman, Caz.'

'I'm a good copper. Committed.'

'Same difference,' Moira said.

Caz thought about Veronica Goddard. She'd been committed too. She'd surfed the danger, and what did it get her in the end? A place in a little hospital in Surrey run by smiling Open University types with round glasses, their white coats discreetly hung behind their office door. Von had been committed and now she *was* committed, sectioned, forcibly tidied away until the drugs worked.

And she went back a long way with Norman Blackside, *loved* Norman Blackside. Had she loved him? Had he loved her?

'Next exit, Mo.'

Or had it been a major sex thing, two coppers on the razz, a couple of plain-clothes taking them off?

'Here?'

'Here!'

No, Blackside had *cared*. Even when he was stuck underneath that lump of furniture he cared. Maybe that was why the wife had never been happy. A touch of jealousy.

Police marriages? They were made in hell!

Three

The last three time Caz had been at Gatwick it was for Valerie – twice seeing him leave her, once seeing him come back. This time she was going somewhere, not leaving, just going somewhere.

She knew all about Club la Santa, Lanzarote. What runner didn't? Every shit Brighton winter she had promised herself that she would go over and spend a fortnight there, getting fit with the sun on her back. Totton Running Club did it, Worthing Runners did it, swimmers did it, cyclists did it, every bloody British athlete except Caz did it. But she was going to, every year she was going to . . .

Linford Christie sharpened up there, Colin Jackson, Mick Hill, Steve Backley. Carl Lewis had run there, boxers boxed there, Heike Dressler regularly long-jumped over twenty-something feet there. But Caz had never been there. Never made it – not quite fast enough to go for free, not quite famous enough to be name-dropped. Till now.

Her letter had been something else and she had wheeled a deal that any market trader would have been proud of. Yes, her letter had said, she had run for England (at seventeen, true, but a vest is a vest) and yes, she was famous (she sent photocopies of her *Sun* cuttings). She would need to be there for five weeks. Could they do anything about cost? She would let the papers know where she was going . . .

34

The letter back from Christian Grøn had been as dry as hers had been slick, but yes, for the price of two weeks she could stay five. Not in a lux apartment mind you, but they looked forward to meeting 'The Girl Who Saved Brighton', and he told her, 'You say my name is Green.'

Considering that she'd got a lump sum from the Police Convalescent Fund (she wasn't saying how much), and considering that she still had the dregs of some insurance money, Caz was peseta-rich, tempted even to pay for an upgrade to some real luxury. But then she stopped herself. She had heard that visiting athletes were so tired at the ends of their days of excess that they didn't *care* where they slept. That the Pool Bar, the Green Bar, and then the late disco just about finished off everyone. If what she'd heard was true, the basic accommodation was a shock day one, OK day two, and brilliant for the rest of the stay. And for sixty per cent off, well . . .

'Caz Flood? Not going to Lanzarote are we?'

She looked up. A man with long red hair carrying a stone and a half, sprinters thighs under Lycra tights.

'Small world!' the man said. 'How are you? Where you off?'

'Ron Jones, right? Totton 10K?'

'This is Debbie, the Missus, going to la Santa for the aerobics week.'

Caz nodded at a slim big-shouldered woman, dark hair, then back to him. 'And you?'

'Oh, yeah,' Ron said, 'I'm going, you couldn't keep me away. With a bit of luck I'll get some sprint training in – not that I'm all that quick at the moment.' He squeezed a roll of fat from his waist. 'Too much mixing it, I think – marathons, soccer and sprinting. I've been out injured for six months. Gammy knee.'

'Tell me about it,' Caz said.

'You injured then?'

'Not exactly.'

Jones sat down, grinning, still talking. 'The physiotherapists at la Santa are brilliant, a German girl and a Danish, both very good.'

His wife smiled politely at Caz. Her smile was the kind someone uses to excuse a simpleton. Caz smiled back, waving at the spare chairs. She sat down too. Caz didn't mind the guy too much, or his family, the two kids asleep in a double buggy next to Debbie. Ron Jones was a runner, from what Caz could remember, a serious veteran sprinter – and the Totton 10K was a well-put-together race. She could do a lot worse; forty yards away from them were three guys with Manchester United shirts spread over their obligatory pot-bellies. They were drinking Stella Artois straight from the bottle. Two of them were smokers. For sure, she could do a lot worse.

'I'm there for five weeks,' she said lightly. 'Winter training.'

'Five *weeks*!' Debbie said, faintly embarrassed as if the thought had slipped out. When she said, 'I wish!' her voice was already trailing off.

'I know,' said Caz wearily. 'It's tough at the top.'

Debbie nodded at the two children. One was stirring and there was a distinct smell of something rotten in the state of Denmark.

'If you want tough,' she said, looking straight at Caz and undoing the smelly one on autopilot, 'try a couple of kids.'

Caz couldn't help but wrinkle her nose. 'Is that what I think it is?'

'I'm afraid so,' Debbie said heavily. Then she turned to her husband. 'Whose turn?'

'Yours, I reckon.'

'Now, why did I know that before I asked?' she said.

Jones smiled. 'Because you're so clever, darling.'

Debbie stood up, a lump of a lad in her arms. She said she was going to the loos. Ron was too interested in Caz. She spoke louder. 'And keep an eye on Bridie, yes?'

Four

Deborah Jones was away for maybe six, seven minutes, the time it took for Ron Jones to run through his list of running questions at a hundred miles an hour and then to be sent away to the bar for a round of coffees. Sending him away had been the lesser of two evils for Caz, since, while he was gone and until Deborah came back, she would be left holding the baby. Caz would be bloody *responsible*, for God's sake, if a fingertip-distanced half-eye on a sleeping buggy was responsible.

Ron was still at the bar when Caz was relieved. She tried her best to look casual, but when she saw the long-striding figure of Deborah zig-zagging towards her through the suitcased minefield of the lounge, her face lit up. She tried hard to make the smile say 'Hi!' but Debbie must have seen an expression not too different from one of those seen peeking over the ramparts of Mafeking. For God's *sake*, Caz had been left alone with Bridie for *three* minutes! What if she had woken *up*?

As Debbie sat down she said, 'Prozac.'

The stress must have been a bit too much for Caz. She said, 'What?'

'Prozac,' Debbie said. 'Ron's on Prozac. For depression. Makes him a bit over the top, too happy almost.'

'Ron Jones depressed?'

'Since the accident – last year – his brother.'

'I'm not with you . . .' Caz said.

37

'Colin Jones . . .'

Caz clicked. 'Colin Jones was Ron's brother?'

Debbie nodded. 'I was five months pregnant with Bridie, this time last year. We took the club over to la Santa as usual. Colin lived in London but we got him to come to make up the numbers.'

Caz vaguely remembered.

'He was a runner, but skinny, not at all like Ron. He wasn't with a club but he was quite quick. He'd had some calf injury, I think, and for a while he was going to cry off the holiday, but Ron persuaded him to come. He said that Colin could get in lots of swimming and get some physio on the leg.'

British Tourist Drowns in Lanzarote.

'He was loving it, he really was, swimming every day and getting treatment. We used to joke about how he must fancy Ina.'

'Ina?'

'The Physio.'

Londoner Colin Jones drowned today when swimming off rocks near the village of Famara, Lanzarote. Mr Jones was a very strong swimmer but ocean currents in this area are known to be treacherous. The local tourist board stressed once again that swimming is quite safe in the sea off the designated beaches. Mr Jones was single.

'He was getting better too. The physio was really working. Then one day he went off for a swim in the sea, that was it. There's a fifty metre pool at la Santa Sport but Colin must've fancied being on his own. They think the undertow got him. Every year on Lanzarote there's a few, different places, blokes who think they're indestructible.'

'I'm really sorry.'

'Oh, it's OK. I just think some people, it's meant to happen. I never saw Colin as an old man somehow.'

'And it hit Ron hard?'

'Like a ton of bricks. It was the last but one day of the holiday. We had to come back to England before they'd found him. The worst bit was that Colin just went off and didn't tell anyone. It was half a day before anyone realised. By then it was too late.'

'But they found the body?'

'Months later. There are all sorts of currents apparently, and underwater caves. Sometimes they come up, sometimes they don't.'

'It must've been awful,' Caz said.

'Yes,' Debbie said. Then she ducked her head. 'Ron's coming back.'

Five

The flight to Arrecife might have been called uneventful except that, in her haste to distance herself from the screaming kids at the front of the aircraft and the smokers trying to recreate Bhopal at the back, Caz ended up in the middle of three seats just behind the engines, no window and no quick exit to the loos.

'You folla football, then?' the Man U guy said.

'I'm a Methodist,' Caz said, grinding her teeth.

The old woman sitting next to her smiled. 'My child, how lovely! And when did you find Jesus?'

The Monarch flight was ready on time – a pleasant shock – and would have been away on time too, if a family called Yonoff hadn't decided to spend an extra twenty minutes in duty-free. But Caz could live with that. She could live with being ten minutes late. She could cope with trainee estate agent Jason, from Basildon, his replays of every Eric Cantona goal. She could cope, even, with Miss Hatpin-Blenkinsop and the pictures of her cats. But when she realised the film was *The Piano* she was ready to scream. Three double Bells later she thought it was quite good, actually. She was watching without earphones and had even got used to Jason letting slip surreptitious farts. Orphans, she called them, whispering in his ear, no pop.

Jason wasn't embarrassed, not even slightly. Caz's body-

40

language, leaning ever-so-slightly away from the cats, the New Testament, meant that she was leaning just as ever-so-slightly towards her Essex hero. He thought he was in.

'So, like, when we get there, Lanzarote, where'r'you stoppin'?'

'Where are *you* stopping?' Caz said sweetly.

'Playa Blanca. Me an' the lads've got an apartment.'

Oh thank you, God.

'Oh, I'm miles away. Over the other side of the island.'

'The other side? There's fuck all there!'

That's why I'm going, Jason . . .

'It's all Lanza-grotty, but the other side, that's all volcanoes and shit.'

'And Club la Santa.'

'What's that then?'

'A sports resort.'

'What d'you wanna go there for?'

'To get fit,' Caz said, then she added, 'To be thin.'

'You c'n do aerobics an' that at Playa Blanca.'

'But I want to get away from it all.' *From people like you . . .*

Jason raised his eyebrows. 'Oh yeah, boyfriend trouble, is it?'

'Hardly,' Caz said.

'So what then?'

'I'm in training.'

'Woffor?'

Now, God. Now I need inspiration.

'It's a bit delicate . . .'

'What is?'

She whispered, 'My training . . .'

He whispered back, slightly perplexed, Stella, peanuts, red wine, 'What kind've – what kind've training?'

Caz tried to look conspiratorial. She leaned a little closer. ''S'fer the Gay Olympics. I'm a synchronized swimmer,

41

practising a secret routine, very hush-hush.' She put a finger to her lips. ''S'where I met Irma. The shot-putter.'

'Shot-putter?'

'But she's doing Karate now.'

Jason burped. 'Karate? Where'd she learn that?'

Caz mumbled something about Holloway, three months.

'Prison!'

'There was this fight . . . this bloke, stitches . . .'

'What over?' Jason said.

Caz tried to look worried. 'The fight? Oh, nothing.'

'Had to be over something.'

'It was nothing. Really.'

'Must've been *something*.'

Caz sighed, glanced furtively. Then she gave a tiny confessional nod.

'Jealous. Irma's a bit jealous.'

'Oh,' Jason said.

'But she's all right now. You could come over, say hello, what d'you reckon? Hire a car and drive across, your mates too. We could go for a run or something.'

'Or something,' Jason said. Then he folded back his table and got up, suddenly discovering an urgent need to pee.

Six

Caz had heard the island called Lanza-grotty, heard talk of a barren nothing-land, of white apartment high-rises, of dusty dead-end roads, beaches of black sand, English pubs, chip shops, trainee estate agents . . .

And when she had creaked undone from the charter jet, queued with the shell-suits for her scratched cases, smiled a goodbye to a relieved Jason and mumbled with the rest past passport control, she thought, so far, my worst dreams. And when a gaggle of tight-eyed mascaraed blondes in various jackets, Cosmos, Intasun, the rest, waved clip-boards at the crowds just inside arrivals, she groaned, pretending it was the weight of her luggage. And when a tall, crisply sexless, green-and-white-shorted Scandinavian woman smiled like a Colgate poster, waved *her* clip-board at the Joneses, she was ready to cringe.

'La Santa? La Santa Sport. There is five of you?'

Ron Jones said, 'Four Joneses.'

'And Kathy Flood? Do I have you, The Girl Who—'

Caz cut in sharply: 'That's me. Is there a bus or something?'

'There is a bus. It is waited. I am Helga, your Green Team guide.'

Caz followed the back of Ron Jones' head, not speaking but thinking, 'Helga? No way! That's a Greenie? Hey, Jones, you never told me they *smiled* so much!'

Outside, eighty degrees and no breeze hit them, the dust, coaches revving, diesel fumes. And how long was this trip, thirty minutes? Caz could see herself on *Watchdog*, already, Ann Robinson reading out her letter and nodding, '*And yet the brochure said . . .*'

The mini-bus pulled away, gear-crunching out of the airport onto a slip-road and grinding through an area of cement-block buildings and gaudy signs, *Supermercado! Vino-Low-Price! Video Slots! Fun!* Caz stared out at it, down-town Mexico, shuddering, wondering just how much it would hurt if she slashed her wrists right now. Outside was roughly Sunset Strip meets Runcorn, with a dash of Soweto. She groaned again as the bus turned a corner and began to labour uphill. This was the moment that Bridie Jones picked to start to cry and even Ron Jones went quiet, presumably running low on Prozac. All he managed before putting his head back was, 'It gets better, Caz.' Then Bridie shut up suddenly, suckered on to Debbie and Caz sighed, resigning herself to her fate.

Five minutes later, Ron must've popped another one because he was manic again. 'Hey, Caz!' he said. 'Take a look. Better or what?'

They were passing through a village, everything white, shut-tered windows all green, those of the odd house brown. Walls were decked with flowers, cacti, people in dark clothes kicking their heels, talking softly. An old man stood at a junction with a grey old donkey sorry enough to be Eeyore.

'If you like that sort of thing, this place is beautiful,' Jones was saying. 'Tao and Tinajo, they're slower. La Santa village is slower still. Everything's white with green windows, a few people get away with brown or blue but the walls are always white.'

'It's not boring?'

'You get used to it. Some artist-architect guy pledged to keep the island's character. Ninety-five per cent of it is as far away as you can get from the Costas. Forget Arrecife. Get yourself a bike and go out. Try Haria, Teguise. There's something about the quiet, the islanders.'

'It's all so dry, so hard, these people . . .' Caz said.

'They're tough,' Ron said.

Caz's mood was low. She thought of Valerie in Florida. Where she was staring out at a dry landscape, dirt, simple white houses, he would be – what, it would be eleven o'clock over there – he would be sitting in some tall office block, stainless steel, glass, music in the lifts. She wondered, torturing herself, if the contrast wasn't symbolic of them. They wanted such different things.

She saw a high ridge, way off to their right, prickled with tall modern windmills, more dusty roadsides, a garage, then, at a cross-roads, an odd modern sculpture, off-white. She dozed, drifted, her eyes open but unseeing, the back of the driver's head tight curls of dark brown hair.

Something ached; physical, mental. She felt suddenly older.

After Tao – more white, more green shutters, black gritty farms, circular walls, the long road – they approached Tinajo, then a final turn and they were sweeping down a hill with a sudden view of the sea to the left and to the front. In the distance, like a cream sea-wall, a speckled mass of buildings.

Ron Jones leaned forward.

'La Santa!'

Seven

She woke next day about seven. For her that was oversleeping in a big way. She lay back, stretching slowly, putting last night back together in her head.

It was about five by the time she'd got her keys, half-past when she'd finally worked out where her room was. Practical as ever, she put off her bath until she had unpacked, did that, then ran herself a deep one and got in. The water, a peculiar brown tint, was soft. She drank a diet Coke and wallowed. She thought of Colin Jones.

She found a pizza place on the campus, went in, sat alone with a bottle of Faustino VII, some garlic bread. When the waiter came back she ordered a ham and mushroom pizza and, in that peculiar sad separateness of eating alone in public, she watched those around her, feeling that every one of them had something she did not.

The first thing she noticed was the men – not sexually, professionally – men who were lithe, with muscle-defined shoulders and eyes with steel in them, confidence, fleshless hands.

Then, even the slim more fleshy because of their sex, the women, their eyes not so fired up but sure, directed, just as confident. So that was the runners. She wondered what the swimmers would look like.

She had finished her pizza, not eating, simply putting bites of food between half-glasses of wine. When the bottle had gone, she toyed with the idea of a second but stopped herself and took a half. This was not a good way to get drunk and she knew it. She was getting lower and lower in the water, and for the life of her she wasn't really sure why.

Was it Valerie? Was it being away from the job five weeks, worry about Tom, that vague, nagging sensation that Moira was making a big mistake? Or was it being injured, being unfit, being aware for the first time in twenty-eight years that her body could let her down? She had no idea, but when she saw faces at a far table that she knew, faces that would light up with recognition when they saw her, would wave her over, gesture, make room for her, she got up quickly, left enough to cover her bill and left.

Her room was bare: simple, red tiles, white walls, a mirror, a poster for the Lanzarote Ironman. She had stripped off, achingly numb, and climbed into fresh sheets, a feeling that still affected her. She was dead tired, dead drunk. And, for the first time in her life, she couldn't sleep.

She slipped out at seven-thirty in the morning, wearing lilac shorts, lilac singlet, Nike ankle socks and white Asics trainers. She'd skipped make-up in favour of some factor eight, and her blonde hair was pulled back and up in a high tight pony tail that would bounce as she ran. The early-morning cold surprised her and she ducked back in to grab a top, more Asics, a light blue jacket with a mesh inside.

She thought about doctors, about Valerie, a man called Avocado, one called Boxx. She thought about how much she cared for Tom MacInnes and she thought briefly about her dad. Outside she could see sun, the sea, sniff ozone. She walked, thought. She thought about Von Goddard, her own decision to ignore her threats and help Norman Blackside, her decision to ignore the real possibility of dying. Then she realised, she had not ignored the threat, she'd welcomed it.

And she thought how the specialist had said she maybe shouldn't race, should never run again competitively. She stepped into the sun and when she felt it, she whipped off her jacket, stuck it behind a wall and took off. She thought. She wondered what dead was, but she knew what being alive was. She didn't take it easy. As someone once said to her, whatever . . .

She wasn't fluid, there was no way she felt fluid, but as Caz built up speed, jogging out through the gates, then turning right, and opening up a bit more, she felt like *Caz*.

She ran past tennis courts, the stadium, embryonic extensions to the site, rusty metal and stunted concrete as if a major build had been put on hold. Then she was passing waste ground, then dropping down a short hill and running towards the sea, la Santa's lagoon to her right, rocks, pockets of sand to her left. A stiff breeze off the sea made her seven minute miling seem quite hard. The same breeze flapped the zipped doors of three or four pup tents, separate among the rocks, all of them with bikes alongside.

The road was a peculiar black, harder than tarmac and lumpy. She could feel the jar to her shins, knees, thighs, despite the cushioning effect of her trainers, but suddenly she thought, 'Who gives a – , I'm out!'

She took a left fork, more of the hard black road, a sweep out towards the sea and back onto the road round the lagoon. As she swung back towards the complex, she passed another small tent huddled away from the wind. Now the wind was no longer hindering but helping, and she ran an exhilarating last kilometre at about six minute mile pace. No one saw her, but her face was spread wide with a marvellous up-yours, pigged-out, self-satisfied grin.

Eight

By the time Caz had finished her run, 4K in seventeen minutes, a sweat raised, but only just, the campus was coming to life, not crowds but a steady trickle, all headed towards the leisure pool. She looked over a wall. The people were mostly in Lycra, a few in running shorts, and they were scattering themselves about on the light brown area surrounding the sharp blue white-bordered pool. In the centre of the pool, a long island of desert plants were in bloom; pink, red, purple, more light blue.

She was beginning to wonder just what was going on when Debbie Jones strolled by and asked was she up to the morning work-out? Caz bit her tongue and said of course.

Later, she was lying face down, long delicate Danish fingers probing her back when Ina Jensen, the physio, said, 'Your back is very tight, it is like the muscles, they fight each other. You have been doing what?'

'Nothing much,' Caz said. 'I ran round the lagoon this morning, did the eight o'clock work-out and had a game of badminton. After lunch I did some track, half a dozen two hundred metre sprints.'

Ina leaned down to Caz and caught her eye, a lovely toothy smile.

'You should stop. This is what your back tells me.'

Caz grunted. 'What do *you* say?'

Ina laughed. 'I say you too, should stop. Not for long though. I can fix you. I think this is your neck and your pelvis.'

'How long is not long?' Caz said.

'Only four, maybe three days.' Ina said. 'Look, I show you. Be still.'

And then she started, Ina, with magical hands. And Caz was in love. Ina did explain which muscles were in spasm, which nerve bundles were under pressure, where probably her vertebrae had been bruised, but Caz didn't give a damn. All she knew was that the other side of the initial pain – Ina's thumbs were surprisingly powerful – was a hot, blossoming pleasure, as the trellised muscles of her back stretched and heaved and tried, still briefly, to get back to perfect diamonds.

'Jeez, Ina, whatever you're doing, don't stop, don't stop! Oh, yes, shit, ah, yes, there, that's where it hurts.'

'Just here?' Another press.

'Yyy-esss! I think I've died and gone to heaven!'

'You have been hurt badly?'

'No, it's OK.'

'Before. This is something bad? Perhaps you have fallen?'

Have I fallen!

'Yes.'

'And this, you have hurt your back.'

'Yes.'

'Okeh!' Ina slapped Caz lightly. 'Get dressed now and I tell you what to do, how often you see me, some exercises, lots of stretches, rest.'

'Do I have to give up sex 'n' drugs 'n' rock 'n' roll?'

'No dancing, and you lie still if you do sex.'

Caz was swinging her feet to the floor. Ina was absolutely straight-faced.

'Ina?'

She broke out in a man-melting smile. 'I am joking, Caz!' Then she looked serious, her bottom lip turned slightly out.

'Though your back, really you should not run until we make you better. And no – no rock and roll.'

'No rock 'n' roll?'

'They teach it here. It's lots of fun.'

Nine

That night Caz met Ina in the Green Bar for a drink. Caz's publicity had preceded her, and a gaggle of Greenies came with the physio to meet *The Girl Who Saved Brighton*. Every single damn one was gorgeous, blonde, thin and fit (and that was just the boys). The girls all looked like Ulrika Jonsson and the boys like far handsomer, slimmed down, ungrossed Arnie Schwarzeneggers. As far as she could see they all had blue eyes. And they knew how to party!

She woke at ten to eight on her second full day, still in what she'd gone out in, but in her own bed and alone at least – which, thinking about the party, was probably accidental. Debbie Jones hardly recognised her at the morning work-out, and when Caz skipped even the gentle bouncing, she hissed sarcastically something about ex-international wimps.

'Doctor's orders!' Caz said, waving her arms.

'Smells more like Southern Comfort to me,' Debbie said.

'That as well,' Caz said.

That morning, Caz did a stretch class, a back work-out and had a long slow swim. When she got out of the pool, she promised herself that tomorrow she'd take sandwiches; fifty metres in water was a llonnnggg way! Her physio appointment was at four. She could hardly wait.

Caz was paying good money for her hour or so of torture

every afternoon – very good money, even if it did come some-what second-hand from the Brighton branch of the Royal Insurance. But she cared not.

Ina (the thumbs) Jensen, physiotherapist extraordinaire, was worth twenty times what she was being paid, and on day two of Caz's holiday, on day three, and on a breathless day four, she bullied, soothed, cooed, pushed and pulled Caz, until the body she was wearing wasn't just mended but was bettered, strange, in tune; a balanced machine, flexing, ready to explode.

There was no absolute need, Ina said that night – they were opposite each other in one of la Santa village's restaurants eating *Mero* – but if Caz wanted to come in every other day, then they could keep a tab on the trouble, make sure that Caz was OK.

'It's tabs,' Caz said.

'I'm sorry?'

'We say "keep tabs on" or "keep an eye on",' Caz said helpfully.

Ina said quietly, 'Keep tabs on the trouble . . .'

'Yeah.'

She smiled. 'Thank you, Caz.'

'You are *joking*!' Caz said. 'It's me that should be thanking *you*. I have *never* felt like this. I reckon you and the boys got me drunk one night and gave me someone else's back while I was out.'

'I'm glad you are feeling better.'

'Better! When's the next 10K? Let me at 'em!'

'You promised, Caz. You must come back slowly.'

Caz dropped her shoulders. 'OK. I'll be good.' Then she brightened up. 'Hey, Een, maybe I could come in once a day. If my back's OK, the hips, the shins, you could maybe give me a sports massage, keep me loose, keep me in shape.'

'Every day you would spend this money?'

'You know how it is, Een, rich, famous, every whim pandered to . . .'

'It is not a problem, Caz.'

'We've got a deal?'

'I am happy to help you. One afternoon I will watch you running, also. To see if you do bad things, make your back a mess again.'

'Can I pay you?'

'Don't be silly.'

'But for the physio, the massage?'

'But of course. For that.'

Ina was grinning. Caz put her hand across the fish dishes.

'Oh, Ina,' she said, 'you have no *idea* what this means to me.'

'Then I will let you pay for the meal. And tonight, when we are back, ten o'clock, we meet some of the Greenies in the Café After Sport, yes? And I let you buy me a drink there also.'

'Hey, steady on, mate!'

That grin. 'Caz, this is a joke. Be lighter!'

'You mean lighten up.'

'This also,' Ina said.

Ten

By the second week Caz was doing daily track work: smooth, twenty-nine-second 200s in the mornings, two or three 400s every afternoon just outside the minute. There was a good crowd, mostly Brits, and every other day four guys, big and sexy – a French 4 × 100 relay outfit – practised running bends and change-overs, dressed in red, white and blue 'lunch-box' Lycra. The sun was out, steady upper seventies, a light cooling breeze; rain was just a rumour put about by the Germans, and every afternoon, Caz got her back work-out cum massage, whether she needed it or not. She *had* died. And she'd gone to heaven.

Gradually, Caz got to know the other regulars. There was a heavy-set computer programmer from Birmingham with knee trouble that Ina was helping with *hand* exercises, and an anorexic Geordie girl called Jenkins, suffering from shin-splints from hitting the lagoon loop too often and not going cross-country for relief. There was a squat Belgian biker with olive skin, round glasses and an over-the-top intensity who paid rapt attention to his Goddess Ina; and a gangling puppet-like German called Ken who had back trouble from one Fosbury Flop too many. Caz was four o'clock, the Belgian half-past. Kenneth came in at five. Caz found the Belgian guy slightly strange. So did Ina. She was an Agatha Christie fan and she called him Hercule, after another funny little Belgian.

Caz knew quite a few of the more serious runners. Ron Jones she knew both as a veteran sprinter at open meetings and as the one time race director of the Totton 10K; other Totton members she recognised from races and the occasional post-race bash. From Worthing there was a guy called Kevin King, a sub-two-minute half-miler, and another runner called Matthew Black – allegedly a bit of a ladies man – that everyone called Matt and who regularly broke thirty-one minutes for 10K.

If Matt was a ladies man, he never took a crack at Caz, but his build, Mel Gibson's, she noted once or twice, particularly when he changed his shorts, or the one time she saw him by the Olympic pool. His buttocks were fleshless muscle, hard as rocks, but what Caz noted was that he was brown; brown all over. Somewhere he sunbathed nude.

By the end of the second week Caz had done it all, been there, done that, got the T-shirt – three or four actually, after her hand-washed sports gear and underwear had insisted on taking on the tinge of the local water. And she had been to Teguise market – 'Cor, you what mate, that's Asda price!' – this from a very black skinny Moroccan who looked a good miler – and she had bought an overpriced carved giraffe that would have been cheap at a quarter of the price.

And she had ridden a donkey in Haria, gone to see the volcanic Fire Mountains, and finally she had chickened out when a few mates went jogging in the altogether on Famara's nude beach. For the first time since she had back-packed round Europe, she had found a way to really, really lay back. She was cool, calm and civilian. And she felt *great*.

Then, Tuesday, a body happened; Kevin King, putting a stop to the morning work-out by being found face down in the leisure pool. He was fully dressed and otherwise unmarked, the best first guess, a drunken swim that had gone wrong. Then, on Wednesday, Matt Black turned up, face down on the walkway near the Spar grocery shop, completely naked, very, very brown and, like Kevin, absolutely, fabulously dead.

Eleven

Caz had missed the discovery of Kevin King's body. At the time she was tucked in behind a German girl, second in the weekly half-marathon as it wound up a dirt track before swinging back on the road up to Soo. She was still taking it steady and the pace felt like about one and a half hours. By the time she and the German girl had reached half-way, Kevin had been removed from the water, pronounced dead and whipped away on a stretcher through a hushed nylon crowd.

'I am so shocked,' Ina said that afternoon. 'Kevin, I know. Often I have treated him for Achilles problems. He is a nice guy, we have a pint once in Pool Bar.'

Caz had stiff back, sore calves and thighs that burned. She had just rolled over on to her back so Ina could work on her quads. The German had been coasting, sussing Caz out. When they had turned at half-way she had clicked up to six minute miling which she maintained all the way back. At the finish, Caz had to run 1:23 to beat her.

'And this too is silly, Caz. You promised no racing.'

'I wasn't racing,' Caz said. 'My PB is one-sixteen.'

'Your personal best is not here,' Ina said. 'Not on the Soo course.'

'It is hilly, isn't it?' Caz said.

Ina dug her thumbs in. 'You are sometimes very stupid, Caz.'

What detail Caz eventually picked up about Kevin King came from her physiotherapist, a little first-hand knowledge, the bulk second hand. He had been drinking Bacardi and Coke most of the night and was full of himself. As soon as the disco opened he was in there for the happy hour and he spent most of the rest of his life dancing, wearing his wireless heart monitor and pulse watch to see how much exercise bopping was actually worth.

'I know Matt, the distance man, his friend. He tells me this. He tells me that Kevin says dancing is worth a good run; sixties music is a steady pulse, about one-thirty, House is one-thirty-five. Kevin said that on a good night he might reach one-forty beats, to Prince.'

'You know Matt?'

'A little. I have treat him. He has hip bursa.'

'Do you treat everybody?'

'On your tummy! No. Matt is one of Ute's patients. Kevin also. But we sometimes treat for each other if we are busy or sick maybe.'

Caz was talking to the bench. 'So what happened? Do they know yet?'

'Kevin was very happy. I hear this. He wants to stay up all night but his friends are tired and one by one they go to bed. But Kevin, he is high as the kite. He dances with everyone, me a few times, Ute a little more, but we go to our room about nearly one o'clock. It is late.'

'The disco closes at two?'

'At two o'clock, yes, the discotheque will be shutted up. Sometimes some boys will jump in the leisure pool. This is dangerous, because it is still very cold and the body, it is different when it has alcohol.'

Caz squeaked as Ina found a tight spot in her calf.

'Then, when the disco is closed, Kevin has a walk to the lagoon. Klaus the barman hears this, and the guards, Carlos and Jośe, they see him go there by himself. This is not unusual, to walk off being drinking . . .'

'Ah,' Caz said. 'Yeah! Just there! Just there!'

Twelve

The day had been sunny and peculiar. Quite naturally, the
Worthing crowd had been subdued and huddles of people had
appeared, in the Pool Bar, on the terraces, on the sides of the
Olympic Pool, sharing half-truths. Kevin King was single and
fairly solitary; his only friend was Matt Black and he, so the
word had it, had gone off for a very long run. At some point,
Caz had picked up a snide remark about 'some friend'. She
knew straight away that the speaker wasn't a runner. The *most*
likely thing a runner like Matt would have done was go off
somewhere, long and lonely, with only the even skit-skit of his
feet for company, the thump in his chest. Three years ago, Caz
had run the fifteen miles from her grandfather's funeral to her
Nan's farm. There had been tuts and whispers then too, but
Nanna had understood. When Caz returned, dark sweat
marking her shirt, Nan had pulled her towards her and whispered, 'Better now, Kathy?'

That night the regular evening entertainment in the square
was cancelled, and in the Café After Sport, perhaps the laughter was not quite so loud, and the jokes, the sexual banter, a
little forced. Ute Fërd and Ina were there, talking quietly, and
Caz sat with them but separate, people-watching, thinking,
nursing a bottle of Rioja.

She saw the Jones family trundling a double-buggy by,
trying to get their children off to sleep, Edward the funny

Belgian, the four black French guys, Karen, the anorexic from Newcastle, walking stiffly. A few people came over, whispered, touched Ute's shoulder, nodded, then walked away. Some stopped briefly, sitting forward on the edge of their wicker seat, not staying, just saying something, touching base.

By the end of the evening, the three of them were sick-drunk, a little ball of arms on the floor of Ute's room, runny noses, sniffing, asking why. When Ute looked up, finally managing to cry, green black lines ran down her face from her eyes.

'Oh, but Caz-ee, he was a young man. Why are they stupid so?'

'It's the bit that makes them blokes,' Caz said, wiping Ute's face. 'There's no explanation. That's just the way it is.'

They put her to bed and then Caz and Ina sat on the floor, staring at a blank wall, their heads back against Ute's mattress. There was coffee between their legs but the effort to sit up and drink it was almost too much. Caz was thinking about Colin Jones, trying to imagine drowning. Once she had come so close, in the sea off Brighton, but someone had dragged her out. She closed her eyes, trying to remember the time but nothing except the first slap of sea remained.

'Accidents,' Ina said darkly.

'What?' Caz said.

'Always, a place like this, we have many accidents. Every week a thousand sports people here, mountain-biking, race-biking, climbing volcanos, doing all sports, always we have accidents. And some tourists, they do not always see the people on bikes, other places on the island. Lots of accidents is because people are at the sharp end.'

'Work for the physios,' Caz said.

Ina looked at her coffee. 'Work for the physios, OK, but not if people die. That is silly.'

'Hey,' Caz said. She pulled Ina's head on to her shoulder. 'Life goes on, mate. Work hard, play hard, die young and beautiful.'

'You think so, Caz?'
'For some.'
'You think so for Kevin?'
Caz lied. 'I think so for Kevin, yes.'
Ina's eyes were closing. She was almost asleep.
'Poor Ute,' she said. 'Sad Ute.'

Thirteen

Caz had woken on the Wednesday morning, foetally cold and stiff, jigsawed into Ina's same shape on the floor, a grey blanket over them, and pillows under their heads. She couldn't understand where the comforts had come from but then Ute spoke from the kitchen as a jug kettle came to the boil.

'Last night, I did not sleep so very long. I got up and put on you a blanket.' Ina groaned. 'And my good friend, like me, she was unhappy also. I left you sleep for the best.'

Caz undid herself, sliding out an arm from under Ina. She had pins and needles. Ina groaned again. Caz got up, wobbling a bit.

'You making coffee?'

'Sure, you want some?'

Caz went to the loos. When she washed she made the mistake of looking at herself in the mirror, her long face haggard, her green eyes like Ina's but, right now, dull. Briefly, she thought about the two girls. Ina was even taller than Caz, with a beanpole black-dress elegance, so different from Ute. Ute was ultra-fit, but she was still wide, solid and big-boned. Right now she was a bouncy, bouncing size twelve, but she was sitting on a lumbering *hausfrau*, the natural big woman inside. And the woman was patient, just waiting for Ute to slow down.

Over coffee, Caz helped Ute put the accidents into perspective. Ina and Ute ran injury seminars, back strength classes, massage courses and courses in reflexology, as well as answering everyday queries on niggles and doing actual remedial work on patients who needed extra help. They probably had direct contact with a quarter of all the sporting visitors to la Santa, maybe as much as a half. Add to that all those people each of them noticed with the *other* physio, people they saw round the campus, in the bars, the disco – they must know a large majority of the guests, by name, by sight, at least to nod to.

'Like you know the man, the woman, who wins the 10K or the man who wins the talent competition in the square. Between you, you know most of the visitors.'

'But my *patients*,' Ute said. 'Now three is dead. I am so unlucky, like I curse them by being me, their physio.'

'Three?'

'There was Mister Jones, here last year who went into the sea. My friend Kevin, now, and Hans, from Stuttgart, also last year.'

'Who is Hans?'

'Not is. Hans was with German bike team, a very good rider. A little trouble with his spine, some knee problem.'

'And he had an accident?'

'All bikers have accidents. Hans, he fell a long way, but not here. He was at the north side of the island, where you can see Graciosa.'

Ina sat up. 'Ute. You are not talking about Hans now? Hans was more than thirty kilometres from here. That was not your fault.'

'I know this, but it is my bad luck when Hans fell.'

'Fell where?' Caz said.

Ina explained. 'At Miramar del Rio there is a beautiful view, very high. There is a restaurant built into the side of the cliff. You can look down at Graciosa Island.'

'And this Hans fell?'

'Yes. He biked to the north of the island, there from la Santa. This was alone but that is not unusual. There he had a break, some coffee. In the evening, they see his bike. Next day they find him at the bottom.'

'Did anyone see him fall?'

'It is not known. People are leaving the island every day. The police put up posters and ask people at the airport for two weeks, but no person says they have seen Hans fall.'

'Isn't this place busy?'

'Always,' Ina said. 'But this day was mist, not very usual. Not so many people go because the view was no good and even on the veranda it is not easy to see everybody.'

'So what was decided?' Caz asked. 'Was the death suspicious?'

'Do you mean about Hans, how he fell? Did he jump? This do you mean?'

'Did he?'

Ute cut in. 'Hans and me had some drinks. He was repressed—'

'Depressed.'

'He was very sad and low. We talked a lot. He had a girl for many years who left him. Maybe he ended it. It is possible.'

'Do you think that's what happened? Hans committed suicide?'

'I think, maybe.'

Ina had stood up. 'But Ute, you *helped* Hans. He was our friend. If Hans did this thing, it is not your fault.'

'I know!' Ute said sharply. 'Every time, I say it is a coincidence but then I feel bad because two people I know die. And now it is three!'

Caz was thinking 'salience and relevance'.

'Ute, think. Think of the hundreds, the *thousands* of people you have met, treated. They're all fine! Maybe la Santa has had a run of bad luck, but there are a dozen people here who could

66

have had the same contact as you. What you are feeling is natural, but that doesn't mean that the deaths of these three lads is your *fault*!'

'I know this. My head knows this. It is my heart that is sad.'

'Ah, that's different,' Caz said. She suddenly realised that *she* knew two of the dead men. 'As long as you remember that there's no logic in what you say.'

Ute nodded. 'You are right, Caz, thank you.' She made a happy face. 'And now I will have a deep hot bath, I think. I am to do the 5K run round the lagoon at eight-fifteen and a back-class at eleven o'clock.'

Caz turned to Ina. 'Fancy another coffee?'

Caz and Ina talked in hushed tones while Ute bathed. Caz harked back to her days studying psychology and the work of Nisbett & Ross, how people's intuitive beliefs about life were usually, commonly wrong.

'Do you read your stars, Ina?'

'Sometimes.'

'And are they usually right?'

'Often, yes.'

'How often are they wrong?'

'They – I – I cannot think when they are wrong.'

'That,' said Caz, 'is because they are only relevant when they are right. The wrong times slip away from our memory because they are not important.'

'What does this mean?'

'That Ute doesn't give credence, sorry, weight, to the thousands of people she has met in her job to whom nothing has happened, because, if nothing has happened, that information is trivial. She focuses on the bad because it's news. Emotionally, it's as if half of the people she has treated are dying. Factually it's maybe one in five thousand. Chance.'

Fourteen

'So there you go,' Caz muttered to herself as she slaked up and down the Olympic pool. 'Little Miss Academia strikes again.' She had sorted out Ute Fërd, put Ina's mind to rest, and solved the case, what a hero!

The sun was blatting down on the turquoise top of the pool like a golden bouncing bomb. She was resting for a minute each end – her shoulders ached like a yoked milk-maid – and every time she rested at the hot end she could feel the sun's heat; a hot towel wrapped round her neck. She no longer needed sandwiches for half-way down the fifty metre length of the pool, but it was still a bloody long way.

She had one huge regret: that it had taken her twenty-eight years to discover this Heaven, that in the late eighties and early nineties she could have been here rather than running through knee-deep grey mud at Parliament Hill or the same depth of snow in Gateshead. She wondered, if she offered, would they make her a naturalised Spaniard? She would soon pick up the language – the way she was going she'd soon be fluent anyway, *mañana, graçias, vino tinto, por favore, hasta la vista, baby!*

She felt great, about her body, about herself. She kicked back from the poolside and floated, her arms lazily stroking like a ray, the sun bright yellow in her face. And I am happy, aren't I? she thought. Then she remembered Val; she hadn't thought of Val for a while, and a flicker of something dark crossed her daydreams. Shit! So was she happy or not?

She rolled over on to her face, a drowning X trailing in the water, her eyes wide open staring at the strangest blue. So was she happy?

She was still face down. 'Define happy!' an executive voice said in her head. She mouthed it to the pool bottom, blowing bubbles of sound.

All Caz knew right now was that she didn't want to slash her wrists or breathe in water. Was that happy? She lifted her head into the air and stroked to the pool's edge. She was feeling the cold but she was not feeling sorry for herself. She thought of Shaw's freezing sparrow. Happy and sad, she decided, they only matter when you think about it.

She was drying by the poolside, her towel wrapped around her against the chill of the breeze, when someone ran past the wall above her head. There was something in the manner, some tension, that made her feel even more cold. Then she heard the scream and more people running. She pulled on a robe, grabbed her flip-flops and jogged in the direction of the commotion.

Fifteen

The crowd had not yet formed. The scream had come from Ute Fërd taking a short-cut past the Spar supermarket on her way to the five-a-side football pitch and her eleven o'clock back work-out. A man had reached her and was holding both her arms trying to stop her shivering. She was white, her eyes wide. On the floor, a body. Naked.

Caz arrived just as the morbid few approached. They were walking slowly, looking around them, then edging forward like nervous cows approach a stranger. Caz's manner was that of a policeman, assertive, positive, taking control, letting her uniformed presence calm things, giving the injured person space. It was only later that she realised that she was barefoot, her 'uniform' was white towelling, and the injured man was extremely dead, his head strangely misshapen and grey-pink matter oozing slowly from one side.

She recognised the buttocks first, their complete brownness, then the body-shape, late of Mad Max, then the hair. She did not, dare not move the head or look at the face of Matthew Black.

Ute Fërd began to jabber and cry. Someone in Caz's peripheral vision came down some steps from the la Santa offices.

'Doctor! Doctor!' Caz shouted. 'Pronto! Pronto!' Then to the man with Ute she said, 'For God's sake, get her out of here!'

Then someone moved Ute away, and Caz saw people coming down the office steps, the uniform of camp security huffing down the service road behind them. They were twenty seconds away and Caz turned back to Matthew. She could hear someone asking in a high pitched voice, 'What happened? Did anyone see? What happened?'

She put her head close to the floor, close to Matthew's bloody mouth. A faint-groaned 'Urrnn' came from him, but Caz knew that could be both a dead sound or pain. She felt for a pulse and, as she did so, someone stepped forward to help. 'Don't touch him!' Caz shouted and the arm retreated, burnt. Then a voice, 'It's Ina, a doctor is coming.'

Caz had felt the faintest of pulses but the beat had slipped away. There was blood, mess on her hands. Now the officials arrived, Christian Green, security. Matthew was neither breathing nor hurting. Around her, suddenly, Spanish, then Danish, Christian and Ina, then Spanish again. Caz shouted, 'Ina, we need space to turn him over.' She heard Ina in Danish again, rapid, definite, then Christian Green, a deeper voice, orders in Spanish, then English, 'Back, please! Please! Back! Please!'

'We should not turn him!' Ina said, now the other side of Matthew Black. She was kneeling in blood and brain, pieces of broken black wood.

'He isn't breathing!' Caz said sharply. 'We've no choice! We have to give him heart massage, mouth to mouth. We have to turn him. Now!'

'Okeh,' was all Ina said. Then she said something to Christian. Two men appeared either side of the body, one she recognised.

'As gently as you can,' Caz said. Then she looked up at the crowd. 'Someone to take his head!' Someone came. To this man, 'When we move him, try to bring the head at the same time.' The man nodded, close to shock but still performing.

Caz caught his eyes. 'Do you understand? Try to stop any more damage to the spine!' The man nodded.

She turned to the rest. 'This must be gentle. As gentle as we can. When I say, we will lift my side slowly, turn Mr Black. This gentleman will try to keep the head and spine in line.'

She looked at the man who didn't look like he was going to make it.

Then Ina spoke. 'Should I take Matt's head?'

Caz nodded. There was nothing now from Black. She felt Ina move, the man move, then everybody ready. She waited three seconds.

'And now!' she said. 'Slowly, slowly!'

And they turned Matthew Black over, saw his face. Wondered for that extra second whether he would want to be brought back.

But Caz had to try. She tried. Her first, the requisite number of pumps to the centre-chest, then her again. 'Ina! You his heart. I'll give him air!'

And she lowered herself on to a man she did not know, his bloody mouth, opened it, hooked a finger of blood and mucus from him, tilted the head dangerously, kissed him, the kiss of life, thinking of a world of AIDS, kissed him, sharing his death, breathed into him, at least tried.

Then Ina, pushing into a chest that was wrongly soft. Then Caz again, not knowing what she looked like, bloody mouthed. And Ina. And Caz. And Ina. And Caz. And Ina. And a bubble of blood, a dim groan. Then someone running, oxygen, a mask, a dumb, bloody Matthew Black, killed but not dead, Christian Green: 'There's an army helicopter coming!' and Caz, falling back, looking at Ina, blood on both of them, laughing, frightened, weak, tears in Ina's face . . .

Sixteen

In the aftermath of adrenalin comes its antagonist, and in the aftermath of action comes remorse. Caz expected to be sick but wasn't; Ina expected nothing and was violently, suddenly, briefly ill.

The helicopter landed at the track, scattering the football trainers, stopping to stare, the walkers, the runners, people booking out bikes. The drilled lovat green of two airmen emerged, wrapped up the flailed body of Matthew Black, sucked him in, then stole away. As the aircraft lifted, dipped to nod its goodbye and tilted away towards the hills, Caz was washing her hands, washing her face for the second time, Ina was in a shower, long since clean but washing, washing, washing.

Then, that afternoon, and all that out-of-sequence night, the re-runs began, the disaster video, the voice-overs, the repeated slow-motion scenes, where each of them did something slightly different, where Matt's eyes opened, where a faint smile said, 'Don't worry, I'm going to make it. Don't worry, you did a great job.'

Or between, they could be cold, a strange joke in the worst of taste rushing in, a laugh erupting with amazing guilt, then joy because they weren't hurt, then an ache, a feeling that if they had been hurt too, everything would balance, everything would be as it should. Then the desire to sleep, to make animal repairs. Then the dreams, the awful, microscopic, techni-colour re-runs. Then the next day, the post-mortems on a man who yet was not quite dead.

A sign was put on the physiotherapists' door. Other signs cancelled classes, massage sessions, the lighter fun and games with Green Team.

But the morning work-out still worked out and the 8.15 run ran, for the show was certain to go on and dangerous thought-ful gaps were not meant to appear. Like the mindless routine on the charter flight to Arrecife – drink-food-film-drink – no one, the people who made plans or the people who followed them, wanted space, time to think. No one wanted a thousand people stopping, thinking, questioning, knocking on doors. Better that they should act; better they should run their long races, play squash, caravan their colours across the island, wheels spinning, tyres drimming, mountains sliding by their bikes to their lefts and to the right.

But Caz was thinking, and Ina was thinking. La Santa's managing director was thinking, and the dark examiner from Arrecife was thinking, nodding as Christian Green spoke.

'Some of the hotel guests use the roof to sunbathe without clothes. The roof is dangerous and this is forbidden, but still the guests will find ways to go up there.'

Caz was quiet, watching. She made Christian – intelligent, grey hair, pale blue eyes, immaculate – to be somewhere either side of fifty.

'At the top of each staircase tower there is a door. This we keep locked always. The door at the top of tower forty was broken open.'

There was a murmur in the room which Christian quickly dealt with. 'But this is not unusual. Unfortunately, guests will do this to get on to the roofs. When we find the broken locks they are repaired, but some people—'

'Couldn't you leave one door unlocked?' Caz asked.

Christian smiled. 'No. The roof is dangerous, people may fall.' He paused, realising what he had just said. 'It is our duty to make things difficult. But as I say, some people . . .'

'We think Matthew Black fell?'

'Oh, yes, most certainly. He was naked and he had left his towel and things on the wall above where he was found. There was his glasses, a book, many other things. A terrible accident.'

'How is Ute?' Ina asked.

'Better,' Christian said. 'Yesterday she was sedated. Today she is with friends in la Santa. The doctor has given her something more and she sleeps most of today.'

Ina made a little gasp as she nodded. Half a smile.

'But you, both you ladies, now we should concern ourselves with you. You did a very good job yesterday and we have news that Mister Black does not have spinal injuries.'

Caz and Ina shared a glance, still this undeserved guilt.

'He is very very sick but he is getting the best care. He was flown straight to Gran Canaria, to las Palmas, and operated on there. He maybe has an angel to guard him. In las Palmas there was a visit from a famous neuro-surgeon to the hospital. Otherwise he would go all the way to mainland Spain . . .'

'Do we know if he will recover?' Caz said.

'No, nor do we know how he will be.'

The Spaniard spoke briefly, dark quick Spanish. Christian answered effortlessly, the words, the accent, the rhythm now foreign to Caz, slow pause-words interspersed between machine-gun sentences. Whatever was said seemed to satisfy the examiner. He said something else to Christian, then, to the ladies: 'Perhaps, again? I hope better reason.'

He shook both their hands, nodded to Christian and left. As the door closed softly behind him, Christian sighed, dropping back in his chair.

He looked at Caz. 'Now we meet, this at last, Miss Flood. I am sorry that I was in Denmark when you arrived.' He glanced at Ina, then back to Caz. 'But Caz, your actions are like your story. This is unusual. Perhaps we need you here if our bad luck continues.'

'I have three more weeks.'

'Already? And are you well? Are you very fit?'

'Both. Ina is an excellent physiotherapist.'

'We know this. And Ute too, though I think she will want some leave now. She may go back to Germany for a while. This will probably be for the best, I suspect. Ina?'

'I think so, Christian.'

He took a breath, then sat forward as if yesterday was done with and now they could look to the future. 'I think, tonight, tomorrow night, that the two of you should be my guests at dinner. I would like to say thank you to you both for the hotel.'

Caz looked at Ina. There was a passive yes.

'Thank you,' Caz said. 'But tomorrow night, perhaps? We should be a little happier then.'

Christian stood up and came round his desk. Caz and Ina stood. He smiled handsomely and held out his hand.

'I thank you again, both of you.' He laughed a little. 'And don't worry! Matthew will be all right. I know this!'

They shook his hand and left. In the outer office Caz said, 'They've given you the day off?'

'Until Monday,' Ina said.

'Let's hire a car,' Caz said. 'Get away from here. What d'you say?'

'I say yes.'

Caz was at the door to the service road. She could feel and see the sun waiting. She took a massive breath and stood taller.

'Right!' she said. 'Let's go!'

Seventeen

They got away about ten-thirty, after a toss-up between the sweetness of a Renault Clio Cabriolet and the potential fun of a four-wheel drive Suzuki. Caz favoured the off-road car but Ina made the point that maybe over the last few days they had had enough excitement. They took the Clio, a neat little green job with a Club la Santa badge splattered on the doorside. Ina was driving.

'So where, Caz?'

'Everywhere?'

'North or south?'

'North.'

They went via la Santa village and the hill to Tinajo, a steady drag that took an extra minute to half-way in the Friday morning 10K. Already there were serious cyclists hammering up it, dark brown legs hairless, their calves standing out. Caz didn't know which was madder, straining to do fifteen miles an hour *up* the hill or coming back down it four hours later at three times that speed.

At Tinajo they swung towards Tiagua, then, just before San Bartolomé they turned for Teguise. And always, the far volcanoes, the post-apocalypse landscape: barren browns, reds, blacks, the stone circled walls, patient fields, dark riven people moving slowly.

They were tootling, only doing about forty miles an hour.

The wind over the open car was enough to lift their hair without slapping the eyes. Caz settled in her seat, her arm on the car door. The sun was high and merciless and she could see herself reddening already. Then she glanced across at her new friend. Ina glanced back – for a professional second, not the fifteen or so of the movies. As she looked back to the road, her face bloomed slowly, first a little smile, as if she had suddenly thought of something, then that toothy grin, the one that disarmed men. She had to shout when she spoke. 'Oh Caz! This island!'

'What?'

'They have something right. There is something old and good here.'

Caz sighed. 'I guess.'

'Are you miserable?' Ina said to the windscreen.

'No,' Caz said. 'I'm thinking.'

Ina laughed. 'Oh dear! This is a problem. Someone English thinks . . .'

'You what?' Caz flashed back. 'Ina, you're a bloody *Dane*; as in fish, as in Lego and social security. What would you know about *anything*?'

'Sizzle!' Ina said.

'What?'

'You forgot bacon.'

Ina was from Copenhagen. Caz was so thick she didn't even know it was an island. Denmark was the bit of the map that stuck up, yes? Over their first dark coffee Ina told her, no, Caz was thinking of Yootland.

'Yootland?'

'Yes. Yay, Oo, Tee and land.'

'*Jut*land,' Caz said.

'*Yoot* land.'

'But that's not where you're from . . .'

78

'I am from Coppenhargen.'

'Is that near Coapenhaygen?' Caz asked.

Ina shrugged. 'You say tomarto.'

Teguise was not the Teguise of the Sunday morning market. Then, it teemed with refugees from the south side of the island determined to buy six plus rip-off T-shirts for two thousand pesetas from one of the Moroccans or from a drug-skinny expat still with his Liverpool accent. Caz had made the mistake of doing the bus trip to the market on her second Sunday. Within half an hour she had realised that everything was crap, the displayed prices were not even ball-park, and the food-stall burgers required a degree in maths and a mortgage to negotiate.

She had escaped, found an almost civilised tapas bar, drunk a coffee then sipped Bud until it was time for the bus back to la Santa. She was late back and some bloke said, 'Couldn't find that dead-good T-shirt stall, eh? *I* did. I got *nine* shirts for two thousand pertaters, brilliant!'

Caz didn't speak. After fighting her way through the beer-bellies and the shell-suits to get her Budweiser and then fighting her way back upstream to get her coach, she wanted to rip this cheerful bugger's teeth out. Then she thought, 'This guy is stopping at Club la Santa!' She'd heard that a few straight tourists were drifting in. That figured. If this guy was at la Santa for sport then he was big in darts.

'A penny for what you are thinking,' Ina said.

'For my thoughts?' Caz said. 'They're not worth that much.'

'Anyway.'

'Well,' Caz said, 'I was thinking about the way the tourists descend on Teguise every Sunday. I met a bloke on the flight over who probably thinks Lanzarote is Playa Blanca and Teguise market.'

'Oh, Caz, you are a cynical! There is much good foreign money spent here and this happens only once every week. The

profits here and from the tourists, they help to keep the island.'
  'Keep the island *what*?' Caz said flatly.

Eighteen

From Teguise they drifted north. No, they didn't, they *drove* north, very deliberately, very specifically, Ina gripping the Clio's soft vinyl steering-wheel and trying not to be terrified as they wound through mountains with ludicrous instant-death drops at their right. A few miles distant was a sea that radiated. In between, pockets of domesticity, the dinky white houses, walled fields, palms, cacti.

The climb above and then the drop down to Haria was a triumph of engineering over sanity. The exactly two-car-widths-plus-a-willy wide road shot towards oblivion every fifty yards, then cut left, ducked right, swung away, just in time. They were looking ahead, praying that nothing would be coming the other way. When it did, they knew they were going to crash, gulped, blinked, and came out the other side.

And then, in the midst of this, Lycraed la Santa bikers would appear from nowhere, free-wheeling past them, brown, oily and brain-dead, with tight grins on their faces, gravel skitting from their wheels on the corners as they leaned away from the *oops!* wrong way to go. As the Clio escaped on to the road into the town, other bikers were starting *up* the hill, quite cheerful, almost normal-looking really. Caz shook her head. 'These are volunteers, right? They don't have to do this?'

'They have charge of themselves, Caz. You know this.'

81

'Their bodies, maybe, but not their heads. No one sane does that.'

'What?'

'Comes down a hill like that. No one does. Did you *see* some of those drops?'

Ina shook her head emphatically. 'Oh no!' she said. 'It is much too much to see. I will close my eyes on the corners. It is better, yes?'

'Tell me you're joking,' Caz said.

'Donkeys!' Ina said.

They skidded on to a gravel car park in front of a huge white and green ranch-style restaurant. There were one or two other cars but, more importantly, to one side, a mope of tethered donkeys, suspect, drooping and grey, but, when they rode them, for fifteen clopping minutes round the shuttered backstreets, stoically strong. Before they set off again, now for Mirador del Rio, they applied more factor sixteen. After a right and left they were purring slowly down a narrow street, the stepless houses with doors straight on to the road.

Ina settled into her body. 'So, Lanzarottay, Caz. You like it?'

Caz answered nasally, suddenly remembering the Man. Utd fan. 'Oh, I dunno, Een. The food's a bit foreign, innit? And the telly's rubbish.'

'But you are inspired by the scenery, are you not, its dark satanic splendour?'

'What, all this bleedin' lava?'

'Our staggering lunar landscape. A reminder of the awesome power of nature unleashed.'

'You mean, like, the eruptions, them?'

'Indeed.'

When the left fork came they nearly missed it, but Ina hairpinned round it late, making the tyres squeal and persuading Caz to suggest that she drove the car back. One of them was a police-trained driver.

Nineteen

Caz hadn't really thought what she was expecting of Mirador del Rio, but roughly, with the mention of great heights and great views, she had imagined some sort of sub-tropical version of an Alpine restaurant at the top end of the ski-lift, glassed out into space with no visible means of support, the kind of thing James Bond dived off or threw a villain from.

What she got was car park, dull stacked stone, no view and a little Spaniard in an orange jacket scurrying round shouting orders to park.

'So where's this bloody view then?'

'Be patient,' Ina said.

Ina clipped her bum-bag on her front like Kanga's Roo; Caz got out of the car wearing hers on her hip like a gunslinger. They went towards the stack of stones, the hidden entrance, dumped a few hundred pesetas in exchange for what looked like a postcard each. Caz looked bemused.

'Stop it!' Ina said.

Then they were walking through white-plastered rock, everything round, César Manrique artifacts left casually abandoned on a sweeping wood-thick shelf. And then they were in an open space, a film set, James Bond again, a great sweeping white-curved room with a polished floor. On the far side, glass, distant blue. Take away the infection of tourists and it was wonderful. Ina smiled.

'How much?' Caz said.

Ina got drinks in while Caz looked out. Even through wind-greyed glass the view was astounding. The sea was a new green, one that Caz couldn't put a name to, and the island below, swathed in light, wide sand, a harbour, a sprinkling of houses, was magically quiet, beckoning.

'Graciosa!' Ina said over her shoulder. 'Doesn't it look lovely?'

'Gorgeous!'

'I have never been. Each time I will go, something happens instead.'

'*We'll* go,' Caz said. 'Before I go back to the UK, we'll go.'

Ina grinned.

They had coffees, a piece of oddly flavoured cake. There was a bar, but when Caz went back up for seconds she actually didn't fancy anything stronger. Over their second coffee she joked about it, but Ina didn't think booze was a laughing matter.

'I drink, have a party, get drunk. I drink sometimes a little for fun. Sometimes I do not drink, have a Fanta orange, maybe, but Caz, you—'

'Don't say it,' Caz said, 'I know the routine already. It's down to my job, I reckon. We say "it goes with the territory".'

'Do you maybe try to stop a while?'

'Stop? Bloody hell, no! Cut back maybe, take a week off, maybe. I'm not drinking now, am I?'

'This is good.'

'This is relaxed.'

'What do you mean?' Ina said.

Caz sat stiffly. 'I mean relaxed. I mean that a copper, a woman in the police, she gets tired, stressed, frightened some-times. The short-cut to calming down after work is a couple of drinks with the boys. It gets to be a habit.' She paused. 'Here, relatively speaking, I'm cool, I'm OK. I'm not chasing some

84

psychotic or telling some poor mother terrible news. Here, I don't *need* it quite so much.'

'We should never *need* it,' Ina said.

'Maybe we shouldn't,' Caz said quickly back, 'but therapy takes too long, running makes you sweaty and sex isn't always convenient. We do what we do, what we have to do.'

Ina didn't answer. She took the last sip of her coffee and put it down. The cup rattled in its saucer and she pointed to outside.

They went out on to the veranda, the balcony. Stone loos were to the left, a thick-barred barrier to the right, a couple of pay-slot telescopes. Below them was a chequered flat with pea-yellow and brown squares, man-shaped pools on the coast next to the fabulous sweet-green sea.

'What are they?' Caz said.

'Agri-Industry,' Ina said. 'Salt things. To make it from the sea.'

'Oh,' Caz said.

Where they were standing, the drop was immediate; there was no mountain sloping away, just space. They moved around the veranda to where some rock tumbled out a few feet down, making the drop one per cent less terrifying. 'How high are we?' Caz said, her hand on the thick banister. She was noticing rust in the supports.

Ina was leaning on the barrier. 'Four hundred-eighty metres.'

Caz did some mental arithmetic, getting fifteen, sixteen hundred feet. Presumably, there had been no rush to check out the German guy, whatsisname. Matt Black had fallen thirty-odd feet and he was a bloody mess, so what did fifteen hundred feet do to you? She felt a shiver, someone walking over her grave. What did it take to throw yourself into fifteen hundred feet of space? What was so dark, so despairing?

Or was it just the moment suicides thought of, the first step;

not the fall, not the long seconds, not the approaching ground?

'Hans,' Ina said. 'With all this beauty that he could do that thing.'

'Yeah,' Caz said.

They had lunch in Orzola, right at the north-east tip of the island. It was from here that the boat left to swing round Lanzarote's head on the way to Graciosa. The harbour bobbed with smacks and bright pleasure craft, all small, but the ferry was large, a white and stainless motor-cruiser that looked like a millionaire's plaything.

They were eating soft white fish, a few fries, onion and tomato thinly sliced on a side plate. They were drinking El Grifo, one of the island's reds, just about OK.

'Do you know Kenneth?' Ina asked quietly. 'He is, he runs the sports side, the events, the Ironman, things like this.'

'I don't think we've met.'

'Oh,' Ina said, then with a shrug, she continued. 'Kenneth has told me, the island Graciosa, this is where someone from Lanzarote goes for quiet and peace.'

'Peace and quiet.'

Ina ignored the correction. She sipped some wine. 'Kenneth says it is such a place, you go there, you sit, maybe you just look at the sea. There is no cars. He says it is fine to be there, everyone should do it.'

'It sounds a bit like Lundy Island,' Caz said. When Ina looked quizzically up at her she explained. 'In England, a little island off Devon. I went there once when I was at university.'

'Like Graciosa?'

Caz smiled, remembering. 'No, not like Graciosa. It's a great lump of granite about three miles long, a mile wide. It sticks up out of the sea a couple of hundred feet and the weather was very unpredictable!'

'Here the weather is always good. We have sun, little rain, and the breeze is always pleasant.'

Caz pushed at the remains of her fish. 'But just every now and then the island blows up . . .'

Ina grinned her grin. 'Is this a problem?'

Twenty

Even if it was a cliché, the next three weeks flew by. Caz continued her physio and her therapy, worked out by the leisure pool, ran the 5K with the boys round the lagoon, got a bit of badminton in every other day.

The events of the first fortnight drifted backwards in time and the faces of the people waiting for treatment changed more than once. She had seen the Joneses off and had seen the high-jumping Ken as he left with a shy 'wiedersehen'. She had seen the not-so-friendly Belgian biker when he was leaving, but he seemed less than happy.

She had no reason to dislike Edward Platt, but she did. He had been in reception tidying up his account as she had been passing through on her way to meet Ina. When all her almost friendly half-smile of recognition drew from him was a poky little scowl, she thought, 'Well, fuck you, Poirot,' and put his problems down to the EC.

They never got to Graciosa. Ute's three-week convalescent break meant that Ina was in demand twelve hours a day and quick-drinking or sleeping for the second twelve. Caz had to make do with bike rides with strangers to Famara and low-impact aerobics. The one session of yoga that she tried she thought was hilariously difficult but gave her some new and interesting views of bits of herself. She trained well though, getting sharper and sharper, and in weeks three and four she came home first woman in the 10K without extending herself.

Then it was time to go.

Saying goodbye to Ina Jensen was a genuine wrench for Caz. As well as missing Ina the person, she knew she would miss Nurse Thumbs. For the first time in ages she had been clocking lap times good enough to be serious, but this time *without* finding herself in pain, inevitable injury coming her way. In five weeks, her stride had lengthened, her knee lift had gone higher and her times had gone lower. She had lost half an inch of waist and put on a pound of muscle. She was *hot*!

Dinner with Christian Green had been in the Restaurant Evento and there had been good news about Matt Black, still out for the count but out of danger. The following day there had been a good-news telephone call from England – Tom MacInnes to tell Caz that Veronica Stallwood was being well looked after not too far away from Brighton.

Ute Fërd seemed fine when she got back to work, and, all things considered, everyone and everything seemed to be following an upward curve. Apart from actually having to *leave*, Caz felt great, fit and loose, at peace with herself for the first time in years. She had exchanged addresses with Ina and knew they would stay in touch.

On her last but one day, Christian Green had given Caz a package for Kevin King's mother, a few personal belongings, stop-watches, a running log, a small amount of money. These had been overlooked when King's things had been gathered *post mortem* and Caz had offered to take them back as a favour. Now, diesling towards the airport, she was sadly mellow; Kevin's tragic death, Matt's accident, the memory of Colin Jones's drowning and Hans Pinke's suicide all somehow wrapped up in this little box as if they were ashes or a folded funeral flag.

III

III

Twenty-one

As the Boeing 757 started its descent into Gatwick, Caz woke up. She had skipped the film, skipped the *plastic dans le plastic* meal and kept herself to just one Southern Comfort and Coke with a little ice. She had never been comfortable enough to sleep on board a charter plane before, but this time . . . And the two people in the adjoining seats, middle-aged, slept. She still wondered vaguely if sometime she'd died and Heaven was a re-run of life with the shit taken out.

The flight-path brought them in over Southampton, the Isle of Wight, then, tantalisingly – she'd left the flat lights on – over Brighton, before sliding in via Crawley. She had phoned ahead from Arrecife, got Valerie and asked him to be at the airport to meet her. He had sounded a little short, maybe because she'd rung only once from la Santa, but maybe because he'd already decided to take the job in the States. Caz still couldn't pin down how she felt about it, about him. She loved him, he made her cry, but she'd hardly missed him while she'd been in Lanzarote and this without the *decisions-decisions* diversion of a holiday fling.

Usually she blamed the job for her lack of commitment. This time she needed a fresh excuse and, as she pictured his face, the hard muscle of his back, she decided that different Cazes needed different things. Other people's selves all stayed inside the one body, but Caz was Jekyll, Hyde, Hyde's valet, his milkman and the bloke next door. If she ever settled, settled with Valerie or someone else, which Caz would the guy get? And if he got one Caz, would the others stay?

She wasn't unhappy, just vaguely uncertain; needing life's accidents to happen to her to give her those obsessively important short-term goals that obscured a central sense of no other direction. She'd read somewhere, or maybe some psychologist had suggested it, that football supporters had a similar papering-over requirement. Why worry about the small things in life like love, poverty and death when you could instead focus on next Saturday, the absolute sexual certainty of one-nil away?

Was that why she was a copper? Give me some villainy, a set of clues, the whiff of danger, point me at the darkness. And while I go through that, while I flirt with the sordid, the frightening, the antisocial, the mad, forgive me my other faults, my weaknesses, for I do this thing that otherwise you might have to do.

And wasn't that what blokes were – led by their dicks from fifteen to twenty-five, driven, another target, another goal, another net, pot, hole? And wasn't it true that when men got depressed they wanted sex and that women wanted warmth? And was that where violence came from, the need to stop thinking, the need not to know where you were never going? Or was all of this bollocks, because, as yet, she hadn't found the right man, the right vocation, the sense of purpose, or was it even more bollocks because she had all three and fuck-it just like Val had said once, they were oil and water?

Her ears were popping. She was thinking, as she blew her nose, as she worked her jaw to relieve the pressures inside. Her own voice was in her head. 'Oil and water,' she heard. 'And mixed they're emulsion.' And emulsions never settle, they separate if they are still. Oil and water. The more agitated, the closer the mix, but the oil and water always separate.

But now she thought about the plane, about this last floating quiet, and then the *batthhumpp!pp!* of the wheels smacked down on England, the metal-metal settle shock into the wings, the screamed reverse of the engines. But flying didn't frighten Caz. So why did she think a load of shit when she was landing? Maybe she'd marry Val.

If he asked her.

She sat still when everyone scurried to let loose their duty-free, sat patiently while they rushed to stand stock-still in a stale-sweat queue waiting for the doors to open. She closed her eyes as a baby whimpered at the front, finally off to sleep ten minutes before the landing, awake again, angry at the nearest thing. Life? Don't talk to me about life.

All she had above her head was Kevin King's little box. There was no need to rush. Once the doors were opened, they would all remember why they went on holiday in the first place, and once they all finally got into the arrivals hall, there'd be a healthy reflective wait for their cases.

And the carousel would start moving five minutes before the first case came out.

And there'd only be one.

And a push-chair.

Then someone's wind-surfer.

A bike.

So what was the rush, eh? And would Valerie ask her? Did her breath smell? Was Veronica Goddard OK? Had Moira told Billy?

95

Twenty-two

Caz had taken two cases to la Santa but she had bought a third, a neat Nike sports bag to accommodate all her newly-bought sports gear. The bag and one of the cases was in the very first batch on the carousel and Caz groaned; that meant that her second case would be the last thing to emerge, probably covered in dust and marked 'not wanted on voyage'.

So when she finally left the luggage hall, last of course, following the shrug-shuffle of disembodied travellers, their trolleys, it was with a smile on her face, the kind of wry smile that comes from suddenly understanding what the hell is going on, what is always going to be. She didn't rush for the shuttle train, there was no need, no point. It was set to British Sucker Time and on automatic; scheduled to hiss and shut the nearest doors just as Caz swung her trolley towards them, goldfish faces the other side of the glass, grey with travel-dust, time.

Val would be starting to twitch. But that was the point. Caz smiled. He was *meant* to twitch.

She was the last Anglo-Saxon through immigration. She waved her British passport and flashed her whiteness – look, it's just suntan. Two suit-uniformed men blocked the other line. One with lowered eyes was flicking through the well-fingered identity of a black man and his wife while another secret policeman hovered in the background. The couple had done this before. They simply waited.

Then she hit customs, now three channels, red, green and try-this-for-a-change. If the new one had been amber it would have made more sense. Red you get stopped and you feel like a drug-courier. Amber you *might* get stopped; you feel like a drug-courier. Green you don't get stopped; you *are* a drug-courier. She picked the middle one. She didn't get stopped.

She came out behind her trolley, trying to feel casual. This is easy? When you haven't seen your boyfriend for six weeks, you were there not so long back when his ex-lover died, you've let him down once but he doesn't know, and now he's just back from America, a new life, with decisions to be made? And you love him like fuck but you can live without him?

If he was smiling, Caz would smile back.

Caz was knackered but she'd had six weeks to prepare for this moment. She was ready to meet her man; prepared for anything from Valerie, a rejection, a declaration of love, a wheelchair, Herpes. Every eventuality had been thought of, considered and dealt with. She had fifteen plans, three lists of alternatives, sixteen sub-clauses, four amendments and a codicil – every scenario covered. Unconcerned, she had slouched into Gatwick Limbo, head down, Miss Super-Cool, apparently not caring who was there or when, when the cold reality of no Valerie stopped her dead in her tracks. She had every scenario bolted down except one – Valerie not being there. And Valerie *wasn't* there!

No fucking Valerie. No fucking, miserable, low down, chicken-shit, chicken-hearted, double-dealing, mother-f, no Valerie!

'*Caz!*'

He came running towards her, but this was no slow-mo beach scene. Her arms were folded, her lips tightly pursed as he belted over, skidded on something, then stopped two feet away before she swung one of her clenched fists in his direction.

'The bog,' he said breathlessly, as if she cared, 'I waited fer *ages.*'

Caz stared. He looked pitiful, trapped in a no-man's-land between laughter and apology.

'I should've gone before, I know, but . . .' Half a smile, then a change of tack. 'I was beginning t'think you weren't on the plane. And then—'

'Arsehole,' Caz said.

'Yes,' he said. Then he grinned. 'Caz, you look fucking gorgeous!'

'No, I don't,' she said. 'And I smell.'

Twenty-three

Valerie had brought the Daimler and was happy to hump the cases over there now, get back, but Caz stopped him, suggesting a drink first. They sat in the odd half-world of late-night arrivals and got to know each other again, drinking orange juice and wondering why there was a bookstall open at eleven p.m. As she mellowed, Caz decided that this was a good thing, a half-way stop between meeting and going. There was time for familiarity to grow thick, time to avoid any silences they might otherwise have taken to the car. They'd done the executive stuff – What d'you want to drink? D'you want to risk one of those pizza slices? – and now they were about to talk. Caz was first.

'So, you're pleased to see me?'

'I love it when you're angry.'

'Clichés aren't allowed.'

'You started it!'

'That's two.'

'Will you marry me?'

'Three. Peanuts.'

'Peanuts?'

'Yes, no and maybe are clichés.'

'You're one cliché behind.'

'Am I?'

'I said "You started it" and "You look lovely when you're angry".'

'No, you didn't. You said "I love it when you're angry." '

He tilted his head, re-ran the tape. 'Same difference.'

'It isn't. One's about me, the other one's about you.'

'So will you?'

'What?'

'Do the I do.'

'If that's not a cliché it ought t'be.'

'Fer fuck's sake, Caz.'

'Cliché.'

'Don't do this to me.'

'This?'

'Jesus! You're a pain, Flood!'

'Yes.'

'Yes fucking what?'

'Yes, I'm a pain, and yes, we'll get married.'

'D'you mean it? You're not taking the piss? You'll let me move in with your pigs?'

'I never said anything about living together, that's a cliché.'

'It's common sense.'

'Isn't common sense a cliché?'

'No, a cliché is an overworked phrase that has lost its original power. Like you saying fuck all the time.'

'But we will?'

'Will what?'

'Fuck all the time.'

'Want another juice?'

'Who pays now we're engaged?'

Twenty-four

Caz was in a bath full of Matey. The water was pink and too hot, and low-grade bubbles piled up between her feet and the taps. She was having a major wallow.

It wasn't until they'd been in the car a minute, the luggage in the boot, that she'd realised Valerie hadn't bothered to kiss her yet. For God's sake, they were *engaged* and the lump couldn't be bothered! She might have called the whole thing off, there and then, but on the dash, in paper, with a bow, there'd been a little package, small enough to be a ring.

'Yours,' he'd said.

When she'd opened it, a packet of Phyllosan, she'd called him an old romantic. He put his finger to her lips and said, 'Let's go home.'

There'd been a fat yellow moon in the distance as they cruised back to Brighton and she'd mentally clicked a shutter on it, time-stamped it; this was the night I decided to get married. Ten miles later, she had a sudden thought, 'Where's home?' but Valerie tapped his jacket pocket, a blue toothbrush protruding, and said, 'Is yours pink?' So he was psychic as well as gorgeous, was he? No, he said, common sense, really – she'd been away for five weeks; she'd have something planned for work, probably laid out on the bed, ready.

So, not psychic, he was a bloody spy!

She was trying not to think, because any vague possibility of pleasure was always threatened by demons, inside and out. Not so long ago she'd sat in this bath behind Valerie, another homecoming, another stumble. She had soothed something from him then, made him sleep, then quietly cried while she was alone, knowing they couldn't have a future.

She shook her head and the thought was gone. She was surprised and tried to pull it back. When nothing happened she turned back to the bath, her body. She felt long and streaky, an eighth of an inch taller, tight and hard and sharp. Work tomorrow, she thought, Valerie tonight. She wasn't that randy but she felt dreadfully satisfied and sensual, as if the misfortune of others in her recent past made her that much more lucky, that the gift-horse in her bed with his lovely mouth was there to be indulged, to be eaten. Why not, she thought, his very special favour? And if he was up to it, afterwards, her as well...

She was up at five-thirty, in her gear and running along the Esplanade before six o'clock. Just an easy four miles, the seafront, a mile along Marine Parade and back, just enough to stay loose. She knew that if she wanted to, she could've pushed it. She had plenty of energy spare. In the end, she had stayed in the bath ten minutes too long. She was pink and sweet when she came to bed. Valerie was asleep.

Waking him was against her principles, and it was definitely *his* loss. Over breakfast she would tell him what she'd intended, every tortured, tantalisingly-tongued detail. If he died of angst, so be it. It would serve the lazy bugger right. She was smiling as she ran. She was actually happy. The sensation that sex could be just something else, that first they would have each other, was new but she liked it. Then she thought, was this middle age, thirty – *thirty!* – rapidly approaching? She kicked hard for a mile. Nah.

Twenty-five

And then she was back at John Street nick, walking down the echoing corridors, sniffing, picking up the vibes again, pulling it all back on to her like an old sweatshirt, a favourite pair of shoes. The stuff she had laid out on her bed five weeks ago had been stock Caz: ice-blue 501s, white top, bomber jacket, Asics trainers. After her morning run she had had a quick shower, put it on, kissed Valerie on the head and left.

She was in early – she was always early – loading up a tray-full of coffees from the canteen, bum-bashing out through the swing doors, climbing the back stairs, dumping the tray on the first surface inside the detectives' barn. There were notes all over her desk, Post-its, scraps of note-pad, a get-well card, and something official – an appointment with the quack to get signed off. Some toss-pot had cut out a photograph, Caz's face, and stuck it on to a cartoon of a nurse with an open razor and a terrified male patient about to lose his pubic hair. Across the top, *a là* the *Sun*, a scrawl: *Caz Flood, the Girl Who Shaved Brighton.* It was Greavsie's writing, she was pretty sure. It could've been Bob Saint's or Billy Tingle's, but she didn't think either of them could write.

She took a second coffee just before the lads rolled in. When they did, she was turned in her chair, stretched out, legs apart, her toes pointing up. She had her arms folded and took all the abuse with a grin.

By lunchtime she had seen the doctor, flown the medical and got her chit. She was part of the team again. There was a professional shoplifting gang doing the biz in the town centre and it was odds-on that Caz would be assigned to the job on that. There were store detectives on the inside but a squad had been trying to film the hand-overs outside. The pros had never been caught on camera actually lifting the gear, and the in-stores were getting a bit pissed off. As soon as the mark left the store, the goods had been walking. Invariably, there was some quick crowd shuffle and confusion, swapped bags, and the evidence was gone. DS Reid's team was parked up in a couple of dark-glass jobs with auto-focus Canons trying to capture the moment on Kodak – so far, without a lot of success.

The other possibility was a Q-Granny job. Some shit had been whacking old ladies for their pensions as soon as they'd left the post office. The idea had come down that a couple of WDCs could dress up as oldies and neuter the bastard. With a bit of luck he'd take a pop at the law and get himself an extra couple of years. If Caz was going to get the choice, she'd opt for the granny-bashing job. Chances were this low-life would bolt. If he did, Caz could go catch him and get some training in while putting another notch on her truncheon.

DI MacInnes called her through about half-past one.

She looked bright. 'So, what's it to be, sir?'

MacInnes was neutral but not unfriendly. 'Today, yer desk,' he said. 'Monday we'll take a look at what we got, see how best t'use yer. Read a few files, see what's going on. There's some organised shopping in town, a mugger or two east side, anna kid-botherer up at Patcham.'

'That Child Protection's, sir?'

'It's everyone's lass, but the CPU is running it.'

Caz nodded, then paused to absorb. Then she mentioned Kevin King's accident, his next-of-kin. Could she deliver his belongings?

'Yer'd say that wuz police business would yer, Flood?'

'It's not personal, sir.'

Tom MacInnes shrugged. 'Suit yersel. Get off out of it about four, then. Do it then. Rest've the afternoon y'll be getting yerself up t'date on these other things, OK?'

Caz nodded, said 'Sir' when she wanted to say 'Tom,' and left quietly, back to the lads, the chat, no doubt another piss-take on her desk.

At four she left for Worthing.

Twenty-six

Kevin King's mother lived on a quiet post-war estate now mostly brown pebble-dashed, the older stained-glass windows replaced by sterile UPVC. The parcel had come with a note saying that Mrs King worked only mornings and that there was no Mr King. Caz's phone call at three o'clock had been answered by a tiny voice, almost loving, a little woman so pleased to hear from someone who knew her boy.

Caz was driving her MX5, but parked three or four houses away from number thirty-two, as if turning up in a bright modern sports car would be somehow inappropriate. She walked the few yards to their drive, opened a sad gate and walked up to their door. As she arrived, raised her hand, it opened.

'You're Detective Constable Flood?'

'Mrs King?'

'Do come in,' the woman said. She was as small as the voice, smaller, a lightweight, blow-away thing. Caz had to marvel that someone so tiny could have given birth to Kevin – no lightweight, certainly not small.

Mrs King toddled down her hall. 'You'll have tea, won't you? You've time for that?'

Caz mumbled something as they went straight to the kitchen.

'I've boiled the kettle already. You said you'd be here for

four. The pot's hot. How do you like your tea?'

'As it comes,' Caz said. 'No sugar.'

'Milk?'

'Yes, please.'

They went through to the lounge. When they were sat down, a cake tower between them, thin bone-china cups, saucers in their laps, Mrs King said, 'Did you know Kevin?'

'A little,' Caz said politely. 'We weren't close friends but I knew his friend Matthew Black.'

'Oh, poor Matthew! Mollie is a friend of mine. She rang me just after we heard about Kevin, and then Matthew had his accident.'

'I'm sorry,' Caz said.

'Thank you, dear. Is your tea all right?'

Caz nodded, glanced at her package.

'Those are Kevin's things?'

Caz sat forward and handed the box across, feeling slightly awkward, though she didn't know why. When Mrs King offered to make her a second cup of tea she accepted, glad that the woman would be out of the room for a short while.

When she came back from the kitchen, the cup and saucer rattling slightly, Mrs King had already opened the package of her son's things. She was holding a black elasticated band, the chest monitor that sent signals to Kevin's Polar watch.

'What is this?' she asked softly.

Caz answered, too quickly, not really thinking. 'It's part of his heart monitor, his watch. Kevin was wear—'

'He was, when he died?'

'I'm sorry, Mrs King.'

'When he died? This thing records his pulse, doesn't it? Kevin paid quite a lot of money for it, I remember.'

Caz nodded. There was nothing to say.

'Then it would have Kevin's . . . Oh, please, take it away!'

'Mrs King?'

'Do you run, Miss Flood?'

'Yes, but . . .'

'You must have the watch. I really couldn't keep it.'

'Mrs King, I'm a police officer. We're not supposed to accept—'

'*Please*,' Mrs King said.

In the end, Caz agreed to take the watch away. When she had finished her second cup of tea, she told Mrs King she would hold it, telephone her in a month.

'I won't want it back,' Mrs King said emphatically. 'You can have it. Kevin would like that, a runner.'

Caz looked into the little woman's face. Deep in there was certainty. She changed her mind. 'OK, Mrs King. For Kevin. And thank you.'

'I'll get you the box,' Mrs King said. 'The instructions are in there.'

Twenty-seven

Over the weekend, Caz caught up on a few things, eating at Armando's, shopping at Marks & Sparks, touching base with Moira and Billy. On top of that, she had six weeks' sex with Valerie to catch up on. That started well, but by Saturday night Valerie was threatening to cry off. He suddenly remembered he had work at home to do and retreated to a corner of his attic with his Toshiba portable computer, a new active-matrix colour job. Caz toyed with the fun idea of making extra demands, but then decided to use the opportunity to go for a run and test out her fancy watch, maybe follow that up with a quiet lunchtime drink with Tom MacInnes.

She was sitting near to Val, a definite distraction, topless and brown, with long brown legs emerging from pink shorts.

'Can't you put something on?' Valerie said, shifting slightly in his seat, maybe thinking of giving up on the computer.

'I'm trying to get this stupid watch to work, rig up this band.'

'You want a hand?'

'Do I?'

'You want a hand,' Val said. 'Out of the way. This needs a man.' He stood up, kissed her neck as he clipped the black band around her chest, fiddled with the watch. 'So what's the problem?'

'It's blipping, see, the little heart thing. But how do I make it record when I go for a run?'

'Follow the instructions?'

'What are you, Val, an anarchist?'

'Where are they?'

'The instructions?'

Val glowered. Caz had them in her hand. She passed them over. He had a quick clever-bastard look through the index, then turned to somewhere past half-way.

'It needs flushing,' he said.

'I haven't been.'

'The watch. The memory's full.'

'Oh!' Caz said.

'So, d'you want me to empty it?'

Caz said yes, then very quickly, '*No!*'

'Yes or no?'

She was thinking, but the sex was making her dull. 'No, as in no, not yet. As in wait a minute.'

'I thought you were going out. I've got work to do, remember.'

'What's it full of, the memory?'

Val grinned, 'Memories?'

'Kevin King's pulse?'

'Was this his watch?'

'No, I just thought his pulse might've got into someone else's.'

'Point taken. You want to flush it or stick it on the computer?'

'Oh, very good, Val. Yeah, stick it on the computer and print me a graph of Kevin's last heartbeats.'

'Now?'

Caz looked suddenly different. 'D'you mean it? Don't joke, Val. This is some bloke who died, remember . . .'

'I'm not joking,' he said. 'This watch has a computer interface, here. And I'll bet you've got the software on a disc in the box, right?'

'There's a disc in there, but I hadn't thought about it.'

'Well, read here. See?' He waved some Jappobabble nonsense-text at her. 'With the interface and the software, you can suck out information and store it on a PC, this PC if you want. You want to do that?'

'Sounds nifty. Practise with Kev King's data then we won't lose mine.'

'You're all heart, Flood.'

'Do it,' Caz said.

'Only if you give me the disc,' Val said.

Twenty-eight

Valerie took the disc from Caz, popped it into the Toshiba's floppy drive, typed a couple of commands. A minute later, he took the watch, clipped it into the adaptor and plugged the lead into the back of the computer. A minute after that, he said, 'You can go for your run now.'

'That's it?'

'That's it. I'll play around with it while you're out.'

Caz went off for her run. It was Sunday, so the run was a little bit longer, but it was Spring, so it wasn't that long. If Valerie had not been a priority, she'd've driven up to the Downs and dashed off a ten. Instead she fartleked, speed-played, for about eight miles, just enjoying herself, her new strength and suppleness.

As she ran, she thought about Kevin King, like her a half-miler, an eight hundred metre runner. He had been sub-two minutes, well under, but had been only fringe county class. Her best, a while ago, was a squeak inside 2:04 – pretty good for a woman. That and two seconds off it, she'd still be in an England vest. She could probably still do it, if she gave up just about everything else. She'd thought seriously about it once or twice, but then, she thought, so had Kevin King. Kevin had tried it, tried it all, including being alone. And now he was dead.

When she got back, Caz undid Val's front door key from her

laces, went straight up the stairs and through to the bog, shouting a Hi! but trying not to bother him. It occurred to her vaguely that before long they'd be the odd couple, but right now she was preparing herself to do battle with his shower.

Val's flat was high-ish in the town and squabbed on top of three-and-a-half storeys. The first time she had been there he had laughably called it a penthouse, but what it was was a converted loft. It was big, yes, but it was still a loft, still a dormer-window job.

Add four storeys to the flat's geographical location and then another six feet to the shower-head and one thing Val did *not* have was water pressure. Val's sluice had cystitis – it *wanted* to go, it thought it was going to go, but when the moment came, nothing but pain, maybe a little dribble. Before she'd gone away she'd suggested a pump. She had told him, 'The bath is OK, but the half-hour it takes to fill, the glugs and burbles . . .' It was more than she could stand.

The shower room was the other side of the bedroom and kitchen, a long way from his desk at the far end of the lounge. She was stripping off when she heard him shout something, and guessing it was 'Drink?' she shouted back, 'Whatever, don't mind!' He was shouting something else as she switched the water on, and, as it hit her full force-nine in the chest, he burst in.

'Watch the . . .'

She was pepper-sprayed, water-cannoned, red.

'Shower?' she said.

He left quickly.

When she came out she was in khaki: vaguely military bottoms with lots of pockets, a Lee Cooper flyer's top, same colour. The trainers didn't go, but then this was Caz Flood. Val noticed but didn't comment. He was thinking about Angola. 'Who wants a drink?' he said.

She had a little Southern Comfort and an espresso, meaty

113

coffee that bit back, just as she liked it before lunch. Val was on one of his big chairs, his eyes sparkling, trying not to laugh. She sparkled back, fighting the urge to say, 'I love you.'

'You going out?' he said.

'If I can get hold've Tom.'

'You haven't rung him?'

'Nope. Tom will be at home, at work or in the Grapes. He's supposed to be at home.'

'So where'll he be?'

Caz sipped. 'Best guess is work.'

She rang him at home, three rings, the time to get from the bookcase to the phone.

'MacInnes.'

'Tom, Caz. Fancy a drink?'

'Ah've got one.'

'In the Grapes, ten minutes?'

'OK.'

'I'm buying.'

'That's OK too.'

She put the phone down and turned back to Valerie, still in his chair. 'So, how much work have you got to do?'

'Coupl've hours, why?'

She was kneeling in front of him, his zip.

'How quick can you manage a quickie?'

It was like pressing a button. Ding!

He stood up with difficulty. 'Oh God, my spreadsheets!'

'Bugger yer spreadsheets!' Caz said. She pulled him down. And by quick, did he mean quick, or what?

Twenty-nine

Caz walked up a shallow hill, gardens to her left, the American Express building almost straight in front of her. Then, at the main road, she turned left and walked down to the Grapes.

She was late – there's quick and there's quick – and when she went into the lounge Tom MacInnes was sitting alone with two Bells, one fat, one second-hand already. He saw her as she came through the door but didn't look at his watch. 'Hello, Flood,' he said.

She sat down. 'Sorry I'm late, sir, something popped up. I came as quick as I could.' She was grinning.

'Ah'll have a large one,' he said.

Caz went to the bar and got a double for the DI, a single for herself with a bottle of Canada Dry. When she got back, MacInnes took the drink out of her hand and swigged half.

'Helluvamonth, Flood! Helluvamonth . . .'

'D'you want to tell me?'

'No. S'dunwith now. But it's bin a helluvamonth.'

'I wish I could say the same,' Caz said, 'but I can't. The last five weeks have been magic. I'm really better.'

'Fit, are yer? Over your problems?'

'I could even work with Bob Moore, sir!'

'It's Tom. We're not working now.'

'Tom,' Caz said. She was thinking about her last proper case.

115

There was a short silence then, as if he was psychic, the DI grunted and said, 'Ah suppose yu'll be wanting t'know about ay that Kingfisher thing, how the young lassie is?'

'Is she OK?'

'The lassie's fine and yu'll be pleased t'know that wuv managed t'sort somethin' out fer the Scots fellah what helped you.'

She smiled. 'That's good news.'

He frowned. 'All's well ends well, ay lass? Is that what y'thinkin'?'

'Sort of, Tom.'

'Well, it isn't! Caz, y'have t'stop doing these things, takin' chances. Y'have responsibilities now. Yu'll be that much mair use to the force if you stay alive, help others. You go to the edge one too many times. Caz, and . . .'

'I end up like Von Stallwood?'

'Or you end up dead. Either way yu'll be no use to anyone.'

Caz had picked up her glass, the double the DI had bought her. She tilted it slowly towards her. 'I know, Tom. And I know it's not just me any more.' She took a breath, then knocked the drink back in one. 'But thanks,' she said.

'Thanks?' MacInnes said gruffly. 'Fer what?'

'Oh, I don't know,' Caz said. 'Just thanks. For saying the right thing. For watching my back, for being there.'

'Away,' he said, waving his boned hand at her. 'So, tell me, Lanzarote?'

Caz lit up. 'The weather was fabulous and I met a physio-therapist who fixed up my back. I got some great training in.'

'Did I tell you DCS Blackside is staying?'

'No. And you haven't told me how Veronica is doing.'

'The DCS has confirmed he's not taking up his post at Scotland Yard and the last I heard, Von was doing fine. Three weeks and she can have visitors. You think you'll go and see her?'

'Yes,' Caz said.

Thirty

Caz sat opposite the other man in her life. Tom looked fluttery, on an edge blunted by his whisky, and he looked even thinner. She worried about him, but she knew his apparent frailty was two-edged – many a villain had made the mistake of thinking Tom MacInnes was weak. There was still a steel core there. He was thinner than he once was maybe, but he was still hard.

He reminded her of the old men who ran in the Sunday Times Fun Run every Hyde Park August. Before and after their age-grouped race they looked wobbly, more than their age, with veiled eyes and time's ache in every joint, but, come the gun, the best of them, seventy-plus, would still run two-and-a-half miles in around fifteen minutes. When she saw them she admired them, envied them. She hungered for that deep strength of character, the John Bull heart that carried them still. They were old athletes, old paras, commandos, sailors; red-faced, red-bereted men, but still out there, not yet given in.

'You don't think you're looking a bit peaky then?'

'Course ah am,' Tom said. 'Ah'm tired. Tired of the CPS, clever briefs, youngsters who'd hit an old lady.'

'You're not thinking of retiring, are you?'

'Every day, but ah'll not. What's there else t'do?'

He sat back as if he ached, as if he was thinking of other places, other times. Caz decided to change the subject.

'While I was on holiday, you know we had two accidents, two lads from Worthing?'

'I heard sumthin'. Not suspicious deaths, are they?'

'Not as far as I know, and it's just the one death. There's a chap called Matthew Black was badly hurt, but he's not dead.'

'Over there?'

'They'll move him by air ambulance when it's safe. God knows when that will be. Poor sod took a nose-dive off a roof. Didn't do his face a lot of good. He was up there sunbathing in the nude, fell off. We thought he was dead but he came round after CPR and mouth-to-mouth.'

'You?'

'And some others.'

'You make a habit of it.'

'No, I don't. The death, the bloke that drowned. I wasn't there at all.'

'I was thinking of the bed-sit murders, that stuff in Shoreham.'

'Water under the bridge, Tom, long time ago.'

'Hardly!'

'Well, it *feels* like a long time ago.'

Caz pulled out a folded sheet of paper from a pocket. 'The guy that drowned, he wore a Polar pulse-watch. This is a recording of his heart-rate the last few hours of his life. I think it might be a first.'

'Happens all the time in hospitals.'

'I mean real-time, in the real world.'

'So, let's see.'

Caz unfolded the paper, smoothed it flat. 'I've not looked at it myself yet, but Valerie—'

'How is he?'

'Val? Oh, he's fine,' Caz said, not looking up from the sheet. 'Anyway, he says that here, across here, this is time. This is King's pulse-rate.'

118

'King?'

'The guy that drowned.'

'Shame they couldna record what the fellah wuz thinkin'.'

Caz glanced at the paper. The trace was wild, up above 150 beats for the part she could see. She fancied a drink.

'Top you up, Tom? Same again?'

'Off y'go, lass.'

When she came back, Tom MacInnes was engrossed, his finger running over the paper, morbidly following King's last moments.

'This here'll be jogging, summat like that, then he runs faster, here, or uphill maybe, something that makes the heart go a bit. He die of a heart attack, this fellah?'

'Drowned.'

'So this is there? His pulse goes a bit higher, right there, even higher there, then, boom, nothing.'

Caz felt intrusive, sacrilegious. 'It's weird, seeing someone, someone . . . No wonder his mother didn't want to keep the watch.'

'She gevv it you?'

'Insisted.'

'So y've tried it out?'

'Went for a run this morning. Valerie was going to put the data into his computer while I was out.'

'This is quite sumthin',' MacInnes said. 'An' you say the fellah drowned, it wasnee a heart attack?'

'I don't know what was done after, but there was a PM and the given cause of death was drowning.'

'I wasnee thinking anything else, lass. Jest, I wuz lookin' here at this thing, seeing the young fellah's heart go. I thought the heart slowed down when a body went in water, tha's all.'

'Maybe he was threshing about or something, trying to get to the side.'

'They checked?'

'Checked what?'

'The pool. An' whether this King chap could swim?'

Caz felt foolish. 'The truth is, Tom, I don't know. The way I heard it, Kevin King got drunk, and jumped or fell into the pool on his way home. Then he drowned. It was nothing to do with me. Everything I know, I've picked up second- and third-hand, but I presume they would have checked for any signs of foul play.'

'Automatic,' Tom said. 'And checked the lungs, water content. You can bet he drowned, Caz. Thing is, *why* did he drown?'

Thirty-one

When Caz got back, Valerie had more or less wrapped up. He was on the point of switching everything off and there was a healthy chunk of A4 in the out tray of his laser.

'I printed off another graph for Kevin King,' he said, 'and one of your run. How hard do you think you go when you're pushing it?'

'Hard-ish,' Caz said.

'So would a maximum pulse of one-nine-five surprise you?'

'Surprise me? It'd frighten me to death.'

'Come see,' he said.

There was a well-touted rule of thumb calculation which said that a person's maximum heart-rate was two-twenty minus their age. For Caz that was one-nine-two. The graph Valerie was now showing her had her at points above that for ten of the fifty-plus minutes she had been out running. Well, it was just a rule of thumb.

'I've printed a comparison graph,' he said, 'you and Kevin King together. Both of you, when you're cruising, you're around one-thirty, one forty, but when you're hammering it, you're nearer two hundred beats per minute. Is that good for you?'

'Probably not,' Caz giggled, a little drunk, 'but who cares?'

'Me for one,' Valerie said roughly. He passed her the paper-work and turned back to his machines.

'Are you sulking?' she said.

'Are you pissed?' he flashed back.

Caz took the graphs and sloped off to the other side of the room. When she crumpled down to take a look at what were basically ECGs she was surprised to see just how hard her body worked when she trained hard. Valerie was in a vaguely miffed mood but not so much that he couldn't offer to make some tea. 'Please,' she said distractedly, trying to make sense of the traces. Some dark feeling was welling in like a slow tide. When she looked up, Valerie was in the kitchen.

'Hey, Thomas,' she said. 'I love you!'

'Cliché,' he said.

And then she saw it, realised. Saw Kevin King murdered.

You could read the dancing, the recorded beats per minute, the one-twenties, the one-twenty-fives, Kevin having a real go at the Irish Rover and clocking one-thirty-five. You could see his alcoholic heart tupping away at one-ten, then one-hundred, and then the late-night, fairly pissed ninety-five as he settled down, as he left, the extra five beats as he walked up the steps past the guards.

Then the high nineties, his walk down to the lagoon, and then, what?

A sudden spike, a frightened one-thirty, then one-twenty, one-fifteen, one-ten. Oh, it's you . . .

But then one-twenty again, one-thirty, forty, fifty, sixty, running. Then one-seventy, one-eighty, one-eighty-five, ninety, running, running, running. One-nine-two, one-nine-four, five, six, seven. Why so fast? Why flat-out running? Why, late at night, drunk, not dressed for it?

Why?

Then one-eighties, tiredness creeping in, lactic acid flooding the body, whoever it was, whatever it was, closing, closing, cornering Kevin. And then the pool's edge, one-seventy, then a brief one-seven-five, thirty, seventy, one-ten, ninety, then a slow sixty, slow forty. Then zero, zero, zero, zero at five minutes to three.

'Tea? Caz? Your tea.'

She was white.

'What?'

'Jesus,' Val said. 'You look like you've seen a ghost.'

Caz felt sick.

'Yes,' she said. 'I have. Kevin King.'

Thirty-two

'You might be right, Flood, but there's nothing we can do.'

Norman Blackside seemed to have lost some of his power. He was just as physically big, but as he sat behind his desk shaking his head for the second time that Monday morning, he was like a giant balloon, not quite filled, no longer straining, just there.

'But, sir, I'm a runner. I know this graph means that Kevin King was either being chased or chasing someone. He didn't just fall in a swimming pool.'

'He was pissed, Flood. There was a PM and no sign of violence.'

'But what about the running, sir? *Something* happened. King was drunk, but to me that makes it even more strange. I couldn't run like that if I was pissed. Something must have frightened him.'

'Tom?'

Tom MacInnes creaked in his chair. 'Ah think the girl might have summat, Norm, but like you, ah don't see wuv got enough.'

'You brought her in here, Tom.'

'There's other accidents.'

'DC Flood?'

'The day after King was drowned, sir, another chap, Matthew Black, also from Worthing, fell from a roof. He was

124

sunbathing. He was in a pretty bad way but he didn't die. In March last year there was another drowning and another fall. One they thought was an accident, the other one suicide.'

'Which was which?'

'The fall was a German chap. He was a bit depressed. There was reason to think he might have jumped.'

'So, if he did?'

'The drowning, sir. A bloke from London, I know his brother vaguely. In his thirties, a strong swimmer. What's a little strange there is that he should go swimming in the sea. The sea between la Santa and Famara is very rocky and dangerous and the camp's got excellent pools.'

'The body?'

'Eventually. The sea gave him up a few months later. Nothing could be very definite. The currents can be rough, there's the rocks and a body in the water for a long time, the fish . . .'

'You don't have to paint a picture, Flood.'

'Sorry, sir.'

'So what've we got?' Blackside grunted as he sat up. 'Two guys from Worthing cop it, one was out of his skull anyway, the other one was where he shouldn't be. The best bet there would be coincidence. The year before—'

'The same fortnight, sir.'

Blackside wasn't amused. '*The year before*, someone dives into the sea, someone else dives off a great height . . . coincidence again. What are you suggesting, Flood?'

'We have three suspicious deaths of Brits abroad, sir, all at the same place. Shouldn't we follow it up?'

'You are looking for another holiday, Flood?'

'No, sir! What was I supposed to do, *not* tell you what I found out?'

'What does this Worthing chappie have t'say, the one that's injured?'

'He's not saying anything, sir. Intensive care, coma.'

'Back here?'

'No, sir, he's not well enough to move yet.'

Blackside filled up slightly. He had made a decision.

'OK, Tom. This week only. Take a look at the backgrounds of these three stiffs, sorry, two stiffs, Matthew Black. Our best bet's going to be the two from Worthing, but run a PNC on this other bloke, the one that died last year. What's his name, Flood?'

'Jones, sir, Colin.'

'Oh, wonderful!'

'We can get the address, sir.'

'Of *course* we can get the address, Flood, we're policemen.'

MacInnes came in as quickly as he could. 'OK Norm, I'll have Flood talk to King's mother again, see what she c'n turn up. An' she can talk to Mrs Black, anyone else that knows him. I c'n do the PNC on Jones without dropping anything.'

Caz coughed. 'What about the German guy, sir?'

'What, Interpol now? You've got a name, Flood?'

She blushed. 'Hans, sir . . .'

Blackside looked at MacInnes. 'She's joking, right? Tell me she's joking, Tom.'

'Schmidt, sir?' Caz said.

'Get her out of here, Tom.'

Thirty-three

Caz remembered that Audrey King worked mornings, so, for something to take her through to lunchtime, she did a couple of traces on Matt Black's family. Other than the obvious one of the running club, the only connection she could imagine between Matt and Kevin was that they were gay or maybe buying steroids. She discounted both very quickly.

Kevin King was single, that was no crime; and Matt Black had a reputation for being a bit of a lad, but, more importantly, Caz had clocked that semi-automatic cross-appraisal that had occurred when she, girl, had met them, boys, for the first time. What she called the sexual exchange, that instant up-and-down, file-it-away assessment of mutual sex-objects, had definitely occurred. She had to close her eyes and look back to an evening at a track in England, again to the track at Lanzarote, but yes, it had been there. It wasn't particularly strong, she guessed due to the context – it's hard to have sex high on the list when you're doing reps – but she could re-run the film of her assessing Matthew – those buns – and she could rewind to note the faint miff that he didn't fancy her. So, not gay.

It wasn't impossible that Matt and Kevin were doing roids, but again, instinctively, Caz thought it unlikely. They were worked out, true, but they weren't pumped up. They were committed but not staring, and they shared the same injury hassles as her, the hassles that came with the territory, the 'My name's not Jason, I'll do it on my own' drug-free scene. So not drugs either.

She went to the Kings' house, found Audrey in, had tea, a nice chat. Yes, Kevin was quite a good swimmer, not a fish, but not scared of water or anything. Audrey had always presumed that Kevin had banged his head or something, you know, dived in and hit his head on the bottom, something like that. Was that what had happened?

'I don't actually know, Audrey. This is just standard procedure. We keep a little file on accidents abroad, not because we suspect foul-play or anything but just in case, looking for patterns, like, say, when there was that trouble in Spain with faulty heaters.'

Audrey smiled. Some lies are kind.

'How are you getting on with your watch?'

'Oh, it's great!' Caz said. 'Really useful. When I've got properly used to it, it should help me with my training quite a lot.'

'Kevin would be pleased to know it had found a good home.'

Caz smiled politely. It sounded like they were talking about a cat.

'Oh, and I flushed everything out. Zeroed everything. There was no . . .'

'Ah, good!' Audrey said, taking in a little breath. 'Yes, good.'

Caz smiled again.

'More tea, detective?'

Thirty-four

Caz got back about three o'clock. There was nothing much to chase and no DI to harass about Colin Jones' record, so she was at a loose end. If Moira Dibben had been around, they might have managed to slope off to the canteen for fifteen minutes or so to grab a quick coffee, but no such luck. Once Caz had made herself unavailable for the shoplifting obbo, DS Reid had pulled Moira on board as his extra pair of eyes, told her to leave her navy-blue knickers at home and to *try* and look like a citizen. Moira had the aspiring detective's fatal flaw. She was one of those coppers who, off duty, looked like a human being, but on, no matter how hard she tried, no matter how she dressed, she always gave off a faint whiff of plod.

Caz thought about ringing Valerie but managed to stop herself, then she had the brilliant idea of ringing Ina Jensen at la Santa. What better excuse to ring an old mate than a possible murder inquiry? Somewhere in the bowels of her bag she had the scrap of paper. When she found it, she copied it out on to a piece of A4 with 'G-28, Lanzarote?' scrawled across the top. If some miserable DS or DI picked up on her call to Isla Canarias, she could point at the sudden death inquiry and smile.

She dialled 01–38 and all the other bits and bobs, and marvelled as she always did when the phone rang, *purred*, in some office just off Africa. Why a bit of water in between should

129

make her think telecommunications were amazing she had no idea, but no amount of use would ever convince her that international calls were anything less than magic.

A Spanish voice, something. Caz immediately spoke English. Then the voice again, 'One moment, please.'

A short wait, then, 'Physiotherapy?'

'Ina?'

'This is Ute, who is that?'

'Ute, how *are* you? It's Caz Flood, bad back, tilted pelvis. I left last week.'

'Caz-ee! It's good to hear you! Are you good?'

'I'm great, thank you.' There was a slight echo on the line. 'But what about you, Ute? How is everything?'

'Oh, me, I am fine now. I kill patients now and then, but—'

'Hey, don't joke!' Caz said. 'You treated *me* once, my back?'

'I am like Jonah, you don't think?'

'No, I don't think, Ute! I thought you said you were better?'

'Oh, I am sorry, Caz-ee. I just have so many bad luck. My patients, all that, an' last night my boyfriend, he gets in a fight in night club in Playa Blanca, gets a big mess of his face made. Some Englishman hit him again after he comes out of disco, piece of wood. He lose some teeth, break his jaw, all swollen up.'

'Oh, Ute! You really are not lucky, are you? Did they catch the man who hit him?'

'Spanish police, yes. Man who had the little fight inside the disco. But they have to let him off. He says, I'm not there when Marco is hurt, I'm already home in bed sleeping it off. Police from Arrecife say they can't prove nothing so this man, nothing.'

'What was the fight over?'

'I don't go to the club with Marco but the fight, it was about spilled beer, only a little fight. Shoving, making faces, Marco says.'

130

'But you don't know what it was over?'

'Beer, I say already, but with boys what does it matter?'

'Cheer up, Oot!'

'I try,' Ute said.

Ina was out in the sun teaching Ute's back-strength class. It finished at 3:15 and Ina would be back five minutes later. Did Caz want Ina to ring or would she ring Ina again?'

'I'll ring at three-thirty.'

'I will tell her.'

'Thanks,' Caz said. She was thinking, 'Just don't *treat* her!'

Caz had time to get a coffee anyway, so she went down the back stairs to the canteen, thinking as she went about 'Ute who lived in a whale'. There was no doubting she was associated with some shit luck, and anyone who read their stars would do well to keep away from her, but Caz knew that she had to avoid putting two and two together and inventing a conspiracy to make five.

No, she thought, be logical; one guy who'd been treated by both the la Santa physiotherapists had died in suspicious circumstances. Two other guys had died, but that was a year earlier, and there was absolutely no evidence of a direct connection between them or between them and Kevin King. This latest thing, some stupid punch-up, a couple of beered-up silly boys, it was nothing.

The old sociobiologist in Caz popped up as she was walking back upstairs with the drink. Blokes fighting! Male mammals! No doubt it was over access to a female or some other kind of sexual display. All that testosterone and nowhere to squirt it. They should run it off, take up boxing, go fight a war or something. Still, she was a good copper. She made a note to check out the Brit, stick his name through the computer.

Thirty-five

By the time Caz had sat down, it was time to ring Ina again. She pipped out the numbers, had her little marvel, waited, then heard Ina's voice.

'Physio! Can I help?'

'Yes, please. My heel-lift is too good and my spikes are leaving nasty marks on my bum. Any advice?'

'Wear thicker shorts?'

'How're you, Een?'

'Fine,' Ina said. 'No one has died this week and it rained for nearly two minutes late on Sunday afternoon.'

'God, it's tough out there!'

'Don't you *know* about skin cancer, Caz?'

'I spoke to Ute before. She still seemed down, depressed.'

'A little, but not because of the accidents. Her boyfriend, he was involved in a fracas in Playa Blanca and was hurt.'

'She told me. Marco. Do I know him?'

'Marco was a Greenie two years ago and last year, then he left to work in Playa Blanca. He is very handsome but I don't think he is very nice. You would say he is shaded.'

'Shady?'

'I saw this on *The Sweeney*. He is a bit of a sharpie. Marco does lots of things. He buys things and sells things. He works in afternoons to sell holiday weeks and he has been bouncing.'

This bloody language! 'He sells time-shares, Ina?'

'Yes.'

'And by bouncing, do you mean he has worked in a night-club, on the door, spotting trouble?'

'I told you!'

'Oh. Yeah . . .' Caz waited a moment, listening to the faint echoes in the line. 'Was Marco working the night of his fight?'

'No. This is what he will have, a boys' night out, every week. This is how it is with Ute and Marco. Once she told me. I said, this boys' night out, does it have girls too? Of course not, she tells me. I tell her she is in cloud cuckoo land, she should watch out for AIDS, other things.'

'Is he a big bloke?'

'Not big like Steve Backley. He is about one-point-eight-five metres but he has good build, good muscle-tone.'

'He works out?'

'Yes. Here and at one of the places in Playa Blanca.'

Caz stopped herself, suddenly thinking how 'copper' she sounded. Her nature was to ferret, ferret, ferret. Sometimes she found it hard to treat friends as just that.

'So what's new at your end, Een?'

'Sex!'

'Pardon?'

'I have a boyfriend, in Copenhagen. Next week I go to see him for one week. When I come back, he will come with me for two more weeks!'

'But Ina,' Caz said, 'you're not *married*!'

The other end ignored it. 'He is not so tall and he is dark. This is the other kind of Dane. Eric will be one day a pilot for SAS. I think we will be married one day, have a clinic, take holidays on the islands.'

'Babies?'

Ina laughed nervously. 'I think we will rent one, maybe two. I am so thin and I have no hips. My mother, even though I was long and slim and only three kilos when I come into the world, she told me that the confinement was very long, a very painful time.'

'You and me both, Ina!'

'What?'

'Childbirth terrifies me too!'

Caz heard a sudden rush of activity in the corridor, someone shouting, someone else running. Then she heard a couple of pandas shooting off, doing blues and twos, lights going, two tone siren blaring. She spoke quickly. 'Ina, it looks like something's on, this end. I might have to go any second.'

Ina said something back. Was there something else? Caz was trying hard not to be distracted. 'Yes,' she said, 'but . . .' Footsteps stopped at the door. 'I was just wondering what Marco's surname was.'

The door burst open, Greavsie.

'Caz, you all that's here?'

'Fraid so, Jim. What's up?'

'Fuck!' Greavsie said. His face was red and excited. 'There's bin a major ruck in the town centre. This shop-knock gang – one of 'em cut up rough and took a dig at Moira Dibben. There's at least four of 'em off on their toes. They're still somewhere in the Lanes, all of 'em, including the arse that whacked Mo.'

In her ear, Caz heard Ina saying, 'Marco, is Harris; Harrison!' but she was already switching off.

'I'll call you back!' she said and slapped down the phone.

Thirty-six

They piled into an area car that was up on the kerb out the front of the station, engine running. The doors were still open as they took off and weren't slammed until they were already racing down the hill. The driver was ex-traffic and was on to the Old Steine before Caz had got her balance. As she came upright she shouted, 'Go the pier end, Jack, we'll work up! Our lot will be coming down from the High Street!'

Jack went the wrong side of the roundabout and pulled up by the ABC cinema, blocking one of the lanes. Caz and Greavsie tumbled out, freeing their radios. As they moved into the lane, the two uniforms secured their car, then stood boot and bonnet, a very quick road-block. The two detectives dived into the crowd, their radios out, listening for info, descriptions, who was where, anything. Caz hadn't used it for ages, but she had her little riding crop down the back of her trousers. If some bastard had hurt Moira she hoped she'd get the chance to hurt him.

Greavsie was one side of the road, Caz the other, walking up towards town, each of them smack in the middle of their pavements, blatant, looking for eye-contact, or people avoiding it. This was instinct time, the time for smelling something, picking up cues, the extra flush, the extra flash of silver in the oncoming face, fear. Ten minutes from now and the streets would be closed off, but now all they had was this, their senses. And they would need luck, too.

135

Caz passed a jewellers. Most of the people she had let go by were the older middle-aged couples; the men with their soft chests poured into comfortable clothes, waistbands that curled over; the women very sensible, corseted, the kind of good old dears who would, when you said 'policeman', still think about asking the time.

A few 'street'-looking kids had gone by – pass. Then a businessman, out with his secretary, twitching when Caz caught his eye as if she was the private detective with the miniature camera he'd always feared. Caz had to make an instant judgement call: a manager and his bit on the side, yes? – or two of a team of six shoplifters, the 'clean' ones? She put her hands in the air for Greavsie, turned, and tapped the woman on the shoulder. As she did so, she clicked. Fuck! No briefcase, no handbag.

'Madam? Sir?'

Get here now, Greavsie!

The woman turned round. She had that practised air of surprise, the look, the half-perplexed, half-annoyed, but still-just-about-smiling look.

'I'm sorry, are you speaking to me?'

As soon as she spoke, Caz just knew. She was a pro. The woman was 'yessing', but too stereotypically, like a bit actor in a bad movie.

'Is this gentleman with you, madam?'

'I'm sorry?'

Greavsie, hurry up, fer Christ's sake!

Caz was smiling. 'I was wondering, would you have the time? As in do you have the time?' She paused. 'As in on a watch. Say on a watch in one of your pockets or something?'

'Pardon?'

'I wonder, mad—'

Then they saw Greavsie coming.

'The fuckin' filth!' the man said. He looked quickly at Jim

Greaves – Caz – then he shoved his girlfriend, hard, straight at her.

Caz took the woman, snarling eyes, the clawed fingers up already. A rough *O Sotogari* put her down, squealing, threshing. As she moved to get up, Caz stamped deliberately on her ankle. Then she went after her male partner, leaving the wounded, winded woman on the ground for Greavsie. As she chased after the man, her last view of the woman haunted her, the face. The change in her had been amazing. From that first false smile she was now all teeth, spittle, gasping, screaming.

'Bitch! You fuckin' bitch! I'll fuckin' *have* yew!'

But she wouldn't, couldn't. Caz was gone and Jim Greaves would already be cuffing her.

The man was about five-ten, five-eleven, average build with dark brown hair cut neatly. All this Caz logged, even as they ran, bobbed, his head bouncing between other innocent heads, moving quickly towards the area car that was blocking the road. The man was moving away, not because Caz couldn't keep pace but because she was conserving energy. Any second now, he would see Jack Carr and his oppo. Then he would turn, cornered. This would be the dangerous moment, the one they wore stab-proof jackets for, the one they half-trained for, the one you never knew you could handle until it happened.

And it happened. Just as they broke into space, the lane's widening mouth. Jack and the other copper tensed, stood taller. There was a barely perceptible blip in the man's progress, then he ran hard, straight at Jack. Jack's oppo moved the same way, Jack's arms coming up. Then, as if it had all been planned, the man dropped a shoulder, a classic rugby feint, changed direction, clipped past Jack's mate and went over the bonnet of the area car. The two uniforms crashed into each other. They were only just recovering as Caz went by them, straight up and over the car. She was thinking, 'I've been here before!'

Mister Dark Brown was noticeably quick but it was adrenalin quick, sprinter-quick, wouldn't last. Briefly he was sixty yards ahead, then, after a glance back, fifty. Then he was the other side of the moving traffic, a slapped car bonnet, forty yards away, thirty, fifteen. Caz went the same way, via a traffic island. She was within catching distance of him now, running comfortably, shouting short messages into her radio.

'King's Parade! West! Sea side! Approaching Conf Centre! Get some ten-ten down here!'

He glanced back, missed her, then dropped suddenly down steps on to the shingle beach. Caz followed too closely, pumped up by the chase and forgetting that all she was supposed to do was knacker him out while the troops came. He was at the bottom of the steps and swung. The only reason the punch missed was Caz's startled slip. As she hit the floor he kicked at her twice. The first shoe hit her hand, her fingers clasped round the radio, the second one clipped her head. Then he was gone, running, rather than finishing the job. As Caz got up, looking for her radio, he crunched into the shingle, slipped, got up, worked away.

He was fifty yards gone by the time Caz was back on the air but she wasn't worried now. The shingle would slow him up. Caz ran on it at least twice a week; it was a bastard.

'White male, five-eleven, dark hair, dark-blue suit! On the beach, heading for The Grand! In pursuit!'

He was slowing dramatically. His legs would now be on fire. Caz got within twenty yards when he stopped and turned round. He was gasping, heaving.

'Fuckin' death wish, have you?'

Caz moved five or six yards closer.

'You giving up?'

His eyes were dark with anger. 'To a fuckin' bird? Are you serious?'

'Well, you better keep running then.'

'Why don't you try to arrest me?'

'Don't need to,' Caz said. 'Coupla big strong boys'll do that soon enough!'

'You smart twat!'

'I'm renowned for it!' Caz said. He moved aggressively forward a foot but Caz knew he couldn't rush her, not on the shingle. 'So, you either run or it's face down on the pebbles. What's it t'be?'

'Fuck you!' he said and turned again.

He had learned a lesson and ran straight towards the wall, the nearest steps. Caz followed cautiously. At the top of the steps he ducked away and darted across the road. There was a screech of brakes, a thump and breaking glass. As she came into view, she saw the two cars and the suit straightening himself, walking briskly into The Grand Hotel.

She clocked her radio, 'Brighton Grand!' – then she turned the set to look at it. No crackle. That was all she needed.

She went up the steps, dragging out her warrant card.

'999, now!' she shouted at reception. A doorman flinched briefly before composing himself.

'Can you lock these?' Caz said.

He nodded.

'Do it! No one in or out unless they show you one of these!' She waved her warrant card again.

A bell-boy came over.

'The man!' Caz said. 'Which way?'

The boy pointed.

She went towards wide, beautiful stairs, not the main ones, just a dozen steps up.

'Where do these go?'

'The toilets, madam, nowhere else.'

'Toilets?'

'Yes, madam. I think hotel security—'

'Yes!' Caz said. 'Soon as poss.' She pointed. 'You're sure?'

'Yes, madam. The gentleman went in the ladies' toilet.'

'You're sure?'

'Perfectly, madam.'

'Can he get out?'

'No, madam.'

'I'll just check,' Caz said.

Suddenly she was scared again. She pushed open the door, solid, gorgeous. The loos smelt wonderful, delicate rose-petals in the air, the linger of expensive perfume. This wasn't out the back of the Grapes. It was mirrors, mahogany, marble and gold, immaculate, except where her man stood on the marble, reaching fingertips for the open fanlight.

'Don't bother,' Caz said, 'there's a dozen cars outside.'

He looked down. 'And you in here? Who you kidding?'

'The boys wouldn't come in. This *is* the ladies'.'

He pulled himself up, his legs dangling. Caz hit him with the whip across the calves. 'Fuck!' he said, but kept climbing.

She hit him again, the calves, across the arse, as hard as she could.

He squealed, 'Jesus!' before he dropped. Caz leaped back.

'Fuck! Fuck! Fuck! Fuck!' he said as he hit the marble sink surround, smacked a gold tap with his head, slid with another double bump-bump to the polished fawn floor. Caz had the door open, ready to back out.

'Jesus fuckin' *Christ*! What *was* that?' he hissed from the floor. 'What the fuck d'you hit me with?' He had made no attempt to get up.

'Never touched you,' Caz said. The riding crop was already back in her waistband.

'I think I've broken something,' he said.

'Oh, goodee!' Caz said.

Thirty-seven

They'd got the whole shoplifting gang, six of them; four women, two blokes. They'd had a tight operation and it worked like a dream, but they'd stayed in one town a day or three too long. The two blokes on the team turned out to be brothers and they looked remarkably similar. There was no way for sure Moira Dibben was going to be able to say which one had attacked her, so she picked the slightly taller one with a scar, the one who had given himself up without a struggle. The other one, Caz's one, had had a bit of a smack and a broken wrist anyway, so she figured picking the other man was insurance. If it wasn't him, he'd have to grass his brother. If he didn't want to, that was his problem. Yes, Moira was certain, this definitely was the man who had attacked her.

Moira hadn't needed hospital treatment but she'd get tomorrow off, no bother. She had a little bruise on her temple and a sore back where she'd taken a few kicks. As they spoke, she hunched forward slightly in her chair as if she was suffering a touch of dysmenorrhea.

'You OK, Mo?' Caz said.

'Just pissed off about that arsehole kicking me.'

'Sore?'

'What do you reckon?' Mo said.

Thirty-eight

After she finished her arrest paperwork, Caz went through to run checks on Mark Harris, a.k.a. Marcus, a.k.a. Marco. She'd been on the winners' rostrum with a Mark Harris once, after a Stubbington 10K, this Harris much slighter, a typical 10K, half-marathon man. While she waited for information back from the Police National Computer she remembered a thrilling finish to a race, the Eastleigh 10K, when Mark Rowlands, an Olympic bronze medallist, had waited until the last two hundred metres and then out-kicked him. Pure class.

'Nothing, Caz.'

'You what?'

'Nowt on the PNC for your punter.'

'You sure, Dave?'

'Don't slam the door on your way out.'

She dialled up Lanzarote again. When she eventually got through, Ina was in her room.

'Oh, hi, Caz. Did something happen? You went so quickly.'

'Just a bit of local excitement,' Caz said. 'We'd just heard we were bottom of the league in the police brutality ratings. Had to nip out and get us a few points.'

'Oh, Caz!'

'Listen, Ina. There's just a small possibility that Kevin King's accident might be more complicated. Have you heard anything there, any whispers, silly rumours?'

'Not an accident?'

'A fight, maybe. Something.'

'But he did not have marks. He would—'

'Have you heard anything?'

'No, nussing.'

'Nothing.'

'Yes, nothing. Nussing is I am nervous.'

Caz thought for a minute. 'Een, last year. The German chap . . .'

'Hans.'

'He died. Colin Jones died. Were there any other fatalities? Did anybody else die?'

'This same time, in the February, Marsh?'

'You're doing it again, Ina. It's *Mar-ch*.'

'Mar-chuh. Do you mean then, that time?'

'I mean any time. In the last eighteen months, there have been three deaths only? And Matthew Black's fall?'

'We have falls from bikes, a little car crash maybe, some things minor like anywhere would have get.'

'Any other major accidents? There were no other deaths?'

'No.'

'Damn!' Caz said.

'Why do you swear? What is wrong?'

'I'm sorry, Ina. It's just a feeling, what we call a gut feeling. There's a possibility something happened to Kevin King before he drowned. I'm trying to find something extra that will persuade my bosses to re-open the case, some reason for him to be attacked, a motive.'

'Kevin was quiet. I do not think he could make someone angry. He just talk, just to me and Ute, have a quiet drink, sleep early, train hard.'

'And you can't think of anything, any reason why someone would hurt him?'

'No.'

'Drugs?'

'No.'

'Sex?'

'No. He was shy, a quiet man, friendly only.'

Caz was exasperated. 'Ina, would you talk to Ute, the other Greenies? Try to come up with something, anything, some reason why, if they were hurt deliberately, why someone might want to hurt them.'

'Caz, you are chasing a goose. There is nothing, I am sure.'

'Try anyway.'

'Bye-bye, Caz.'

It was nearly six o'clock, lights on outside, the dull burr of cars going home. Caz thought Moira was long gone but then she came back into the room. Caz looked up. Moira looked terrible.

'Caz,' she said, 'I'm bleeding.'

144

Thirty-nine

They went round to Caz's. Caz made Moira lie down on the sofa, went through and brought out a duvet, some pillows. Then she made tea.

'You needn't fuss,' Moira said. 'It could just be a show, nothing to worry about.'

'Whatever you say, Mo, but you get off that settee I'll have to break one of your fingers.'

'Billy,' Moira said.

'It'll be sorted,' Caz said.

She got on the phone. Valerie was between buildings and Billy Tingle hadn't yet arrived at Mo's. Then it occurred to Caz that maybe he was at the station, looking out for his girlfriend. She got hold of Jim Greaves and asked him.

'Think he's off on a prisoner escort, Caz. Bit've overtime. You want me t'check?'

'You'd do that for me, Jim?'

'Oh, Caz,' he said, 'anything.'

'Fuck off, Jim!'

'Ring y'back,' he said.

Billy was out – on overs until nine o'clock. When Greavsie came back it was to read out a note; there was a message on Moira's answerphone with more info. Caz tried Valerie again, caught him at home, told him she'd be with Moira for a while.

That was no problem, he said, he was up to his armpits in paper anyway; kiss-kiss.

Caz turned back to the sofa, her friend putting on a brave white face.

'You look shit, Mo.'

'About right, Flood! Cheers! Where'd you learn your bedside manner?'

Caz did a straight-arm salute, a finger moustache.

'Nah,' Moira said, 'they'd've thrown you out. You're far too cruel.'

'Oh, cheers, Mo!'

'Any time,' Moira said. Then she closed her eyes, peristaltic pain sweeping through her. 'Oh Jesus, Caz!'

Caz sat on the floor, held her mate's hand and waited. It clenched a second time.

'OK, Mo,' she said. 'Half an hour, you still hurt, as agreed, we call out the doctor.'

Moira grunted, long, slow. 'Twenty-nine minutes.'

They were still like that at half-past seven. Caz's head was resting against their joined hands and Moira was asleep. Caz was dozing, dreaming, someone chasing someone else, blue water splashing, white borders, bright colours, a Hockney nightmare. When she realised where she was and moved her arm, Moira came with it, moaning lightly, but not in pain. Inside her head, Caz whispered, 'Hang in there, Albert.'

At nine o'clock, Caz made another cuppa for them both, came in to the lounge, sat down next to Moira and rang Tom MacInnes.

'Caz?'

She was whispering. 'You knew it was me?'

'Who else phones nine o'clock at night?'

'I was wondering . . . the computer checks on Jones?'

'Clean.'

'Bugger!'

'Don't fret, lass!'

'I can't help it, Tom. The more I think about it, the weirder it gets. That graph, King's heartbeat – it freaks me out. At the very least he was hounded to death.'

'So what's t'do?'

'You're the DI, Tom. That's why I rang. Can't you think of a way for us to get out there, some pretext?'

'We need another accident, another injury. Something to persuade the DCS to let a coupl've detectives go out there.'

'A couple?'

'Ah need a holiday.'

'That's a holiday?'

'Mebbee not to you, lass, but it's sunshine, somewhere's a change. It'll do this old man.'

'There's been another attack, Tom.'

'Where?'

'Disco. A former Green Team member, swacked with a bat or something. Name of Marcus Harris, no form. Also, he's connected to one of the two physiotherapists.'

'The disco, you say?'

Caz crossed her fingers but the guilt was the same. 'As he came out. Someone came out of the dark and hit him with something.'

'What did the local police do?'

'Interviewed one guy, a Brit. Insufficient evidence.'

'It's something, Caz. I'll try the DCS tomorrer. Speak t'you first thing. We'll put it down on paper, give it a run.'

Caz had never lied to Tom before. Maybe her voice wavered. 'What do you suppose our chances are?'

'Mebbee just the right side of fifty-fifty, lass, the day's just right an' nothin' major's hit the air conditioning.'

'But?'

'But, ah'll go along with your gut feelin' an' that thing y'said

147

the once about coincidences, three's pushing it, but four an' five, yewhat? Now, that's taking the piss.'

As Moira stirred, Caz put the phone down, exchanging a sense of guilt for one of concern. When Moira asked was there any tea she told her, 'Just made!' and lifted a cup. A weak, different Moira took it.

'How are you feeling?' Caz asked quietly.

'Like I've been run over by a bus.'

'That good eh?'

'It was a big bus.'

'I should ring Billy now? Get you home?'

Moira nodded.

'I still think we should call out a quack, Mo, look after little Albert. He can't be in a very good mood.'

'Give it tonight, Caz. If I tell the quack then I'm public in the nick. Public in the nick means crime stats and phones for four months, and me written off for even longer. No thanks.'

'Billy's not going t'be pleased.'

'No, but it's not his insides, is it? I'll just tell him it's the kicking I got; lay it on a bit, get him to mop my brow.'

'But I should ring him?'

Moira smiled. 'Yeah, why not?'

Forty

Before she took Moira home, Caz rang Valerie. Yes, he was still hard at it and no, he didn't mind stopping, doing something. Had he eaten? Yes, but if she meant did he want to go out – let me guess, Armando's – he could chew some garlic bread while she got pissed.

'I need to eat!' she said.

'Eat and get pissed,' he said.

Billy was sweet, their sofa already made up, a box of Ferrero Rocher on a table next to it. He'd got two videos out, *Die Hard 2* and *Terminator*. Caz wanted to cringe but Moira said, 'Brill, Billy!' She left as soon as Mo was comfortable, Billy in the kitchen, whistling.

'Where I'll be,' Caz said and gave Moira a piece of paper.

Moira looked puzzled.

Caz smiled, trying to be casual. 'Need a girlie, you ring me, doesn't matter when.'

They kissed and she left.

Forty-one

Valerie had sorted them out a table, got there a bit early and ordered a bottle of Il Grigio. When Caz arrived he looked up and smiled, shuffling through some suspiciously Amex paperwork. She stayed upright until he got the message and slipped it away, a black leather folder.

'How's Moira?' he said.

'Surviving,' Caz said.

'You don't want to talk?'

'No.'

Caz ordered turbot and, at the last minute, so did Valerie, skipping the garlic bread and the breath problems that would have cleared the seventh floor of Amex House tomorrow. Caz drank her first glass of Chianti without tasting it, snatched at a mouthful of her second.

'What's wrong?' Valerie said.

'Us,' she said.

'Us? We've only just got engaged!'

'Where's my ring?'

'You want one?'

'No, but you haven't bought one I can say no to.'

'*Que?*'

'And I don't want babies.'

'What?'

'I don't want babies.'

150

'Do I?'

'Or you saying, "Don't do that, it's dangerous, can't one of the blokes do it, you're not big enough, you're not strong enough." '

Her fingers were hurting; make-up hid the mark on her head.

'Caz, when have I ever said—'

'Or, "I wish you didn't have to go away, Caz. Not another course, Caz. These courses you all get pissed, end up fucking around . . ." '

'Caz. What's the fuckin' *matter*?'

She poured some wine back into the bottle. Some spiralled round the neck. She wiped it, licked her finger. 'Val, why did you propose to me?'

He looked at her. 'Why did you say yes?'

'You made me. Because I love you. You were there. I didn't have a choice. Why couldn't you have fucked off to the States?'

'You mean that?'

'I'd've only been miserable then.'

'And what are you now?'

'Confused.'

'I could still go,' he said.

'No, don't!'

'What's the *matter*, Caz?'

'Babies, having them, not having them.'

'You've already said you don't want any.'

'I should've said I'm not having any.'

'There's a difference?'

'Yes, there's a difference. Not having doesn't mean not wanting. I didn't say I didn't *want* to have babies.'

'Just tell me what you want, Caz.'

Forty-two

'Do turbots go out, Val? I mean are they, like, shoaling along one day and one turbot turns round, says to another one, "D'you fancy doing something tonight?"' She was playing with her food. 'Is this someone's boyfriend, girlfriend? Are you going t'fuck me tonight?'

'No, you'd be using me to masturbate. You want us to make love, that's different.'

'As soon as we get in? Behind the door?'

'You sound like me, Caz. You sound like a bloke.'

'How d'they do it, have sex? They squirt eggs on the floor like sticklebacks, what?'

'We'll go home, Caz, we'll kiss, we'll talk, we'll listen to music. You can play "Blue Eyes" if you like, make yourself cry. You can undress me. I'll undress you. We can love each other. I'll pretend I never asked you to marry me. In the morning you can go running and hurt yourself.'

Caz felt so heavy. When she looked at Val she felt ugly, unwhole.

'Tonight, Val, Moira was on my settee, waiting, hoping for the best. She might have lost her baby, Val, she might have been losing it. I was talking to my DI. She just went to sleep, hoping it would all go away. She wouldn't call a doctor out – she couldn't, that would fuck up her job. I sat with her, rang Tom MacInnes.'

'Caz, she did what *she* wanted.'

'No, she did a Caz, Val. She denied herself, Albert's rights.'

'You were there for her. What else could you do?'

'I could've said, "Call a doctor – you've got to see a doctor!" I could've rung Billy, got hold've Billy, told him. I could've rung a doctor myself.'

'But you didn't. In the end it was up to Moira. Maybe she was letting God decide what was for the best.'

'What d'you mean?'

'What happens happens. Like us, Caz. This hurts because it matters. You were just a great bonk, it'd only matter then. It's something else, more, then it starts to hurt. We go looking for hurt, hurt's the real bit, the rest of it is just marking time, scuffing yer heels on a street corner.'

'*Do* you love me?'

'I plead the fifth amendment.'

'Val?'

'Caz, I want to marry you.'

'Yes but—'

He was holding her hand. 'Look, Flood, I'm being paid a lot of money to take you off the streets, right? Give the other girls a chance. This is purely a financial thing.'

'That's yes?'

'And some day, *some* day, I wouldn't mind having a crack, you and me, at making a couple of Olympic milers, carpenter . . .'

'This is babies again, is it?'

'Only sort of.'

'So are we still engaged?'

'Have you called it off?'

'No.'

'Good!' he said. 'Then you can pay the bill while I'm in the bog.'

Caz ached.

Forty-three

In the morning it was Spring, the sun bright yellow, light, bright blue sky, windows flashing. Caz was in late, rebellious, at twenty-past eight, ten minutes before the lads, best part of an hour after Tom MacInnes. When Billy came in, he winked at Caz and told her Moira was taking a day's freebie. Her back was sore, he said, and she had a headache. At half-past nine, Blackside called Caz through.

'You want to know, Von Stallwood's much better. The stuff she's on takes a while t'work, but she's looking good now. I went to see her last night and she asked after you. She likes you, Flood, said you showed an edge when you got me from under that cupboard.'

'I can't really remember, sir.'

'I'd rather forget too, falling for an old trick like that.'

Caz waited. The DCS sat forward. He looked a little bit better.

'Lanzarote, Flood. You've wangled your holiday.'

Caz thought of Valerie. 'Oh. When, sir?'

'There's a flight Thursday, charter from Gatwick. All cleared with the Yard. Tom MacInnes is going the same day, different plane.'

'Where's he now, sir?'

'Doing something, Flood. We've had an idea.'

'Is, sir?'

'You undercover, detective. How'd you like to be a running coach?'

Forty-four

Caz was still coming to terms with the idea, telling Valerie, when Tom MacInnes knocked and came in. 'Caz, Norman.'

'Names, Tom?'

'Three, Norm, you take all five incidents. Just the first four an' we're talking best part of a hundred and fifty, not including the staff.'

Blackside spoke to Caz. 'The DI's been on to this Mr Grurn at Club la Santa. They ran a check for us on their computer, people that were at the complex both years, both weeks, that's the hundred and fifty. This latest incident, if it's connected, brings us down to just three names, plus the Green Team, security, the admin staff.'

'It's pronounced green, sir.'

'Is it? Tom and I have been talking. I'm still not convinced we haven't got a series of unconnected accidents, but Tom's persuaded me and I've persuaded Scotland Yard that the King death at least is odd, odd enough to be a G28 overseas.

'Point is that, these deaths, there turns out to be something, then the most likely source is the staff, the Green Team. Our idea is that the DI goes over there on an official basis, you get slipped in undercover.'

'But they already know me as a copper, sir. When I was over there last, they'd picked up on all the stuff in the *Sun*.'

'Already thought of that,' MacInnes said. 'Christian Green

will be in the know, but no one else. You're taking a two-year sabbatical to train for that England place, a special dispensation. Tom will let slip that you're under some sort of cloud and this is the next best thing to you being out on your ear.'

'I'll be an *ex*-policeman?'

'In one, Flood.'

'There's a couple of the girls over there, sir, Ina Jensen and Ute Fërd, the physios. I've got to know them both quite well. I was talking to them both only yesterday about the attack on Marcus Harris.'

Blackside was short and sharp. 'No more confidences, Flood! Use your brain a moment; the connection turns out to be the Green Team, one or both of these girls could be it.'

'I'm not arguing with you, sir, but it'll be a bit tricky. How are Ina and Ute going to believe I just suddenly made the Green Team?'

'You've been negotiating with the director for weeks. The trouble back home in England, you were looking for an out.'

'I lie, you mean.'

'You're a copper, Flood. You might be about to catch a murderer. Yes, you lie. You got a problem with that?'

Caz paused, but only slightly.

'No, sir, none at all.'

'We'll work out you and the DI, some way that you can liaise without being compromised. Talk again this afternoon.'

'We could talk on the morning run, sir.'

Tom MacInnes was *not* amused. 'Dinna be stoopit, Flood!'

'Aerobics, sir?'

Now he grinned. 'Me in Lycra? Oh aye. An' give up the drink too! Get out've hee-yuh, Flood!'

IV

Forty-five

Valerie got a couple of hours off work to take Caz to Gatwick. Enough time to drive her there, himself back, but not enough time to sit and be squidgy in departures; just as she liked it. He stopped on zig-zags, dumped her cases as quick as he could, kissed her on the nose and said, 'Go get 'em, champ!' As he drove away, there was that ache again, deep, deep, deep.

No matter how often she jumped on a big-silver-bird, man-come up-the-sky, Caz would never get rid of that excitement, that 'I'm going to be half, a quarter the way round the world in just a few hours' feeling. All she had to do was drive past Gatwick, Heathrow, see a Jumbo slipping in on the sky or roaring out, and the old urges, the wanderlust would leap out and caress her.

She went in, looked at the queues, thought, 'Sod it!' and sloped off to one of the bars. She'd read somewhere about on-board dehydration, so bought a Miller Lite and sat down opposite Tom MacInnes, a stranger, a thin-looking man, wrapped around the second of two double whiskies.

'I wonder,' she said, 'if you could tell me the time.'

'Go away!' Tom said.

'Oh, I'm sorry,' she said. 'I thought you were a policeman!'

'Flight wuz cancelled,' he said. 'An' you, don't you *dare* laff!'

Caz didn't go. Instead, she stayed and tormented cloak-and-dagger Tom, a new-found angle on their relationship to be

161

exploited. So, the three names, was he going to tell her now? No, he said. She would be at la Santa looking from a different angle. If he told her the names, she'd be out there, creeping around, tripping over his feet, making a mess of things, maybe taking chances.

'Jess you get yer feet well under the table, detective. An' leave the serious detecting to the professionals.'

'Detective? Did you say detective? I'll have you know I'm an aspiring Great British athlete. Maybe I used to *vaguely* be involved with the police but I'm just a runner now, hold the Bow Street.'

Tom wasn't smiling when he said, 'Where's yer warrant card?'

'Blackside's desk,' Caz said.

'I can't watch your back, Caz.'

She stiffened up. 'No, Tom. I'm sorry.'

'Be safe is all I ask, that's sorry enough.'

She got another drink in, a virtuous single for MacInnes.

'So what's the score with your flight now, Tom?'

He dug out a number. 'M-O-N one-one-nine.'

'Oh no!' she said, her hand to her mouth. 'You'll have to cancel that, Tom, that's my flight!'

'Ah've bin here three hours already. There's as much chance ah'll be giving up whisky.'

'Does that mean we could sit together?'

'What do you think?'

'Is "no" close?'

'Yer couldnee be closer, lass.'

She turned over her lower lip.

He grinned. 'Less, of course, it happens by chance . . .'

She beamed. 'But what'll we talk about?'

Forty-six

Tom MacInnes and Caz were the last two passengers to book on to the flight. There was absolutely no chance of sitting together. Tom took the seat in smoking and Caz took the one right at the front, the one squashed in next to the window, where you couldn't see the video screen above the aisle, and they fobbed you off with an edge-on view, all browns and yellows, of a tiny liquid-crystal joke they called a personal viewer. That was the negative. The positive was the guy she sat next to, sun-browned and hard, like an outbacked Aussie.

'Hank,' he said, his hand out, little white smile.

She shook the hand. 'That figures. I thought, Hank, Burt . . .'

'My real name is Harry.'

'Caz.'

'D'you talk or sleep?' he said.

'See how it goes,' she said. His smile widened.

He was thirty-three, full name Harold Carry. Yes, he *had* heard the joke about ritual suicide, that was why he was now Hank, not Harry. The day job, he was a graphic artist; on holiday he was a 'twitcher', a man who liked to spot feathered birds. There was a single breeding pair of Egyptian vultures, *alimoché*, in the Fire Mountains on the island. He would be helping out with their protection for a few weeks, a chance to see them. No, no hotel, he said. He'd be camping out – a lot less pesetas.

163

What did he do? He went looking at birds! Where? Anywhere, everywhere. When? As often as he could. When he could afford it. Was that all? Of course that was all, what else could he possibly need? He read about birds, took photographs of birds, studied birds. He had quite an interesting job, but it was what *paid* for his life, it wasn't his life. And every weekend, every Bank Holiday, he went somewhere, saw something new, something real.

'So tell me where you've been,' Caz said.

'You're joking. Everywhere – well, nearly everywhere. I've still to get to Madagascar and the Galapagos Islands, Darwin's finches and all that.'

'I studied some birds once, kittiwakes, on Lundy Island.'

He laughed. 'Lundy's my second home! I go there when I've got the time but no money. What did you do?'

'I was at the north end, Puffin Gully. All the literature said that the adult birds never left their offspring alone. First day there I'd clocked a couple of empties, so I spent a fortnight sitting with my feet dangling off the cliff, getting sunburnt and checking them out. Anyway, turned out they do, leave the kids, that is. The books are wrong. I ended up giving a paper on it at Oxford.'

'So you know the pub, the Marisco Tavern?'

'And Millcombe House, the Barn, the Blue Bung, Tibbets . . .'

'You ever meet Peter de Groot?'

Caz was laughing now. 'Tall and skinny, beard. Behind the bar in the Marisco. Got his PhD studying finches in Africa.'

'It's a small world.'

'Very,' Caz said. She was thinking.

The drinks trolley was nearby. 'You want something?'

Caz looked up at the hostess. 'A couple of Southern Comfort 'n' Cokes, please!'

'Thirsty?' Hank said.

Caz was clicking her drink open when Hank asked her the obvious. 'So, Caz, what do you do?'

'Do?' She fussed with the top of her bottle. 'Do?'

You tell lies. She tried it. 'Starting a week ago, I'm a full-time athlete. I used to be a civil servant but I've given up the day job. I'm going to Lanzarote to train. I'm quite a quick runner but I want to be quicker.'

'Winter training? Like Linford Christie?'

'At Club la Santa.'

'Oh, I know it,' Hank said. 'I went up there a couple of years back, camping out. It's a big complex, yes? Built round a lagoon?'

Caz nodded. 'So who's following who?'

'I'm sorry?'

'I was joking.'

'About what? Did I miss something?'

Caz sighed. 'It's not important. I'm just . . .' She undid her seatbelt and got up to go to the loo, stooping to avoid the overhead lockers, nodding quite close to Hank's face and then the man in glasses in the third seat, glancing up from his paperback.

'I'm . . . just going to the . . .' she said, feeling foolish. The man looked up. Behind the gold specs cold blue-grey eyes, like an SS officer. He flicked a straight-line smile at Caz; on-off. Caz smiled back. The paperback was a Jeffrey Archer. 'Couldn't find a book, then?' she said.

Caz folded the loo doors closed, popping up the light. Toilets on a charter, God! Never mind the claustrophobia, get the smell! She didn't actually want to pee but she did one anyway, for something to do. She had just felt the need to get away for a minute, she'd had to get away. Now, as she washed her hands, the mirror was streaky. She cleaned it with a paper towel, looking at Caz Flood. She felt vaguely unwell. She thought of Moira, Veronica Stallwood, Tom, Valerie. Why exactly did she suddenly feel so bad about herself?

One of the best bits about flying to Lanzarote was the length of the flight – four hours – long enough to give the feeling of distance, of a point to it all, not so long that boredom, dehydration and stinking toilets took the edge off the holiday.

Caz went back to the three seats, squeezed past the bony knees of the *Obergruppenführer* and Hank, sat down, grabbed her second Southern Comfort off Hank's tray, clacked it open and poured it over the remains of her ice. 'So, tell me,' she said, 'what do graphic designers do?'

Hank told her, they drew pictures. What a boy with A level Art couldn't do . . .

'This protecting the birds, why d'you do that?'

'Some things are precious. You have to keep bad people away.'

'People would kill the birds?'

'They might,' he said. 'The egg-thief's ultimate dream is to get the last two eggs ever, then see the bird extinct. It's not a pretty obsession.'

'So you do what?'

'Make sure no one gets too close, no accidental tourist, no egg-nut.'

'And you get paid?'

'No, Caz, I love birds. I love being out there. Of *course* I don't get paid. If they paid me, I'd donate the money straight back.'

'Oh,' Caz said.

'You seem surprised. What's so wrong with giving a bit back now and again?'

Caz objected. 'Hey, you grew up in Thatcher's Britain too!'

Hank looked at her, not cold exactly, but firm, as if he'd had this argument once too often. 'I don't vote, but I never joined in when they built Docklands either. You were a civil servant;

you must have seen the country get harder, colder, the last fifteen years. You seem too decent to vote Conservative.'

'People vote Tory,' she said.

'People vote Tory, but human beings couldn't.'

'So you haven't got extreme views, then?'

'Caz, I just want to get along, go away, look at birds, see new places, feel at peace for a while. I don't do anything about things, even those things that I think are bad, except I try to protect birds. I think I could, but in the end I wouldn't be someone I'd be comfortable with.'

'But precious things should be protected?'

'You don't think birds can be precious?'

'All I can remember about the kittiwakes is that they were noisy and they shit everywhere. Nah, I can't see it.'

'But they're still precious, Caz. Would you rather there weren't any? Does that seem right to you? Would you have them exterminated? Call them vermin and unleash something like myxomatosis on them?'

'I wouldn't do anything. I'd just let them tootle along like they've always done. But they're just interesting. I wouldn't say precious.'

'Life's precious. But life's not you, or me, or mankind, or man, his food animals, his pets. The whole thing is everything. Take something out, the machine is different. No one knows which bits are crucial.'

'So you're an environmentalist? A Friend of the Earth, Greenpeace, protesting, all that?'

'No, Caz. I just try to be interested in birds.'

Forty-seven

They touched down late afternoon. Warm. The plane gently halted on concrete scattered with equipment, light wind, articulated buses taking plane-loads to arrivals. There was a softness, a different air. Coming back, Caz knew the people would be browner, talk a little more, smell a little better, but right now they were still on the London Underground, every unconnected point in space painfully interesting. Caz was standing with Hank but they weren't talking. As the bus filled, she brazenly looked around, looking for eyes, making the avoiders stretch to avoid even more, looking for the few that weren't so isolated, so distant. These were usually the couples; booked in for more sex in two weeks than they usually managed in a month.

Caz hadn't avoided Tom, but she hadn't seen him either. She spotted him just as the shuttle began to caterpillar slowly towards the airport building. He was standing by the doors at the other end of the bus and looked desperately thin. Despite the warmth packed around him, the crush of people, she saw how cool he looked, how separate. Then she saw him again. Lonely.

Later, they nodded to each other by the luggage carousel, managed an 'Oh, again!' smile at passports, then muttered to each other under the skirts of the la Santa Greenie while they waited for the others to congregate. Mister MacInnes was

going to the resort on business. No, he would have very little
time for sport, unless they had crown green bowls; did they have
crown green bowls? Caz smiled. Did he not do a sport when
he was younger, perhaps? Well, there was a time . . . he played
a fair bit o'fitba, once, middle o'the park. But that would've
bin before she was born, wouldn't it? And what did she do?

'Oh,' Caz said, 'I'm going to la Santa to be the new running
coach. I'll be part-time. I'm going there to train for an England
place. I'm an eight-hundred-metre runner.'

'Haff a mile, two laps?'

'Aye,' she said.

'How many times round is that?' he said.

They sat together on the coach. MacInnes was nearest the
window but he saw nothing, just the land dumped between
the airport and the hotel. Beyond him, Caz could see the white
walls, the green shutters, bent backs, the green shoots thrust
out of the black soil. She could imagine softening again, forgetting she was a copper. Maybe that was why Tom saw
nothing; to retain his heart of glass.

They had checked in by six-thirty. Both of them had
messages waiting. Inspector MacInnes could see Christian
Green tomorrow at ten a.m.? That was OK? And Kathy
Flood? Ina Jensen was in physio, finishing at seven o'clock.
Did she want to drop in?

'I'll say good-bye then, Tom. Perhaps we'll see each other
round . . .?'

'It's not impossible,' MacInnes said.

Caz had a sudden thought. 'You've not been here before,
have you? Where are you eating tonight? I could—'

The DI tapped his briefcase. 'I'm fine, miss, but thanks.' He
tapped the case again in explanation. 'Sandwiches.'

Caz left to go and see Ina. Tom was joking, wasn't he? Then
she thought. 'Hula Hoops more like, and a duty-free litre of
Whyte & Mackay.'

169

When Caz opened the door to physiotherapy, she could hear the sounds of making love, the deep, near-pain groans, the occasional grunted yes! She tried to imagine waiting for Valerie, the other side of the screen, underneath Ina – at least she presumed it was Ina – the muscled flesh rippled, the hands, fingers, the aromatic oils, the clean white smocks . . . She shook her head, the stuff of movies, very blue.

A male voice expressed air suddenly. 'Ah!'

'You run again too soon!' Unmistakably Ina. 'You run again, one, two days too early. You do this thing, ignore good advice, soon you be an old fat man who limps!' There was a sound of Ina's slap.

'Oh, Ina!' the voice said.

Caz listened, thinking the accent. The voice, it were fr'm up north, Blackburn p'raps, Clitheroe mebbee, or Burnl-eh. 'Oh, Ina. Marry muh,' it said. 'Let muh tek yuh back t'England, so yuh'll do this just f'me?'

'Get dressed!' Ina said.

'Yuh'll not marry muh?'

'Next week,' Ina said casually.

The curtains were sliding back and the man was coming out. 'So, cannah play footie wi' this thigh or what?' he was saying. Ina glared, half a joke. 'Ah'm gone!' he said, scampering a stiff eight feet towards Caz and away from Ina's withering look. He was a big, Blackside-styled man with a large square face and an impish grin. To Caz, he said, 'Magic! The gal is magic!' Then he hissed, 'But for Crissakes din't tell her ah said so; she's bad enough now!'

'Hi, Ina!' Caz said.

In was wiping her hands. 'Caz! How's the back?'

Ina had already heard about Caz coming to la Santa Sport as – as she put it – 'half a Greenie'. She was thrilled that Caz would be able to meet Eric, especially as Eric was now coming for an extra week and Ina wasn't going to Denmark for a little while.

'Poor Ute. She is miserable for her boyfriend. Like today she goes to Arrecife to see him. He is not in hospital no more but he is still not working because his face is so sore.'

'So you cancelled going home?'

'To see my boyfriend, yes . . .' She paused, then laughed suddenly. 'And instead he will come here, to la Santa!'

Her happiness was infectious. Caz was smiling.

'So, Een. What're we doing tonight?'

'We eat, drinking some Rioja. Then we come back from the village, to Cafe After Sport, the disco. This is all good?'

'Tiring!'

'It is good to be tired, then to sleep heavy.'

'I could sleep heavy now,' Caz said.

'No, none of this rubbish! I have some more friends you want to meet. There is Petter from Denmark and Blodwen, she is not from Denmark. She is—'

'Blodwen? Did you say Blodwen?'

'I did say this, yes. She is Welsh.'

'Oh, really?'

'She is from Wales. I can go there. To Swansea, Mumbles.'

'There's no such thing as Mum-bulls. They're called cows.'

'No, silly! Blodwen lives there. It is a place. A place that is Mumbles.'

Caz left it. 'Is she a Greenie?'

'No. Blodwen is admin. She works in the offices. She will do bookings, find out if there is room for people to stay, book groups who will stay at la Santa, things like that. She is tall and she is lots and lots of fun. She does not speak like you at all but she is still lots of fun. She lives in the village, behind Los Charcones.'

Caz clicked. 'Blodwen what?'

'No, Blodwen Griffiths. But she is nice. I promise you this.'

Forty-eight

'I kid you not, Blod, his name was Harry Carry and he was *very* tasty!'

Blodwen made to disembowel herself with a steak knife. 'Caz? As in, Arry Carry?'

'In one. He called himself Hank 'cos've people like you!'

'He should've changed his bloody surname to Kurcheef while he was at it!' Blodwen blurted loudly, another glass tipped up at her face. 'Yer get it, yeah? As in Hank Kurcheef?'

Ina said, 'I'm sorry?'

Caz said, 'Mr and Mrs Key and their daughter Ann?'

Blodwen said, 'I'm Mister Bates, this is my wife Missus Bates and my son Master Bates.'

Caz dived in. 'Oh, we'll soon put a stop to that, Mister Bates!'

'I'm sorry?' Ina said.

They were back at Blodwen's, behind the restaurant, very Spanish, red tiles, white walls split by wooden carvings, a crucifix. They were getting badly pissed on cheap local wine that worked out about a quid a litre. It might have tasted like shit but they were too far gone on the OK stuff from earlier to notice. Now they were swapping 'Mr & Mrs' jokes and Blodwen knew a thousand. Ina just couldn't get them.

'Mr & Mrs Hardon and their son, Ivor!'

172

'Mr & Mrs Eedick and their dog, Spot?'

'Mr & Mrs Itcheeass and their son, Ivan!'

'Mr – no, no! Stop, stop, stop!' Caz squealed. 'For fuck's sake, I'll be ill. We've still gorra get back tonight. Issa mile and a half!'

Blodwen stood up. 'Issno problem, buttee. I'll drive you. I gorra car.'

Caz waved her finger and shook her head. 'Y'carn do that, Blod. Nope! I'd 'ave to arrest you f 'drinken driving.'

'What letter comes before Y?' Blodwen said.

'What?'

'A-B-C-D. What's the letter before Y?'

'What the fuck're you on about, Blodwen?'

'The alphabet. Uh, Why, Zed.'

'EX.'

'Exactly, Ex!' Caz stared, slightly foolishly. 'As in EX-copper, Caz.'

'Oh, yeah,' Caz said. 'It's an old habit. Sorry!'

'I'm sorry?' Ina said.

Caz glanced Ina's way – back to Blodwen. 'You gorrenny coffee?'

Blodwen had a lot of Teguise Market giraffes. One small one for every boyfriend – not including one-night stands – and a large one for every guy who'd found her button. Of the eighteen giraffes she'd accrued in fifteen months, two were biggies, the rest disappointing little ones. The two tall animals were her current boyfriend – five months and getting stronger – and, out of the blue, she suddenly said, Colin Jones, the guy from last year, the accident.

'Oh, shit,' Caz said. 'I'm sorry, mate.'

'Oh, it's awright,' the Welsh girl said. 'It wasn't love or nothing. We just 'ad a few laffs, like you do.'

'It's still shit, though, bud, isn't it?'

Ina fell asleep while the other two girls were drinking their second coffee, so in the end they decided to crash until six o'clock in the morning and drive back to la Santa Sport then. No, Blodwen said, she would not have a problem waking up. She had a digestive system more efficient than Port Talbot steelworks and there'd be no hangovers tomorrow, she'd be as right as rain.

'So what exactly happened to Colin, again?' Caz said.

'They reckon he went swimming in the sea,' Blodwen said, 'but I can't see it, m'self. Colin was a very sensible bloke. Even though he was a good swimmer he wouldn't have tried that. He was spending all his time getting physio, doing his exercises and working out with an aqua-jogger, one of them float things, in the big pool. Swimming in the sea – not only is it bloody dodgy, but it would take a lot of effort, 'cos've the currents. He was taking it easy, doing what the physios said he should.'

She glanced across at Ina who was snoring delicate little snores. 'Colin thought Ina was wonderful,' she said quietly. 'He'd been carrying his injury for years and suddenly someone was curing it. Een may be a bit of a dill sometimes, but she's bloody good at fixing injuries.'

'She's a genius,' Caz said.

'Ay, steady up!' Blodwen said, very very Welsh, 'she's bloody *Danish*!'

Before they went to sleep, Caz asked, apart from the German guy and the Worthing runners last month, had there been any more grief?

'You are *not* kidding,' Blodwen said. 'Someone turned a Suzuki over, March last year; broke his leg 'n' wrist. Someone else had a nasty fall on one of the back-door routes into the Fire Mountains, and there was one unlucky sod, a biker, who got swatted by a car door as he went by on his bike. That was in March as well, and all blokes. Presumably, that's 'cos women're that much more sensible.'

'Presumably,' Caz said.

Caz tried to sleep but was flying a small biplane blindfolded. She didn't fancy throwing up, so each time the sensation came she clicked her eyes open and stared at a cast of light on the ceiling.

'You're awake,' Blodwen said, somewhere around three.

'Sorry, mate. Was I disturbing you?'

'No. I was disturbed already. I started thinking about Colin. You're a copper, right? Could someone have pushed him in or something?'

'There's no evidence, Bee.'

'Well, me, I'm like a bit psychic. In school they used to call me Gypsy Lee. I just don't think Colin drowned.'

Caz went for it. She sat up. 'We could do some checking, Bee. I'm not actually on the force any more, but I know about major investigations. If you want, we could do some checking on the QT.'

'What sort of checking?'

'Who had accidents, when. Who they knew, whether they were connected. But it really would have to be QT, Bee. I'm on two years off. I do something gets me into trouble here, I'm back in the UK and in uniform as soon as I'm off the plane.'

'Awright, Caz. Lunchtime tomorrow, we'll sort something out. I c'n tell you one thing, though . . . You know that Matt Black, he was always up on the roof warming his bollocks. He fancied himself something rotten and wanted to be brown all over.'

'And was he?'

'Oh, aye. *Including* the bollocks.'

'You know this?'

Blodwen chuckled. 'He's one of the little giraffes.'

'Oh,' Caz said.

Forty-nine

Caz managed two, maybe three hours sleep. She woke with her own hangover and her host's as a bonus. Blodwen had got out of bed at five-thirty, and was now clip-clicking around the kitchen with a gorgeous background smell of coffee following her like an aura. She was singing.

Caz couldn't believe it. 'Blod-bloody-wen!'

Her face came round the door. 'What?'

'Yer singing!'

She looked surprised. 'Am I?'

'Yes.'

She disappeared into the kitchen for a few more clangs, then she started again. '*Oh, I've got an Auntie Kitty . . .*'

Caz shouted through. 'You got any razor blades, Blodwen?'

'*And she's oanlee got one titty . . .*'

'Only, if I've got to listen to Mary Bloody Hopkin . . .'

'*And it's very long and pointed . . .*'

'And it's not even six o'clock . . .'

'*And the nip-ple's double-jointed . . .*'

'It's a straight toss-up between my wrists an' your throat.'

Blodwen came back into view, grinning. '*Did you ev-uh see, did you ev-uh see, such a funny thing before?*'

The toast and marmalade the three of them managed for breakfast was calorifically unimportant, but, as ballast against fermented grape juice it was OK. Ina was out of bed but she

176

was still asleep. Her eyes were open but there was nothing getting back to the brain yet. When they'd tipped her off the sofa she had gone to the loo on her hands and knees.

Blodwen was sickeningly alive and when she wasn't talking she was humming to herself and grinning, a sort of Principality version of Winnie-the-Pooh. Caz was guilty, a feeling that almost always came in tandem with a hangover.

On the way back to la Santa Sport, Blodwen suddenly became serious when she asked Caz, could she really mix last night's kind of boozing and serious training?

'I do,' Caz said.

'What I mean is, can you make it big time?'

'No,' Caz said.

'So what you gonna do?'

'Train harder.'

'Drink less?'

'Maybe.'

As they pulled up at reception, four bikers were just wheeling out their racers. They were hard brown men dressed in the kind of colours that anywhere else would look effeminate. One bike had a saddle suspended in space on a long cantilever support. It looked expensive.

'That looks expensive . . .' Caz said.

'Saves yer bum,' Blodwen said. 'It's about four grand.'

'For a *bike*?'

'See you at one o'clock,' Blodwen said.

When Ina emerged from the back seat her face was blank. 'I'm in charge of the 5K this morning,' she said slowly. 'Will you carry me?'

'To your room?'

'No, round the 5K.'

It was twenty to seven.

Their room was three hundred yards from the Olympic pool. When Caz suggested they should use it to wake them-

177

selves up, Ina went white but started getting undressed. When they got there, four lanes were already full; a swimming club from Birmingham; forty swimmers following each other up and down fifty ice-blue metres by four, forty perfectly shaped bodies steered by very tiny brains. Caz said they had to be cerebrally challenged; no one with a brain would do forty lengths before breakfast! She dived in. Jesus! And not in this. Stuff the blue, what about the ice?

They had more coffee at seven-fifteen, counted their fingers until they got to ten, had another coffee. At ten to eight they went out for the early-morning warm-up exercises by the leisure pool. When they got there, a Greenie called Dorte was already setting up the equipment. She was so good-looking Caz wanted to spit; five-four max with great brown legs, blonde hair like only the Danes did it, and a smile that could have warmed the pool.

'She is a champion wind-surfer, a tri-athlete,' Ina said, and she is reeling out a CV she knew would hurt. 'And she is also teaching rock and roll and playing in the Green Team Band.'

'Does her breath smell?' Caz said hopefully.

'No.'

'She gay?'

'No.'

'I'm going to kill her.'

Ina glanced down at her non-existent chest, then at Dorte. 'You must get in the queue, Caz.'

They were both grinning when the music started.

Fifty

At ten-thirty Caz went to see Christian Green. The la Santa offices were up a few steps just along from the *Supermercado*. As she walked there, she could see Matthew Black, the people coming, shock, the slowly oozing blood. She shook the picture from her head as she walked in. Strangers at computers pointed her through to the back. When she got there, a secretary stood, smiled and said that Christian was busy. Outside his office he had a mountain bike and a racer, a helmet dangling from the handlebars. Caz could see the DI through the glass.

'Is that Mister MacInnes?' she said innocently.

The secretary smiled quickly. 'Yes.'

'We met, coming here. He's a nice man.'

'Yes,' the secretary said. Then Christian saw Caz and waved her in. His secretary looked slightly surprised. 'Please . . .' she said.

As Caz came in, Tom MacInnes stood awkwardly, smiled and offered his hand. He was wearing a light-blue cotton suit and light-brown canvas shoes. As far as Caz could remember she had only ever seen him in dark blue, charcoal or black. He was still 'white-collar and dark tie', though, reflecting the immaculate hotel director opposite. Caz was in turquoise Lycra bottoms and a top that said 'Pigs in Space'.

Christian looked quickly up and down her and smiled. 'We

179

must get you your Greenie uniform, Miz Flood, I think today.'

Caz grinned sheepishly and glanced down. 'There's something wrong with this?'

'Of course not, Miz Flood, but the Green Team—'

'It's not a problem,' Caz said quickly. 'I've always wanted to see myself in uniform.'

'Caz!'

'Oh, Mister MacInnes . . .'

'We're in private now, Flood. Let's get serious.'

'Yes,' said the director. 'I know why you are here, and so do my secretary, and my colleague, Kenneth Gasque.'

Caz went to speak, but MacInnes was quicker. 'We decided that the secretary was essential, Caz. If you started sneaking round to see Mister Green, the rumour-mill would start here. Kenneth Gasque is another director and you may need to talk to him.'

'Is that it, sir?'

MacInnes looked at the director.

'And my wife, Mrs Green . . .'

'Is *that* it?'

'You may come into my home. My wife, it would be easier . . .'

Caz felt flat. 'I understand.'

'Right, Flood!' MacInnes said snappily. 'I will be looking at the dates and the people here. At the moment we have to consider the staff and the members of the Green Team. Mister Green assures me he has a wonderful team but it has to be done.'

'Yes,' Christian said.

'Has t'be done. Ah'll be discreet. What concerns us is if something's going on underground, a drugs thing, something like that. You should be on to that, Caz.'

'OK, sir. And if Mr Green could furnish us with *all* of the major incidents, accidents in the last two years . . .?'

'You think there are more, Flood?'

'One of the four-wheel-drive jeeps crashed, sir, a cyclist was hurt, someone had a bad fall in the Fire Mountains.'

MacInnes took it well. 'Christian?'

'These, true, and some more, some not so serious. But Tom, you must know with so many activities, and so many people for so long, there will be accidents, deaths even. This is nature, yes?'

'They may still all be accidents, Christian, but you must let us decide what is important and what is not. Do you have an accident book?'

'A log.'

'Can we see it?'

'Of course. This will be arranged.'

Caz had the bizarre sensation that she was in a Dick Francis novel. Was some mysterious organisation trying to cause difficulties for the hotel? If these were racing stables, someone might be about to nobble their top horse ... She heard MacInnes.

'And we have considered one other possibility, Caz, that of some outside agent seeking to discredit the la Santa company. That has already been discounted. One, the place's reputation is secure. Two, every accident has been down to the individual and no blame has been attached to the hotel. Three, there has been no offer for the complex for many, many years and the only use of a place this far out of the way would be as a sports retreat. To discredit it would be illogical; they're not going to build an airport here or discover oil under the lagoon.'

Christian spoke. 'I still believe only that we have had some accidents. And only because they are together, near in time, does this seem strange. The death of Mister King perhaps is odd. I have used these Polar watches to monitor my heart when I train, they are very good.'

Caz sat up. 'You've seen Kevin's trace?'

'Yes. Inspector MacInnes has shown me. It is certainly odd, but then I am not a doctor. Perhaps these things can be explained . . .'

Fifty-one

'No, you look cute, Caz,' Blodwen said. 'Green really suits you!'

They were in the Pool Bar, lunch. Caz was wearing her Green Team uniform, a heavy T-top, green and white horizontal stripes, vertically striped shorts with a generous cut. On the other girls the outfit looked comfortable and sexy, but Caz felt a bit silly without knowing why.

'I just feel a bit naff, you know . . .'

'That's your individuality,' Blodwen said confidently. 'By tomorrow you'll forget all about it.'

They were drinking lager, pints, some island stuff with a slight edge but nice and cold. On Blodwen's recommendation, they had ordered two Pool Bar salads and now they were waiting, small talking about la Santa, letting the sun burn down on them out of a sharp blue sky.

Confident, laid-back groups sat at plastic tables all around them on the patio, open-legged and brown, a few different accents, Danes, Brits, Germans, the lilt somewhere of French; a lot of blonde heads, good-looking women. The bar had a peculiar air of relaxation, a sensuous, sated atmosphere, that came either from sex or, more likely, the morning's hard workouts when endorphins flowed and mellowed away life's sharp edges.

What Caz noticed was the physiques: the swimmers, big

shoulders and hard flat bellies; the skinny distance runners; the footballers with extra hair, chunky, their shin pads flapping out of ankle-dropped socks; the serious bikers with red-brown bands of sunburn striping their big thighs; the colours, the white sun-blocked noses, 'cool' sunglasses.

'So d'you make it round the 5K, Caz?'

'What? Oh yeah, no problem! We went for a swim beforehand – that got rid of the effects of last night – had a bit of brekkie, some coffee, did the morning work-out . . .'

'Ran fifteen minutes for the 5K . . .'

Caz smiled. 'Hardly. Ina and I started off at the front and led the group out at five minutes a K, nice 'n' easy steady running, by the book. It would've taken us around twenty-four, twenty-five minutes.'

'But . . .?'

'Oh, about half-way four or five guys got testosterone overload and started to push it.'

'Germans?'

'Yeah, how did you know?'

'Doesn't matter,' Blodwen said. 'Ziss is known, it is usually Germans.' She paused. 'Or, yer knaw, wukking-class blokes from Newcassill.'

Caz was grinning at Blodwen's quick-change accents. 'Ina stayed with the main group. I went after the lads.'

'You didn't *beat* them, did you?'

'Only sort of,' Caz said. 'I got back to them as they came off the loop, came up alongside and gave 'em a sweet smile.'

'Weren't you knackered?'

'A bit, but what you do is take a few really deep breaths beforehand, then make it look like this is all too easy.'

'And then?'

'As we went past the squash courts, they went for it. It was just me and these two guys from Dusseldorf. I wasn't really in the mood for any eyeballs-out stuff, so I let them beat me, five

yards or so. Then we got to the stadium. They were done in, so
they stopped, but I just kept going. I went straight past 'em
and ran on to the running track. I shouted something to
'em, like, "Thanks for the warm-up, lads!" and went off to do
some fast laps. When I came round on the end've the first one,
they were still getting their breath!'

'You'll have to be a good little girl tomorrow, Caz. You're a
Greenie now. Can't have a little girlie beating those nice young
men . . .'

'Why are they nearly always Germans?'

'They're not. Geordies, good vets an' welders do it as well.'

'Welders?'

'Blokes seem t'think winning's important. They forget that
the early morning run is just a loosener, like the work-out by
the pool.'

'You said welders . . .'

'No, I didn't. How was the water this morning?'

'Freezing! Brass monkeys. It was OK once we'd got going
but it's a bit've a shock when you first jump in.'

'That's *heated*, Caz. You want to try the leisure pool. Now
that is just silly. You get blokes, you know, pissed up after the
disco, middle of the night, they jump in off the board, get
the shock of their lives. Spring 'n' early summer it's still very
cold, the water temp is a season behind the weather. When
they jump in, they're sober in milliseconds.'

'D'you think that's what happened to Kevin King?'

'What, he jumped in and the shock killed him? It's possible.'

'Or what?'

'He was with some lads, they chucked him in, a joke went
wrong . . .'

'Or?'

'He topped hisself for some reason.'

'Why would he do that?'

'I don't know. I thought you were the copper!'

'I'm an ex-copper, Bee. Remember?'

Blodwen took a lungful of lager. 'So you say. This is why you want me t'burgle the files, yeah? Dead of night stuff, a pencil torch, rifling through the cabinets . . .'

'I thought it was all on computer?'

'It is.'

'Well what're you on about, then?'

'Being a private eye, a spy, you know. I've seen *The Big Sleep* four times. I c'n just see me now, all the black gear, Purdy, the Avengers . . .'

'Oh, piss off, Bee. All you've got to do is look at who was here the time that Colin went swimming and Hans Anderson fell off Mirador del Rio. Do the same for the fortnight Matt Black and Kevin King were here and see how many visitors were here for both.'

'There'll be hundreds! Most of the clubs come here the same time every year.'

'And *then*,' Caz said, brandishing the 'then' slowly, 'and *then* you can see if any of them were here for any of the other incidents.'

'You don't want much, do you? And why can't I just whack in all the dates?'

'*Because*, Blod-wen, if one of the accidents actually *was* an accident and someone *was* playing silly buggers, and he wasn't here when the accident happened . . .'

'He'd be eliminated.'

'You're getting the hang of it now, buttee!'

'You've got all the dates?'

'Oh, yeah!' Caz said sarcastically. 'And where would I have got them from? What do I do, go into Christian Green and say, "Hey, Chris, I'm secretly checking up on people? Can you help me out with a few dates?" '

'You know we had an inquiry like this last week, do you? The police in the UK were asking. We had best part've two hundred names to start with but then they gave us another date to cross-check. There was only three after that.'

'Were,' Caz said.

'What?'

'Were. There *were* only three.'

Blodwen simply shrugged. 'I can do this, tonight for you, when I finish. D'yer fancy a quick drinkie before I go home?'

'Half-six?'

'Sounds about right. You're buying.'

'OK,' Caz said.

Then Blodwen said, 'It depends whether the three's three individuals or one group containing three.'

'If you say so,' Caz said.

Fifty-two

As soon as Blodwen had left, Caz strolled over to the running track, her new office. When she got there, saw the brown-orange artificial surface, the old butterflies came straight away, the urge to try it out, to kick a few hundreds. She decided she had time to jog a few easy laps and wash the lager through.

Her brief was to coach, to talk running, not so much to experienced runners but to beginners, typically the dragged-to-Lanzarote husbands and wives of serious sportspeople who'd finally arrived at their Holy Grail, warm-weather training. She was to devise running-plans, advise on shoes and clothes, look at running styles and counsel against overdoing it early on. There'd be short runs or track work with some joggers – this the worst bit – where she would have to suppress her natural urges and shuffle round, sometimes as slow as ten minutes a mile.

Not that she disparaged joggers, beginners. Some of them turned into seriously good athletes. There was a Scots woman she'd met once who'd taken a year and a half to train for a marathon and then trudged round it in about five hours. Her second marathon was about four hours and her third three-and-a-half, respectable club running. She wasn't built for the long one – what *was* her name? – but in her next race she broke three hours and in the one after that, two-forty-five. Now she was running for Scotland and knocking on the door of two-and-a-half hours.

And there was Gareth Jones, a plus-forty at Southampton University. He'd started out a lunchtime jogger, looking for fitness. A year later he was winning things, running third-fourth in races like the Totton 10K, picking up vet's prizes most Sundays. No, Caz was thinking, there but for the grace of big G goes anyone, including me, distance people who should've tried sprinting, sprinters who really were actors, failed actors who should have written plays. Some of those who made it to the top of their chosen tree, she thought, barked at the bottom of it because there was never anything else they were going to do, but some tried that one over there instead. And maybe they did OK, well even, but, but, it was the wrong tree.

And I'm a copper.

She came round towards the bike sheds, her fourth or fifth lap. A gaggle of race-bikers was gathering. She envied them their colours, the tight Lycra tops, the flash headgear and the trendy shades. There were about fifteen, twenty; straddling saddles, leaning, tinkering, chatting, with that air of confidence that came from being in charge of the body. Caz knew the feeling and knew it was delicious. She was smiling when a family emerged from the shed's darkness, the husband in awkward whites, the wife floral and the two kids wobbling on little single-geared street-bikes, white crash helmets on top of slightly pink faces, making them look like mushrooms just off on a jolly.

The biking group moved away from the bike sheds, languorous, slow pedals, solid legs. The bums settled down, the bikes paired up, then the murmur of their conversations changed to a new rhythm and they were gone. Caz walked into the shed. To the right, the little boy had just taken a tumble and was whimpering. The man in white was attending while his wife and little girl watched, leaning on their handlebars.

Outside on the track, the sunlight was absolute and unforgiving, so the hut's inside came as a dark-brown shock, as the eyes rapidly adjusted, then the skin, the cool contrasting with the rayed heat of the stadium. There were two guys working, a Greenie called Otto, and a handsome little islander she didn't know. There was a bike up on a rack and the little guy was adjusting something to do with the gears.

Otto said hello. 'Cazzy, right?'

'It's Kathy; call me Caz.'

'Cazzee?'

'Just Caz.'

'You wanna bike, Caz?' Otto asked with a little smile. His accent and delivery was strange, some German there, some American, bits and pieces of lots of other places.

'No, thanks, Otto. I'm after some advice.'

'Shoot away. What I don't know about mountain bikes, fuh, not worth knowing. And if it's road-racing, fuh, then Yoseph, he is your man!'

Caz nodded to Joseph who smiled bashfully back through the bike frame. 'You know I'm going to be working as a running coach, Otto? Well, I'd like to know a bit about cross-training, long-distance biking for runners who are trying to stay fit but can't run.'

'Knees, Achilles?'

'Whatever,' Caz said. 'I'm just curious for now.'

'With the knees, sometimes biking is good. Fuh! If the problem is the jarring, the hard road making the knee sore, for example, fuh, then the bike is great! But, if you have ITB or other soreness, sometimes to get on a bike is worse, then you are completely fuh.'

'Do a lot of runners bike?'

'Fuh, yes! And they do always much too much first times. Big surprise, next day they cannot walk! I warn them but they all say, fuh, bike is easy. Next day they change their mind.'

'Do they get injured very often? I mean falling off, that sort of thing? The last time I was here, I went up to Tinajo and back. Coming down the hill is a bit frightening.'

'Soon you get used to going fast.'

'Yes, but do they fall off very often?'

Otto was full of it. 'Fuh! They fall off all the time. We take people out on the official rides, they must wear helmet. We say, no helmet, fuh, you don't go. The roads, lots of them is volcanic black rock ground up. Iss very hard. You don't want to hit this.'

'I heard sometimes people have accidents with cars . . .'

'Fuh! You're not kidding! Tourists, fuh, they haven't got a clue! They are looking at their maps, look up, fuh, there's a bike, bang! It happens! We say bikers, watch yourself, tourists, fuh, they are all brain-dead, no fuh-in' idea. Last year we had biker, straight into a car door, wallop, two fortnights in hospital before he can go home.'

'Two weeks?'

'Two fortnights. Fuh! He was a mess. Was doing maybe thirty-five K when the car door hit him. Zup! he is over the top. Messed up face, broke collar-bone, ribs all bruised, well fuh.'

'And he was in hospital for fourteen or twenty-eight days?'

'Fourteen. Fuh, Caz. I tole you! Two fortnights.'

'Was the car-driver prosecuted?'

'What is prosecuted?'

'Did the driver get into trouble with the police?'

'What for? Fuh, no. This guy was from la Santa, he was not even a tourist. He is a Belgian guy called Edward, a biker too. He was pretty stupid, opening his door, so he brings the man here in his car for the doctor. Car Hire is pretty pissed off, there is blood on the seats. It won't wash out!'

'Do you know the driver's second name?' Caz said casually.

Otto looked up at the ceiling. 'Maybe, but fuh, what d'you want to know for? Ask Car Hire.'

'So, anyway, I can get my runners on bikes if they're injured?'

'Some, yeah.'

'And you can advise me. It depends on the injury?'

'Fuh, Caz! No problem!'

Caz grinned, then smiled at Joseph. He looked shy again.

'Bye Joseph!' she said, and watched him pink. Then she said thanks and goodbye to Otto.

He grinned. 'Fuh! You come again, Caz! No probs!'

Fifty-three

The car hire office was closed, a Spanish lunch and siesta combined with common sense – who wants to hire a car at three in the afternoon? Caz had an hour, so she went back to the room for a shower, sluiced down with the water a notch above cold, stretched, then lay down in the curtained bedroom to think.

So one of the accidents really looked like an accident. True, if this Edward Braindead turned out to be Edward Platt, he'd've popped up for the second or third time – but if a weasel like that was some sort of nutter knocking off sportsmen, he'd hardly knock one down then pick him up and bring him in to la Santa and say, 'Look what I did', would he?

She wondered what Tom MacInnes was up to right now. He could get his lists and cross them with the various incidents; he could re-open the incidents themselves, see what was on record here, maybe talk to the victims. 'No, plonker,' she whispered to the ceiling, 'the unlucky buggers are all back home now. Tom is hardly going to go shuttling round Europe just to chat to people who *might* have been hurt deliberately!' She suddenly thought. 'So why is Tom here? What can he really do?' Then she realised. 'Oh, fuck. He's here to keep tabs on me. To watch my back.' She sat up and grabbed the phone.

The DI wasn't likely to be in his room in the middle of the afternoon, but it was the only place that Caz could ring without having to bullshit. She dialled on the off-chance. The phone trilled one long ring.

'Tom MacInnes, yes?' Much softer than his usual voice.

'It's me,' Caz said.

'You not working, Caz?'

'Four o'clock, sir.'

'Hey, it's Tom, remember?'

'Can we speak, sir?'

'I think we are, Flood.'

'I mean, can I come round?'

'Ah'm in 16A,' he said, slightly harder.

Caz dressed quickly in her green and white stripes, brushed her hair back then tied it into a pony-tail. Her socks were 'Lanzarote Ironman' from the campus shop and her trainers were her favourite white Asics. She took one last look in the mirror before she left. She decided she looked good except for the scowl. Valerie was a liar, she looked *awful* when she was angry.

MacInnes had left the door open and Caz went straight in without looking round. She had learned to forget the furtive glances right and left. She knew that the best way to hide is to be obvious. People are tuned to see odd behaviour, not normality. The best way to steal was openly, with broad gestures that didn't catch the eye precisely *because* they were in plain view.

'Good t'see y', Flood. What can ah do f'yer?'

'Can I sit down, sir?'

'Tekk a seat, hen.'

'Thank you,' Caz said. She noticed the bottle on the table.

'Y'want some?' MacInnes said.

'I'm working,' she said.

'We both are, Flood.'

'At what, though?' Caz shot back.

MacInnes sat down, white chair, white table. He looked

small and hard with a lid on his anger. 'Well, for a start, Caz, Matthew Black's sunbathing habits.' He seemed to be making a point of saying 'Caz' rather than 'Flood'.

'Which are?'

'Wanna go see?'

They went out, locked up, then MacInnes turned to walk towards the campus shop. Caz dropped in alongside. In soft holiday clothes and shoes MacInnes seemed to walk differently. Gone was the tipper-tapper click-clack always-thinking quick-step. Now the DI shuffled along, his heels flapping occasionally. He was relaxed. But he was still thinking.

'While we're getting there, Flood. You lied t'me.'

Caz had been waiting. 'Yes,' she said.

'Set me up, could've made me blot my book.'

'No, sir.'

'What would you call it then?'

'Are we talking about Marco Harris?'

'Aye.'

'I just heard he'd been attacked. It was another la Santa connection. I just said.'

They were at one of the off-cream towers.

'Up here,' MacInnes said. As she went to go past him he stopped her.

'You didn't "just say", Caz. You *lied*. You said "the disco". You knew ah would think you were meanin' the disco here.'

'But I didn't say where it was, Tom.'

'It was a lie, Caz. You lied t'me. You an' me, we don't d'that. Never. And we din't never again.'

She looked him in the face. There was love-hurt-hate spinning like gaming machine fruit behind his eyes. She felt like a lover had just discovered her cheating. The next words . . .

'Tom, I'm sorry. I was floundering. I knew something. I wanted to get back here. It didn't seem that bad when I said it.'

'Anyone else it wasn't, Caz.'

'I'm so sorry, Tom. There's no excuse.'

He put a lightweight fist playfully to her cheekbone.

'Behind us, DC Flood. Just din't do it again!'

'I won't,' Caz said.

'Gidd!' he said.

They went up spiral concrete steps, an interior, a feeling that reminded Caz of going up the lighthouse on Lundy. Her DI was behind her, his breath rasping, a funny sort of echo of her own. She stopped at the top floor.

'Keep going,' MacInnes said.

'Wha?'

'There's stairs to yer left.'

There were more stairs, just round a fawn pillar. Caz found them and went up, one more twist of the spiral. They came to a door, splintered wood, some sort of thick cloth protruding near the damaged lock.

'Tom?'

'Give it a good tug.'

Caz pulled and nothing happened. She pulled harder and the door moved. The folded sheet that had helped to jam the door now dropped to the concrete floor. Bright heat, the roof waited.

'Go out there,' MacInnes said.

On the roof, apart from the occasional modern artifact, aerials, clothes lines, pipes, Caz had the sensation of an adobe Indian village built into a canyon, thick brown-cream walls that could have been whitened mud, nooks, crannies, odd barriers, the sensation of separateness, of being above the world, defended.

'It's very quiet.'

'First thing ah thought,' Tom said. 'A place yu'd come to be alone or with someone.'

'The lock, sir?'

'Awriddy asked. Happens regular. They want t'bathe on the roofs, they break the locks. Maintenance mend them regularly. Means nowt.'

She had called him 'sir', still feeling guilty. 'So where exactly was—?'

'Black used t'lie here,' MacInnes said sharply as he stepped over a low wall. He was still speaking as he flicked his body up on to the outer wall and stretched out theatrically on his back. Caz's stomach flared sudden anxiety. Shit, she loved this bloke! MacInnes turned his head. 'He lied right he-yuh, jest like this!' Caz looked. It was eight to ten feet and a blind turn from the doorway, three steps, a jump, a shove. Tom was lying back, soaking up sun, talking. 'Black could've bin pushed, but he jest as easy could've fell.' He leaned out slightly, looking down. Caz almost lifted her hand. 'Easy murder t'do, if murder's what it were.'

Caz was surprised. 'Murder? Is Matthew dead?'

'Nay, lass. Figure've speech. What's the difference between a murder and not, anyways?'

'About ten years?'

'Y'see we still punish according t'the *result*, not the intent. Try t'kill someone an' succeed, it's murder, life. Try t'kill them and fail it's attempted murder, mebbee as little as three, four years. Whyfore, because you were inefficient?'

Caz was thinking about psychology lectures, the attribution of blame. 'Never thought about it, Tom, but you're absolutely right.' She was still smiling but she was thinking, *Will you please get off that wall*?

MacInnes grinned, a slightly nasty, odd grimace that Caz couldn't read. Then he said, 'Ah, what the fuck!' sat up and swung his legs into space. For a dizzy, horrible, illogical second, Caz thought he was going to jump. She spoke his name.

'Nay worry,' Tom said as if he was talking to someone else. He was looking down, bewildered by his new perspective on the world.

'You gonna jump, or what?' Caz said. 'On^ly it won't half cause a lot of paperwork if you do.'

MacInnes looked round, his head slightly down, looking back at her. He smiled a thin smile. 'That's very funny, Caz.'

'I do my best,' she said. Then she sat down, splayed out her reddening legs and felt the full force of the sun. She relaxed slightly. She suddenly thought of Val and a flutter of sexual need flowed up through her.

The sun was baking, lovely. Caz was thinking, *Sod skin cancer, this has to be worth it*. Eventually, Tom swung his legs back inside the wall and away from the drop. Caz then got up. When she moved to the edge and looked over, what struck her most was how absolutely isolated this world was from the one below them. She remembered a discussion she'd had not so long ago. *People don't look up!* She was fascinated by the view, the five-a-side court, the lagoon, the roads the other side, the top of the laundry layered with rubber piping picking up God's free heat. It was a great place for a terrorist, a last stand. Maybe it wasn't an Indian village, maybe it was Masada and the colours marching on the five-a-side pitch weren't aerobic wannabees but legionnaires, their shields flashing in the sun, red favours fluttering in the breeze . . .

She would have dwelled on all of this, soaked up some more kiss-me-deadly UV but MacInnes broke the spell. He sounded almost angry again. 'You're not doing that well this time round, Caz.'

'I said I was sorry.'

'Not that. Ah'm not on about that. It's your man Marcus Harris. A record as long as yer arm.'

Caz was shocked. 'But I ran a check on him, all his possible first names.'

'The Mark was right, but the surname's Harrison.'

Harrison? *Bugger*! She was trying to remember the conversation with Ina. It was when the shoplifting ob blew up, Moira, all that . . .

'Mark Robert Harrison. Last UK address was our patch.

Used t'be based in Crawley. He's got an ABH against him but that could've been explained away as self-defence with a better lawyer. There was a GBH that the CPS never got to court and a sniff he might've been involved in protection. But the big iffy on his file is he's been connected to drugs.'

Oh, shit!

'He was shifting speed small-time we think but he was being watched for other substances when he suddenly decided to up sticks for the Canaries.'

'Substances?'

'Performance enhancing drugs. Steroids mainly. The Squad picked up a whisper that he had access to some sort of muscle builder that was undetectable. They thought he was shifting it around the clubs but they hadn't managed to get any evidence by the time he took off.'

'Took off being literal,' Caz said. 'Maybe there was no evidence.'

'Well, he upped sticks pretty pronto one morning 'n chartered out here. Then he took a job at la Santa.' Caz looked up, about to speak but MacInnes was quicker. 'And yes, I already checked. The dates fit.'

'Then he didn't do a sudden runner, Tom.'

'Why not?'

'He went on a charter. You don't get a seat last minute to Lanzarote unless it's a stand-by. And second, if he came here to a job, he must've planned it, discussed the position with Christian Green.'

'You saying he's not iffy?'

'I've no idea, Tom. I'm just betting that it wasn't a rush job coming here.'

'Do I get odds?' MacInnes said.

'Nope!' Caz said.

'Awright. Bottle of Whyte an' Mackay says I'm right.'

'Bottle against a litre,' Caz decided quickly.

'Why's that?'

''Cos when I win, you'll drink my winnings anyway.'

'Yer a cruel woman, Flood.'

'You taught me,' she said back.

Fifty-four

Caz's first day as super-coach hadn't been too taxing, and she felt light and solid as she walked over to the Pool Bar to meet Blodwen. The sun was still warm, but now with its hardest edge removed and the faintest of breezes drifting in from the sea, it was just about perfect. This, this, Caz decided, long deep breath, I could learn to live with.

When she arrived, the outdoor bar was almost deserted, just a couple in one corner, something being negotiated. It looked like he was trying a little bit too hard and she was enjoying herself deflecting. Caz bought a Southern Comfort and Coke, lots of ice, tall glass, and sat down to wait.

According to MacInnes, the jurisdiction thing was border-line. If he was investigating Mark Harrison as a murder suspect then there'd be little problem. Anything else and it popped up, he was likely to run foul of protocol pretty damn quick.

'What I'd like t'do, Caz, is just accidentally bump into the guy. Have a wee chat, gloves on. See if he wants t'tell me who clobbered him.'

He wanted Caz to try to set it up?

'Aye, why not? That way yu'll be doin' somethin' useful, 'stead of jest gettin' brown, sharpening thaise lang legs on the running track.'

'You don't know the half of it, Tom.'

'No,' he'd said. 'Mebbee not. But I can make a pretty gud guess!'

'I'll talk to Ute tonight,' Caz had said.

They had gone back down the tower steps as far as the first floor. Caz had gone left, towards the lagoon, MacInnes had sloped off right, into the centre of the complex. As far as Caz could tell, no one had seen them.

She had been close to late for her first-ever stint as la Santa's running coach so she'd jogged sharply over to the track to hold the meeting. There were eight there, a thin-faced Brit with a grey beard who looked like he'd probably keel over and die first lap, three fattish German ladies, two Danes, husband and wife – unfit – and a couple of young kids, English, who should have been in school, not lapping up the sun.

She'd gone through the motions, all of them walking, jogging, walking round the track, all awkward, all trying too hard. As the group spread out she didn't try to stop it. Instead she used the gap from front to back as something to sprint across, keeping them all interested, chatting pig-dinnish BRITLANG with them all, keeping up a smile like a synchronized swimmer all the time. Her mind was elsewhere during all this and suddenly, unfettered, it had popped off back to her first flight to Arrecife and her silly statement to the Manchester United fan about the gay Olympics.

She'd almost said out loud, 'Serves you bloody right, Flood!' Instead she'd heard herself shouting, 'Hey good! That's good! Relax those shoulders! Think about those arms!'

They had gone away sweaty, the adults with deep red in their cheeks. By default, Caz had managed to inspire them, and tomorrow they were all going to do the 3K in the morning, her session in the afternoon. She was trying hard to make herself think about villains but the utterances of the mundane had always had the uncanny ability to dominate her head. Instead of strategy and deep thought she found herself with verbal diarrhoea, issuing little verbal strokes gem-like, as if they sold by the pound. 'Good!' she'd shout. 'Hey, Great!' 'That's the way!' 'Move over Seb Coe!'

When the eight had walked (not jogged) away, she turned back to her real head, but the inside, the serious stuff, was layered over with platitudes, her real purpose temporarily smoke-screened out of existence. She was going to do what for Tom MacInnes? How? Nothing came, so she ran one flat-out lap, exchanging confusion for buzzing calves, tightness in her back and a last fifty metres gagging in her throat. She was on her knees close to heaving when she remembered. 'Flannel Ute into a night out, her and this Mark bloke. That done, bump into MacInnes, get the two boys together, see how it goes.' She thought about Marco. She wondered if his lumps had gone down yet.

Fifty-five

Blodwen arrived at five to seven, slightly flustered, carrying a striped beach-bag and looking as guilty as hell. When she spoke she was *very* Welsh.

'Bloody 'ell, Caz. I bin shittin' myself the last 'alf-hour, you bugger. Kept thinkin' someone was goaner come in an' catch me at it!'

'You were nervous,' Caz said deadpan.

'*Nervous*!' Blodwen blurted out loudly. She ducked towards Caz and whispered, not much quieter, 'Nervous! Christ Caz, if Christian come in, ee'd've 'ad my guts fer garters.'

'I'll get you a drink,' Caz said.

'No, I'll gerrum. I can't sit down yet. Jees, I feels like a valley chicken coming up to Easter. My 'eart's still goin'!'

'Where's the stuff?'

'In the bag,' Blodwen said as she turned away. Then she turned back. 'You're not going t'look at it *yur*, are you?'

Caz smiled. 'Course I am. No one will notice.'

'Oh, bloody buggering 'ell!' Blodwen said, turning away again. 'I must be completely Harpic, toop, round the bend!'

'I'll have another Comfort!' Caz shouted.

Blodwen waved a hand as if she was too scared or embarrassed to look round. Caz grabbed the bag and looked in.

Inside was a day-trip to Porthcawl; sun-cream lotion, after-sun, sunglasses, a damp swim-suit, goggles, Blodwen's red

Filofax, pens loose at the bottom with brushes, combs, some pesetas, her contraceptive pills, a pack of ciggies, a paperback (*The Godfather*), and there, a big fat brown envelope. Blodwen came back just as Caz emerged with it.

'I see you got the stuff, Caz, but I doan reckon it'll be a lorra use t'you. Far as I c'n see there's no one that's been 'ere for all of the accidents, even half of 'em.'

Caz was opening the envelope. 'Let me have a look, then we'll see.'

'Coupla names I know were here when the two blokes died last year and again this year, but there's more than a hundred like that. Soon as you add one more accident you've just got three, if you add any other accident you get no one.'

'So who are the three?'

Blodwen pointed. Straight away Caz saw Edward Platt, the funny little Belgian. 'The fifth accident,' Blodwen said, 'this is the biker hit by the car door?'

'Yeah.'

'Well, Platt would be involved, wouldn't he? He was the bloke who actually caused the accident!'

'Yeah, I know,' Caz said. 'He brought the biker in.'

'He wasn't here for any of the other accidents though.'

'Nor anyone else, so you say.'

'You gorrit!'

'So that means, if something's going on, it's . . .'

'Someone from the village?'

'Or someone on the staff . . .' Caz said slowly.

'Nah,' said Blodwen. 'Can't see that. Everyone's too nice.' Then she thought for a moment. 'Hang on. The last sheet, that's which Greenies were here for each accident. You start off with a lot but each time you add an accident, a few of 'em were away on leave, see?'

Caz looked. Almost all of the Green Team and admin staff had been on duty the day of the two deaths last year and the day of the night that Kevin King died. But a few were away for this accident, that accident, and the list gradually shortened. Five of these filters from the end, Mark Harrison was still on the list. So was Ina, Ute, Blodwen, a chap called Alan Sapsard, two guys from security, and two Spanish names, both workers from the offices. In the next filter Mark dropped out, one of the guards dropped out. Blodwen was looking at the list. 'Miguel is sixty and walks with a stick, you c'n scrub him. Fatima is four foot nothing and couldn't do damage if you gave her a flame-thrower.'

'So who's this Alan Sapsard?' Caz asked.

'Footballer. Used to be a semi-pro. Teaches a bit and runs the five-a-side. He's all right.'

Caz looked up and raised an eyebrow.

Blodwen shook her head sadly. 'Little giraffe.'

Caz was trying hard to think. If she presumed that Ina, Ute and Blodwen were not villians and Mark Harrison was more likely to be a victim or a dead end, then they were down to one guard and this Sapsard guy. Failing that it had to be someone from outside.

'What's this Alan Sapsard like?'

'I told you. Disappointing.'

'Blod! I don't give a bugger what he's like between the sheets. I mean what kind of bloke is he? Could he have had anything to do with these deaths?'

'Norra chance!' Blodwen said. She smiled knowingly. Caz was joking, yes? 'You could probably check dead easy but he'll've been on duty most of the time. He wouldn't have been able to go off the site and do damage to someone.'

'So what else?'

'Well, there's the villagers and there's the engineering and cleaning staff. I don't have rosters for them so I couldn't tell you much. But a villager floating around all the time would definitely be spotted. One of the things that the guards do is to keep an eye out for outsiders trying to use the facilities without paying. I reckon you're down to the engineers. The cleaners are all either sweet little *señoritas* or mamas. Either way I can't see them being baddies.'

'Then it must have been you!' Caz said.

Blodwen looked up.

'That's not even remotely funny, Caz!'

Fifty-six

The next morning was the dullest that Caz had seen in the forty-odd mornings she had witnessed, her two stays at la Santa. The sky was a solid, uniform grey, threatening rain, and the cool breeze was nearer cold with no sun as its counter. Whatever, the girls had jobs to do and Caz and Ina were walking down towards the leisure pool to loosen up before taking the 5K run. They were wearing track suit tops, green and white of course. Caz was thinking how trim and sexy they both looked.

'So, Ina, you know Alan Sapsard? The footballer?'

'I have treat him once or twice. A little bit tough man for me. He is a friend of Blodwen.' She rolled her eyes, the look of a despairing mother.

'I never see him around much in the evenings.'

'No, he has a very serious girlfriend, from the island, she lives in Haria. If he is not with her, then he is studying Spanish.'

'What kind of man is he?'

'He is a bear. He was a bear, a very big man. Billy Goat Gruff. But his little *señorita*, she has tamed him. Now he is coochy.'

'Coochy! Who taught you that word?'

'Blodwen,' Ina said, almost hurt. 'Is it not a nice word?'

Caz went to say something cutting but then she managed to stop herself. 'No, Ina, it's a fine word.'

It was one minute to eight. The warm-up music started.

On the 5K, Caz took the fast boys and blasted it in under eighteen minutes, pushing it from the start. Ina took the rest of the group and sauntered in on twenty-five. Caz was grinning, just finishing her warm-down laps and stretch.

'Was it fun?' Ina said.

Caz grinned again. 'One of the buggers went and beat me!'

'Hah!' Ina said. 'Good for your big head!'

Caz was scheduled to help with a stretch class at ten o'clock, thought about a shower but decided not to bother. After her stretch, Ina said she was going to get some breakfast in. Caz said she'd follow shortly. She wasted a few more minutes as the grey sky miraculously folded back, then she left the new sunshine for their room. On her way there she dropped in on Tom MacInnes.

He opened first knock as if he'd been stood there waiting at the door.

'Flood, I was just mekking coffee. Y'want some?'

'Thanks.'

He turned back to the kettle. 'Any joy with this Mark chappie?'

'Not yet, Tom. I went out with Ina last night and didn't get to chat with Ute.'

'Soon as yer can, lass.'

'Of course,' Caz said.

Over coffee Caz ferretted gently. How was Tom enjoying his break?

'It's no break, Flood, it's work. But so far, ah canna see any way a guest was up to somethin', anythin' to do with these accidents. Ah've come to the conclusion if there is somethin', it's the staff, or this Mark fellah.'

'Couldn't it be an outsider, someone from the village?'

'Nay, lass. Security would pick up on them too quick.'

Caz smiled inwardly. 'So what's next, boss?'

'This Mark, an' then ah'll need t'talk to the head of engineering, check out some of the site workers.'

'So you're getting there?'

'Not really, Flood. No better than you. Seems t'me there's something we're not thinking about. Seems t'me we're not going to have much luck the way we're looking.'

'Why, sir?'

'There's too many ways we could miss summat. Like what if one or mair o' these accidents *was* an accident?' He paused. 'Ah'm thinkin' maybe that we should try a different approach.'

'Like why, you mean? Like what's the motive driving everything?'

'That'd be good, Caz, but motive usually means the villain's alriddy dead to rights an' yer jest trying to show why he done what he did.'

'Then the connections between the victims?'

'Better. If we find there is one, then we're almaist there. Chance is that the connection gives us a motive, no?'

'Yes,' Caz said. She was thinking again about Ute, her connection with at least five of the victims. Notwithstanding that the physios *would* know an awful lot of people, it seemed pretty obvious they should check to see if Ute knew any more.

'I'll sniff around my end, Tom, see if Ute knew any more guests who fell over, but thinking about it, wouldn't it be better if it came as a direct approach from you? You can produce your list and directly ask. It'll be much trickier for me.'

'Awreet,' MacInnes said, 'but a browse through their files some time . . .?'

'What for?'

'Case they're holding out on muh.'

'And why would they do that?'

MacInnes grunted. 'They might if 'n they had summat to keep secret.'

Fifty-seven

Ina had bought fresh crusty bread from the bakery, some smoked ham and, for afters, two outrageous Danish pastries sprinkled with almonds. They devoured them with coffee, not even thinking about the calories. One of the great bonuses of their active lifestyle was that they could eat to their hearts' content without ever feeling guilty. Caz felt guilty about something else, being a liar. She was beginning to feel mentally softer, easier, liking this lady so much, loving the sun, the daily sport, the companionship of bright-eyed, fired up people. Meanwhile she scurried behind them in shadows, manipulating, snooping. And some day she'd be leaving. It would hurt.

Ina was speaking. 'Caz, you are unhappy?'

She came back. 'I was just thinking.'

'Two pennies for your thoughts?'

Just say something she'll believe.

'My boyfriend,' Caz said slowly. 'I was just wondering how he was.'

'Oh, Caz. My Eric will be here very soon. I am being so happy and I was not thinking of you.'

Caz snapped, 'Don't think of me, Ina. Don't be nice!'

'What?'

'There's no need. I'm all right . . .'

The stretch class was fun, blazing sun, slow four-bar music on

211

the big speakers, swaying stuff for the flowing moves. It was Ute's turn out front, chanting Germanic English instructions into her clipped-on radio mike, switching effortlessly into her native tongue, then again into French with her big-boned, tooth-led grin. She was big, beautiful and warm-eyed, her infectious smile almost laughing as she led about fifty Lycra-clad wannabees through torture.

'And so! And *slow*, and *slowwwlly* stretch, feel the stretch, yah, here in the groin, ah, iss good, and *hold* . . .'

Caz helped during the session, adjusting postures, demonstrating the various stretches. Afterwards she helped wrap up, smiling at the sparkling Ute, moving in with her own agenda.

'That was great, Oot! I really enjoyed it.'

'Thank you, Caz-ee. It is fun to be doing things which is also doing your body so much good.'

'You know your stuff.'

'Of course, we are professionals.'

Caz rolled up a wire. 'So, how is Marco?'

'Oh, he is better now, only little marks on his face. Last night we ate in la Santa. He was not miserable.'

'So when do I get to see him? Soon, I hope! Why don't you let me buy you both a drink one night?'

'Tonight he is coming over.'

'Tonight then?'

'That would be nice. Thank you, Caz.'

'Don't thank me,' Caz said. 'We're all mates, aren't we?'

Fifty-eight

The guilt came in waves. One moment Caz could be thinking about the sun, laughing at a joke, then she'd see Ina's face or Ute's face, their eyes, trust built-in. But it wasn't trust, not quite, she knew that, because trust, like faith, was unborn until the moment doubt had slipped inside. If she closed her eyes she could see the look, a child's, automatic, in the girls.

But that look wasn't in the face of the DI. When she closed her eyes and thought of Tom MacInnes, she didn't see it. Tom had eaten shit, trodden in shit, listened to shit all his life. He knew what life was like – cheating husbands, cuckolding wives, liars, frauds, molesters, thieves. What was left to believe in for him? Caz? No, she had already let him down, conned him to get here, and now here, she dug in the same dirt he dug in, tried to second-guess him, moved in his shadows.

Caz was in her room. She fancied a drink or a run. The drink was easy, the run would hurt. Ten miles would be enough.

She came out of her room in light nylon shorts, a nylon top, ankle socks, soft cotton. Everything was white including her Asics shoes. She was already stretched and by jogging through the complex she warmed up. When she reached the road that ran to la Santa and Tinajo, she was already loose enough for fast running. She set off aiming for six-minutes pace. In this sun she would not be able to keep it up.

213

She ran quickly, out, past a parked Clio, then down a brief hill, before hitting the concrete road linking la Santa village and la Santa Sport. Earlier, she had thought about turning off on to a dirt track, the half-marathon course, but she had realised that, after la Santa, the road to Tinajo would be tougher, a bigger test, almost 3K steadily uphill.

The sun was bell-ringing hot and here she was out in the open, no breeze that she could feel, sweat already beading on her forehead, waiting on her eyebrows, then either wiped away or nipping the sting of salt into her eyes each time she was too slow with the back of her hand.

It was hot and her legs felt strange and leaden. She wasn't enjoying herself. *She* felt strange and leaden. A car passed, a Renault. She felt empty, deficient. She knew it was the hill, her speed, the sun, and she knew she should slow down, but as the little car purred away and disappeared she was swearing at herself, still trying to maintain six minutes a mile up the hill. Her head was filled with chattering voices: Ina, Ute, the slower, sober Scots of the DI, Val whispering in her ear, bed, Val again, the unknown but imagined face of Alan Sapsard, Val *again*. Shit, she hadn't phoned him for days! Then villains, bodies, a burning car . . . She was definitely running too hard, then *ziiipppp*! and she was through the other side, a space-ship jumped into hyper-space. It was all gone now and she was sailing on endorphins, the hill was slackening, she was back in control, white buildings either side. Tinajo. Fuck, that was hard!

She passed a sun-darkened field-worker, clad in black, who looked up vaguely before returning to his onions. Then, in the street, an old man who caught her eye, waved back, calling '*Ola*!' as she passed with a wave of her own. A dog barked on a roof; chatter in a foreign tongue spilled from an open green door. Far off, another dog barked, and a grey donkey trawled slowly across a black field back-dropped by red-brown cliffs as barren as the moon. Calm! This was six-thirty pace and here, here was, was, *Lanzarote*! She almost giggled.

Halfway through Tinajo she took a right, skitted on tarmac past more green-shuttered houses, parked cars, then found herself aiming at a road that swept along below the red cliffs.

Then she was out of the village and flowing again, the road fractionally downhill, she guessed towards the sea. A car passed her and she glanced at her watch. She was intending to turn at thirty-two minutes then aim to be back on the hour. She would have the hill in her favour, but it was too hot, she wouldn't do it. The thought annoyed her but she shook it away roughly and concentrated for now on maintaining her pace. Ahead, the car disappeared round a bend.

It was probably a touch of dehydration but she still didn't feel great. She found herself glancing at her watch as she got further and further from the town, trying to urge the digits forward past thirty. She got to the bend just as twenty-eight finally arrived, and as she grinned and grunted she saw the car. Something made her stop.

Fifty-nine

She dropped to her haunches, waited, then leaned forward slightly to play with her shoe-laces. The road was dust, grit, sudden isolation. When she glanced up she could still see the car. It was half-hidden – parked if you weren't paranoid. The paranoia came from the sudden clicking into place of images, Clio, Renault Clio, parked Clio, passing Clio, and now, waiting Clio. They were so damn commonplace on the island; they could have been one two three four five different Clios, all the same colour, a quiet blue, but somehow, some nagging little how, Caz felt they were all the same. What to do?

The trouble with a long run was not tiredness, though that might be a factor near the end, but blur, the soothing, gently insidious blur of exercise endorphins. Once Caz had dealt with a child cyclist injured by a speeding car. Then she had been half a mile from home, sixteen miles behind her at eight-minute pace. She had walked out into traffic, soft, serene, feeling that she was gliding, almost a swan. She had dealt with the kid, saved his life maybe, but it was the detachment that she remembered afterwards, the lack of bite, the hardness gone, the edge she needed to survive.

But adrenalin was here now, *phtt-phtt*, good old flight-fright-fuck juice. There was a flush, a little dizziness, a confusion of hormones. Then she was decided. And the car was still there. She stood up.

216

Sixty

She started jogging again, then running, not so fast now but something inside eights. After this turn there was another, to the left, above that a slight hill and a right-hand sweep, then a blue-yellow flash of sea. Now she couldn't see the car, so where it was parked *was* hidden. She had seen its rear, just chance. When had she read that snipers either hit the head or the rump, the two bits of body left on an unlucky horizon? It was something to do with body-awareness, a lack of it, something to do with not being able to stand outside and think.

The blue Clio had passed her, pulled off the road and then backed up out of sight. Why? If she was la Santa's next accident, she could already be dead, seriously injured, swatted from the road, slammed against a dark wall, in a ditch. It hadn't happened.

Or was this something else – if it wasn't just paranoia – a couple looking for privacy, perhaps? An island salesman, time off? A cruising rapist? A rapist? Maybe. Slim girl, out on her own, it was quiet enough, long legs, medium brown, sweat-wet, glistening. This was the stuff of centrefolds (if she had tits). This could be a stalker, someone working up the courage for something more serious.

She didn't run, as in run away, partly because there was nowhere to go, partly because something in her made her look for these men, these things, these sticky handshakes with danger, death even.

She knew, as yet, that she didn't want to die, but the darkness, the dark sexuality of evil, facing it, that kind of death, that, intrigued her. And it was an obstinacy, too, some pigheaded refusal to be a woman, the weaker, the put-upon. Evil was male and fuck them! Some shit, one day, yeah, he'd manage it, kill, rape, cut her, but he would grab a screaming cat in a sack. It would be face to face and the blood wouldn't only be hers.

She passed the car's shadow, tried not to stiffen, tried to look seaward, to stay relaxed. The back of her head buzzed, ear across to ear, and she was thinking, whispering, 'OK, you sad fuck. I'm here.'

Now she felt the prickle of the preyed, the stand-up buzz and burn, skin rising. She was speeding up, against her will, huffing little asthmatic half-gasps between forced breaths, dust, her feet lift-scuff, lift-scuff, a slight soreness where the flesh of her arm sweat-wiped, skin-rubbed her side. She listened; no engine, no creaking car, hand-brake off, rolling her way.

She didn't have eyes in the back of her head but she could see him now – it was always a him – dark, dark glasses, maybe darkened glass, always hiding. Out of her blue past she popped a vision of *Duel* – a great black truck, a snorting bull, headlights, teeth, following, following.

'Oh, fuck this!' she said suddenly and turned. The arsehole, he could put up or shut up and he could do it now! Now there were four hundred yards between them, but the gap was closing. He was metal and glass, she was flesh, blood and bone. But he was waiting. Caz wasn't. She wanted this more than he did. She looked. Her hate was for the car, eyeball to headlight, *Duel* again, but she was confronting it, him, bringing it to a head. And she was closing, coming. She heard the engine start. Red light rushed up through her.

Sixty-one

Behind her was the sea, empty sea, cold bubbled lava, wasted beaches, black. This was now. Ahead, a mile, maybe two away, there would be people, the soft brown smiling eyes, shy nods, a tentative, bewildered help. But that was Mars. This was Caz. And the car. Him.

Caz was two hundred yards away from where the car had slithered off the road. She looked hard at it as sunlight flashed on the fawn mirror of his windscreen. Then the car moved. She was still too far away to decide what she could see, but anger-sharp, she looked anyway. Just a shape, a small blur; different light in light behind the glass.

She was ready to turn, maybe a hundred yards from the cut, when she heard the engine rev, heard-felt the skitter of stone, saw the change in the car as it smoked forward. She stopped, tensed.

It came out on to the road, skidding, the rear flicking as it spread legs, snarled and snaked for her. Caz stood her ground, staring. There was no fear, just calculation, an anger. The Clio, him, went right, left-left, then racing straight, was a flashed second, and then he had passed, swerving, diving, ducking away from her face as she stared him down. Then he was gone, dust, snarling, rrammppping away between walls, swinging up towards a horizon, left, beyond Tinajo, towards the middle of the island. A coward. She'd guessed a coward. Time now to feel sick.

She walked rather than ran. She had forgotten the sun and now she imagined she was being burned, beaten down. She hadn't seen the man – it had to have been a man – and the car was tinted-glass, half-hidden half-mirror. She'd taken no plate number – was it removed or covered? – and she'd seen no markings, a garage, the name of a company . . .

This had to have been planned. But Caz was animal. She had been ready. He had blinked, spoken first and lost. A coward or a warning? She thought a coward. So why her, and how? Then she suddenly thought, *Shit, another filter*!

She began running.

The first steps were pain, the next few discomfort, her joints and muscles washed through, no blood there yet, only waste. She stuttered, her feet touching lightly, then the knees only nagged, then they softened, then, as she ran everything through in her head, the pain soaked away, her body, everything oiled again, alive, on top, going for it.

She got to the village, looking for a phone. Shit! Were they red, black, yellow, what? Double-shit! How d'you make a call? Emergency? No, it'd bring in the local gendarmes, not a good idea. She was about 5K from la Santa, twenty minutes' running in this state, about nineteen too long. She found a shop. Phone, phone, where's the fucking phone? A sweet old dear, dark brown. She knew *Ola*.

'*Ola!*'

The woman smiled shyly. '*Buenos dias, señorita.*'

'Er, yes. Thanks. Telephone?'

'*Telefono?*'

'*Si, telefono!*'

The woman pointed over Caz's shoulder, '*Por alli.*'

'Pardon?'

'*Por alli! Si! Telefono!*'

Wunderbar! Now all she needed was money.

She pulled out a sweaty thousand. '*Gracias. Pesetas?*'

'*Si!*'

'Can I have some?' Arghh! She mimed coins and dialling. '*Pesetas?*'

Hand is a phone. '*Telefono!*' Coins in. '*Pesetas, por favor?*'

'*Hah! Si! Si!*'

The old woman ducked out of sight, then back. Then, from a thin hand lumpy with brown rheumatic knuckles she dumped coins on the glass counter.

'*Pesetas! Telefono!*'

Caz grabbed the coins and turned away. The woman looked shocked. Caz turned round. 'I'm sorry. *Gracias.* Emergency! *Emergencio!*' It was a guess but it sounded right.

'*Emergencia!*'

As she popped in coins she heard the woman moving and talking quickly. It was a babble. She heard '*turistico*' and '*loco*'. She went to dial then realised she didn't know the number. Oh, fer fuck's sake! More guesses. '*Er, como esta? La Santa Sport. Numero? Telephono?*'

The woman stared. Her mouth was slightly open. Suddenly she snapped into life, walked round the counter, shoved Caz aside and grabbed the phone. As Caz moved towards her she was waved away and the woman started speaking. '*Es la Santa? Es recepción?*'

There were a lot of words, some '*Si's*', a few '*locos*', a '*senorita*' and at least one '*turistico*'. Then the old dear was shaking her head, the phone was back in Caz's hand and someone was speaking to her.

'*Para cuantas noches?*'

'You what?'

The voice suffered, 'You are English?'

'Yes!'

'How many nights do you wish to book?'

'You what? No, I . . .'

'Is that Miss Flood?' The voice was soft educated Spanish.

Caz sagged. 'Yes?'

'The Girl Who Saved Brighton?'

Caz managed not to scream. 'Yes,' she said.

First she asked for the DI's room. When there was no answer she asked instead for Christian Green. He was busy, in a meeting, they said. Caz shouted. They interrupted.

Christian's meeting was with the DI. Within two minutes, phone calls had been made, duty-staff were being checked, all vehicles in and out stopped and their occupants noted. While they were doing that, someone from admin was on the way to meet Caz. When the car arrived it was Blodwen.

'You've caught the sun!' Blodwen said as Caz got in the car. Then she said, 'So what's up, Buttee? Taken over a bit funnee, was you?'

'Something like that,' Caz said.

They drove away just as the old woman came out.

She was shouting, '*Cambio! Cambio!*' after the car.

Caz was buckling up. 'What's "*cambio*" mean?'

Blodwen grinned. 'Oh, nuthin',' she said. She was changing gear. She grinned again. 'Roughly, it's like, "Thank you. Please come again." '

It was probably funny, but Caz wasn't there any more. She was standing on the road, facing that car. She could feel the driver, imagine his breath. Blodwen was saying things but they were like tinkling muzak far, far off. Caz was trying to decide. She had stood her ground. He had swerved. But what if he hadn't?

Sixty-two

'No, sir. I knew *exactly* what I was doing. I figured that standing my ground was safer. I was ready to jump out of the way. I wanted to stay on top of things, see if I could clock him or the number of the car.'

'Why do I get the idea that you're keeping something from me?'

'Because you're paranoid, sir?'

'Not, funny, Flood.'

'No, sir.'

They were in Christian Green's office. His handsome face was still grey with the news, a mix of worry and relief and not being the one in control. He was a manager, powerful. The sensation was new to him.

'We checked that our staff were all here, as they should be, Miss Flood. All the Green Team members were accounted for except our football coach.'

'Alan Sapsard?'

'You know him?'

'Of him.'

He paused as if recording something. 'And we were able to discover all of our technical staff, our carpenters, our electrical workers, all of them, except Giuseppe Castellano. He is in charge of the pools.'

MacInnes broke in. 'He should be here, on duty?'

'Si, yes.' Christian said. He spoke precisely, excellent English. 'Giuseppe works for us in the mornings and in the evenings. He cleans the pool areas and checks the pumps, the chlorine levels and heating.'

'And he's done a runner?' Caz said quickly.

MacInnes glanced her way.

'This we do not know,' Christian said. 'At this time we would expect to find Giuseppe in the maintenance area for the Pool Olympic. This is a cellar, a basement. It is very large. You will find it where our odd things are stored, behind engineering. There is a compound there.'

MacInnes spoke sharply as he stood up. 'Thank you, Christian. Everything here is as quick and efficient as always. If Mister Sapsard turns up, can we arrange for him to be detained by your security staff?'

'Of course.'

'And the same for this Mister Castellano?'

'Again, we will have him brought to my office. My secretary will give you a radio. If either of these men appear, we will call you immediately.'

'Thank you, Christian.' Caz was still sitting. 'Flood?'

She was slightly distant.

'You coming with me, Caz?'

She turned her head, still faintly lost. 'Oh, yes. I'm sorry, Tom. I was thinking something.'

'Wanta share it?'

'Sorry, what?' Caz was now standing, limp.

'You were thinking.'

'Oh, yes,' she said, still distracted. 'I was thinking.' She turned to Christian Green. 'Christian, would you know if Mister Castellano ever worked late at night?'

Sixty-three

Caz and the DI left together, going out through the offices, down a couple of steps and then along the service road past the place where not so many weeks ago, Caz and Ina had resuscitated Matthew Black.

At the end of the service road were the site engineer's offices, a room where carpentry was carried out, and stores. They went in there, made themselves known to the chief engineer then left, turned right and went through two large gates into the storage areas.

After the efficient cleanliness and painted lines of the complex, the yard was a sudden contrast; a jumble of wood, paint and metal, a clutter of bits-to-be-kept-just-in-case, a squirrely man's back shed taken to a manic extreme, multiplied by twenty and then some.

'Ah hope yer man's no underneath tha',' MacInnes said. He had stopped just inside the gates, a shaft of sun across his face coming through a stack of planking.

'If he is,' Caz said, 'I don't fancy meeting the guy who put him there.'

A couple of the la Santa cats watched them from beneath particular shades. One Caz recognised, a scrawny black and white Tom with a missing front paw. As they came closer the cat raised a tired arm and vaguely hissed, as if it was saying don't mess with me, but had done it too many times now and was bored with it.

The pool basement was down six concrete steps, one and a half levels below the pool surround, maybe thirty metres from the water and yet a world away. The double doors leading in were the ubiquitous Lanzarote green, solid at the bottom and louvered at the top for air. Right now the ventilation was superfluous as the doors were wide open, revealing the innards of the building and the low vibrations of non-stop maintenance. Caz had heard the numbers that keeping an Olympic pool generated. She hadn't quite believed the cost then. Now she did. She looked at dials, pipes, nooks and crannies, a raised metal gantry, ladders, stainless steel tubs. The tubs made her think of breweries. The smell of chlorine was very strong and MacInnes sneezed twice, cursing himself.

The place was immaculate and ordered. Even the brooms and dustpans were stacked in a line on one wall. By the door were two metal dishes for the cats, dry as a bone. Neither Caz nor the DI felt anything. They could not feel that Giuseppe Castellano had been here.

'Did we check if yer man was in this mornin', Flood?'

'It was an obvious question, Tom.'

'But we didna, right?'

He stepped into the light and spoke into the radio.

Caz wandered. She felt strangely, delicately, aroused. It was this place. In a vague, illicit way, secret places like this often made her think of sex. She didn't know if it was association or some deep, Freudian thing. Or it might have been some throwback memory from her childhood, a well-felt hormonal rush that, because these days it was more likely to be linked to a flesh encounter she now wrongly read as erotic.

She had ducked under the gantry, her nose twitching. Presumably the place had not been searched. The foremen would have been told to check on all the staff, but they would have popped in or phoned across. They would not have come with a search party to look in cupboards and see what was hidden.

The most likely explanation for Giuseppe's absence at this point was a cheap wine hangover or an unbooked visit to the doctor. The thought that maybe he was in some corner, blood flowing, was B-movie, a dark thought from Caz and the DI's gloomy experience, not actually likely.

Except it smelled that way to Caz.

'Where are ye, Flood?'

'Under here, sir, sniffing around.'

'Let's get outa here, Flood. These hey chemicals are gi'ing me jip!'

Caz was coming out, ducking her head. 'Sorry, Tom. Curiosity killed the cat.'

'The cats're fine,' MacInnes said. 'Ah've spoken to the chief engineer. He tells us wuv ought t'check a place called the submarine.'

Caz was out. 'The what?'

'The submarine. It's hey place under the leisure pool. Same as thisun only different.'

'Oh, fine,' Caz said.

MacInnes was already leaving. 'Shut the door on yer way out.'

The submarine was accessed through a wire mesh door in the side of a blob of cream-painted concrete that stuck out like a sore thumb near the edge of the kiddies' pool. At a certain time of the day it must have cast a shadow where most of the topless sun-eaters, Caz occasionally, lay with their curly paperbacks. Caz could not believe that she'd never noticed it before, but then she remembered the saying, 'There's none so blind as those who are concentrating on something else.'

This was a quieter week but there were still four or five people lounging one bare side of the door, a dozen or so the other, the women topless, the men solid. The air was a salad of ozone, chlorine, perfumed tan oils, after-sun, laundered towels. Caz looked at the books, Jackie Collins, Wilbur Smith, Dick Francis, John Grisham . . .

'That's it!' MacInnes said.

Caz clicked her brain back. 'And it's locked.'

'It's supposed t'be,' MacInnes said.

'Why's that?'

'Dangerous. Chief engineer says it's a nasty wee drop, fourteen feet.'

Caz looked in and down. She could see nothing.

'Yer see owt, Caz?'

'Nope.'

'Yer wanta jog over t'get the spare keys frai the offiss?'

'We want to go down there, Tom?'

'Nay, lass, ah jest like the sound've they jangles.'

She suddenly thought. The DI was heavy on the accent this morning. That usually meant stress or booze.

'You seem a bit edgy, Tom.'

He frowned. 'What makes yer say tha'?'

'Oh, nothing,' she said. He was standing at the door with her now, looking down into the darkness. She felt more than smelt the faint blur of whisky under his peppermint breath.

'You OK, Tom?'

'Gay get thaise keys, lass,' he said.

Sixty-four

The chief engineer was a big, self-indulged man, about forty, with one of those red-round faces, always half smiling, that made you think he knew something funny that you didn't. When she had been in the building before, Caz had been nosing around and the DI had done all the talking. Now she realised she didn't know the engineer's name. It was on the door. She knocked and when he called her in, she smiled, 'Ah, Arnie! We need some keys . . .'

'It is Arn-eh,' he said flatly. 'There is no "i".'

'Arn-eh,' Caz said.

'That's good,' he said and gave her a little smile.

'The submarine. It's locked. Do you have the keys?'

'Giuseppe has them. But I have a master. You can promise me you won't lose it?'

'No,' Caz said.

He grinned and passed over a massive bunch of keys that must have weighed three or four pounds. 'Here!'

They felt like a shot putt to Caz. 'You're joking, right?'

He feigned innocence. 'This is the keys.'

'These are,' Caz said. Then she asked which one did she need?

Arne grinned again, put out a hand and magically pulled one key from the rest. It was large and sellotape around it covered paper and the word *submarino*.

229

'I suppose we couldn't take it off the bunch?' Caz said hopefully.

'I am sorry,' Arne said. 'I do not do this. If I do this and the keys are broken up, there would be trouble. These are my keys.'

'Would a "please" help?'

'It would make me feel good maybe.'

'Twenty minutes!' Caz said. She thanked him and left.

Caz decided not to jog back. It was never a good idea to mess with your running gait and the welter of keys in one hand, their weight, would certainly do that. Blokes into punishment did that, army types, blokes who loaded rucksacks for the extra weight, the increased training effect. And they were always surprised when the injuries came. Pain junkies.

She came past the Atlantico restaurant and the crazy golf. The sun was high bright and yellow, dark glasses time. The fawn walls were bright, the sky was bright, everything was bloody bright. Caz was due a headache and she fancied a day off.

She dropped down the steps towards the sun-bathing area. Tom was staring up towards her, looking pink, she thought, with the sun. When she got to him, he snapped at her.

'The fick yer bin, Flood? Ah've bin gettin' mair and mair dutty lukes, they peepul here. They're thinkin' ah'm a peepin' Tom and ah cannee blame them.'

Caz waved the keys.

'Yer luke like a Barlinnie keep,' he said.

'Aye,' she said. Then she looked pointedly at the various bare breasts, the oily, slowly-cooking flesh, and realised that Tom was pink, not with the sun, but with embarrassment. She couldn't resist it.

'And Tom, hey y'had a nice time, spying all the lassies, while y've been waitin on muh?'

Tom was not amused. 'Gey fuck!' he said.
Then he took the keys.

Sixty-five

MacInnes had grabbed the bunch of keys and now he was fumbling. Caz leaned forward and pointed to the sellotaped one.

'Ye could've done that f'me to start with,' MacInnes said coldly.

She left it. 'I'm sorry, Tom. Didn't think.'

Behind them was sunshine, blue-silver water, the squeal of splashing children somewhere, glasses tinkling up at the pool bar. Ahead of them was darkness, some sort of hidden cold. For a second Caz thought about the difference. Then she followed the DI through the door.

Inside was strangely cold, strangely separate. To go down they had to use a ladder-stairway as steep as a ship's gangway. Cast in a tiny low-watt lamp, they could see very little below them, but Caz went down with her back to the ladder, wanting to be looking in the face of anything. Confined spaces made her feel weak and she hated feeling weak. When she got to the bottom, she let out a tiny rush of air.

'Ah know what y'mean,' MacInnes said.

The room was perfectly circular, the roof domed, the whole thing maybe forty, fifty feet across and about twenty-five high. Like the previous room, there were pipes, gauges, taps and vats. It was as if they had stepped into some Orwellian nightmare where St Paul's Cathedral had been taken over and turned into a power station.

'It's weird!' Caz said slowly. She was spinning on her heel, her eyes sweeping round the ceiling. She felt like she was inside a concrete ball. She managed not to say it, but she was thinking, '*Fucking* weeeirrrdd!'

MacInnes interrupted her. 'Let's hey a luke round.'

She stopped spinning and dropped her gaze. It took a few seconds for the room to stop with her. She flicked her head to clear it. 'I'll go east,' she said. 'Which way you going?' MacInnes just pointed.

They looked under, by the side of and behind, but wherever Giuseppe Castellano was, he wasn't in *Unterseeboot Ein*.

'Seen enough, boss?'

'Aye,' he said.

They came out into sunlight that cut slices out of them. Their eyes had adapted to downstairs, and were wide, ready for the smack in the face they duly got. Now their pupils were like pinholes but it still hurt. MacInnes locked up while Caz waited, idly taking in nothing, bodies, sun-tans, water. Then she saw someone looking down, watching them from the Pool Bar. Her eyes were still smarting. She put a hand to shadow her brow and looked again. Edward Platt, the ugly Belgian. Then she saw Ina standing next to him, smiling, waving. She waved back and Ina gestured hand to mouth, drink? Caz made a huge exaggerated nod. Oh, God! Yes please!

Tom MacInnes came up behind her. 'Yer friend, Caz?'

'Ina Jensen, sir.'

'Yer betta go, then.'

'It's all right?'

'It's all right aye. We're no gonna find hey fella today.'

Caz hesitated. 'Ring you later?'

'You do that, lass.'

'Thanks, Tom,' she said. Then she left him.

Sixty-six

Caz jogged around the beach side of the pool, past the divers' school and up the ramp at the back of the disco. The Pool Bar was heaving and when she found Ina and Edward, they had already bought a drink for her, a massive Southern Comfort and ice, Coke thrown in. She nodded as she came to the table, glancing pointedly at the drink. Edward stood as she approached and nodded politely in a somehow foreign way.

'This is a surprise . . .' Caz said flatly.

'I am surprised to see you also,' Platt said.

'When did you arrive?'

He smiled, not particularly nicely. 'Fifteen minutes ago. Today I flew in from Belgium and Ina was in charge of the bus from the airport.'

Ina flashed a very quick grimace just for Caz. 'I was on the airport run, we arrived at one o'clock.'

'The service here is so goot,' Platt said. 'I am barely off the aeroplane and Ina is saying already she will help my injury to be better.'

Ina spoke now. 'Edward has a recurrent hip bursa. This is from much of his biking. I have tol' him he should maybe rest a little more.'

'But I do not!' the little Belgian said. He was grinning and Caz forced a polite click-smile back.

'So I am manipulating the joint for Edward two times each

day, to make it help much as I can, but . . .'

'Ina is wonderful!' Platt said quickly. 'Her hands are like magic.'

'I know,' Caz said. 'In fact, Een, I was hoping there'd be a slot tonight for me. I went running this morning, had to stop. And then I started again. I'm a bit sore.'

Ina shrugged and went to speak but Platt was quicker.

'Ina is fully booked. My hour was the last today.'

'That true, Ina?'

Ina nodded. 'Edward is right, Caz. All of my slots is filled.' But then she smiled. 'But we can sort something, can't we? Come round at eight o'clock. Edward will just be finishing.'

'Oh,' Platt said. 'Am I not to buy you your thank you drink, then?'

Ina put a hand on his arm. 'Of course, Edward. But at nine o'clock instead.'

He huffed slightly. 'Then I suppose I will shower and change.'

'Good idea,' Ina said.

Caz took a long, too-cold bite of her Southern Comfort. She could feel its one-off taste in the roof of her mouth. She had the urge to get pissed and then sleep the afternoon away but she remembered her coaching duties, four o'clock. Ina said something.

'Caz, that man you were with?'

'He's a policeman, Ina. I know him.'

'What was he doing in the submarine?'

Caz hardly blinked. 'Looking for some workman, I think. I didn't ask.' She looked towards Edward, allowing him a share of the conversation. 'I know him from way back, from when I worked in Brighton. I bumped into him in the supermarket this morning. He said he was going down to this submarine thing and did I want to look inside.'

'When was this?' Edward said.

'Was what?'

'You met the Inspector.'

'Half-nine, tennish, why?'

'Oh, nothing,' Platt said. 'I am just surprised a nice lady like you would go to such a place with a man like him.'

Caz was perplexed. 'Like him?'

'An older man. I do not think you would go there with this, an older man.'

'He's a friend, Edward.'

'I am sure, this is so. I am trying to make a joke.'

'A joke?'

'Yes. Have I offended you?'

Caz took another swig of her drink. She was thinking, and this bloke really pissed her off. 'No,' she said calmly, 'you haven't offended me. When they want a skin graft for a rhino, they send for me.'

'I'm sorry?'

Caz sighed. 'No, Edward, I'm not offended.'

'Ah goot!' Edward said. 'I will buy you a drink then.'

'Thanks, but I can't have any more this lunchtime. I'm on the track at half-past three, and training some joggers at four.'

'Another time?'

'Thank you,' Caz said. She looked up at the sky, cloudless bright blue. She smiled again but she was thinking, 'Yeah, next time it snows.'

Sixty-seven

They ordered salads, and at some point the little Belgian went up to the bar for more drinks. While he was there, Caz leaned forward and whispered conspiratorially to Ina. She was keeping a half-eye out.

'You don't *like* him, do you?'

'No.'

'Then how come you're all smiles and having drinks?'

'I don't know. Edward just seems to invite himself. It is difficult to say bye-bye.'

'He's a lurker, you mean?'

'A pest, I think you say.'

'He's that all right. Cramps your style a bit, doesn't he?'

'Cramp?'

'Edward. When he's around, it stops you having fun.'

Ina smiled and leaned forward. 'Sometimes I will hide. Sometimes, I see him and I think, oh no, and I walk the other way. Sometimes I will sit in the corner and wear dark glasses.'

'He gives me the creeps!' Caz said. 'A sort of poison dwarf. How come he's here again so soon?'

There was a movement up at the bar. Edward was still waiting.

'He is quite rich. He sells farm things, I think. Often he will come here for more physio and to take some sun. I think though it is just physio.'

'Must have more money than sense.'

'He has both. He is a clever man, I know.'

'Well, he's not that bloody clever, Een. He swiped that biker last year. He wasn't clever enough to look in his wing-mirror.'

'He has the drinks now.'

'Oh!' Caz said. She looked up at him coming and let out a laugh for his benefit. 'You're a natural, Edward!' He looked slightly sheepish and his head tilted in query. 'The tray, Edward. You could be a waiter.'

'I think not,' he said flatly.

As he sat down Caz let out a low laugh. 'Ina and I were just talking about that biker you hit last year. Must've been funny!'

'It was not a matter to laugh about, Caz. The gentleman was badly hurt and he was lucky not to have been killed. This was my fault completely and I feel very bad about it.'

'So what happened exactly?'

'I was on the road from Soo down to Famara. I had stopped to look at the view. I was to get out and this man coming down the hill, very fast, he is too close to my car and he hits my door.'

'You opened the door in front of him?'

'Yes. I was careless.'

'Then you brought him back to la Santa?'

'Yes, here was close. I do not speak much Spanish. Here was help.'

'You did well, apart from your initial mistake.'

Platt scowled, looking even uglier. 'I do not like people to make jokes. This man I might have killed and people make jokes. I am very guilty even now.'

For a second, Caz actually believed him. 'Yeah, OK. No more jokes.'

'Thank you,' Platt said.

Sixty-eight

Ina had to go back to work and Edward offered to walk part of the way with her. Caz still had the urge to stay in the bar and get stupidly drunk. Then she thought of Tom and followed them, before hanging a right to her room.

As soon as she got in, she picked up the phone and dialled. When Tom answered, another edge was off his speech. He would need more peppermint later.

'Hi, Tom. Little bit of news. One of the accidents last year, the biker who got clobbered by a car door . . .?'

'I know it.'

'The guy that did it, Edward Platt, he's a businessman. Happy to chat about it. Think we can put it down as an accident.'

'Oh, and why's that, Flood?'

'He wasn't on the island this morning, Tom. He flew in late on and got the bus from Arrecife to la Santa.'

'You've checked?'

'What, checked he came to la Santa?'

'He flew in.'

'Ina Jensen said she picked him up at the airport, sir. That means he must have booked his flight arrival and informed la Santa.'

'Well, that's all right then.'

He sounded funny.

'Yes it is, sir.'

'That it, Flood?'

'I guess so, Tom. I presume we haven't heard from Alan Sapsard or the pool guy yet?'

'Not when I asked.'

'Sapsard's got a little Spanish girlfriend.'

'Actually she's a *Conejera*, an islander. They've phoned her place, but there was no answer.'

'D'you think Sapsard could be in the frame, Tom?'

'Ah don't think anything, Flood. Ah'd just like to speak to the fellah.'

'I suppose he's in deep shit, not being on campus when he was supposed to be?'

'No one's said so to muh, but ah wouldnee be bettin'.'

'Maybe he's gone off to see the girlfriend and he's just dropped unlucky. You don't usually expect a roll-call in the middle of the day.'

'Always expect the unexpected, Flood. You know that.'

She laughed a little. 'Right-oh, Tom. I'll do me bestest.'

'OK, Flood.'

She thought for a minute. She could sense some sort of ache in his voice, in the things he wasn't saying.

'I've got an hour and a half, Tom. D'yer fancy a short drive?'

'Where to?'

'Thought we might nip over to the rocks near Famara where Colin Jones went into the sea.'

'Aye,' he said. 'Why not? Ah'll see you in reception, two minutes.'

Sixty-nine

When he arrived, Tom had changed. He was in white shorts with turn ups and a white shirt, white socks and orange-brown sandals. She thought of something out of *The Great Gatsby* but Caz's Gatsby was Robert Redford and Tom's too-skinny, black-haired white legs lacked a certain *je ne sais quoi*. Caz was dressed the same as before except that she'd swapped her trainers for a slightly more substantial pair. She carried her track spikes in case they were late returning. In the back offices behind reception Caz thought she heard Blodwen's shrill laugh.

Tom had the use of a Suzuki four-wheel drive and they took the half-marathon course, a dirt-track and then the hill over the top of Soo and down towards the sweep of Famara's beach. The breeze was up, fanning the heat over them in a soft, sensual way, smelling faintly of the ocean. To the left were onion fields. Caz knew that just beyond those was a village, squeezed in against the water. She had stumbled on it while running one day, white, dusty and deserted. She had stopped near the first buildings, looking at a ghost town, fully expecting a gunslinger to step out of the shadows and face her down the main street, the heavy whistle of something by Ennio Morricone somewhere in the background. That was the funny thing about this island, people, places, quietly waiting, not hiding but just not seen.

241

When they arrived at Famara they crossed a half-finished car park and drove down onto the beach. They turned back towards la Santa, the back of Famara village, and stopped when they reached the rocks.

They got out and worked their way towards the sea. It was difficult underfoot and Caz was worried that Tom might stumble. She knew to help him would be absolutely the wrong thing so she went ahead and stopped herself from looking back. When she reached the real sea's-edge and did glance back, he was happily skipping from rough stone to rough stone in a zig-zag, stopping often, looking and thinking. When he got to her, he said, 'Plenty of handy rocks, eh Caz? One o' they on the head and you might go swimming.'

Caz had already thought of that. 'That's the way I figured it too, Tom. The hardest one to work out is Kevin King. How d'you frighten someone that much, get him dead without touching him?'

MacInnes crouched and looked into the sea. He didn't answer. Lost, Caz stepped down towards the water. Foam and bits of flotsam jerked into a dirty gap between two rocks. It was greasy and dangerous and she could feel the ground sliding from her. She put a hand down to balance, out of the sight of the DI. When she looked up, he was still communing. She looked at the sea again, feeling a vague urge to get wet, to walk away. Was that how it was, Colin? A rock, a slip, an angry throw, no more than an insult? An insult which suddenly was much bigger? Had that happened, Colin? A bang on the head, some jealous gesture and you fell in? Was it frightening?

MacInnes was calling her.

She turned and climbed back up and the DI gestured for them to walk back a way, away from the water.

The DI was back on top of his accent. 'Forget King,' he said as they walked. 'That's problem one. Think of the rest instead. Think of the sequence, of what your man must have been like.

Did he kill people or did he just hurt them and then they died? Did he *try* to kill them or just to annoy, to injure them? And did he, each time, go just that little bit further? Did he suddenly realise he was getting away with murder?'

Caz felt cold. 'What are you saying – that he killed Colin Jones by accident? I was just thinking the same thing.'

'It's a good bet, Caz. A rock thrown here, a little push from behind on the German chappie up at the north end, a shove on that laddie in the Fire Mountains, a quick wee shove for yon Matthew Black, they are all accidents, they're all sneaky, like yer man is a coward, small and sly.'

'I know he's a coward, Tom. I thought that this morning.'

'You *bet* that this morning.'

'I was right.'

'It wasn't a good bet, Flood. Doesn't matter you won.'

Caz just kept walking. They got in the jeep and started back. All the way she kept thinking about that little weasel Platt. She had the unprofessional thought that she would have liked the murderer to be him. It even felt like it *ought* to be him. It was a bloody shame he wasn't on the island for some of the accidents, wasn't around this morning when she faced down the Clio. Then she had another thought.

'Did we get any further with the connection between the people who had the accidents, boss?'

'Only one we can find is being here, being at Santa Sport an' most of 'em knew the physio, had had some.'

Then a word she'd thought came back to her – 'jealous'. Someone who didn't want people to be near Ina and Ute? Someone like Edward Platt but someone who was here at the crucial times? She couldn't imagine the old maintenance man. That left Alan Sapsard. But why should some guy who was apparently besotted by his little *señorita* be angry and jealous at all these people? She couldn't see it.

They arrived back at la Santa and parked outside reception.

Tom was muttering as they got out of the jeep and Caz only half-listened, still wondering. She was still like that when Christian Green suddenly appeared, his face pink. 'Inspector!' he shouted. 'We have Mr Sapsard!'

Seventy

'I already told you. I went to see Maria. I know I shouldn't've, but I did.'

'What car were you in?'

'I got a Clio.'

'Where is it?'

'Just opposite reception.'

'OK, show us,' MacInnes said.

The DI, Caz and Sapsard went out, down the rear service road and back out on to the lagoon road. The footballer was worried, not about the policeman's hassles but that he'd been caught nicking some unofficial time. 'It's over here,' he said as they approached a grey car.

Straight away, Caz shook her head. If she saw the right Clio she would *smell* it. In the *dark* she'd know it.

'I don't suppose you've got *two* cars, have you?' MacInnes said.

Sapsard didn't think it was funny. 'I can't afford this one.'

'Didn't think so,' MacInnes said.

Then Sapsard said, 'I suppose this means they'll give me the 'oof from the Green Team?'

'That I wouldn't know, laddie, but it was you that buggered off on the sly. There's no one to blame except yerself, I reckon.'

The lad growled back, 'D'you think I don't know that?

D'you think I'm not kicking myself?'

MacInnes wasn't interested. 'It was your bed, lad. Dinna luke at me.'

Seventy-one

When MacInnes told Caz she'd better run along now and go do her coaching job, she was frustrated. And when she hesitated and he barked an order at her, she was upset. He had to remind her she was supposed to be an ex-copper and the job wasn't over yet. He was a DI. He could deal with young Mister Sapsard, continue the hunt for Giuseppe Castellano *and* keep a check on the still slightly iffy Mark Harrison. As a passing shot he reminded her that when she called up the Police National Computer she could have entered Mar dot-dot and Harris dot-dot, both open-ended names. Then, he said, she wouldn't have slipped up. She couldn't understand why he was being like this. Her face was flushed when she left.

She was still stiff from the morning but as soon as she hit the track she started pushing. In the first two hundred yards she thought she felt the tweak in her back again, the pain like just before she had blacked out in Von Goddard's house. In the second two hundred yards the tweak flashed like a red hot knife up to the roof of her head and back down again. She felt it, then she was a heap in the track's third lane. For a second her legs were somebody else's and then felt like hers again. She decided that she had tripped, not concentrating, thinking too hard about the DI, Alan Sapsard, Marco Harrison and the ugly little Belgian.

She got up and walked. Her back felt fine. She stepped off

the track to do her normal pre-run stretching exercises, her hamstrings, quads, both the calf muscles – two different stretches on each leg – her shoulders, fingers, arms, and then her back, her buttocks, her back again. The only sensations she felt were normal ones. She began to believe she really had tripped.

She had a few minutes before her coaching class was due. One or two were just drifting in through the stadium gates. She pretended not to see them and tried a gentle jog – nothing but a slight tightness like she used to get when she raced. Maybe she did trip.

The session was fine. The Danish couple arrived in matching red kit, the half-dead bearded Englishman had bought himself new trainers and the three German ladies had brought a couple of husbands along to see the wonderful new coach. Caz promised herself she'd crack no more towel jokes for the rest of the week.

She persuaded them to run loose, to settle down at the pace where they could just about chat and to learn that it was speed and not distance that killed. For fun, every second lap she got them sprinting a hundred metres or so in the finishing straight and the least fat German woman found she could not only outrun the biggest German man but every other newcomer as well. From the beaten man, Caz learned how to say '*scheisser*'. By the time they had finished she had forgotten her fall. She went off for a shower in a mood only just short of OK. She figured a few phone calls to England and maybe things weren't too bad. She didn't know it, but as she loped along the grey-floored corridors to her room, she absently rubbed her back, just on the waistband. And later, when she soaped herself in the stinging hot shower she lingered there, where her shorts met her vest, deep rain finger-drumming into her spine. Again, she didn't notice.

Seventy-two

She stepped out of the bath and switched the shower off. Water had been steadily getting through on to the tiled floor and she had to throw a towel down for safety. She dried her hair enough to stop the drips then combed it out while staring at herself in the mirror, trying to decide who she was. Her hair was water-dark but she knew it was blonder, a sun-blonde, a throw-your-head-back, be-a-filly-and-enjoy-it blonde. She was beginning to think about not going home, not being a copper. Sometimes, and she hated this when it happened, sometimes, she wondered whether she should leave catching villains to somebody else, maybe let herself fall properly in love, take in some sun, re-read all her favourite books, buy another one. She looked at herself close up, her eyes lit by the shaving light, the whites white, the centres bright green. There was no edge in there. She was going soft.

She tramped naked through to the little lounge and walked over to the patio doors and pulled the curtains closed. A male head, passing on the first floor, half-turned, half-saw but wasn't sure. She grinned, now in darkness, went over to the sofa and lay down with the telephone. She dialled for an outside line, dialled again to get an international line, then started with double-four for England. She figured, try Valerie at work first. As usual she'd just missed the ideal time to phone. He would be in the gym or running somewhere, having a pint or something.

'Val Thomas.'

She pinched her nose. 'One mimont pliss. I have international call for a Meester Thomas from Meece Flude in Hawaii. Will you take zee call?'

'That's pathetic, Flood.'

'You can do better, Thomas?'

'Anytime.'

'You still want to marry me?'

'Want to, no. Have to, yes.'

'You're pregnant?'

'No, Caz. But I have to have you.'

'Makes me sound like one of your cars.'

'Well I want to be inside you, twiddle your gears . . .'

'Are we gonna talk dirty? Only I'm naked here. I'm lying on the sofa in the dark.'

'Don't, Caz!'

'Don't what? Don't hold back, d'you mean? OK, Val. I'm lying on the sofa in the lounge, it's long and blue and it has a dark blue cover that's rough and is leaving little squares on my naked back, that's *naked* back. I've worked out three times today; I'm long and lean and brown. I've just stepped out of the shower and I'm wet in places . . .' She paused and let a long long breath go. 'Oh, look there are droplets of water *just* there! Oh Valerie, you should see. You could kiss them away.'

'You're probably wearing wellies, cleaning out a cess-pit, Flood.'

'No I'm not, I'm lying on the settee, I really am!'

'Well it's not working. I don't believe yer!'

'But Val, I need *you* to talk dirty to *me*. I'm all alone, feeling long and sexy, the curtains are drawn. I really am lying here naked. You could say nice things to me while I console myself.'

'You dirty little bugger!'

'I are aren't I? D'you still love me?'

'Yes,' he said. He did. He said so. Said he missed her like

hell and didn't like her going away on open-ended jobs. Said he wished she was an accountant and she worked nine to five for Ernst & Withey and did aerobics in the evening. 'I miss you like fuck, Caz. Come home.'

'Can't,' Caz said. 'But it won't be long now. There's only three people in the frame for the trouble out here and DI MacInnes of the Yard is hot on the heels of villainy as we speak.'

'You take care, Caz.'

'I will, Val. I've got something to come home for now, haven't I?'

'What's that mean, you love me or something?'

She wasn't going to say it. 'You have to work it out, Val. It's part of the process.'

There was a few seconds' silence. She could feel a vague disquiet.

'Did I tell you they brought that Worthing runner back by air ambulance? It was in the papers. He's still in a coma but he's stable. The parents wanted him here and signed off the risk.'

'Where is he?'

'In the General. His parents run a B & B on the front.'

'Did it say anything else?'

'The paper? No, just "Local runner injured in tragic fall flown back from holiday isle," et cetera.'

'At least he's alive.'

'Depends what you mean. If he's brain-damaged and can't run, how alive is that?'

'He'll run again!' Caz snapped. 'I know it.' Caz didn't know it, she couldn't, but she knew if there was anything she could do, she'd do it. 'He was too good a runner not to fight back. When I get back there I'll have to promise him my body to bring him out.'

'That's not funny, Caz.'

'It wasn't a joke, Val.'

Caz put the phone down after Val said a testy goodbye. Right, so she'd cocked up one relationship for the evening, time to call Moira Dibben and put her foot in it there, probably say something about Catholics or women in the club. She picked the phone up again.

She got through straight away. 'Hello?' Very quiet, very sweet, slowly. It didn't sound like Mo.

'Is that Moira?'

'No, I'm afraid not. This is *Mrs* Dibben. Who is that, please?'

Oh.

'Oh, it's Kathy Flood, Mrs Dibben. Is Moira there?'

'She is, child, but I'm afraid she's a little poorly, right now. She's . . .'

'Is the baby all right?'

'We hope so, Kathy, but it's still early days yet.'

'Is Billy there?'

'Young William? No, I'm afraid not. He is working from two o'clock until ten o'clock. That's why I'm here, to keep an eye on Moira.'

There was a pause then more of this slow melodic speech.

'But perhaps, if you left a message, then Billy, when he arrives . . .'

'No, it's all right, Mrs Dibben. Just give Moira my love and tell her we'll speak soon.'

'Of course. Kathy will ring again, love to Moira.'

'That's it.'

'Righty-oh, dear. Bye-bye then.'

'Goodbye, Mrs Dibben.'

Seventy-three

When Caz went round to the physiotherapy clinic both Ina and Ute were working. She was fifteen minutes early but had run out of things to do. She had failed to get hold of Billy Tingle back in Brighton, failed to drop off to sleep when she tried, and, after she had dressed – her Max Wall Lycras and a white top – she had failed again when she'd trolled round to see Blodwen to ask her something about the computer.

Behind two screens, as usual, there was something definitely sexual going on; the deep groans, the oohs and ahs. The oohs were Belgian, the ahs were non-specific. It made Caz ache just thinking about it. She sat back, listening. Edward Platt was talking between grunts.

'So what – other – injuries – are you treating?'

Ina told him, a footballer's knee, two runners with Achilles problems, an older woman with a frozen shoulder.

'So none like me. They need much regular work?'

'Only Caz, my friend,' Ina said.

'Ah, yes,' Platt said.

'You know,' Ina said slowly, 'really this injury is better now. I can do little for you. Only rest now is what you need. You like, you could save some of your money.'

'I think not,' Platt said.

When Ina finished there was a low silence, a murmured exchange between her and Edward, but no frivolity, and no lightness. The victim on the other couch was talking quietly in English and German as if he and Ute were now chatting socially, no longer nurse and patient. Caz couldn't explain it, but she could feel tension in the room.

Then Platt came out from behind the curtain and Caz saw a little light come back into Ina's face, something like the look on the person rescued from the office creep at the works Christmas party.

'Ah, Caz!' she said loudly, a trifle too loudly. 'Come on in. Let's see what we can do about your back!'

'I will just go now,' Platt said heavily.

'Yes, yes!' Ina said. 'The Café After Sport. OK!'

It didn't come up spontaneously so Caz didn't talk about Edward Platt. But he seemed to be one of those guys that somehow managed to inveigle themselves into a woman's company without being so gross that the woman could just say fuck off. What happened then was that she would have to go through hoops to avoid him when really it was all his fault for not knowing or refusing to see when he was not wanted.

Ina was kneading away at Caz's spine and there was a low deep burn across the small of Caz's back. 'Oh, jees that's sore.'

'It feels a little strange, Caz. What have you done? Do you go climbing mountains or something? You have to let your body be in charge sometime. You cannot keep it pushed like this.'

Caz was stomach down, her head sideways on a thin pillow. She was at a disadvantage in an argument.

'Can't keep pushing it, like this. Can't keep pushing it.'

Ina snapped. 'Please, Caz! Don't tease me. You must stop running if you hurt yourself. Otherwise you . . .'

'Ina?' Ute's voice, her head through a split in the curtains.

'Oh, hi, Ute.'

'Marco is all done. If Caz-ee does not mind . . .'

Caz was hardly naked, just a touch of bum cleavage showing. 'Oh come on in!' she said from the pillow. 'Pleased to meet you.'

'So you've got a bad back?' Marco said.

Ina was still working those thumbs. Caz grunted. 'Yuh, I mean nuh. Ugh. I do this instead of sex.'

'I know the feeling,' Marco said. He had a large, full, happy voice. 'First time Ute fondled me, it was a hamstring problem. I had to train her to move up and round.'

Caz turned her head to see him. She thought instantly, rogue not villain. 'Hiyah,' she said. 'So what's the real name, Mark, Marco or Marcus?'

'It's Marc, but with a cee instead of a kay. My dad was half Welsh. He was a Marc.'

Caz grunted again. 'I see you're nearly over that fight.'

'It wasn't a fight!' Marc said quickly. 'Some little twat hit me with a lump of wood as I was coming out of a club. I hardly saw a thing. But it wasn't a fight. I've not had a scrap for years.'

'You said little.'

'That's all I saw. It wasn't a big bloke. The locals picked up a Brit for it but I told them right at the start that the guy who whacked me was a short-arse.'

'Nice term.'

'You know what I mean. It's Caz, int it?'

'Yeah, but with a cee not a kay. *My* Dad was a Londoner.'

She held up a hand to shake his, just as Ina found the precise spot. Marc took it just as it began to tingle. 'Caz, right!'

There was a pain. 'No, wrong! Jesus, Ina!'

'Ute says we're having a drink later. Café After Sport? That true?'

'Sounds like a good idea to me.'

'What d'you drink?'

'Whatever gets me pissed. Red wine, G & T's, whisky.' She grunted again. 'And I can get *badly* pissed on Southern Comfort.'

'I can get booze cheap.'

'Don't tell me about it. I used t'be a copper.'

Marc never batted an eyelid. Ute said, 'But not any more, right?'

'Right. How much is the Comfort?'

'Five quid a bottle? A thousand pesetas?'

'Really? It's not knocked off?'

'Believe it or not, nope. Some tosser on the Costa Teguise got into a bit of a cash-flow prob and wanted to make some quick bread.'

'I'll believe you, thousands wouldn't!'

'That's up to you, Caz. But the booze is straight.'

'You got any whisky? Bell's, Whyte & Mackay?'

'I got Teachers, forty-five quid for ten bottles. That do you?'

'Christ!' Caz said. 'I don't know if I'll be here that long.' She realised her mistake as soon as she'd spoken. Quickly she said, 'If I had ten bottles that cheap, I'd kill myself with the first five.'

'So d'you want any?'

'Two, three bottles?'

'Six quid each, twelve hundred pesetas. There's some in the car.'

'I thought you said four and a half?'

'For ten, yeah. Each is six quid. That's still bloody cheap.'

'OK,' Caz said. 'I'll have three, thirty-five hundred per-taters?'

'Done!' Marc said. Caz grinned. Crook, yeah, but not a villain.

Ina was splatting some oil on Caz's rump. 'Now we have it, Caz. Nursey make the bad pain go away. Just *here*.'

'I'll go and get your stuff,' Marc said.

'Urrrrnnnn,' Caz said.

Seventy-four

There was a good bunch of Greenies in the café and talk of going on to some party way later after the disco. Caz and Ina arrived to see Marc and Ute already commandeering a table and desperately trying to hang on to their seats. In the court-yard bowl beneath them, the Green Team band was limbering up for practice, playing a few blues riffs and one-two-one-twoing, *phutt-phutt!!* into the stage mikes. As they sat down Edward Platt materialised like a goblin out of nowhere and Ina's smile wobbled. 'Hello, everybody!' he said. 'And it is my round for the drinks, yes?' This was about nine-fifteen. MacInnes arrived at nine-thirty and came straight towards them.

Caz whispered to Marc, 'My ex-boss, don't mention the booze.'

'A copper?'

'Detective Inspector, bit of a shit. One of the reasons I left the force.'

'Well, he better not come any shit here, he's off his beat.'

'He won't,' Caz said. She stood up. 'Tom, what a surprise!' As she stood she heard Platt say, 'The man in the submarine this morning.'

Briefly the conversation stuttered into awkward but Tom MacInnes quickly got pissed, or let the table think he was pissed and they loosened as he did. Why was he here? Oh, it

257

wasn't official. He knew the mother and father of Matthew Black and was coming over anyway . . .

'So what, exactly . . .?' Marc said. Platt was watching but quiet.

'Matthew's mammie and dah. See, he'd bin heying some domestic strife at haim. They think their laddie mebbee *jumped* off the roof.'

'Suicide?'

'Aye lad, seems like as no the laddie jumped. He owed a fair whack o' money, 'mungst other things. Ah jest said to Jess and Jack ah'd try t'help. Ah told them ah'd tek a look see what ah could find oot.'

'You go very Scots when yer pissed,' Marc said.

'Aweh! I dint . . .'

Marc grinned. 'No, I suppose not.'

Platt sat forward. 'I remember when Mister Black fell. I helped Caz here and Miss Jensen. Miss Fërd was there too. She was quite shocked.'

MacInnes gave him a slit smile. 'A nasty t'do reet enuff, but ah hear the laddie's a wee bit better every day. Any luck at all now an' he's oot o' that coma.'

'Oh, I do hope so,' Ute said. 'Matt was really nice.'

Platt seemed surprised. 'You hardly knew him!'

'Yes, she did,' Ina said. 'We both knew him. He had so much physio with us he was like family, and we would have a friendly drink too.'

Platt huffed. 'Well, look where *that* got him!'

'What does that mean?' Caz said quickly. 'Are you sick or something?'

'No,' Platt said, 'I am sorry.' He looked at his glass. 'I think perhaps I have drunk too much.'

As far as Caz could remember, Platt had drunk almost nothing. God, she did not like him! 'Yeah, well,' she said slowly. 'People here, some of us care. Matt Black was all right . . .'

'I know,' Platt said with a quick breath. 'I think I am mistaken and I should leave now.' He nodded to Ina. He looked close to tears.

'Well if you must,' Caz said. She felt triumphant.

He slid away.

The atmosphere changed slowly. The awkwardness of Platt's departure put a small dampener on the table but one drink and ten minutes later they were all having fun and Marc, now Marco again, had told this MacInnes bloke – who was all right really, fer a copper – all about his few brushes with the law. No, he said, he'd never gone near drugs, but this rasta bloke he'd crossed had promised him a stitch up and he did a bunk for the Canaries once he realised the drug squad were obbing him.

'They must've been new at it, I reckon. One of the guys had a new pair of Levis on and he looked *bloody* uncomfortable. I don't think I'd have clocked Caz here if she didn't want to be spotted.'

'If I'd been undercover,' Caz said.

'You haven't? Not ever?'

'Coupla small jobs, looking for shoplifters. I don't think that counts.'

Marco smiled. 'Well, no, it's not exactly *stake-out*, is it?'

Ute finally spoke. 'What's it like, being undercover, Caz? Is it like being a spy, something like this?'

'No, Ute. It's more like having leprosy and trying to hide your stumps.'

'But it is exciting? You catch bad people.'

'No, it's nasty, dirty and frightening and I don't want to do it.'

'*Didn't* want to do it,' Marc said.

'Yes,' Caz said, puzzled. 'Why, what did I say?'

MacInnes stepped in quickly. 'I think you were confusing your tenses, lassie. Anyone wid think you were undercover *now . . .*'

'You're joking,' Caz said. 'I'm well glad to be out of all that.'

She slugged back a double mouthful of Southern Comfort. This was peculiar. She was losing track of what she really did want.

'Are we going to the disco, or what?' she said.

'Soon,' Marco said. Then he turned to MacInnes.

'So, Tom, you want t'buy some cheap whisky?'

Seventy-five

Later, someone – when Caz tried to remember, she thought it was Ute – someone made a half-hearted attempt to drag Tom along with the group to the disco. But it was one of those 'Of course, well, it's not really, but then, and you probably wouldn't, but, but would you like to come with us to the discotheque, Tom?' offers. He declined.

Caz, Ina, Ute, Marco, half a dozen Greenies and Otto went. 'Fuh! Great idea. Happy hour, fuh!' The conversation was manic, the slapping hands and cuddling arms interchanging, in that dizzy, narrow window of studenty camaraderie, sexy but not sexually intent. Caz realised she was fit and pissed, her ideal body-confusing state.

The music choice was Manchester House. If you tried really hard you could just about notice when one track ended and another began but even then, three people would have disagreed. The floor was half-full and, from the bar, Caz watched a stick-insect Poole Runners 10K man, a dark-haired woman with calculating eyes and another runner – she didn't know him – in a classic 'OK which one slinks home alone?' scene.

The Poole Runner was older, gangling and didn't have a clue how to dance, but for some reason the younger better-looking guy seemed to be dipping out. Caz turned back to the bar, away from the ultra-violet.

'Skip the ice in the Comfort, Klaus. And wet it with a dash of Coke!'

She ended up on the floor with Ina, moving round, something a cross between St Vitus and a second coming. Ina danced with a far-off self-satisfied smile. She was fluid, graceful, like a woman on something and dancing to some other music. It vaguely pissed Caz off.

'What you so happy about?' she shouted.

Ina slid back. 'Eric! Tomorrow night he will be here!'

Caz forgave her instantly, suddenly thinking of Valerie.

'What time is it?'

'Twenty-two forty!'

'I'm going to go soon!'

'Are you not having fun?'

'I want to ring my boyfriend.'

'OK. One more drink, I come witt you.'

Caz managed a smile as the Poole Runner went past like a praying mantis on stilts. She looked for the younger guy. He was either gone or at the bar.

Seventy-six

Eleven o'clock, a balmy Lanzarote night, a gentle breeze, the lagoon dark, rippling, the sky a shotgun spray of stars, nothing at all like England. When Caz came out with Ina and up the few steps past the Spanish guards, it hit her, the romance, the lack of tension, the shorter route to God or whatever you called 'it'.

'I really could live here, Een. I wish I had the courage to make the break.'

'The break from what?' Ina said. 'You have two years here, you want.'

'But I'm still "from England", Een, and "over here". I'm not *part* of all this, am I? I'm visiting. I'm still on the outside looking in, hanging on to my Anglo-Saxon roots.'

'Is that bad?'

'Yeah, it's bad. It's not real. I don't know what is.'

'You want we should go for a little walk, Caz?'

'Where?'

'Round the lagoon? To the sea? I do not mind. Where the lights are not, you can see the sky even better. It is very beautiful.'

'It is very beautiful from here.'

'This I know.'

They walked down the steps towards the leisure pool and past the diving school. White plastic loungers were scattered under shrunken palms and someone had left a beach-bag behind. The pool was a half-lit sullen light blue and Caz had a fleeting death-image of Kevin King. She shook her head. 'So, Een, when will you and Eric . . .?'

'As soon as he has showered!'

'You dirty little Dane! I *meant* when will you get married?'

'Next year, maybe. Or maybe one year more when Eric is finished his studies.'

'Me too, me and Valerie. I reckon eighteen months or so.'

'But you will still be here, still be training?'

'No, I'll have gone back, I reckon.'

'Have you lost some heart, Caz? I do not understand . . .'

Caz stopped, looking across the beach, the lagoon, rocks.

'Lost something, Ina. I just fancy trying "nice".'

'Nice? Like my ice-cream, it is nice?'

'Nice, as in pleasant person. As in honest, as in decent, as in caring.'

'But Caz, you are these things.'

There was a hint of doubt in Ina's voice.

'Oh yeah? You think so? You don't ever wonder about me, Ina?'

'No.'

'That just makes me feel worse.'

'It must be something English. All I think is wrong with you is you try a bit too hard some time and some time you are the head of a pig.'

'Thank you.'

'This I mean, pig-headed.'

'Oh, I'm that all right. Sometimes it's an asset.'

'When you were a police girl?'

'We say "woman", Een. When I was a police-*woman*.'

'When you were this. Was not being a pig-head a good thing? Do you not some time have to be, be *dour*, like Sherlock Home, Mr Watson?'

'It helps sometimes.'

'Well, see? And when you are with your friends, with Valerie, then you can stop being a pig and be lovely. Iss easy.'

'*It's*, Ina.'

'Then you stop being hard-nose and be soft girl instead.'

Caz was going to say 'It doesn't work like that', but Ina had suddenly raced down the beach to the edge of the lagoon. She was such an open damnably-happy person that Caz was frightened for her. As she followed, she saw trainers and socks flung, then Ina stepping into the water, squealing 'Ee, ee, ee!' and something Danish. She jogged up.

'Ina, you're a child!' she said, trying to be deadpan.

'This is true!' Ina said. She was so nice, it didn't even occur to her to splash. Caz sat down and watched her. She could see fifteen years on, Eric and Mrs Eric, four daughters, all sylphs, all dancers, crisp water, green fields, a sunlit house, white planking, love.

Ina was laughing. Innocent. It depressed Caz.

Seventy-seven

Ina came out of the water with blue-cold feet but an undiminished grin. They walked for a while, as far as the sand would allow, and then they made to go back up to the complex and the brighter lights. Caz's urge to confess had subsided, but not her disquiet. She decided that maybe she needed a heart-to-heart with Tom MacInnes. But then she thought, 'What's a DI going to say to a DC who says she maybe doesn't like some of the things she does?'

As they came through the beach-gate, they went left instead of the right that would have taken them back past the disco. As Ina said, still smiling, this way was shorter, like Eric.

To the right, the bare rows of plastic, nothing but white; ahead, the kiddies' shallow pool, the short curve of their water-slide. They rounded this, climbed steps, past the sun-trap, the submarine. Up the next steps was the Atlantico restaurant and the slightly seedy crazy-golf course. As they got to the top of the steps, Caz stopped, one of the near-feral cats scritching quickly past them. She turned, cold. Something . . .

'Ina, you got a torch?'

'It is small but powerful. What is wrong?'

'Can I borrow it?' she said. 'And would you wait here?'

Seventy-eight

There was something else, but it hadn't surfaced yet. Caz went quickly, following the cat's footsteps, a sound, the *grawesh!* of raised territorial claws. Then she saw the door-head of the submarine, the unclasped lock, the inch-opened door. She tensed, and, like the unseen cats, her hair stiffened, her skin raised.

On an instinct, she walked first past the door and round the corner to where the paperbacks and sun-oils filled the day. Nothing, no one there. She didn't want someone behind her if she went down the sub's steps.

Old trick, breathe very deeply, till the ribs protest, the belly rises. Again. Now she was calmer. She could hear the cats, and, somewhere, the other side of the pool, the Pool Bar, faint sounds, the disco still going, a man's voice – Otto? – just emerging, laughing, fuh!

She ran back to Ina. The smile had gone, the eyes were wider.

'Ina, go get Otto! If you miss him, bring a guard, quick! To the submarine. He's at the disco, just coming out. Quickly!'

'Otto?'

'Otto! Yeah, go! Schnell or something! Hurry!'

Like with Matt's accident, Ina didn't really need telling twice. As she ran, she shouted, 'Hey! Otto! Hey, Otto!'

As Caz went back down towards the submarine she thought, a reply. 'Fuh! Who is dat?'

Seventy-nine

OK, Caz, so now you wait. You wait. And Otto comes with you, Ina goes for security, for Tom MacInnes. No need to go down there . . .

She pulled back the door. The cats, at least three, were going crazy at the bottom. She shouted.

'Thanks, Otto. No, it's OK, you and Klaus stay by the door!'

She stepped in, to the top step, tried the light switch. When it worked, she was startled. Below, in the low light, there was a flicker of fur, more hissing. She went down, sliding like a seaman, as quick as she could before her fear made her spastic. For speed, her back was to the room, but as she hit the bottom she was already turning, hiss-ready, anger-fright her energy and her defence. One of the cats snarled like a mountain lion and loped into a shadow which moved.

And then, above her, she saw the rope, the peardrop noose, the spent pendulum, and Giuseppe Castellano. And on the floor, the step-ladder kicked away. And on his chest, a note, something. Then, on his back, screeching, one of the cats, his body swinging again, and Caz, revolted, the ladder upright, swinging at the cat with the torch, more hissing and it, they, rushing from there, and Giuseppe Castellano slowly turning round to stare at Caz, an ordinary, quiet face, not yet bloated, and the note, *lo siento mucho*, turning with him.

Eighty

When Otto and Ina came, Caz was huddled at the top of the ladder and just outside the door, suddenly very cold, but not frightened, just dull, as if she would never love, never feel, never smile again.

Two booted, key-clinking guards came, a little nervousness, then a rush of aggressiveness and rapid Spanish, Caz standing to step in front of the door, blocking it, shouting, slapping her chest, '*Polizia! Prohibio!*'

Her guessed Spanish slowed them but one raised a truncheon. She was a drunk, she should move. He said something that sounded like 'Alij-arse!' and Caz stood taller, resorting to English. 'Emergency! Get Christian Green. Get the police! I can't let you down there!'

Then Ina came good, stepping alongside Caz and rattling quick-fire, calming Spanish at the larger guard who turned, barked something and sent the other guard clumping away. Now Otto stepped up to the two girls and the guard shook his head.

Then it was five minutes later, then ten, and distant sirens, and Christian Green, dressed but in flip-flops, quietly organising things, the security guards now controlling the late-night post-disco crowd, one of them steering a leather-trousered motorcycle policeman towards the scene. More Spanish, then Christian saying in English, 'Everything is all right now. An officer is coming.'

Eighty-one

'It is difficult, Miss Flood, Caz. We have not had the *autopsia*, the post-mortem. Until then . . .'

'What Christian is saying, Flood, is calm bloody down. No one is going anywhere.'

Caz looked at Tom MacInnes. There was still just a hint. He was still very definitely not buying her anything for Christmas.

'I did a bit of forensic pathology, sir. Giuseppe Castellano was choked, not neck-broke, the tongue, the eyes. If he really *had* kicked away that step-ladder he'd've dropped almost six feet.'

'Leave it to the locals, Caz. He was one of theirs.'

'He could have been winched up there. We don't even know he died there.'

'They can tell from the marks, Flood.'

'No, sir. That experiment was done years ago, a bloke called Casper. String someone up within two hours of their dying and the marks are exactly the same as a real hanging.'

'So?'

'I just think his neck should have been broken.'

'Wait and see.'

No one had thought to wake up Tom MacInnes. As Caz had come down from her high mix of fear and drink, she might have thought about it, but she had felt ill and Ina and Otto had taken her to Ina's room.

Someone had done the instinctive – but utterly wrong – thing and lowered Castellano's body to the ground, so exact measurements of the scene, of the death, by whatever hand, were instantly meaningless.

Caz had failed. Confused, a little pissed, she had been led away to throw up once then need the loo. In the hour or so she took to get herself back into some kind of shape and go round to knock on the DI's door, the damage had been done. He had snapped at her then and gone quickly past to get to the scene. When she had offered to follow he had said roughly, 'Get to yer bed, girl. Ah'll no be needin' y' the night!'

And was the note pinned on in the way a man would pin something to himself? MacInnes didn't know, but yes, they would check that. And was there any sign that the body had lain elsewhere, any blanching? MacInnes didn't think so, but it would be checked. There was nothing there, no clues? Clean as a whistle. No sign of any scuffle? Just the cats. And prints? On the keys? The door, the ladder, the winch? For God's *sake*, Flood, no, in hand, what is *wrong* with you?

What was wrong was the mistake. What was wrong was walking away. What was wrong was that something, something stuck in her head and she had been too drunk, now too hungover, to drag it out.

'So where was Alan Sapsard last night?' she asked flatly.

'Don't know,' MacInnes said. 'That's being checked too.'

'Then I can go?'

'Y've got work to do?'

'A run.'

'Y'might as well, then, lass. But not too far, ay?'

She felt like crying.

Eighty-two

Eric was due into Arrecife at 14:10. When Ina asked Caz did she want to come to the airport, she said yes straight away. Her coaching session, all her Green Team duties, were cancelled for the day and if she didn't do something like that she'd end up blasting up the hill to Soo again and making herself ill.

They left shortly after one o'clock, another sharp yellow day, in a borrowed Suzuki jeep, courtesy of one of the mechanics, married but sweet on Ina. They were quiet, last night hanging over them. Ina was sad, as if a cloud might fall on her and Eric.

'Don't worry!' Caz said. 'Soon as you see him, I'll bet you'll be right as rain!'

'I hope you will like him,' Ina said. 'Until Saturday he will be loose-ended and I was hoping you could guide him.'

'Look after him, you mean?'

'Take him places, Playa Blanca, Haria, Teguise. To Mirador del Rio and Orzola and to the Fire Mountains.'

'In two days?'

'No, I mean one, some of these places, or Los Jameos del Agua. There is a museum there of natural things.'

'So you know I'm resting for a few days?'

'Of course. Blodwen tells me this. I know maybe before you do. La Santa is amazing grapevine, no secrets.'

'None?'

'Silly! If I know a thing, then it is not the secret any more.

But if there are still secrets how could I know this?'

Caz was trying to think of a neat put-down. Something like, 'Blimey, Ina, that was profound for a Dane!' but Ina was just changing down to swing round the bright Lycra of a la Santa biker. Caz recognised the body shape of Edward Platt. She turned to stare and then waved her hand when she realised how gross she must look to him. He nodded.

'That was your friend, Mr Platt!' Caz said loudly, into the wind.

Ina shook her head. 'Not my friend, just a patient.'

Caz felt slightly malicious. 'Well, he hangs around a lot for "just a patient". I think I might need to discuss him with Eric.'

'I am not amused, Caz.'

'I don't suppose Eric will be either.'

'This is not funny. Eric would like that I was not here, that I was home in Copenhagen now.'

Caz was apologetic. 'Eric's jealous?'

'No, because I am trusted. But he would rather I was home again. He says, people who love each other, these should not be apart.'

'Can't argue with that, I guess.'

'You can argue any time, Caz. This is how you are.'

'Oooohhh! Viking talk!'

'Please, Caz, stop this all. It is hot and I am worried.'

'About Eric?'

'Yes. And all these things happening. Is why I would like you to take my Eric to places.'

'You want me to look *after* Eric? Like a bodyguard?'

'This is silly? You are a trained police *woman*, not girl. Of course!'

'Oh, Ina!' Caz said. 'If that wasn't tragic, it'd be funny.'

Eighty-three

Arrecife airport was a manic, pressured mess of dust, hot tourists, bulging coaches, itchy-batoned policemen and railing trolleys. The fact that no matter how good the holiday, Caz would have to re-negotiate this hell filled her with woe. Vaguely she wondered about ferry trips to Tenerife or Gran Canaria and flights to points north from there. Whether those airports groaned under the weight of all this tourism she had no idea, but surely nowhere could be crazier than this?

When Eric emerged he was dressed in a lightweight rumpled cream suit, linen that looked good on a film star, dross on anyone else. He was like a stumpy version of Our Man in Havana, but his big silly eyes-'n'-all smile made up for deficiencies elsewhere. Ina called him 'Eck-wick'. When he kissed her he called her 'Ee-Ee'. Caz waited.

'And I will bet you are Caz Flood?'

She grinned. 'The same!'

'You run, you're quick, you have a bad back and you swear a lot.'

'If I was a book, that would be my jacket.'

'And I would read you,' Eric said softly.

'So, you have everything?' Ina asked. 'We shall go?'

Eric waved two haversacks.

'Which one's the Lego?' Caz said.

274

Eighty-four

That night, Ina and Eric turned up late at the Café After Sport. Caz had presumed they'd been hard at it on top of the sheets, but no, Ina said, they'd spent a romantic two hours in the Evento.

'The rumby-tumby, this we do already. This afternoon. Fun!'

Caz got them both drinks, a big one for herself.

She'd gone to find Tom late in the afternoon. He wasn't there. She'd wandered over to the running track, back to the Pool Bar, the Green Room, the two swimming pools, the beach, but either he didn't want to be found, Caz didn't want to find him, or he actually *was* somewhere else. Vaguely miffed, she decided he'd gone off on some jolly, maybe gone to Arrecife to see the police, talk about the dead Spaniard. Either way, whatever bridge between them had caught fire, there was no way Caz was repairing it till the DI returned. She was depressed. She went back to her room, stripped off and dialled up England. Three calls later she fancied a drink. Valerie was in a conference, Billy was out and Moira was still on the sick, staying at her mother's.

She had wandered over to the Olympic pool, slid in, and done seven or eight very slow, leisurely lengths, thinking, trying to work out what she might have done to offend Tom. There was nothing. Nothing.

Each end she had rested, the cold around her, a peculiar loneliness on her despite the breath-voices of people all around. She still didn't understand swimmers. Compared to running, the club fun, the long slow chatty runs, swimming was like solitary confinement; all ozone, blue, cold, wet and waiting. Anyway, she didn't have the shoulders to be a swimmer.

There was some sun-cream, a bit of block wrapped up in her towel. She had decided to wander over to the leisure pool, get a little bit of topless sunshine now the burn was five o'clock moderate. For some reason as she walked, she'd noticed her feet, no bumps, no wrong childhood shoes. Some long-ago thought had come wafting, a man, older, massaging her feet and saying how sexy they were. Oh yeah! And did she? Oh yeah, one of her first big giraffes . . .

She'd been smiling as she cut through, past the *Supermercado*, closed, past where Matt Black had landed, past where she, Ina, Edward Platt, Ute, had all been suddenly together, the cow-crowd shuffling forward, beach clothes, beach gear, flip-flops, bare feet, bags . . .

They'd done pretty well that day, Ina especially, even Edward Platt. Ute had freaked, but, the way her week had gone, maybe she'd had an excuse. Someone took her away, left his bag, her bag?

She had looked up to the top of Tower 40. This way it didn't look so high but she knew, looking down, *falling*, was different. Then it was a long way. On the beach, by the pool she could go top-off but up there, up on the roof she could whip off her pants and get some botty-sun. It felt vaguely naughty so she went into the tower and up the stairs.

At the top of the stairs, the door, obviously repaired, had been broken again, sun-worshippers who would not be denied. She had thought briefly about the kind of vandalism that was done for executive purpose but was vandalism just the same, then thought about the kinds of people who would cost the hotel money just to be all over brown.

But then she was out on the roof, over one wall and laying out her towel. Then de-topped, bottomed, hot, she had lain face down, the one wall beside her her first line of modesty should some buck with buttocks decide it was micro-wave time too.

Caz hadn't dozed, only closed her eyes. Dozing was not something she did; she either slept or she was awake. After fifteen minutes or so, she had turned over, her belly, pussy, sunny-side up. She could feel the sun's heat on her, in her. She had felt sexy, outrageously, deep-down, right-inside, damn-fuckably red-sexy. Maybe she should go to her room. She was sure the feeling came from the slight adventure, the little illegality of being on the roof, the faint ever-so chance that someone might happen upon her but, what the hell, she felt *nice*! To help things along, she'd tried to let erotic dreams come floating in, tried to think of Valerie, but, though she felt the right way, something, something, green, red, yellow, stripes? had kept intruding, something that was, wasn't, something to do with Germans, towels, missing.

First she had cursed, a sexual pleasure denied her by a trick of the mind. Then she had wondered if the girls, Ina, Ute, Blodwen, ever came up here. Then she half-saw the stripes again, a beach bag, peripheral, where Matt Black's blood had seeped on to the road, and again, by a deserted pool-side then gone, then gone, *to the right, the bare rows of plastic, nothing but white* . . .

Eighty-five

'So, Caz. You are running very well now?'

'What?'

'Ina says that you are getting your best-ever training times. You are getting ever so bloody fast.'

'She's right, and it's all down to her thumbs.'

'She is good. She is very cruel also.'

'This I know,' Caz said.

Eric caught the joke instantly. 'So, Caz, you like Lego?'

'My back is niggling again,' Caz said to Ina as she dumped more drinks.

'Well, *my* back is fine!' Eric said, a little grin.

'So much a shame, tonight you have to cancel the physio,' Platt said.

'Why's that, then?' Eric said. No grin.

There was only a second's silence, a little breath, but it was there. Then Platt said, 'Today I cycled one hundred-ten kilometres and I was sore a little. Some physio . . .'

'What was wrong with Ute?'

'Ute was busy, she is very busy.'

'Well, Ina was busy. With me.'

'Yes, you have said this. But I am still sore. This just means I am unlucky.'

Eric scowled, morphing into a light grin.

'You fall off your bike? Crash somewhere?'

'No.'

'So why do you say you have no luck?'

'Because I am sore. I have not had massage.'

'Maybe you should go and have a lie down, some rest?'

'You think so?'

Eric stared. 'I think so.'

'Perhaps one more drink?'

'I think it will be bad for you.'

Platt hesitated. As Caz looked up, his eyes flickered, catching hers. She looked away. 'Perhaps, I will go to my bed,' he said. Then he said, 'Ina, my book for tomorrow, this is OK?'

Ina looked up. Another Ina.

'Yes,' she said coldly.

Eighty-six

In the morning, Caz got up from a sleepless bed, dressed quickly, drank some orange, stretched a little, then jogged through the quiet half-open corridors of the hotel, out through reception and on to the main road. She tossed a mental coin, lost, and started for Tinajo via la Santa village. She wasn't in the mood to run, the miles conflicted with her sprint training, but she *needed* to run, end of story.

She started easy, around eight-minute pace, loping past the stunted second phase of the complex and down the hill. The rhythm, easy, easy, slap, slap, slap, was exactly right for thinking, for cruising, letting her body and her mind come together to do something more than either could do alone.

When Edward Platt had slunk away, Caz had felt sorry for him. This she had found amazing because, up until then, she had quite disliked the little man. She decided it must have been because she had an automatic empathy with the underdog, or the fact that she didn't like the subtle bullying coming from Eric or the surprising coldness that Ina had displayed. All this, and her own woes, MacInnes, missing Valerie, worrying about Moira, her own crazy mixed-up head, and she really wanted to get sad-bad pissed, crawl away and sleep black and heavy.

But, 'Oh, fuh! No way! Fuh!' Otto had said. 'Fuh! The disco tonight sixties-seventies shit, you me, we dance like crazy maybe bonk after.'

He wasn't joking. They went over, got a bit more pissed, danced a bit – Beatles, Stones, Manfred Mann, Pickety-Witch, Hollies – had another drink, danced a slowie, Long John Baldry – Otto had a spare bicycle pump in his trousers – went a bit silly to some Glam Rock, including a bit of head-banging, then were finally slung out when the bar shut. Then, giggling, 'No, not your room, Otto, no, no, no!'

He had crawled home, no doubt with blue-ball. And she had lain in her bed, her hands between her legs, thinking what would've, what *would've* been so wrong? Being married, being sensible, being twenty-eight. She wished to fuck she knew who she was.

La Santa village was quiet, a couple of dogs, looking up at her from yards away, then she was on the hill, working to maintain a pace around seven-fifteen a mile.

She had stayed in her room rather than go knock on the DI's door. If she had gone back out it would have been to leap on Otto, but when she dialled Tom MacInnes' number it rang and rang and rang across a long and lonely night. It was two o'clock when she rang Valerie. His phone rang a dozen times before it was picked up, dropped, picked up again.

'Val?'

'Baby?' Fuzzy with sleep.

'I know it's late, but . . .'

'Snot late. Three o'clock. You OK?'

'I just wanted to hear your voice.'

I nearly fucked another bloke tonight.

'I miss you, Val.'

'Come home, then.'

'OK.'

'When?'

'Soon.'

'I miss you too.'

It was better, but she still didn't sleep.

Three-quarters of the way up the hill into Tinajo is a two-storeyed green-shuttered restaurant and the slope eases. When Caz reached this she turned to go easily back down towards the campus and the sea. The sun had broken through the early morning haze and was just beginning to feel noticeably hot, but she was twenty minutes out, no twinges and as smooth and as fit as Seb Coe at his best.

The beach-bag worried her. It was there when they went down to the beach, when Ina went paddling, not there, or missed, when they came back up, when Caz had seen the door to the submarine, found Giuseppe Castellano hanging . . .

But it was there, was it, there when she rushed to Matt Black's side? Was it commonplace, rare? Would she recognise it for sure? Was it some sort of evidence or just a tired, slightly pissed, messed-up Caz's brain doing overtime?

That was why she'd wanted to talk to Tom. Why she couldn't sleep. Why she'd tossed and turned, drunk coffee at four in the morning, thought about Otto again, had a long shower, picked up the phone to ring Valerie again, stopped herself.

When she got back to the complex, she turned left into the stadium, jogged to a halt, and stopped her watch. Then she walked out, across to the middle of the track and, on the centre-spot of the football pitch, laid herself out in an X like a pinned insect and silently screamed.

Eighty-seven

They left at five-past ten, Caz and Eric, five minutes after Ina's first booked physio session. Eric had hired one of the Suzukis for two weeks as soon as he'd arrived, parked it out back in the staff spaces, and was ready to go wherever his appointed guide suggested.

Caz was in a slightly better mood. 'We'll go over the top to Haria, go see Mirador del thingee, then drop over the back, have lunch in a little fishing village.'

'Orzola?'

'Clever boy!'

Eric wiped his brow, affected. 'Iss nussing.'

'Then after lunch we can go to Los Jameos del Agua. I've not been, but it's supposed to be brilliant. I've seen a few postcards.'

'This is fine. It sounds great. And gently should I try to seduce you all day?'

'So Ina and I can compare notes?'

'So whatever.'

Caz laughed. She hoped it sounded less hollow than it felt.

Eric drove. By the time they had got to the village she felt OK again.

They followed the same route that Ina had driven the day after Matt Black's accident. There was almost a sense of *déjà vu* about it all, a trip out following a death, but instead of

283

the long languid Ina, her flowing hair, Caz was now being chauffeured by the stumpy but powerful Eric, his short-cropped dark hair hardly moving in the splitstream of their passing. They talked, with a very slight awkwardness that Caz thought was due to her generally dark mood. Eric was OK, he said, but really, now Ina had done her time abroad, he would prefer her to come back to Denmark.

'Also, last year when we had the accidents, the German man who fell, the man in the sea . . .'

'You know about that?'

'Ina would tell me, wouldn't she? Did she not tell you also that I was here for when it happened, when it was?'

Caz spoke slowly. 'I thought this was your first time here.'

'This time is my three four, fourth, time now. Last year I am here with Ina three times. I get cheap flights and come to see her. Once maybe twice she will come to see me.'

'So why are you so keen to have her back?'

'You know why. She should be with me now. This is right, the way it is. All the time she is here, with doing the physio, she is . . .'

A car blared past.

'She is what?'

'She should be with me now. This is much better.'

They were climbing, approaching the top of the hill before the hair-raising descent into Haria. On the right was a restaurant. Eric suddenly said loudly, 'A drink, yes?'

'Sounds good to me,' Caz said.

'Great! And I will check the tyres, the wheel. Some air maybe we need.'

Caz hadn't noticed anything. 'Shall I go in and order?'

'This is good. I will be a few minutes only.'

They had coffees, in the end two straight ones with a little milk. Caz had seen someone at another table having a dark brown milky concoction she remembered from a holiday in

Barcelona – espresso and condensed milk. In Barcelona it had tasted wonderful. This one she couldn't finish. So she ordered another *con leche* to drink with Eric.

He came in, a very lightweight concern on his face.

'You drive, Caz, yes?'

'Of course.'

'OK, when we finiss, you drive. You try out the car, tell me, is it all right. Me, it feels funny, sloppy or something.'

Caz sipped her coffee and smiled. 'The Suzukis get a bit of a hammering, but I'm sure they're well-maintained.'

'OK. But you try. You tell me if everything is fine, is OK.'

Caz smiled again. Then, with a melodramatic look on his face, Eric said, 'Too many accidents are happened. I don't want to be one more.'

Eighty-eight

Inside, the restaurant had been shuttered-gloomy, the heat banned. When Caz came out with Eric, the heat and light was like a hammer. She had the keys in her hand, walked round the car, looked at it – fine – and climbed in, started up.

Eric stood a few feet away and shouted, 'So try the wheel, go right. Is it funny, you think?'

Caz went into first gear and pulled away, the little jeep reacting easily and normally, maybe with a bit of play in the steering wheel.

'It seems fine!'

'OK. Take it round the car park, try to do brakes!'

Caz was winging round on gravel. She braked. 'It's fine!'

Eric climbed on board. He looked a little foolish. 'I am schizophrenic, yes?'

'Schizophrenic?'

'You have paranoid schizophrenic, yes? I am paranoid?'

The engine was quite loud. Caz thought it all quite funny.

'No, Eric! Just paranoid. Schizophrenic is something else.'

She was still laughing as they set off.

Eighty-nine

Caz took it more slowly down the hill. In the Clio with Ina it had been horrific and it was no better now, in a Suzuki that Eric didn't trust. Yeah, he was being a plonker, but slow, slow, slow and in third gear wouldn't hurt, would it?

She laughed, touching the brakes. 'So you think we're gonna die, Eric?'

He apologised. 'I am sorry. I think too much.'

She gave the brakes a second spongey touch. 'They're not that good, though!' Then, as the brake pedal, her foot, went suddenly to the floor, no back pressure, she shouted, 'In fact, they're no bloody good at all!'

They had been doing about twenty-five, thirty miles an hour and had dropped back to nearer a cautious twenty as they hit the hill. Caz was thinking, 'Oh no! Cliché, cliché! Dick Francis!' as she pulled on the hand-brake and tried for second gear. There was a scrunch but it went in, the engine wheeing but otherwise OK. The brakes had failed on the second corner. On the next they were OK, tootling; the next was more hairy; the third, space to follow, was 'Oh shit!' – and then they were rolling, rolling, rolling a little too quickly, screaming engine, but in a straight line into Haria itself.

At the bottom of the hill was a T-Junction. No way! Instead, Caz chose the huge restaurant forecourt where the donkeys waited. There was a nice soft-looking fence, a little rising ground, some of the donkeys' straw. She aimed there, not for the donkeys. Somewhere she'd read that hitting a big animal was worse than hitting a brick wall.

They bounced across the gravel.

'You – are – doing – good!' Eric grunted. Then blat. Windmills. The fence exploding, wood flying, the jeep bucking, stopping, Eric standing up, flying away. The windscreen. Smack, smack. Someone over there, donkeys braying, pulling at rough ties, a dark *Conejero*, his sharp stick flashing . . .

Caz opened her eyes.

'ERIC!'

Then his face in the shrubbery.

'Caz? I am on my arse, yes? This is not funny?'

'No seatbelt?'

'No seatbelt.'

Caz grunted, sagged, back into her seat. Then she made a funny Helga-Danish voice. 'Do you sink mebbee that the car is not OK, Cazee?'

Eric straightened up, an odd grin on his face.

'I say to you about it, I did.'

'OK,' Caz said, this time straight. 'You warned me.'

Then – she couldn't resist it – the Helga voice again.

'I sink *now* mebbee the car is not OK, Eric!'

Ninety

The presumption was 'Well, that's the day buggered,' but it was not so. All Eric had lost was a little dignity and Caz some skin off her chest, belt-burn. The jeep was driveable, or would have been with brakes, and after a few quick phone calls – Eric spoke great Spanish – someone said they would let them have a hire car if they could wait half an hour. Someone else was arranging for a breakdown truck and would liaise with la Santa Sport about returning the Suzy.

They got two Cokes from a machine and went back out to the jeep. Caz got underneath and poked around inexpertly. She was still looking at pipes and things when she heard the dark *brudder-brudder* of the police-bike and saw the dust-over-polish of the patrolman's boots.

Above her, out there, something was said, a question. Then Eric spoke quickly. She thought she heard '*fluido*' and, between what sounded like jokes about women drivers, something like '*fracaso*' and '*freno*'. As she slid out from under she caught a haloed view of black leather, white helmet and the obligatory mirrored shades. Did this copper fancy himself, or what?

He grinned, one brown tooth. '*Ah-ha! Señorita! Boom!*'

Caz stood up, dusting herself down. 'If you say so,' she said.

The only car available turned out to be a Range-Rover, a bit big for Caz and Eric but better than walking. Eric waved some plastic and everything was fine. Between them, her being little-girlie and a copper, he being very slick with the Spanish, they had got rid of the policeman before the hire-car had arrived and had found time for another *café con leché* before continuing. In the restaurant Eric pointed out the little bump Caz had picked up.

'I've had worse,' Caz said. 'Goes with the job.'

'Being a Greenie? Running?'

'Being a policewoman, when I was.'

'Oh,' Eric said.

The Dane drove and Caz had the map, but when they got to the turning for Mirador del Rio, he took it slickly, almost before she had shouted 'left'. When they got there he said, 'Where is it?'

'What?' Caz said.

'The thing, the view.'

She pointed at a short queue.

Inside, Eric seemed lost, as if he couldn't actually see the long, long window, the blue beyond, the backs of tourists' heads bobbing, pointing out and down, the sea, Graciosa.

'So where?'

'There's a balcony,' Caz said.

Outside was glorious. God had pasted a pretty neat sun in a sky the colour of a PC's shirt and the early morning dampness had done for any haze. Graciosa was picture-perfect below them, and, with the breeze, the world was not far off comfortable. Apart from a sore head, Caz was feeling all right. Eric was a few yards away looking at the safety barriers, over, down at the island.

Caz drifted up. 'Ina and I were intending to go down there for a day out, take some mountain-bikes or something. You fancy that, Eric?'

'Sounds cool.'

'Maybe get a few of the Greenies to come, maybe Sunday.'

'OK.'

Eric seemed detached. Caz asked if he was OK.

'Oh yah.' Suddenly he sounded very Danish. 'I am just thinking. We joke, are happy, but now we could be dead. The car, the brakes not vurking, so easy maybe we had crashed are dead now.'

'I don't think so,' Caz said. 'Your being vaguely worried made me a little cautious, and anyway, if I had really thought I was going to lose it, I'd've turned the car into the wall or used a fence to slow us down.'

'You are a good driver?'

'I should be!'

'The policeman made some jokes . . .'

'Water off a duck's back. Male coppers, they're like that all the time. You just get used to it.'

'So we wouldn't have died?'

'No, Eric.'

He smiled and let out a little pointed sigh. 'Ah, good. I think mebbee it is here, this place, a long way down, gives me to be gloomy. Here where the German man falls last year?'

'Over there,' Caz said.

He moved. 'Here?'

'About there,' Caz said.

Eric looked over. 'Wow! Is pretty bad long way to fall! Yee! Not crazy to be on here.'

'Are you scared of heights, Eric?'

'Just here. It is unlucky. I would like a drink.'

'Ah,' said Caz, 'now yer talking!'

Ninety-one

Later they drove down to Orzola, the long, thin, dead-ended village on the top right-hand knuckle of the island, mostly restaurants but with a delightful rainbow-splashed, boat-bobbing harbour. Caz was slowly discovering Eric, but his chat, though always accompanied by a light and flirty smile, was somehow controlled, unpeeling him to order. Like the fact that he ran and was club-level good – Caz's speed and faster, up to a mile. She found the fact that she hadn't known that before vaguely disconcerting as though Eric played with her, let her know tid-bits about him but never the whole man.

'You kept that quiet!' she said across their fish.

'I just never am talking about it, running.'

'When do you train?'

'Most days. But I come here, sometimes I doan run at all. This is not why I come here. I come to make sure Ina is OK, she is safe.'

'Safe?'

'Happy.'

'Some more *vino tinto*?'

'*Si!*'

The trip down the eastern coast, scrub to one side, rock and sand to the other, looked more like a post-holocaust landscape – of the wrong buttons pressed – than the clash of continental plates. It was hard to imagine such power, such devastation only a mile away, under them, lurking, moving through the islands.

Not much driving and the sign for Los Jameos del Agua appeared, inviting, but not at all inviting, among the scrub, glimpses of ordinary sea. Caz turned anyway, feeling a little flat, the result of half a bottle of wine in the middle of the day.

'Del Agua, yes?' she said, vaguely hoping that Eric would suggest a slow drive back to la Santa.

'You are the boss,' Eric said.

The entrance looked equally unpromising, postcards, cheapie plastic things on sale in the shop, a long queue of shell-suit types, their suits exchanged for nylon shorts. They went in, paid.

'So where . . .?' Eric said.

'Follow the cellulite,' Caz said.

Immediately behind the entrance was an awkward square-spiralled stairway, cut-away rock, shuffling feet. Caz was feeling foul now, looking for Bo-Peep and wanting to scream. When she saw the bottom, rock walls, a restaurant floor, something like a bier-kellar, she thought, 'Oh, God. Oh no!'

'Drink?' Eric said.

'Nope!' Caz said. What was this?

They walked over to one side, a cavern thrown back, black water, carefully positioned lights. Nowt much. Right, done that – next? The other way, steps down to clear, cold water, UV lights and strange scurrying albino crabs. OK. Then along the edge of this pool, stairs up and light beyond. Should they try that? Why not? She followed Eric.

The stairs zig-zagged up towards light, a typical Lanzarote bare-sun afternoon, harsh and blue. Eric was walking in front and for some reason Caz noted his body, very hard, very chunky. If he really could do the 4:20 mile he said he could, his power must be awesome, pushing that weight through sixty-five second laps.

'Oh, hey! Oh wow!' Eric said.

Caz was just behind. 'What?'

'Here,' he said just as she reached the top. 'This is nice!'

Caz stepped out into a brown-cliffed saucepan, the lid off, flowered shrubs, a palm tree. But it was the centrepiece that had wowed Eric – another Cesar Manrique land-sculpture, bright blue water, a white kidney of contrasting slope, two rocks, perfectly placed. Beautiful, just like the postcards. Eric turned.

'You do not say that this also bores you?'

'No. It's very nice.'

'I think so too. Here would be a good place to be marri-ed.'

'I can think of better,' Caz said.

They passed the blue-white pool, more steps back up through flowers to low white buildings and beyond these, more steps, another cave, an amphitheatre, magical, completely enclosed, the kind of place where you wanted to shout your name and hear the echoes. And everywhere the Manrique touch, curves, wood and stone, white and contrasting dark, a strange serenity. The coolness as well. Caz felt at home.

When they went back up, Eric steered Caz into the museum, again cool, again with sweeps and curves, a sense of space. It was interesting but Caz was no buff. She was always at the doorway to the next room well before Eric, muttering, 'Oh, I'll just be through here, um . . .'

It was in the third room, something about wildlife, that she saw the bird photograph and stared. Then she heard a voice, close to her ear, sexy, '*Alimoché, Guirre*. It's an Alpine vulture, my little protected baby.'

Ninety-two

Caz turned round. Hank Harry-Carry grinned at her, a lovely, friendly big-lad grin, him on his own territory now, even more at-home sexy-confident than when they had met on the plane. 'They're breeding,' he said. 'Great chick this year. See here, the picture . . .'

He leaned past with his left arm, cutting the cord to Eric.

'Er, this is my friend,' Caz said.

'Friend?'

'Eric. The fiancé of one of my friends at la Santa.'

'Good,' Hank said. He paused a quarter-second and then turned to just-ready-to-scowl Eric. 'Hi, Hank Carry.'

'I am Eric,' Eric said. They shook hands but they might as well have not bothered. Hank shrugged and turned back to Caz.

'Never saw you as the tourist type.'

'Well, you know,' Caz said confessionally, 'sometimes a girl's gotta do what a girl's gotta do.'

Hank glanced at Eric then turned back to Caz. 'We've got an office just . . . you fancy coffee?'

'It's free?'

'Cheap. You have to talk to me.'

Caz spoke to Eric. 'Coffee, Eric?'

'No thank you,' Eric said.

Caz stopped for a moment. She had just presumed. 'Oh,

OK.' She was thinking, 'Why so snotty?' Then she decided. 'So where shall I meet you?'

Eric glowered, then it went.

'At the car, one half-hours. Then we should go back to la Santa.'

'How very generous of you,' Caz said.

'One half-hours. I meet you then.'

There was an awkward moment, then Hank said, 'You sure I can't persuade you to have a drink, Eric?'

Eric stiffened and began to move away, looking at a map. He turned his head, the instant on-off scowl again. 'Yes,' he said, 'I am sure.'

Hank decided to write him off. He smiled at Caz.

'My office, ma'am?'

Ninety-three

'So, what's with the little dark fella?' Hank said.

Caz was laid back in a chair looking at the bookshelf. 'Quite honestly, I don't know. He must have something on his mind.'

'He seemed more than a bit pissed off with the idea that you could want to talk to anyone other than him. More like a jealous boyfriend than a mate's fiancé.'

'You think so?'

'I think so. All that turned-inside anger, all that repression. I should think he's probably nasty when he loses it.'

'I'd agree with that. It was only a little thing, but I saw him come the subtle heavy with a little bloke one night at la Santa. Made me think.'

Hank came over with two coffees. 'Yeah, well, he's gone now. So how are you doing?'

'Running-wise, do you mean?'

'Whatever.'

'Well, running-wise I'm doing pretty damn OK. I've run some training PBs and I'm feeling pretty hot.'

'PBs?'

'Personal bests. I think the Yanks say "personal record".'

'And your love life?'

Caz grinned quickly. 'None of your business.'

'Of course it is. I just rescued you from a dark and dangerous man.'

297

'Oh,' Caz said. 'Well, in that case, it's all right. My boyfriend is back in Brighton.'

'It's OK that your boyfriend is back in Brighton?'

'Did I say that? Are you hitting on me?'

Hank grinned, raising his coffee mug slightly. 'Yeah, I guess. But only by the numbers. When you recognised me, when you turned round, your face said "Oh, it's the hunk. I could do but I won't." '

'You got that in a second?'

'Does it take longer? Tell me I'm wrong.'

'Fer fuck's sake!' Caz said, trying to mute the swear word even as it emerged. 'You want me to admit that I wouldn't mind sleeping with you, that I fancy you but have already decided not to?'

He laughed. 'See, I told you so!'

'You're outrageous!'

'No, I'm not. If you *did* want to sleep with me you'd call it a refreshing directness.'

'Honesty.'

'Honesty what?'

'I'd call it honesty. I like it.'

'So you'll sleep with me?'

'Can I ring my boyfriend first?'

'What for?'

'To check it's all right.'

'You need permission?'

'He needs reassurance.'

'He's jealous?'

'About average, I'd say. Not a freak-out, but I think he'd rather I went back home untainted.'

Hank nodded. 'Funny old thing . . .'

'What, jealousy?'

'Yeah. And trust and all that stuff.'

'I think jealousy's a pretty normal emotion, don't you? Aren't most blokes jealous?'

'I can only speak for those blokes I've seen, me, my dad when he was around, a few mates losing it at the disco. They always seem worse just after they've split up with some girl.'

'Well, drink and hormones . . . a bad mix.'

Hank was sitting on the side of a desk. He slumped very slightly and paused, as if making a decision. His coffee was finished and he turned the mug in his hand. When he spoke it was with a little and gentle smile. 'So what do you think of my little baby *alimoché*? Isn't she cute?'

'That scruffy thing more fur than feathers?'

'The first chick born here for a century. She can be as scruffy as she wants to.'

'OK, but she still looks like the ugly duckling.'

'True, true . . .' Hank said, slightly distant.

'You're really keen, aren't you?' Caz said gently. 'Talking about her makes your face soften like a woman talking about her baby.'

'Is that a compliment?'

'More or less. It's just, when you stop showing off, you . . . you . . . well, you give off something you don't see very often in a man.'

'And what's that?'

'Well, it's not just caring, it's protective, maternal.'

'More than you, do you mean?'

'Oh, definitely more than me. I'm a hard bitch. I haven't got time for motherly love.'

'Oh yeah?' Hank said quickly. There was distinct disbelief in his voice. 'And what does the boyfriend think about that?'

'Not a lot. I think he thinks I'll soften.'

'And will you?'

'Soften? Who knows? I suspect I won't but how can I know? Maybe we'll hang through it, maybe we won't, but I can't *not* marry him.'

'Seems a lousy way to start out together.'

'I know. As I said, I can't not marry him.'
'You said.'

Ninety-four

Hank took Caz out from the office after half an hour and out of the museum fifty minutes later, leaving the building's inner cream-cool for the car park's sun and bustle. On the way, he showed her the place where four circular mirrors, above, below and front-back allowed Caz a million different views of herself. One view made her think about out-of-body experiences. The others reminded her of yoga classes.

They broke into the sad-dusty heat, looking for the car. It was a full five minutes, a systematic trawl up each lane for the Range Rover and the unhappy Eric, before they were certain they weren't there.

In the end, they sat down near the car park's entrance. After thirty more minutes they began to think that Eric wasn't returning. Ten later they went back inside, Caz vaguely confused.

She rang la Santa, got through to Ina.

'Caz?'

'Yeah . . .'

'Where did you *go*, Caz? Eric says he waited till one hour and then he was fed up and went to find you. Then you was gone from the office and you had go somewhere with some man about some bird or some sing.'

'What?'

'That you went off and left Eric.'

'What!'

'So Eric come here about half of one hour ago. He got something wrong he says and you go off with this man together. He didn't realise.'

'Where is he now?'

'He is here.'

'Put him on.

'Is that you, Eric?'

'Is me, yes. I look for you. Where are you now? Where did you go?'

'Nowhere, Eric. You said an hour and a half. How am I supposed to get back to la Santa?'

On the other end of the line, Eric sounded bemused.

'But, Caz, we said one half hour. I wait for nearly more than one hour and you, when I go to see, are nowhere in museum or in the gardens. I give up after maybe one hour and twenty minutes and sit for a longer while in my car. Then I come back to la Santa to wait for you.'

Caz was furious. 'You *what*! You said one and a half hours. You've fucking *dumped* me here? I can't believe you would do that.'

Behind her, Hank said something about a lift. She shook her head, dismissing him. Eric was bleating about a misunderstanding. Caz was happy with this man. Eric thought he should take himself out of the way. And no, he had said one half-hour to her, not one and a half hours.

'Caz, I can get you back,' Hank said.

'One half hour. This is how I say it,' Eric said.

She slammed the phone down.

'Jesus!' she said. 'This is fucking crazy!'

'We'll go the pretty way,' Hank said.

Caz wanted to punch something, both fists clenched too

tightly. When she finally let out the anger it was the long 'Rrrrraarrrggghh!' of a trapped tiger.

Ninety-five

OK, in the end it *was* worth it. Hank had the use of a jeep and they went down the island, bypassed Arrecife and drove via the south-west coast and into the Fire Mountains, stopping only once, out of their way, true, but worth it, Hank had promised, at a rock chimney risen from the sea where waves, randomly united, would suddenly explode into the air, green and white, regularly unpredictable.

'Neat eh?' Hank said.

She was leaning over. 'Can we wait for a few more?'

'Not if you want to see *ma jolie bébé alimoché* . . .'

'Just one?'

'One, OK.'

There was a crash, rolling waves, but then, no spout.

'How's about two?'

'No *alimoché* . . .'

'OK,' Caz said. She was thinking how the explosions were sexy.

'I'll stand back,' Hank said. 'Close your eyes and guess the wave.'

When they got back in the jeep he said, 'You thought it was sexy, right? All that power, the danger? Water is sexy to you?'

'I don't know,' Caz said honestly. 'But I feel primitive some-how, as if I'd like to jump in, take my chance with the waves.'

'You'd die,' Hank said.

Ninety-six

Caz had been to *Montañas del Fuego*, the Fire Mountains, once already, this on an organised trip from la Santa, a coach into its heart, another coach round the sculpted road, looking through glass at the mountains of the moon, spangling electronic music whispering through the bus. It had been part of a hard long day in the middle of a hard long month and she had looked, half-seen, wondered, then filed the images away. All she could remember now was that she'd thought Pink Floyd should have done the ambience.

'Now, Caz, this is very special . . .' Hank said as he slowed the jeep down, turned and rucked off the road. Up to their left a mountain swept away, browns and reds and golds creeping rainbows in the late sun.

'Notice no notice, no "*prohibido el paso*". This area is out of bounds and into a little bit of danger. There was a sign, but at least once a week some plonker with a four-wheel drive would fancy going this way simply *because* it said no entry.'

The jeep was bucking like a mad thing, Caz hanging on and wishing she had a fatter rear. 'If – you – say – so,' she said.

'It gets better when we're over the ridge,' Hank shouted. 'Then it's a bit of a walk, I'm afraid.'

He glanced away from where they were going and down into the wheel-well, at her trainered feet. 'You'd've been better off in some boots, the ground's actually warm where we're going. Rough too.'

Bump! 'Thanks for – reminding me.' Bump! 'Next time I'm going out to lunch I'll take a haversack!'

'Point taken!' he shouted. 'But I don't recommend you stand still for too long!'

Then they were over the worst and bumping on to what was almost a track, then they were into a fine sand-like black grit and coasting.

Hank spoke again, loud, but no longer shouting. 'A couple of feet down and the earth is hot enough to cook your tea, four hundred centigrade! You've seen the little trick they do with the water at the restaurant?'

'The water spout?'

'Steam, yeah. Water down the tube, God's furnace and whoosh! There are hot and very hot patches very close to the surface. One of the reasons they like to keep the tourists out.'

'The whole area is amazing. Primeval is the word. What must it have been like when it happened?'

'The eruptions? Pretty damn scary, I should think. Some priest wrote about it at the time, villages disappearing, cattle dropping in the fields poisoned by gas, the sea boiling . . . major stuff.'

'My bum is getting sore. Is it much further?'

'Nope!' Hank said.

Ninety-seven

They left for the north end of the island just after six o'clock, after a whispered hour huddled into a brown canvassed hide, near to the cliff nest, them and a smiling, sweet-faced Spanish student, another Marco, he to study ecology, to save just a few animals now, this is all, all, he said, we have left.

They were intimate, close, and not intimate. Caz was warm, deeply interested in the secret little birds, and Hank was strong, comfortable with himself, and knowledgeable. But the last one per cent was not there and Caz, under every false pretence, sniffed at the man, touched him, took sideways glances, still slightly bemused, perplexed, expecting the quiet *ding*! and only ever hearing, feeling, a slightly off-key thud.

'I expected you to click,' Hank said as they topped over Tinajo and saw la Santa Sport again.

'Click?'

'About me, that I was gay. You seem the sort to just know.'

'I am!' Caz said, very surprised. 'I am, I was. I'm just, I'm . . .'

'Off-colour? Out of tune?'

'I can't believe this! You're gay? I fancied you!'

'You didn't fancy me, Caz. You were floundering around. So who or what is it that I was an escape from, might have been? The boyfriend?'

'Valerie? Oh, no,' she said, and then she thought some more, pulling together strands, half-hearing the *bunnnrrhh-zhlapp* of the jeep, the road, watching la Santa grow in the distance.

'You can stop? You'll let me buy you dinner?'

Hank was smiling. 'This goes without saying.'

'Good,' Caz said. Then she thought a little harder, about Eric, about Edward Platt, about Ina and Ute, about Mark Harris, his scams, and Alan Sapsard, sneaking out of school to see his *señorita*. Her eyes closed, she felt the lift and lower of the road as she thought as well about Blodwen, about her giraffes, and finally about poor Giuseppe Castellano, hanging there and the cats. He was a plaything, dangling meat, waiting to be ready.

The engine note changed. Caz came round. The jeep was cutting up the little hill just before the complex. She glanced ahead and said, 'I just want to shower and change, make a couple of phone calls, check with my boss.'

'Your boss?'

'My *ex*-boss. A guy called MacInnes. He's on holiday here.'

'Ah-ha!' Hank said.

'Yeah,' Caz said. 'I haven't seen him seems like forever, and I've got this feeling he thinks we're eating out tonight.'

'We could make it three of us.'

'We could?'

'Unless you think you have a chance of converting me.'

'I'm not that sort of girl, Hank. I have enough trouble working on my own head.'

'Aye, aye, what's this?' Hank said.

Ninety-eight

There were two police cars, a police bike, its front wheel turned in, lights flashing, and somewhere, the special crackle-bark of quick-talk radio Spanish. An average gaggle gawked, pizzas on temporary hold.

'What the hell's going on here, then?' Hank said.

Caz might have answered, guessing, but then she heard Ute's raised, crying voice, something in Spanish, and two khaki policemen came out of reception with Marco Harris, closely followed by Tom MacInnes.

'You are a pig, you do this! A pig!'

MacInnes shrugged and stepped away, towards the flashing lights.

Ute spat. 'Only one way a policeman can be. Pig! *Schwein-hund!*'

Caz saw Tom flick a glance behind him then ignore the girl. Then he sighed, stretched to his full five feet seven and watched as Mark ducked into the second police car. Now Ina was there too, and, lurking, Eric.

Hank had stopped the car. Caz heard the *sckranck* of the hand-brake. 'Give me a minute,' she said.

She went over. The DI looked up at her, but somehow, his eyes were still lowered. Behind, Ina looked expectant, Ute wild and frightened. 'Hah!' she shouted as Caz walked quickly up to Tom. 'See, they stick together like *Scheissen!*'

309

Caz ignored it. 'What's going on, sir?'

'Harris has been a bit of a naughty boy. The booze he was flogging wasn't exactly his. I've been talking to the locals in Arrecife. It's tight as a drum. They've booked him, already.'

'Jesus!'

'And we need to talk.'

'Now?'

'Now.'

Caz nodded and said something loudly. Quickly she hissed, 'I'm still under?'

'I guess so, but your friends aren't that impressed.'

'How *could* you, Tom? Marco was a good bloke!'

'Don't be stupid, Flood! A villain's a villain. Suntan changes nothing.'

'Well, fuck you, MacInnes!'

The DI smiled, almost loathsome. If he was acting, Caz didn't see it.

'So what do you want of me?'

'A wee chat. For a start, where have you been?'

'Where have *I* been? What the fuck's it to do with you?'

'Ah'll tell y'that when y'tell me where y've bin the day.'

'I've already said, it's none of your fucking business!'

MacInnes motioned to one of the policemen who stepped up and took her elbow. Caz stiffened but managed not to shake herself free. She was genuinely angry now, her face dark.

'I've got a friend with me,' she said.

'He can wait in reception.'

'Oh, thank you!' Caz said.

MacInnes didn't even bother to reply. He just walked ahead, into the hotel. The policeman gave Caz a little squeeze and push.

Caz jerked away. 'You get your fucking hands *off* me!'

She walked stiffly after the DI, her nose high, ugly with anger.

Ninety-nine

Caz stepped through the green double doors between reception and the two public phones, took a couple of paces past stacked boxes and a photocopier, then walked into the bookings office. She had removed her first mask of anger but underneath was another. She was faintly confused. As she had passed Ute, the German girl had flashed a look as vile as the shoplifter Caz had brought down in Brighton. That confused her too.

'Yer friend in the jeep, off the airplane, right?' MacInnes said.

'Chap called Hank Carry, sir. He's working in the Fire Mountains.'

'Your Valerie know about him?'

Caz looked up, not pleased. 'What, you as well?'

'Nothing to do with me, Flood.'

'So why bring it up?' Caz said, spite there. Then she added, 'Sir . . .'

MacInnes shrugged. 'This chappie Harris. I took a day over the other side o' the island and did some proper detective work. Sims yer girl Ute's bin hangin' round with a minor Mafioso; he's mair than a wee bit bent.'

'I was sure . . .'

'Well lucky fer us, I wasnee, Flood. Burglary, mebbe some protection, and very probably drugs, despite what he telt us.

311

The examiner telt me the lad should get five amore years, any luck.'

'Jesus! Ute will be shattered!'

'Not my problem, Flood. Wasnee me that chose t'do villainy.'

'All the same, sir . . .'

'All the same what, Flood?'

Caz relaxed, resigned. 'Nothing, sir.'

There was a knock on the inner door, a creak, Blodwen's head. She saw MacInnes first then reacted to Caz. 'Er, those . . . Oh, hi'yah buttee.' She waved some paper. 'The print-out you were after, Mr MacInnes.'

Caz smiled. 'It won't be on there, Tom.'

'What won't?'

'The name of your man.'

'It won't?'

'They don't log guests, sir, guests of staff.'

'Try me again?'

Caz smiled a second time, turned to Blodwen.

'You keep tabs on boyfriends, girlfriends, when they stop here, Blod?'

She was very Welsh. 'Norron the computa!'

'But you keep them?'

'In the bonk-book, yeah.'

'Any chance of a borrow?'

Blodwen looked vague. 'Yeah, sure, but you'd never . . . there never would've . . . I mean, none of the boyfriends would . . .'

Caz was cold. 'The book?'

'All right, keep yer 'air on!'

'I will,' Caz said. 'You want t'give me that print-out?'

Blodwen dropped the green and white sheets into Caz's fist and spun away, half-anger in her stiffness but mostly confusion, just like Caz. As soon as the door closed behind her, Caz said, 'Gut feeling, sir, but I think our man is Eric, Ina Jensen's boyfriend.'

One hundred

'You're going t'tell me why, I suppose?'

Caz sat forward. 'He's the only person who was here for every attack, that's a good start. And there's something very dark and nasty about him. He's as jealous as fuck and really strange. We were out today and he—'

MacInnes cut in. 'Was with you when your brakes failed, tampered with.'

'I know that, sir, but before we went down the hill, Eric asked me to check the car out, drive it round the car park a few times.'

'And did you?'

'Yeah. I wasn't sure. The brakes seemed to work all right. It was just, well, as if Eric wanted me to drive the Suzuki, as if he knew the brakes would go on the hill and that I'd cope.'

'You're a woman. He'd've rather driven himself surely?'

'Unless he knew about my driving skills. The *Sun* article on me, all that "Girl Who Saved Brighton" stuff, in there it said that I'd been in traffic and had done some rallying.'

'So he could have known?'

'That's what I think.'

'It's pretty extreme, though, Flood, isn't it? Fixing your own car and taking a chance on getting killed?'

'Not if he trusts me it isn't. It could have put me off the scent.'

'But why should he think you would be on the scent in the first place?'

'Because Ina told him I was a policewoman. He figured out maybe that I was undercover and he was trying to clear himself in case I got too close.'

'That is piss-weak, Flood.'

There was another door-knock, Blodwen again. Caz ignored it.

'After we'd crashed, Tom, I crawled under the car. I'm no mechanic but I'd've said that the brake pipes had only just been undone.'

'Meaning?'

'Meaning that Eric would have had to do it himself. He had the opportunity. If the brakes had been tampered with at la Santa, they'd've gone before we got to Haria.'

'They did.'

'You know what I mean.'

The door was knocked on again, louder this time.

Caz shouted, 'Fer fuck's sake, Blodwen. Get yer ear away from the door and come on in.'

Blodwen crept in, hunched. 'I wasn't lissnin', 'onest.'

Caz was dismissive. 'Yeah, and I never play with myself.'

'Burr I wasn't!'

'Is that the book?'

'Yeah, last three yurrs in there. Who's it you want t'know all about?'

'Ina's fellah.'

'Eric? You're joaken, right? He wouldun, he . . .'

'He's a wonderful guy, Blodwen. Just tell us, you got the dates of the accidents. Any he wasn't here for?'

'You mean *all* the accidents?'

'The big ones, the deaths, the nasty stuff. The stuff where someone might've been pushed instead of fell.'

'But there's loads. The blokes that come yurr, they do some

315

really hairy stuff. You know that. They're always falling off things.'

'OK, just for my boss then, was Eric here last year when Colin Jones drowned?'

Blodwen scrabbled.

'Yeah.'

'And Hans the flying Kraut?'

'Yeah.'

'The accident in the Fire Mountains, the bloke that slipped?'

'Oh, 'ee was defin-ately 'ere then,' Blodwen said. 'I know 'cos him and Ina and me and my bloke went down Playa Blanca. I remember it.'

'And when the jeep turned over?'

'I'll check.' Pages.

''Well?'

'Where's the bloody fire?' Blodwen said quickly. ''Old yer 'orses will you?' She turned another page. Her lips moved as she read.

'Well, bloody hell!'

'Yeah?'

'Yeah,' Blodwen said.

Caz turned back to MacInnes. His face had not lit up.

'But! But!' he said firmly. 'But! Yer man Eric wasnee here when the King chap died, was he? Or when Matthew Black had his fall . . .'

'I know,' Caz said, the excitement draining from her, 'I'd left that bit till last. I was hoping I might get an idea.'

'But you haven't managed it?'

'No.'

'So yer've got naywhere?'

Caz sagged. 'No, I guess not.' Then she sat up again. 'But he's an iffy bastard, Tom. There's something. Today, he left—'

'Left you at Jammy gardens?' Blodwen cut in to say. She

was looking through the book absently. 'I 'eard, but I didn't believe it.'

'Yeah,' Caz said. 'He came out with a really feeble—'

'Bloody 'ell!' Blodwen said.

'What?' Caz said, the DI said.

'Eric,' Blodwen said. 'He was supposed to've been here for those two weeks when Kevin and Matt had their accidents.'

'Supposed to be here?'

'Yeah, but Ina had a load on and she put him off.'

'But he didn't come?'

'Well no, stupid. That's why he's here now, isn't it?'

Caz folded up. 'Fucking *shit*!'

One hundred and one

'Let me think about this, Flood. We've other ways to go yet. That's what I want to talk to you about.'

He seemed to be ignoring Blodwen who just stood there, eyes popping like someone was just about to be awarded a big giraffe.

Caz looked pointedly across.

'Oh, thank you,' MacInnes said.

'Sawright,' Blodwen said. Then she looked at Caz. 'What you up to tonight, Butt? Fancy a drink?'

'Meet you outside in five,' Caz said.

'Yeah, you will,' Blodwen said, fifteen questions in her tone of voice. She opened the outer door. 'I'll be in the foyer.'

MacInnes waited as Blodwen moved through the room. As the door closed behind her he spoke to Caz. 'Giuseppe Castellano *was* a suicide.'

'It was?'

'It was. There was a letter in his place; in his kitchen. He was having family grief, problems with cash. It was a long note, his handwriting. No doubt about it, and there was absolutely nothing suss found at the PM except he'd taken tablets as well.'

'He killed himself . . .' Caz said. She waited as if trying to make the fact solid. 'Tom, could he have been responsible for the accidents?'

'We're working on that,' MacInnes said.

318

'We?'

'The locals have adopted me. They liked the present I gave them.'

'You mean Marco?'

He smiled a thin smile. 'The tea-leaf bully.'

Caz's voice softened, then darkened. 'I'm sorry, boss. It's just that I didn't see Mark as a real villain. I'd've bet my life on it. I got to quite like him. In fact, I liked him more than his girlfriend. He's locked up and I feel shitty about it. I just can't make myself feel he's bad.'

'It happens, Caz. He's a criminal and a con-man. Like tricksters and child molesters, first you get the victim's confidence.'

'I know that, Tom. You know me, usually I can rely on my sixth sense. I come here, it's blown away. Sudenly, I'm rubbish as a copper. I'm something, somewhere else.'

'An' what? Ah'm a no-good pig-dog all of a sudden, reet?'

'What Ute said? No, Tom.'

'So what is it?'

'You're my other side, Tom.'

'What?'

'I can do it, sir. But I don't see a very rosy future.'

'Y'mean the light's at the other end of the tunnel but it's on the front of an oncoming train. Summat like that?'

'No, sir, I don't. I mean I feel like yeah, there's a tunnel, and it's well lit, but I don't know if I like what I see down it.'

'Meaning what, exactly?'

'Meaning, most of the time, catching bad bastards is easy. This time it's involving my friends and I feel like a shit.'

'It's the name of the game, Caz Flood. You came here as a lie. You lied. What exactly is yer problem?'

'My problem is I still want to feel decent.'

'Your problem is in Brighton, then.'

'What?'

'Valerie. Your boyfriend.'

'What!'

'You're going soft, Flood. You're confused.'

'Well you are A-one fucking right there,' Caz spat. Her voice was raised. Now it lowered. Now she spoke deliberately. 'But what is going on between me and Valerie is between *me* and Valerie.'

'Until it affects the job,' MacInnes said.

A light, black-beamed in her head, clicked on for Caz.

'Until it affects *you*, you mean.'

MacInnes took a tiny, deliberate breath.

'I *said*, Flood.' He paused for control. 'Until it affects the job. *The* job.'

Caz surged inside, sure she was about to lose a friend.

Overwhelming panic.

'I'm . . .' Then she realised. *You bastard, you're making me decide.*

She put brakes on it. 'We need to talk again, sir.'

'Do we, Flood?' His eyes were hooded.

He's jealous. Is he jealous? Jesus!

'Yes, sir. We do. We need to talk.'

How long you been celibate, MacInnes? Fifteen years? Is that what makes you such a good copper?

'Just tell me when, Flood.'

Caz felt sick.

If I fucked him, would things be different?

If you fucked him, Caz, you would destroy him.

Destroy him?

Yes, that's how much he needs you.

MacInnes needs me?

Of course. He guards the gates. He wants you to let him die.

There are few left like him, like you.

But I don't want to be like him!

You don't?

I want to do what he does but I don't want to be like him.

Then you're going to be cut in half.

'Flood?'

'What, sir?'

'You OK?'

'No, sir.'

'Can I help?'

'What would help is for me to get very badly pissed with you.'

Will you fuck him then?

'This is not new, Caz.'

Caz managed a smile. 'Soon as we wrap up Eric?'

'I thought we decided it wasn't Eric?'

'No, sir, just we couldn't figure out how if it *was* him.'

'This your radar, is it, Flood?'

'I just *know*, Tom.'

'But you've only just told me that you're completely off-beam at the moment.'

'Meaning?'

'You could be *wrong*, Flood.'

'No, sir. This is to do with jealousy. He's hurting people who get too close to Ina. I'm not wrong.'

'Don't bet your life on it, Flood.'

Caz was still angry. Out slipped, 'You care?'

Mentally, Tom bit his lips. 'You decide, Caz. You decide.'

Then he sat back, took a breath. Flatly he said, 'I shall clear these accidents up by tomorrow night, Caz, six o'clock. And if you want – if this old man is not too much for you – we'll go out somewhere, eat, come back here, and get drunk.'

She hated him.

'Fine! You do that!'

'Oh, Caz . . .' he said softly.

She loved him.

'Yeah, right,' she said. 'Show me how fucking clever you are!'

One hundred and two

When Caz came out, Blodwen was in one corner of the foyer, talking intently to Hank, presumably making estimates of his giraffe potential. Another girl missing signals. She went over.

'How you doing, Blod?'

'Do I know you?' Blodwen said.

'Giraffes!' Caz said.

'Oh,' Blodwen said, 'I know you.'

'We've been chatting,' Hank said with that nice deep voice. 'Blodwen hasn't eaten. I suggested she might want to come with us.'

'I still need to shower.'

'No problem. Blodwen says she'll show me one of the bars.'

Blodwen grinned.

Caz grinned at Hank. 'Keep your secrets. Ask her about giraffes. I'll not be long.'

Caz went quickly. Now she had the chance to, she realised just how disgusting and sticky she was. She ought to have been depressed, but a little switch had gone over somewhere, and seeing Blodwen's hammer about to meet Harry Carry's brick wall had cheered her up a little. She decided to see life's bright side. It lasted as long as it took to get to her room. It was wrecked.

Almost before the door opened Caz knew. Some sixth feeling, some strange smell, the wrong electricity, dust that wasn't hers, something. Whatever it was she knew as she turned the key. Fuck! Life! Here we fucking go again.

She pushed the door against broken china which *scraccked* on the tiles, making her wince. There was what looked like jam on the wall, stuck-broken glass, water on the floor from the lightly trickling taps.

'Oh, bollocks!'

She closed the door behind her. Water was running in the bathroom, coming to meet her. She left it running. The bedroom. Bedclothes on the floor, clothes scattered, some ripped but not that bad. In the louvered cupboard some of her clothes still hung, not slashed, not defiled.

She stepped back into the lounge. A book was ripped in half, another one wasn't, half the food in the kitchenette was spilled, half left. There were some broken dishes, some intact.

She checked her runner's watch, noted the time to the minute. Then she turned off the tap in the kitchen, pulled out the plug and went through to the bathroom with a litre jug.

In the bathroom she switched to 'stop-watch', pressed go, and put the jug under the taps. The jug base dipped under the brimming water and a little more flowed over the bath's edge. She watched the racing hundreths of seconds, then seconds into minutes as the jug slowly filled. It took a while. Once the jug was full, she pressed 'stop'.

She could have emptied the bath, well nearly, then let it refill, to work out the earliest possible time the rooms had been ransacked. But that would have required her waiting around. This way, she knew how quickly the bath would fill. At least she would once she knew the size of the bath.

Why she was bothering with this was another issue. She already knew that it was Ute who had wrecked the place. Only a woman would do such a lousy job.

But her radar needed overhauling, so the DI said. The time to fill the jug would give her an 'earliest possible', nothing to do with guess-work. As she grabbed something to go out in she was muttering to a distant but present MacInnes.

'I wouldn't be surprised if it was you, you old bastard. Anything to keep your apprentice hard.'

The bath was now gurgling down to empty. She banged in a plug and switched the taps back on. She was pulling her T-shirt over her head when a gentle knock came on the door. This would be Ina.

'Caz? Hello? Is it all right? I come in, OK? Oh my!'

'I'm in here, Een,' Caz echoed. 'Come and have a swim.'

One hundred and three

Caz was stripped now. Ina came in timidly, her footsteps crunching and slapping.

Caz grunted as she stepped into the light brown water. 'I'm just taking a thirty-second bath, Een. Don't stand on ceremony. You want to talk, right?'

'Is it OK, I come in, yes? I mean . . .'

'Come *in* for Christ's sake!'

The bathroom door opened.

'Oh, Caz! My friend! What has happened to your room?'

Caz looked out from the water.

'My first guess is one of the physios.'

'I am sorry?'

'Ute, your mate. I presume she thinks I had something to do with Marco's arrest.'

'You did not?'

'No, I did not! I was bloody well surprised when I got back and the cars were everywhere. I'm an *ex*-policewoman, Ina. Remember?'

'But Eric said . . .' She stopped.

'Eric said I was still a policewoman, right? He said I was here undercover?'

'Eric says you act like a police person will be, that you maybe still could be a police person.'

'And this gets my rooms wrecked?'

325

'My Eric did not, my Eric is not . . .'
'I already said I think Ute did it, Ina.'
'Not my Eric.'
'Do me a favour, would you?' Caz said. 'Chuck me a towel.'

One hundred and four

As Caz stood up Ina said, 'I have come to see you.' Caz took the bathtowel. 'I have come because of my Eric.'

'Eric sent you?'

'He says you will be angry for him. He says you are not cool.'

Caz stepped out of the bath. 'Your boyfriend is full of shit, Ina.'

'This may be, but he is sorry. Caz, he says so sorry, can he buy you dinner and make up a bit?'

'He couldn't ask me himself?'

'You are cool?'

No, I'm fucking mad as hell.

'I'm OK.'

'Then you will have dinner with Eric?'

'Why not?' Caz said.

Ina beamed, relief bursting out. 'Oh, Caz-ee, I am happy at this. We must be friends. I am glad.'

Caz smiled back. 'And I'm glad too, Ina. Really.'

Ina frowned. 'Stand up straight, Caz, a moment.' She looked Caz up and down, taking the towel. 'Yes,' she said.

'Yes what?'

'Your pelvis is tilted. What is wrong with your running now?'

'Nothing. I'm fine.'

'Cowshit. Do you have pain?'

'No, I don't.'

'Tomorrow at seven-thirty a.m. you come round to me and get done again. You have twist in your back. It must be sort out, Caz. Why are you stupid?'

Suddenly Caz burst into laughter, a thought about circumstantial evidence hitting her.

'What is it?' Ina said, half an infected smile wobbling on to her face.

'I'm just thinking, Ina. Here's me, standing naked. We're alone. You're on your knees in front of me. Someone walks in and . . .'

Looking up, Ina blushed profusely.

Caz felt malicious. 'But hell, seeing as you're down there . . .'

'What?'

'Give us a kiss.'

One hundred and five

In the end there were eight walking to the village. As well as
Hank, Caz and Blodwen, the quiet Eric and his Ina, they
had picked up Otto and one of the twins, and her triathlete
boyfriend. Caz had even tried ringing the DI but he didn't pick
up the phone. Ute was sleeping.

The walk to Restaurant la Santa was a little over a mile, a
drifting sea-edged, star-skied friends-amble of half an easy
hour. The early tentative steps between Eric and Caz were
done and she had drifted in the pack to talk to Otto and the
triathlete. Blodwen was knee-deep in seducing Hank. Otto
was his wonderful, simple, long sexy self. The first thing he
had done when they had met was groan and glance at his own
Lycra'd groin. In the back of Caz's head was the thought that
maybe tonight she'd put him out of his misery.

'Fuh! What a lady!' he was saying to the tri-guy. 'Drive a
man to fuh himself, she could. Jesuh!'

'Give it a rest, Otto,' she said. 'You know I'm out of bounds.'

'Hey fuh, inside someone else's fence is damned sexy too.'

Ina spoke up from behind. 'Otto, you are a rude man.'

He turned round. 'You did not say that last night.'

Eric's face blackened.

Otto laughed. 'Hey fuh!'

Caz half noticed the little tug Eric made on Ina, the extra
stiffness momentarily in her gait. For Ina's sake, she suddenly

329

grabbed Otto and slid a hand round his hip. The back of her neck tingled with darkness.

'Oh Caz!' Otto said. 'You love me?'

'Fuh!' Caz said loudly. 'You are crazy man!'

One hundred and six

By ten o'clock and six or seven empty bottles of *El Grifo* there was a good atmosphere. Caz was sitting opposite and one seat to the side of the over-eager Otto: 'Fuh. Why do you take my Caz away from me?' Hank was one side of her and the bronze triathlete on the other. Directly opposite her was Ina, subdued, and to her right was Eric, full of broad gestures and *bonhomie*, but broken up by the occasional deep-cutting remark at one or other woman's expense, once at Hank's. The graphic artist was too much of a real man to respond, but a few minutes later he said, in another context, 'My mother taught me, "Take an insult from a fool as a compliment." ' Everyone laughed.

Seven of the laughs were real.

The local fish, *Mero*, was particularly cheap and most of the plates were that, with a delicate sprinkling of chips and a finger-pinch of salad; healthy. Caz had intended to order the same but at the last minute had asked instead for the fish of the day. When it came it was orange and sat up on her plate like a large dog, its head and tail hanging over the plate-edge, its teeth bared, one staring eye following her wherever her head turned. She decided it was a boy-fish and called it Cedric. The meat was dark-white, chewy. She needed more wine to help it down.

As Caz entered blur-world, the oasis between too-sharp and too-drunk, she heard Hank talking, his solid, dark English voice.

331

'The name is *alimoché*. It's a type of vulture. Just the one pair, but they have managed to breed. We're very pleased.' Blodwen's fantasies right now would make a table-napkin stand on end. Caz, gently pissed, thought it funny, but then, just sober enough, she thought it was about time she put the girl out of her misery. There was just enough time for Blodwen to switch her attentions to Otto.

'So is that where you took Caz?' Eric said, almost neutrally.

'Into the Fire Mountains, to the hide, yes.'

'Very cosy,' Eric said.

Hank turned very slightly towards Caz.

'My mother said always . . .'

Eric was about to say the wrong thing but Caz cut in to stop him.

'Hey!' she said quickly. 'I got a story! Have I told you all the one about circumstantial evidence?'

Ina shook her head.

'No,' said Blodwen.

''S'good, you'll like this one,' Caz decided. 'And I'll tell you just as soon as someone tops my glass up.'

One hundred and seven

Someone poured some more red wine. Caz sat up slightly.

'There was a farmer. His wife didn't give him much. One day she sent him to the barn to milk their cow. Now, the farmer knew the cow was a bit temperamental and sure enough, every time the farmer tried to milk it, the cow would move, kick or try to bite him.'

Caz took a swig.

'This pissed the old farmer right off.

'After the second kick, the farmer had the idea to tie one of the cow's legs to the side of the stall. He managed it, but then the cow started kicking out with the other leg.'

She took another sip of her drink.

'So the farmer ties the *other* leg to the other side of the stall. Now, he thinks, milk – but no, the cow thrashes about, it won't keep still.'

Another sip, most of the glass.

'So the farmer uses another rope to hobble the cow's front legs. Now she's on her knees, her rear end is up in the air, she can't move. Finally, the farmer can milk her. He's sweating, he's tired. He's just about to get the bucket underneath the cow when he realises he needs a piss.'

Caz paused, had another drop of wine and put down the empty glass.

'So there he is, cow, legs tied, pulled out, front legs bent, arse in the air, and his dick is out.' She waited a second.

'And his wife walks in. Now what d'you want to tell me about circumstantial evidence?'

One hundred and eight

No one bothered with sweet, but when Bepe, the little waiter, produced a complimentary bottle of an odd fruit brandy it was quickly snaffled by Otto to make certain none went back to the kitchens. That and the extra two bottles of wine had moved Caz and everyone else out of the oasis. Caz, in particular, was being stupid.

Earlier, she had dragged Blodwen out to the toilets on some feeble pretext, and had tipsily tried to tell her mate that Hank Carry was gay. What she had actually said, giggling a little too much, was that Harry Carry was a waste of time, a dead end. At that, Blodwen had snorted and said Caz was pathetic as a comedienne. All was lost.

Six of them walked back to la Santa Sport. Blodwen had persuaded Hank that it was *far* too late and he was far too drunk to drive to his hide, his tent. She had a sofa and, it was all right with Caz wasn't it, he could crash there? It was, Caz said. She was gone, hanging on to Otto and looking forward to the disco, where, she figured, she was going to sober up. As Hank and Blodwen leeched into the tall man, Caz suddenly thought of Valerie. She shook her head and the image was gone. She grinned as a thought came to her. 'Fuh! Otto! The disco tonight, house 'n' garage shit. You, me, we dance like crazy, maybe bonk after, yeah?'

'Oh, yeah,' Otto said.

One hundred and nine

Caz woke in a room smelling of man; after-shave, toast, a faint smell of sock. Oh, Jeez! There was a pain on the inside of her left shin and the most amazing firework display going on in her head. She decided not to open her eyes and felt around for Otto's body. She remembered nothing. She felt nothing. When she tried to say his name, her lips untacked, dry, with faint yellow stickiness at the corners of her mouth. First time, nothing. Then she sat up, grunting, 'Otto?' Silence.

There was nothing for it but to open her eyes.

'Otto?'

'He's gone for a run,' a voice said.

'Jesus, where am I?' Caz said. She thought the room was full of smoke.

A voice walked through. 'Oh, very nice,' it said.

Caz realised she was topless above the sheets. As she pulled the clothes up, her head banged again.

'Are you Dave?' she said.

'Yeah. Otto's gone out for a run. God, you were crazy last night.'

'I was?'

'You had a soccer match going on the five-a-side pitch.'

'But I don't play soccer.'

'So Otto said. You whacked yourself, I believe.'

Caz felt her leg. 'There's a lump.'

'Cancer,' Dave said.

'Oh, thank God for that!' Caz said. 'I thought it was shin-splits.'

'You want t'get up?'

'I guess. What happened last night?'

'What happened? You mean you don't remember?'

'Not the details.'

'Which details?'

'Well, like anything that happened after eleven o'clock.'

'You're kidding me?'

'Nope!'

'You don't remember what you did when you got back here?'

'Was I bonking?'

'Only a couple of blokes.' There was no smile.

'Two blokes?'

A hint of a smile. She lifted the sheets and looked down.

'What you doing?' Dave said.

Caz's voice came out muffled. 'Checking.'

'Checking what?'

'You're lying,' she said as she re-emerged.

'How d'you know?'

'Easy,' Caz said. 'Cobwebs.'

'Yer right,' Dave said. 'You were in no state to do much more than throw up, which is exactly what you did. In the garden, just outside.'

'Oh, shit. I have to clean it up?'

'The cats will have eaten it.'

'The cats?'

'Vomit and mice. What more could a cat ask?'

'I threw up?'

'Oh God, yes. Then you came in here, rinsed your mouth out and asked us where we were going next.'

'Then what?'

'You flaked out where you were sitting.'

'And?'

'You snore. Like a ruptured diesel.'

'Oh.'

'And we put you in bed.'

'Who's we?'

'Me and Otto. And the old bloke. The one with the Scots accent.'

'Tom MacInnes? What was he doing around here?'

'If that's his name. You were being a bit silly then you had your turn and went to throw up. I guess it was a bad one. Maybe you sounded like someone was hurting you. Out popped the Scots bloke. For a second we thought he was going to attack you.'

'Tom wouldn't attack me.'

'No, I know that now. But last night, when you were losing your dinner, he came from nowhere and bloody quick. Otto went for him but was on his bum before he knew what had happened.'

'Tom *hit* Otto?'

'No, he just sort of put him on the floor. It was quite nifty actually.'

'And you put me to bed?'

'Well, sort of. You were wet from when you went in the pool. The old bloke got you out of your clothes and put a sheet round you. Then we stuck you in Otto's bed. You never moved.'

Caz groaned.

'And you talk in your sleep too.'

Caz was imagining things. She didn't want to ask.

'You're not gay, are you?' Dave said.

'What?'

'You're not gay? Only you kept moaning, repeating the names of a couple of girls. Someone called Moira? Someone called Valerie?'

'Yeah, I'm gay.'

'Fucking hell. What a waste!'

'Of course I'm not gay! Have you asked Otto? Moira's my best mate, a copper, and Valerie's my boyfriend.'

'You've got a boyfriend called *Valerie*?'

'It's Russian.'

'Oh,' Dave said.

Caz sat up. 'Can I get dressed now?'

'Your gear's still damp.'

'Oh fucking *wonderful*!'

Dave grinned. 'It's true, ay? Blondes have all the fun?'

'Piss off,' Caz said. 'But sling me my kit first.'

One hundred and ten

Caz might have had worse sensations, but pulling on damp knickers and then wet leggings over a bruise the size of an egg ran the worst very close. At least she didn't have to do a wet T-shirt impression. Dave had slung her one of his tops, getting another quick flash for his pains, and she limped out, grateful for small mercies.

She'd forgotten the trashed room but remembered as soon as she opened the door. After yet another groan, she went to the bathroom, started a bath and then went through for some dry kit, her favourite pretty running outfit, Nike lilac, shorts with a good loose cut, the top exposing the belly, designed to drop away from the breasts, whatever they were.

It was seven twenty-five when she stepped into the bath, seven thirty when she left the apartment and seven thirty-five when she tapped on the door to the physio clinic. Footsteps came and then Ina opened the door.

'Caz! You are here! After last night I expected you would not come! Last night, you know, you were crazy person, very silly.'

Caz grinned sheepishly. 'I've just been told.'

'*Very* silly.'

'Then punish me, Ina. I should pay.'

Face down on Ina's bench, Caz felt like a specimen. Ina had asked her to strip down to her knickers so she could check out her spine, and now she was attempting to pull Caz's left leg out of the hip.

'You – couldn't – do – that – just – a little bit gentler, could you?'

'Caz, this is bad. Something here . . .'

'It doesn't hurt, Ina.'

'For an hour now, I make it hurt.'

Ina pushed Caz's face down into the hole at one end of the leather couch. Caz wanted desperately to say something funny, but somehow the moment didn't seem quite right. She stared at the concrete floor and thought.

'See here, it is . . .'

'Yee-hah!'

'Very tight.'

'Oh, really?' Caz said.

Ina tweaked again and something flashed up into Caz's head.

Dark red.

'I think maybe that here is a problem for a doctor, something touches I think.'

'No, it's fine, really. Just loosen me up, give me a massage.'

Ina was soothing but firm. 'Caz, my good friend. Massage I can do. And I can loosen you also. But I think something in here is not so right. I think maybe you must see your doctor, see someone special.'

Caz grunted as she felt the fingers, thumbs. Ina hadn't finished.

'And I do not see how when you run, nothing has happened. This I feel. How you can run, I cannot understand. You have no pain?'

'No. Nothing,' Caz said.

'OK. I will massage first, make you as loose as is possible. Then we will see how it lies, the land.'

'Uh-huh,' Caz said, and the magic hands moved over her.

341

The tall girl's healing fingers moved into Caz, over Caz, up and down the dull piano of her back. Caz's eyes were closed, gently shut by warm breezes, lullabied by flowing grass. Her groans subsided into the dull brown sensuality of after-sex when everything is skin and untouchable; dull heat. Then she was asleep.

It was then that the naked body of Ina moved down on her, slid over her, when the long, long body of her friend slid over Caz's buttocks, up to her shoulders, lips gently, gently touching her neck. Their room was red and pink, perfume wafting, and somewhere music tingled, harps or guitars, violins, muted rock. Deep inside, heat made her wet, and the fingers, the fingers, and someone was whispering, *shhh, shhh!* It's all right . . .

And then Eric! The room harsh with white light. His dark face roaring, but no voice, his hand lashing into Ina's face! No!

'Caz?'

'Shit, I was alseep.'

'You back is stiff again.'

'I was dreaming. About Eric.'

'My Eric? You dream about my Eric? I hope this was good, not sexy. You don't dream sexy about my Eric?'

The memory rolled back. 'Er, no,' Caz said. 'Not exactly.'

'Your back is softer now. So hey, you roll over and I do you on the front.'

Caz pretended a laugh, expecting a slight embarrassment as she rolled on to her side, then on to her back. Face up now, she grinned, back to being Flood again. 'So, Ina . . .' she said.

'Yes?'

Caz was impish now. She caught Ina's eye. 'Be gentle with me.'

One hundred and eleven

Caz didn't fall asleep again – she thought it best – and was awake and mellow when the door was lightly knocked on with the weight of a man's fist. Ina's moving thumbs stopped – Caz was on her front again – and with a gentle slap, she whispered, 'I must – one moment, Caz.'

She moved away and Caz did a log of the sensations she felt. Everything was soft and elastic now, but somewhere just above her waistband there was a point, almost imperceptible, that didn't hurt but simply wasn't as smooth, as right, as everywhere else. She had the sudden vision of the princess and the pea. When everything else was so right-right, the wrongness, whatever it was, muted, hidden, cried out.

'Oh hello,' Ina said. Then Caz heard the deep brown voice of Hank.

'Is Caz here? I just wanted to have a word.'

The pair of them came through and Caz could hear their footfalls outside the screen. She sat up, grabbing her top and pulling it on. Ina was muttering, a little more Danish than usual, as if she was slightly embarrassed to be found alone like this with Caz. The curtain moved.

'Caz, we can finish now. Your friend, the man of the birds. He is here.'

Caz swung down, her long bare legs flapping on to the floor.

She felt lithe and rubbery, flexible enough to slide under a door.

'With you in a sec, Hank!' she shouted, and pulled on her shorts.

When Caz came out, her running shoes in her hand, the big twitcher gave her a huge damn-sexy smile. Like Dave, her first instinct was to think, 'What a waste.' But then she simply smiled and said, 'Mornin'!'

'I came over to get my jeep,' Hank said. 'I wanted to say goodbye and have a quick word.'

'Time for a coffee?'

'You *mean* coffee?'

'You offering?'

'What do you think?'

Caz smiled. 'Yeah, I mean coffee, long-life milk or black.'

'Yick!' Hank said.

'Hey, come on!' Caz said. 'You're a big boy, you can take it.'

She sat down, pulling on her shoes, leaving the laces. As she was sat there, Ina came out and suggested lunch.

'Twelve-thirty?'

'That is good. We meet here, yes? Go to Pool Bar?'

Caz nodded, said thanks and goodbye, then, as she took Hank's arm to leave, she said, 'So, Harry . . . you get to see Blodwen's giraffes?'

'Oh, yes,' Hank said, grinning at Caz like a chimpanzee. 'Apparently, Sunday she's off to Teguise to buy a big one.' Smile. 'A *very* big one.'

Caz's face dropped. 'Tell me you're kidding. You're kidding me, right?'

They were approaching the *Supermercado*. Hank stopped, his hands spread, one two or three feet above the other. 'You did that?' Caz said.

'Why not?' Hank said. 'It didn't hurt. And Blodwen's *very* happy.'

Caz made a face, her teeth together, talking only with lips. 'She is *dead*. I am *not* amused.'

'You're not jealous, are you, Caz?'

'Nope!' Caz said. 'But stupid, maybe . . .'

One hundred and twelve

They went in the Atlantico. Caz nodded to the girl on the tills, whipped her man quickly in, avoided the queues at the breakfast buffet and came away with their drinks. As they sat down, Hank said, 'Blodwen told me about the accidents, how you were both trying to figure out who might have been here when they happened.'

'Yeah?'

'Well, I had a thought. I know it's teaching yer grannie to suck eggs, but why does the guy have to have been here at all?'

'Sorry?'

'Whoever did it – why did he have to be here?'

Caz looked perplexed. 'I know it's only half-eight in the morning, Hank, and I know I got badly pissed last night, but . . .'

'Caz, you're presuming that someone was here, actually here, on the la Santa campus, right? And you've not found anyone that was.'

'Yeah . . .?'

'Well, why do they have to be *on* the campus? Why do they have to be *staying* here?'

'Am I being thick or something?'

'At the moment, yeah. It's the alcohol.'

'Tell me again,' Caz said.

'Caz, am I here or not here?'

'Is this a trick question?'

'I'm here as in here, but Caz, I'm not here as in *booked in* here, am I? If I were a villain, you'd have no record of me stopping at the hotel.'

'Oh, Jesus! But that means we're nowhere. We've presumed all along that our way of getting a shortlist of suspects was to check out everyone who *could* have done it.'

'And there's no one, right?'

'Right.'

'Well, who'd be stupid enough to knock people off on a regular basis and leave you to spot that he'd been here every time? Would anyone?'

'So what are you saying?'

'You remember the hide? You remember watching the *alimoché*?'

'Yeah . . .?'

'After we went in, Pepe left, right? As far as the birds were concerned we weren't there, unless they can count.'

'Jesus, I think I better give up drinking. I still—'

'Caz. If you want to con the birds, you leave, then you sneak back, or you sneak in when they're not looking. If they think you're gone, they relax. We do it all the time, walk up openly, walk away openly. Just that sometimes the in and out numbers aren't exactly the same.'

'But if it could be a complete outsider, someone who never stops here . . .'

'I thought of that. It's unlikely, surely? I could hardly pop on and off the campus time after time and never be spotted. No, what you want is someone who was here for *most* of the accidents and away for some, especially if those accidents were just after they've left.'

Light slowly dawned on Caz. She spoke slowly. 'Or just before they arrived . . .'

'What d'you think?' Hank said.
'Oh, Hank,' Caz said. 'I wish you were straight.'

One hundred and thirteen

Caz really wanted him to stay but Hank had to go. He was
saying this even as he finished the second coffee that Caz had
forced on him. He was saying how he had to go and protect his
bébé alimoché and how, if anyone went near her, he might just
get violent.

'It's been great, Caz, but I'm back to England next week. I
need to do my bit looking after the chick, mum and dad. It's
why I came here.'

'I guess so,' Caz said. She was thinking, *I have to protect my
baby.* She was thinking how Ina's jealous pig of a boyfriend
Eric, Eric with the violent streak, Eric the bully, must have
slipped into la Santa, hurt the guys that got too near to her.
She was thinking about how she could prove it.

'That's not a nice look on your face, Caz.'

'What?'

'You're scowling. It's ugly.'

'I was thinking,' she said. 'Sorry.' She clicked the light back
on, sat up. 'Hey, don't mind me. I'll walk you to your car.'

'My jeep.'

'Same difference,' she said.

When she waved him away, it was with a twinge of regret.
He was a nice man with a good set of values. He really seemed
to have his life sorted out. As the jeep prutted away and out of
sight, she envied him.

One hundred and fourteen

Hank's jeep had been parked behind the Pool Bar close to the stadium. Caz was fuzzy still, both in her head and in her thinking, and she walked slowly through, intending to gently jog round the running track while her sinuses cleared. Last night – this was last night. The poison was not yet worked out of her. She was still mixing booze and training, still holding herself back from really breaking through into the athletics big time. It suddenly occurred to her that maybe it was deliberate, that running, like loving Valerie, might get in the way of her career.

She didn't bother stretching but went straight into a really light jog the wrong way round the track. A soccer team were training on the pitch in the middle of the oval and she half-heartedly watched that, a brick-legged full-back with crunching power clattering in against a skinny winger, the ball scuttling out from the tackle towards her.

She stopped, picked up the leather ball, trotted over and tossed it to the defender who grinned at her, four of his front teeth missing. The grin reminded her of pictures of Nobby Stiles. She blew him a kiss.

As she settled into her running she mentally looked at her back, looking for that dull mark that pointed to whatever slight trouble she had. But there was nothing. She was long, tensile, and easy, flowing round the lanes, picking up the pace in the straights. A gazelle.

It wasn't ten o'clock yet. As Caz ran, she thought about going to check in with the DI and work through the ideas that Hank Carry had prompted but she didn't, still smarting at the memory of last night, her embarrassment with Ute and Ina. MacInnes had said he'd produce the villain by tonight at six, so fuck him, he could do it on his own.

Every other lap now she put in a fast one, one minute-thirty seconds, six-minute miling. Again she looked for the pain. Again, nothing. There was absolutely no problem anywhere that she could feel, except the usual vague tightness in her lower back and upper buttocks that she got, always got, whenever she pushed at all.

So Eric, he must have come over to Lanzarote when Ina put his trip off. It figured. He would've already bought the airplane ticket. He was jealous, probably obsessively so, and when Ina gave him her genuine excuse, knowing him, he would have imagined all sorts of things, all sorts of dark images, lovers, crazy parties, Ina drunk and abandoning herself in sordid, debauched couplings.

She kicked into another slightly faster lap. It figured! It figured! Eric came there, to la Santa when they didn't expect him. And then, what? Then he hid himself somewhere? Crept around at night? But what if he had stumbled on to Ina, or Ute, or anyone else who knew him? How would he have explained *that* away? Shit! And wouldn't Ina have phoned him in Denmark? It didn't make much sense. But it *had* to. It had to be Eric. She didn't know *how* it was Eric, but it was Eric.

Caz was hardly aware of her body and she was running faster and faster. Her quick laps were seventy-five seconds, her easy ones inside two minutes. Over and over, over and over. How was she going to pin Eric down, how was she going to fix him, catch him? Could she get flight logs for that fortnight, check that he had indeed left Copenhagen? How would it be done, how would MacInnes do it?

Then she heard a distant shout, '*Watch out!*' and a football whistled past her face *flacking*! loudly against a wall. She woke, startled that she could be so far away. How would MacInnes do it?

'You all right, luv?' A footballer, the full-back, thunder-thighs.

'You what? Oh, yeah. Working too hard.'

The footballer grinned. 'In case you're interested, our centre-forward fancies you. His name's Jay. You want 'is phone number?'

Caz glanced over, a lanky awkward-looking guy with big ears and white legs grinned at her. He looked like he had an IQ in the nineties.

'Pass,' she said.

The chunk-hunk grinned as he picked up the ball. 'You did right, sweetheart!'

He turned to take the throw-in. The lanky guy was bawling in a naff Yorkshire accent and pointing to his forehead.

'Dildo! Dildo! On me nut!'

Dildo took a couple of steps back and wiped his hand on his shirt, left, then right. Then he spat.

Caz shook her head and jogged away.

One hundred and fifteen

For no particular reason other than avoiding her wrecked room, Caz turned left instead of right as she exited the stadium and went towards the Pool Bar, then down the stairs to the leisure pool, the disco to her left. The sun was high now, the wake-up haze burned away, and the microwave-suicides were laid out with their fat Tom Clancys, hardly a lounger left anywhere without a burning body flopped on it or the ritual it's-booked signal of a towel, no doubt of Prussian origin.

There were a few kids in the shallow water, screaming, splashing, being kids, and way over the other side, in the deep water area, a brown, triangle-topped diver wearing bugger-all shiny trunks that wouldn't cover a decent erection. As she walked that way he boinked once on the springboard and flipped into the blue hardly raising a ripple. She hoped his trunks came off.

There was a spare lounger in a shadow. She dragged it into the light and dropped on to it. With nothing between her and the white-ribbed plastic, hard against her back, she struggled for a comfortable position, found one, then allowed the sun to briefly cook her, crisp up the little bit of sweat she'd raised on the track. Whatever else, she suddenly thought, her eyes firmly shut but a grin across her face, this, *this*, was definitely the way to do detective work.

She was hardly sleeping. Even through her eyelids the sun

353

was red and far too bright for that, but she nevertheless was cruising her brain, letting angst trickle away, letting various perplexities unravel themselves in their own sweet, inexorable way. Aware of the sun, she thought some cream would have been sense, then she thought about the rigmarole of the beach, the gear, the flip-flops, towels, the paperbacks, the sun-stuff, all squeezed into some prattish carry-all beach-bag. She got near to dozing.

Stripes. Her back was two-inch stripes. The legs on tanned bikers were different reds, stripes; beach-bags were stripes, flowers, canvas, logos, Union Jacks, but stripes, some were stripes.

She thought she had it, but the memory was dancing. It was there as long as she didn't look, but if she looked it went, shimmering, lost, like Captain Kirk beaming down on to the nearest planet. Stripes. Give me stripes. She tried to dream, relax.

Plastic loungers, a striped beach-bag, nothing else, and the same stripes, the same bag, another bag, just there, a suggestion, somewhere in the background where Matthew Black leaked grey cells outside the camp shop. And who was there? Strangers, Ina, Ute, Christian Green, the yikky Belgian whats-isname. She was getting it now. Black on the floor, someone taking Ute away, picking up her bag, *her* bag or *his* bag? It was all so peripheral, she was just trying to get the body shape, come on eyes, come on head, cones for colour, rods for periph-eral movement, bollocks, the shape, the shape. Marco? Could it have been Marco?

She tried again, relaxed, a little self-hypnosis. She was swim-ming, those long, long, slow lengths of the Olympic pool, the sun on her neck each end. Fade to drying. Now she was drying herself, feeling not so bad except that the breeze felt cool on her wet back. Now she was swimming again, the long, long . . . No! Get out of the pool! She was drying again and, above, someone was running – and someone was running. Yes!

But tall? Heavy? Short? Light? See! Someone was running, now the footfalls, toe-landing, not a heel-striker. Fast? No, fastish, but easy. But on the balls of his feet, yes? Covering ground quickly but not sprinting, not obvious. And not Marco Harris. No, not as tall.

And you're walking round that way, Caz, feel the sun, you're jogging, you can feel the floor hot and rough under your feet and someone is screaming, someone is shocked. *Ute* is screaming and . . . and what else?

There are people around you, you know that, people murmuring, people offering to help, people about to. *'Don't touch him!'* and people aback, people melting away. They are all around you, these people. And Ute is leaving now. Who took her away? And Ina is helping, and Platt, the Belgian is helping and there are guards, and there, on the other side of the road, it's nothing, just someone who doesn't care, someone who isn't involved and the shape, look back, look again. You didn't know him then. Look now. It was Marco, wasn't it? Wasn't it?

In the shadows he moved and refused to come back into view. She could feel the blood, the brain, smell death and ozone, see Matt's poor face, but each time she raised her mental eye to look for Marco's shadow it grinned and dissolved. All that was left was tall. The long lost tallness of a man who should have been interested. A tall man who wasn't interested enough.

She sat up just as someone splinged into the water. The board wanged. 'But it's you, isn't it, Marco? It's you?'

And a made-up face, rebuilt, stepped back into her memory, not the original but Caz's own creation. Out from the shadows he stepped, tall, hard, roguish.

'Hi, Caz!' he said. Marco. He was smiling. Not a nice smile.

'Even if you're right,' he said for her, 'forget you even thought it.'

She sat forward, cold despite the sunshine.

He wasn't smiling now. 'Forget it, Caz,' he said. 'You'll *never* prove it.'

One hundred and sixteen

When she got back to her room, there were three cleaners there, three low-flying, sweet-faced *señoras* in light blue skirts and tops and white plimsolls, scratching quickly around and grunting low Spanish at the mayhem, the only recognisable word being *pesetas*. From their collective manner, Caz knew that by *pesetas* they meant repayment or a fine, and by their studious avoidance of any eye-contact or even the most cursory *'Ola!'* they obviously thought that the wreckage of her room was the afterbirth of a particularly bad and debauched Green Team party.

She tried *'Bandido!'* and *'Burglaroso!'* and a grimace and gesture that was meant to indicate the violence met upon her room from points unknown. It worked, they understood. They responded. Instantly the three were one, brush-handles like crosses as they backed out of the room three-strong, a phalanx-defensive, the heaviest mama of the three last out, dark-eyed as they disappeared, rears first, into the corridor.

'Hey!' Caz thought. 'My Spanish knows no bounds!'

She went across the room, picked up the phone, and dialled the DI's room. As expected, he wasn't there so she went through to the toilet, flicked on the taps and prepared herself a consolatory bath.

It was still running when the phone rang. She picked it up. Blodwen.

357

'Hey, Caz!' she said. 'You'll never guess what 'appened!'
'Wanna bet?' Caz said.

One hundred and seventeen

'But how could you possibly know?' Blodwen said. 'I only just found out myself.'

Oh, not giraffe-talk. 'Know *what*, Blod?'

'You 'aven't 'eard, then?'

'Blodwen! You've just bloody told me I couldn't have!'

'They sacked Alan Sapsard. You remember, he was off-base, AWOL that day you got chased by that car out past Tinajo?'

'I remember.'

'Well, I just 'eard. He'd got his girlfriend in the family way and he was lifting stuff and flogging it to get enough money together to get married. When you rang for us to do that check-up and we caught him off-base, we didn't know then, but he was nicking all sorts of gear, tinsa food, welding equipment, all sorts. Marco Harris was buying it off him.'

There was a second's pause before Caz replied. 'And they were hiding it on the roof,' she said. 'Up out of the way, somewhere near Tower Forty, right?'

'How the buggery did you know that? Yeah, it was stashed under tarpaulin. Right opposite the site offices. If you said Christian Green was a bit pissed off you'd be understating things just a bit.'

'But Alan was just seeing his girlfriend that day, the day I had my run-in with the Renault Clio?'

'Far as I know, yeah. Your ex-boss, MacShit, the miserable

Scots guy. He had someone ring up Alan's girl that day, the day when they caught Alan playing silly buggers and going missing. She gave him an alibi straight away, and when the local police went up to check it out, he had an army of witnesses. All the villagers like 'im. Alan and his girlfriend thought they were keeping their little thing a secret, but everyone including the mayor knew about 'em.'

'So, Alan . . .?'

'He's in the police station at Haria.'

'What'll they do?'

'I 'aven't gorra clue, mate, but genrully speaking, the Spanish don't piss about when they catch people.'

'But his girlfriend's pregnant.'

'Well, the silly bugger should've thought of that before he started nicking stuff, shouldun 'ee? Or 'ee should've started his crim career by nicking some condoms about six months ago.'

'I guess,' Caz said slowly.

'An' anyway, it was you that blew the bloody whistle, weren't it?'

'Were it?' Caz said. 'All I did was to say I'd had the frighteners put on me by some twat in a Renault. We checked out the staff just in case.'

'Well, you did a fuckin' good job, Caz. Giuseppe Castellano is dead, you've got rid of Alan, Marco is banged up for all sorts of stuff he's supposed to've done in Arrecife, and I heard this morning that Ute Fërd is packing up and going home.'

'This is my fault?'

'Well, we were doin' all right before you got 'ere, sunshine!'

'Are you serious, Blod?'

'What'cha mean?'

'Are you blaming me for Alan Sapsard's problems or for Marco? For Ute? What am I supposed to do, look the other way? Some fucker tried to *kill* me, Blodwen. He didn't manage it and I rang in here. It's not *my* bloody fault we took the scab off a sore, is it?'

'Well, you know what they say, Caz, me old china.'

'No, enlighten me.'

'That thing about an ill wind blowing.'

'And that's me is it, an ill wind?'

'Well, it has bin suggested.'

'You think that, do you?'

'Oh no, Caz. *I* don't think it. *We're* butties.'

'And if we weren't?'

'Whatcha mean? What kind of question is that?'

'It doesn't matter,' Caz said. 'I've gotta go. There's a bath just about to come to meet me.'

'You all right for a drink tonight?'

Caz sighed. 'Yeah, sure, Blod. Who needs a liver?'

One hundred and eighteen

Caz sank into a bath that was yellow-brown and flowery, a combination of bath oil and the local water colour. Her head was a mess, inside and out, and she needed to shampoo, first her long blonde hair and then a couple of pounds of grey matter. The first was easy, the second a little trickier. Once she had washed her hair and flashed cool shower water through it to rinse, she lay back slowly, trying to allow out the knots inside her head. Some things were easy.

So she *had* glimpsed Marco that morning outside the Supermarket, Marco Mark Harris, sliding away in the shadows. Good ol' Marco, good old local-heavy Marco. Marco, the thief, and now Marco the murderer, or near-murderer, the man who Caz now thought had given Matthew Black the wrong kind of nudge. Into thirty feet of space.

And Marco had realised, guessed at Caz's instincts. But she had left, gone back to the UK, and he must have thought he had got away with it. But then she had returned and he must have then decided she was a danger. So he'd waited for her, watched her, waited for his opportunity. Had sat in his car and followed her, waited until she was isolated, far away from help. And then he had gone for it, finally gone for it, driven the car at her, driven to kill her.

And swerved away.

And that was her problem. Why *did* Marco swerve away?

Decency? No balls? She couldn't see either. He liked her? So what? If he was a killer – all right, a near-killer – and her knowledge threatened him, was he going to hold back? Surely not?

She soaped down slowly, trying not to think about it, her hands down her long, long legs, her fingers working between her toes. She soaped her arms too, her underarms, her breasts, her stomach, down into her lifted pubic hair and underneath her, still confused.

But it must be him! Must have been him! It was so obvious! There wasn't the slightest doubt he'd go down for the assault on Matt Black and, if Matt died, be done for his murder. So why did he follow her and not do it, not finish the job?

God, this was hopeless, hopeless! Forgetting she had rinsed her hair, she slid slowly away, down into the water, closing it over her, her bent legs up somewhere by the taps and the wet world shutting her away till there was nothing. Nothing but the drip, drip, drip, of the shower-head, clubbing to the second its droplets, dull-splott dull-splott, dull-splott forever, dull as it dull-dripped into the bath, as drip-dull as Caz, drip-stupid Caz, stupid, stupid, stupid, underwater Caz.

One hundred and nineteen

So she was stupid? So what? When she had got out of the bath and rubbed down, she drifted through to the bedroom half-dressed in two towels – head, tits and bits covered up, pulled shut the curtains, and flopped on to the bed.

Take out, presume it was Marco, the Clio up on the top road. Then last year there were the two deaths, Colin Jones in the sea and the German who sky-dived from Mirador del Rio. Maybe a thousand people could be lined up for that one, maybe six hundred who could be eliminated. But then this year, when Kevin King was hounded to his death, many of that thousand, the four hundred, would still be around, could have done it. But then, when she added the other accidents, the fall in the Fire Mountains, the jeep accident, the others, the suspects dissolved, except one, Ina's Eric.

'But Eric wasn't here!' she said out loud.

'But booked, he was booked to be here.'

'We've been through that. He was booked in here. OK. And maybe he sneaked about the place, maybe he did things at night.'

'But,' one of her other voices whispered, 'but what a risk! What if he had bumped into someone he knew? He couldn't do it, not on his own. If he was here, he would have needed help. Needed somewhere to hide.'

One hundred and twenty

Somewhere to hide, someone to hide you. Somewhere to wait, someone to watch for you. But who, where, when, and for that matter, why? How did someone find someone to hide them? A Greenie? No, they all shared rooms. Someone from admin? No, they all lived off-site. A techie? No, they all lived off-site too, they had no . . .

They had nowhere to hide someone . . .

Except the lumber yard.

Except the storerooms beneath the complex.

Except, except, the pool-maintenance rooms. Just like the feral cats who came and went, almost invisibly, who ate their tinned fish beneath the Olympic lanes, or Giuseppe Castellano, late-night dragging the leisure pool, dumping his gear in the submarine, smoking a quiet cigarillo, not wanting to go home, while rock-music dropped over the Pool Bar wall, and late night heat wafted on the water.

Like . . .

A man who needed money, a man that, maybe over some time, a Spanish-speaking Dane could get to know, could manipulate, could suggest, 'Hey, Giuseppe, my girl, you know, I'd like to make sure I'm not imagining things. If I could stay near, maybe hide in your place, and you, while you were out there, if you saw something . . .'

And Giuseppe was dead, so sorry, but dead.

And Caz, here it was now, the beach-bag, the stripes, the stripes she'd seen before, overlooked, out there by the pool-side, there then not there the night Giuseppe Castellano died.

Now Caz knew. She could see Eric, the hidden Eric, Eric the dark eyes, Eric with his quick flash of black anger, the hand-grip too tight. Eric who controlled his Ina, Eric the bully, Eric the jealous, so jealous he couldn't even let Caz talk to Hank Carry, who went off in a huff, a crazy huff, left her to fend for herself. Left her, to rush back to Ina.

She realised, jealousy. It explained everything.

'I have you!' she hissed in the half-dark. 'I have you!'

She closed her eyes, smiling, relaxing now. Before she allowed herself to sleep she thought briefly about Ina, but it passed. Poor Ina, like Ute, the wrong man. Maybe for a second, she paused, but then she remembered Tom MacInnes, speaking softly but firmly, a glass of Whyte & Mackay in his hand.

'We catch 'em, Flood. Is all we c'n do. We jest put the bastards away. What happens happens. No one makes them do the crime.'

Satisfied, she let sleep roll darkly up her body, knowing that in thirty minutes she would sit up and set about the arrest of Eric Ortollo.

In her sleep, both Valerie and Ina visited her. Ina was sad, but Caz held her close. Then Valerie entered the room. She went across and slipped into his bed. He was smooth-shaven, smelling of Cacherel. His hands were between her legs briefly but then she raised herself, swung on to him like a fairground horse and allowed herself to use his still piston as she climbed and fell on him, quickly going close then falling slowly away. On the other side of the room, Ina watched impassively.

One hundred and twenty-one

She woke with a start. The fucking bag. If the bag she'd half-seen when Matt Black was discovered was Ute's, the same bag seen the night Giuseppe Castellano died, and if Eric was around then, when the old man had hanged himself, been hanged, and was using Ute's bag, Ina's bag? then one or both of the girls had to know he was around. That was crazy!

So Eric wasn't around for Castellano's death? He had nothing to do with it? But he'd hidden there, in the submarine? When? A few weeks ago, when Caz had been there the first time, when Ina had said she was going to Denmark to see Eric. When she was going *to* Denmark, not the other way round.

When, Caz had decided, Eric had somehow killed Kevin King. And how, for that matter? Kevin was pissed, yes, but he was still quick on his feet and fit, reasonably handy at looking after himself. So how? So how? It was Eric, she was certain, but how, how had he done it?

'You're forgetting the bag, Caz.'

'I'm not.'

'You are. You're trying to ignore it. MacInnes wouldn't.'

'I'm not MacInnes!' she said aloud and sat up, stood up, before the little voice could laugh and say, 'Yet!'

She left to look for Ina.

The first place Caz tried, the physios' rooms, were locked. Second try was the girls' shared apartment, locked too. She walked once round the corridors, then over to the track and then via then slowly-filling Pool Bar along the top towards the crazy golf, then cut through to the Olympic pool. As she walked she looked down at the burning bodies and sun-oil. Unless the girls were on the beach they weren't sunbathing. But then, thinking of the one time Ina had discussed her naked body, trying to laugh about having a chest tattoo – 'This way up in case of rape' – perhaps it was no wonder that the girls weren't outside, baring all.

Not on the five-a-side pitch, and not playing badminton or squash – she bumped into Edward Platt, the Belgian, while she was looking – the girls had hidden themselves well. Caz was on the brink of giving up. She thought about the day she had searched for MacInnes like this, only to discover he was out playing Spanish policeman. Then she thought, 'Oh, they're off somewhere' but then she thought, 'No, Ina's meeting me at twelve-thirty.' So probably not off camp either.

She cut through by the *Supermercado* and passed Tower Forty. It was possible, so she jogged up the spiral steps as far as the roof door. The door was still damaged, held shut by a rag jammed in the lock. The rag suggested no one the other side, but Caz pulled anyway, let in the light and stepped out on to the fawn and grey roofs.

One hundred and twenty-two

Ina and Ute were over the first wall, hidden away in the same place that Caz had chosen, her one off-duty time up on the roof. To say they were hiding would have been putting things a little strongly. True, they were out of sight, but the music they were whacking out of a ghetto-blaster, rock, Alice Cooper's 'School's Out', was hardly out of mind. What surprised Caz was that she had heard not a whisper, not even a pebble, from the other side of the stair door.

She was standing by the low wall when she spoke, aware that, presumably, she was still not exactly flavour-of-the-month with Ute.

'I was looking for you,' she said to two very different naked backs.

Ute turned her head and looked up neutrally, no actual malice. Ina turned, pulled away a pair of sunglasses and said, 'It is good here, Caz. Here we can be unclothed without being bothered by Peeping Thomas.'

Caz swung herself over the wall. There was a striped bag.

'Came up here once myself. It's so peaceful.'

'Yes,' Ina said.

'But sometimes you get bothered by outsiders,' Ute said.

'That's a neat bag,' Caz said. 'Yours?'

'Why do you ask?' Ute said.

'No reason, just liked it.'

'It is mine, a present from Ina.'

Ina smiled. 'I bought some, all the same, special offer from in the club shop. Me and Ina we have one, and my Eric also, and also Marco.'

Four! Caz could throw herself off the roof now.

'Henry who run the shop, he got eight of the bags only, very special. Then they don't sell at all and he want to get rid of them.' She paused, shifting slightly on her belly. 'You miss out, Caz. It was just the day before you come here. If you I know were coming, I could have buy you a bag also.'

'Baked a cake,' Caz said.

'Pardon me?'

'If I'd known you were coming, I'd've baked a cake. Don't suppose you know anyone else who bought one?'

'Was only four left. I buy them all. The others I doan know about.'

Ute lifted herself slightly. 'Why are you asking questions?'

Caz was about to lie again but, suddenly, she felt tired.

'Because it's my job,' she said.

There was a beat. Ina's face changed to one of slight disappointment, Ute's to one of anger-disgust.

'Ha, so you and the Scottish man! I said this! Marco was right!'

'Yes, Ute. Marco was right. We were trying to find a murderer.'

Ina spoke. 'So you have lied to me, you cheat me by pretending?'

'No, not cheat, Ina. I just didn't say. I was doing a job – my job.'

'And you are my friend, but you pretend to me? You make me feel we are friends for a long time and we are not? Only someone bad would be like this. I diddun think you were like this, Caz. The Scottish policeman, yes, but you, I did not think so.'

'I was doing a job, Een, my job.'

'This does not matter to me. I know only if you tell me lies, if you pretend to be my friend.'

'But I *am* your friend, Een.'

'My name is Ina. You should call me Ina, Ina Yensen. This is who I am. You investigate me? My Eric? And you investigate Ute's Marco?'

Both the girls had swivelled into sitting positions now. The heavier German girl was pulling on a top. Caz was vaguely angry, but really at neither Ina nor Ute. She spoke harshly.

'I am a policewoman. A *police*woman! I came here to catch someone who *murders* people. You both understand this word, murder? I liked both of you when I came here on holiday. I thought of you as my friends, I still do. Both of you. I like you Ina and I like you Ute. Yes, Ute, I like you. Enough not to have you arrested for wrecking my room.'

'Your . . .?'

'Room. Room. The room you trashed. Where you ripped things, smashed plates, turned on water . . .'

'No, Caz. This I did not do.'

'I'm not going to report it. It's done. You thought I'd got Marco arrested. I understand.'

Ute was standing up, then pulling on shorts, trying to maintain eye-contact with Caz. 'I have tol' you. I do not wreck your room. Do you understand?'

A slowly dropping penny. The truth was in Ute's face.

'Caz-ee. All day I could not be going to your room. All day they talk to my Marco and I stay there, just outside the room and will not go away. Even when they threaten me, I stay. All day, you understan' me?'

'Ina?'

'It is true, Caz.'

'Why didn't you say? Yesterday afternoon when—'

'You were very angry, very stupid, Caz. It did not matter

whatever I say. You have a bonnet with a bee in it and you are chasing wild gooses. Because I think I am your friend I think I will wait for you to cool it a bit. Then we all get very drunk that night and I forget.'

'Holy fuck!'

'And I say often to you, that you say fuck and words like it much too many times, Caz. You are not a lady like this, Caz.'

Oh, for fuck's sake . . . . 'I'm sorry.'

'And we are sorry too. Because you lie to us.'

Now Ina was dressing, stretching to pull on a top and innocently exposing pubic hair. Caz felt a flutter of something. She coughed and half-looked away. Ina picked up her shorts.

'There are a couple of questions . . .' Caz said.

Ina looked blankly. 'From a friend or a police person?'

'Both. I need your help. Please, Ina. Please Ute.'

They were stood together.

'OK,' Ute said.

'OK,' Ina said.

One hundred and twenty-three

'Please don't presume anything, Ina, but I need to ask you a couple of little questions about Eric.' They were still on the roof.

'What should I presume? What is this word, presume?'

'Can I ask you about when Eric was supposed to come here but you were very busy? Ute was unhappy, unwell after Matthew Black's accident . . .'

'You are mixed up. First I was going to Denmark, then I was going to bring my Eric back to la Santa.'

'But you didn't. You had to do extra work because Ute took time off.'

'Yes and I ring Eric every day and say I am sorry but it is my job.'

'Every day?'

'Of course. Do you not ring your Valerie every day?'

'In Denmark?'

'Caz you are climbing off the wall now. No, I ring my Eric when he is in Timbuktu of course! You are being very strange. If Eric is in Denmark I ring him in Denmark. Have you banged your head?'

'You rang the usual number. The same one as always?'

'YES!'

Oh, fuck!

'Every day?'

'Caz, you should lie down a little. Little words for you I will say. Every day, because I stop Eric. Because I have to say to Eric that I miss you and we have to wait for rumby-tumby, every day, every single day, I ring him at the college and say so. Are we together now?'

Oh, FUCK!

'I think I'm getting there, Ina.'

One hundred and twenty-four

The sports shop was closed until noon and, unlike in books and films, there was no convenient manager inside tidying racks. Caz thought of Dick Francis again and thought, 'If this *was* a book, I'd've been in there and out again by now, with four names. And the murderer would be the fourth name on the list no matter how many times they were shuffled.'

It was pathetic, but she walked down to the leisure pool, wandering around on the off-chance, hoping the bag would just pop up next to a sunbathing body. Her behaviour was a little too obvious and, if she had been a man, she would have looked like a tit-gawker, a new arrival not yet used to everyone being topless. As it was, she probably looked like a cruising dyke. One girl in particular, aware of Caz's one-second-too-long gaze, sat up, round breasts dropping, and gave Caz a particularly deliberate smile. She made her excuses and left.

She wandered a little more, then she spotted the little runty Belgian, Edward Platt, again, this time just making himself comfortable on a recliner with a towel round his neck and a thinnish-looking paperback in his hand. For nothing better to do for the next hour, she walked over. The book was a Dick Francis, immaculately un-read. For a split second, glancing skyward, she thought, 'God, you are now taking the piss!'

'Edward?'

He looked up, squinting. She had the sun behind her.

'Eh?'

'It's Caz. What are you up to, Edward? I'd've thought you'd be out somewhere on your racer, doing two hundred K or something.'

'Ah, Caz!' he said, shading his eyes now. 'No, I have had some physio from Ina and I am resting. Ina has told me off for not resting, so I am trying to be a good boy. Would you like a drink?'

'Don't mind.'

There was nowhere to sit and Caz glanced around.

Platt realised. 'Oh, I am sorry. I should be polite.'

He stood up and shuffled the recliner out, beckoning to Caz to take half.

'Why, thank you, Edward.'

She was surprised that she was almost taking to him. This, presumably was fall-out from when Marco had bullied him. She always went for underdogs. Maybe Poirot was human after all.

'I know,' he said, 'Ina tells me. She tells me you have seen the rare bird, the *alimoché* in the Fire Mountains.'

'Ina told you that?'

'Yes, I have told her I am also twitcher and I like to see birds.'

'Not these ones, I'm afraid. I know one of the men looking after them so I was lucky, but the whereabouts of the nest is kept secret.'

He looked genuinely disappointed. 'Then I am sad. Because I come here, to the island, many times I have wished to help. My work is I supply farms, even here, many things. Though I have money, I am rich, I am what you call, Green?'

'An environmentalist?'

'Yes. A little I am. I would like to give some money to the people who look after the *alimoché*. A little back, it costs my company little.'

Fucking hell, a generous Belgian!

'Well,' Caz said, 'I've got a number I could ring.'

Edward beamed. 'You would do this thing for me? Thank you! And in return maybe I buy you some lunch somewhere nice, we have a little wine . . .'

Hey, steady on, Poirot. 'Perhaps,' Caz said. 'The number's in my room.'

One hundred and twenty-five

They walked back up together, Caz explaining that she knew Hank Carry after meeting him on the plane over. The little man was listening politely but only half there as if sun-touched or slightly drunk. When they reached Caz's room, he said, 'I will wait here. A lady's room, I think I will wait outside.'

Back to weird. 'OK,' Caz said.

She came out with the telephone number and her bum-bag. Caz had already said they should skip the meal but a drink in the Pool Bar would be fine. The bum-bag was so she'd have money of her own. One thing a sensible girl never did was to let the guy buy more than one drink.

She had left her door open and she saw Platt look up and deep into the room. 'Oh,' she said. 'Do you want to use my phone?'

He made a little grateful gasp. 'This would be all right?'

'Sure,' Caz said. She swallowed a grin. 'But I'll stay out here so you won't be compromised.'

Platt nodded, missing it. 'You are very kind, Caz. I wish I had know you more earlier, we could have—'

'The Pool Bar's open . . .' she said.

'Oh, yes. I am sorry. Please excuse me.'

Platt went in, straight to the phone, dialled quickly, then began to speak in soft quick Spanish. Then it seemed as if someone was asking him to hold. He had his hand over the mouthpiece and was signing to Caz, 'I have to wait . . .'

Caz waited, smiling, wondering how Tom MacInnes was getting on with his investigation. Inside the room, Platt was very comfortable, nodding and speaking quickly to the other end. Outside, Caz was poking her toe around half-heartedly in the gravel garden where flecks of suspicious orange lingered, missed by the cats. Then louder, she heard 'Si! Si! Muchas gracias!' and then Edward Platt put down the phone. As he emerged, she grinned to herself and then smiled at him.

'And they say you can see the birds?' she asked, looking at his broad smile.

'You know this?' Platt said.

'Because you are smiling,' Caz said.

'Ah!' Platt said, suddenly understanding her. 'You are so kind. I am a little sad you cannot let me have you lunch. I would be nice to do.'

'When did they say you could go?'

'Today in three hours. Someone will meet me where is the restaurant in the Fire Mountains at fifteen hun'red hour and take me there.'

'Where?'

'To see the birds, alimoché.'

'You are very lucky, Edward.'

'Only a little. But I would be very lucky if you would let me pay for you lunch, some wine. This would be very lucky. And saying thank you to you, this would be right too.'

She shrugged. 'Yes, but . . .'

'A special meal?' he said quickly. 'Cooked from the fires of the earth. Your word is barbecue-grill?'

'You mean actually in the Fire Mountains?'

'You know this restaurant?'

'Yes, of course, but it is very expensive.'

'It is nothing. Money only. You will let me say thank you. I

379

also have the company of a pretty woman. This is not bad.'

'When you put it like that . . .'

He beamed. 'You will let me?'

Caz smiled. 'OK, but if it's that restaurant I'll need to change. Can I meet you in fifteen minutes?'

'Of course,' Platt said.

'Outside the sports shop, then?' She glanced at her watch. 'Shall we say at ten minutes past twelve?'

'OK!' he said, very loudly. His gesture was very German. In shoes his heels would have clicked together. As soon as he had nodded formally he turned and walked sharply away.

Caz had seventeen, eighteen minutes, hardly enough time.

One hundred and twenty-six

When Caz emerged from her room she was no longer in shorts and top but in light khaki cotton bags and a soft, green-silk open-necked shirt. Instead of running socks, now she was barefoot and instead of trainers she wore a delicate pair of shiny silk slippers, a gift from a friend who had been to Thailand.

She got to the sports shop one minute before opening time and was first in as the door was unlocked. Her conversation with the manager was very brief, his response mostly spread hands accompanying a shaking head. But Caz had one direct hit, after a pointed question, an 'Ah, yes! This I remember' from him and a head-nod before an offer to check his credit-card returns.

'No,' Caz said, looking out anxiously. 'You've told me enough.'

She nipped quickly out, went to her room, glanced in to check, and left to walk back to the square and Edward Platt.

One hundred and twenty-seven

Edward had changed too and, as she hurried towards him, she saw a thin but muscled small man in an expensive denim shirt and jeans, a thick brown leather belt pulled in to what she reckoned was a twenty-eight-inch waist. He was wearing tan leather shoes and carrying a small black attaché case, slightly larger than a briefcase.

'Ah, Caz!' he said brightly, glancing up and down her appreciatively. 'You are only one minute late! Like a lady, only just so!'

Caz looked past him at the shop manager who raised his eyebrows, then at Edward. 'You must tell me again how you will get back.'

They were walking through the complex towards reception.

'Robert has said that I will be dropped back at the main gates to the *Parque Nacionale*. There I will leave my car. I can be back here in only half of one hour. This is excellent.'

'And I come back by taxi?'

'Yes, is this not good? From the restaurant. I did not ask for you to come again to see the birds but perhaps if we ask once more?'

'No, there wouldn't be room in the hide.'

'You are right, Caz.'

'And anyway,' Caz said. 'Y'seen one scruffy vulture y've seen 'em all.'

As they entered the reception, they bumped into Otto and Arnold, another biker-Dane, bass-guitarist in the Green Team group and even bigger than Otto. They were pushing a pair of very expensive looking racing bikes and clacking on the tiled floor in metal-bottomed cycle shoes. Otto winked at Caz and she felt a little tweak of excitement. She couldn't help it when she said, 'Tonight, Otto. Only one or two drinks. Then we go to the disco, and *after* . . .'

Otto must have said, 'OK! Fuh!' but the pair were already clip-clapping out the door, as if in some great hurry.

Behind the counter, Blodwen was busy with something. Then she looked up to see Caz and said, 'Oh, hi-yah, buttee! There's some mail in yer pigeon, did you know?' Caz didn't, but excused herself to Edward for a minute, walked over, waited a few odd seconds for Blodwen and then took a couple of envelopes.

Edward was waiting placidly but watching. She looked across, then tapped her wrist-watch with the letters, a question. Edward nodded with a tight smile and looked at his own watch. Caz quickly opened the first envelope, read. Then she said something, a quick joke to Blodwen who laughed. The second envelope, from England, she left till later.

'Right!' she said to Edward as she turned. 'I'm all yours, now!'

Platt was smiling. He seemed a perfect gentleman. Saying something softly in his own language, he gestured Caz out through the door.

One hundred and twenty-eight

It was an 1812 cannon-blasting high-noon when they stepped out, the sun white-hot above them, no shade at all, the breeze minimal. Platt told Caz that his car was just over the road, a Renault 19 he had hired his second day on site.

'I waste some money really. I do not use the car much. But maybe some evening I go to la Santa for some fish or perhaps one afternoon I go to see a client, then . . .'

'The grey one, is it?' Caz said.

They walked past a couple of four-by-fours and another of the viral Clios and stopped at Platt's car.

'Could I sit in a moment?' Caz said, meaning the driver's side. 'I've always fancied one of these. Seen the ads on TV.' She play-acted. 'Papa? Nicole?'

Platt leaned past her to unkey the door. 'Please . . .'

Caz slipped in and behind the steering wheel, thanking Edward who walked round to the passenger's side. As he sat in himself she said, 'I don't suppose I could drive, could I?'

Platt showed the first signs of displeasure. 'But the insurance . . .'

'Not a problem!' Caz said brightly. 'This is a la Santa Sport car and I'm staff. It's OK.'

He looked vaguely miffed. 'We can go now if we do this?'

Caz slammed her door with a flourish and made a show of

384

moving her hands up and down on the wheel, then adjusting her seat.

'Great!' she said, and put her open hand out for the keys. Platt dropped them into her palm and clunk-clunked his case open, glancing inside very quickly before shutting it.

'Please,' he said. 'Lunch . . .?'

'No problem!' Caz said and started the Renault.

One hundred and twenty-nine

Caz took it slowly as they pulled out of the car park and down the hill. She remembered loosely the Renault Clio that had waited for her the day she went running.

'It's very smooth,' she said as they trundled on the concrete towards the village. 'Very easy to drive.'

'Yes,' Platt said, 'and it can go quite fast too.'

At the top of the hill to Tinajo, Caz swung right following the signs for *Montana del Fuego*. The lads on their racers must have been working hard because they were still ahead.

They broke out on to open road, long and narrow, looping away into the distance. There were small walls both sides, and circular wind-break enclosures spotted the lined rectangular fields of black and brown. Green onion shoots spattered up from the grit like machine gun puffs in the earth. Ahead now they could see cyclists working hard.

Caz began to speak blankly, strangely, staring ahead. 'My Inspector, my *ex*-Inspector, thinks that by tonight he will have the man who caused the death of Kevin King.'

'Kevin King?'

'He drowned one night.'

'Ah, yes. He was a runner.'

'Ina liked him.'

'I think I know this.'

They were approaching the bikers. There were four of them. It looked like Otto and Arnold had worked very hard to catch up to the group.

'Green Teamers!' Caz said. 'They're the two guys we saw in reception.'

She heard the clunk of Platt's briefcase.

'And MacInnes says that the creep who killed Kevin must have killed the German guy last year and the Englishman, the man from London.'

'Colin Jones.'

'That's right, Edward.'

She swung round the four bikes. There was another group of five or six two hundred metres ahead.

'He was a swimmer, that one, but not a fish.'

Caz tooted the horn. 'And a friend of Ina.'

The briefcase lid came up.

'They all were. All were.'

'But not as good a friend as you, eh, Edward? You were her protector. You protected Ina, didn't you?'

The car was slowing. Ahead, one of the bikers looked to have a flat. Otto and the others were close behind.

'I had worked everything out, Edward. Everything. I had worked out how Eric Ortollo had been here for almost every accident. I had worked out that he had slipped back on to the island for the other times. I had guessed, but did not know, that he persuaded Giuseppe Castellano to help him, bring him into the site in his van, hide him in the submarine.'

They had stopped now, bikes and bikers in front of them and behind.

'I knew it *all*, Edward. I could see Eric. I could see him, Edward, see him sneaking through the night, silent, burning with jealousy, determined that anyone, anyone who got near to his beloved Ina would suffer. I knew exactly how it had been done.'

Otto had stepped off his bike and was tapping the window.

'That's Otto,' Caz said. 'He was a good friend of Kevin King.'

Platt wound the window down, strangely calm.

'You see, Edward,' Caz said. She was still staring ahead. The other cyclists had lain down their bikes. 'You see, I had almost everything worked out. I understood the motive, jealousy, possession, possessiveness. I knew why these guys had been hurt, why Eric had felt the need to kill.'

'Hello, Edward,' Otto said.

'The one thing I'd got wrong was the *man*. I'd got everything right but I had the wrong man. And do you know *why*, Edward? Do you know *why* I had the wrong man?'

'Because you are stupid?'

'No, Edward, because I was jealous. I was jealous too.'

'Hah!'

'You see, Edward, I did not like Eric, and Ina was closer to Eric than me. You see, Edward, I *understand*, I understand what you did, why you did what you did.'

'You know nothing.'

'But I think I know *you*, Edward. You stalk. And, Edward, I know that you lie. I know you cheat. And I know you had no intention of taking me to lunch today, that you were no more interested in the *alimoché* than I am in ever seeing you again.'

'Do you want to get out of the car, Mr Platt?' Otto said.

'Nothing. There is nothing you can know.'

'But you rang the museum at los Jameos del Agua, didn't you? I gave you the number?'

'Yes.'

'And they arranged for you to meet one of the park rangers.'

'So?'

'But the number, Edward. I gave you the telephone number of police headquarters in Arrecife. I presume you did not ring it at all?'

'But . . .?'

'If you had rung the number . . .? It was a mistake. I'd simply given you the wrong piece of paper.'

Otto's face was no longer bland. 'Please, get out of the car.'

Platt glanced his way. He seemed to give in.

As he went to get out of the car, Caz asked about Matthew Black.

'What is it that you want to know?'

'He fell. Did you push him?'

'Do you think I pushed him?'

'You were there, Edward. I think, perhaps. But my Inspector will think it is someone else. It might be someone else, someone else who had a reason to be on the roof. Another man.'

'You have made one more mistake. It was not a man.'

The door was open now. He looked back. 'I think you should say Mister Black fell.'

'And you helped him?'

'I did not.'

'Then . . .?'

'You say it yourself. Someone else who was on the roof.'

Otto growled for Platt to get out of the car.

'*No, Otto, wait!*' Caz said. 'Edward, were you on the roof?'

'I go there. Maybe I think I can help this man Matthew Black to fall. Always he lies on the wall for sunshine . . .' He paused. 'This I would have liked, but instead he has a real accident, some justice.'

'I don't . . .'

'He has surprised a lady with no clothes. She is angry and she throws something. When Matthew Black ducks he slips from the wall.'

Caz spoke slowly. 'Who was it, Ute?'

For the first time, she looked at his face. He had turned, almost out of the car. He stared, waiting for her to guess.

'Ina? Was it Ina?'

He smiled, his eyes peculiar.

Caz should have realised. If this was Ina, was Ina . . .

Edward Platt would only smile.

One hundred and thirty

Caz pulled the key from the ignition, and was looking out and forward when Edward finally stepped out of the car. She was vaguely aware that he still had his attaché case on his lap and that he was bundling out, slightly awkwardly. Then he or Otto grunted something and she turned, the key now in her hand. Otto had stepped back slightly, his controlled anger making way for what seemed like perverse politeness, and then, just then, Platt dropped the case, the contents spilling.

She saw only the back of the Belgian and then his raised arm, and then a shout, something Danish and 'Fuh!' as Otto jumped backwards and fell down. And then, stupidly, stupidly, Platt was gone, over a wall and running across a field of onions towards the sea.

'Oh, Jesus!' she said.

She had been slow to realise. She was pitifully slow emerging from the car. Two of the guys were jumping over the wall now and running hard, chasing after Platt across the field; another was helping Arnold with Otto. The rest were picking up their bikes, slightly lost before deciding which way to ride to cut off Platt when he finally reached a road.

Caz was making decisions. She shouted to Arnold. 'Is Otto all right?'

Arnold nodded.

She jumped the wall, and when she landed she was two

hundred yards behind the two Greenies, another two hundred yards behind Platt. As soon as she started running, she looked at their style. Neither of them was going to catch him.

As she ran, trying to get the pace exactly right, she thought about specific fitness. These guys were bikers, but Platt biked *and* ran. He was small and wiry and had developed his running muscles. The two guys she was already gaining on were super-fit but not running fit. If they'd known anything at all about what it would take, they wouldn't have set off across the black field.

Far over to her right she could see a road that swung up towards the mountain directly ahead of Platt. Four bikes could be seen going that way, their colours flashing. She had to bet that Platt would turn away as soon as he saw them and she turned herself, diagonally, embarrassed now that her short-cut meant she was treading on onion shoots instead of running in lane. The two Greenies, pumped up but tired already, were taking the straight line shortest route to the Belgian, focused on his back but nowhere near close enough to seriously imagine catching him.

'Ignore it!' she told herself. 'Ignore him! More than one way to skin a cat! More than one way to catch a fox!'

She was heading for the far corner of the huge field. Platt was now at one edge and, yes! He had seen the posse on their bikes and was turning, away from the road and towards the same corner as Caz. He would see her in maybe twenty seconds. In his hand he had something; something like a short stubby car aerial.

Back to her right she saw one of the lads stop, heave, then start again, jogging, desperate to recover. Ahead of him the other Greenie was also faltering. 'But I'm not, you evil fuck!' she said. She was well within herself, five-miling for economy not hero-sprinting for effect.

And now Platt saw her. He was breathing heavily but trying

to pace it, trying to get to the corner first and over into the scattered rock, the faint edge of the lava fields, the foot-start of the Fire Mountains. They were eye-on-eye for seconds and Caz knew he'd be there first. Then she realised that she was running barefoot, her gold slippers long since forsaken. This was the first time she felt the pain. She didn't look down.

Platt was at the corner. He stopped and climbed the wall, waving the funny wire-stick in his hand and taking the few seconds to stand higher, look around and take in the enemy. It was obvious that he was discounting Caz and that he had figured that all he had to do was get away from the roads.

One hundred and thirty-one

When Caz reached the wall she hurdled on to it, now just getting truly into her stride. The peculiar, moving black gravel of the field would have been hard on ordinary legs but back in Brighton, Caz had trained on the shingle of the beach every other day. The man she was chasing hadn't. She figured she had to be less tired than him.

The Belgian was maybe a hundred yards ahead of her now, running between the rocks on what looked suspiciously like a man-made track, S-curving both ways between jagged black lava splashes. Her feet hurt like hell. She was praying that Platt would stay off that lava.

On each bend, for a second, Platt was disappearing, then she was rounding the bend herself just in time to see him striding round the next. It occurred to her that on one of the turns the Belgian might stop to ambush her and she readied herself for the possibility, going wide on the curves, forcing him, if he did try, to cross a few extra yards.

But each time, each corner, there he was again, frightened, running, running, making himself keep going but now in real pain like a novice in a 10K who had started off far too fast.

Caz could catch him whenever she wanted.

But she chose not to. Instead, she kept her distance, her cool. Like a Masai warrior jogging, chasing the antelope until it dropped, she kept hounding, stalking, harrying the Belgian, close enough to see him, far enough away that he thought he had a chance. She was torturing him and she wanted this to last.

Again he turned, ducking away from her view. Again she rounded a bend and caught sight of him. The road was climbing now – she'd only just noticed – and they were high up to the right of a plain, a sea of spiked black, and something familiar in front of her, red-grey grit-like sand. She felt *déjà vu*.

Then, quite suddenly, Edward Platt stopped. He was small, not a six-foot man, and it was hot, not an English April, but Caz was on Brighton Beach again, facing the man who had hurt Moira. She shook her head. Platt was desperately sucking in air with a look of total hatred deep in wet eyes.

'I must hurt you,' he said.

'With that thing?' Caz said. He was gasping, she was not.

'It is for cattle,' he said, waving the orange coated metal. 'For cattle it is painful; for you, enough to shock you, make you fall down.' He heaved again.

They were twenty feet apart. Platt looked weak.

'You are a little shit-fuck,' Caz said. 'A fucking sick little shit-fuck poison dwarf. I doubt if you could even lift that thing.'

'Is a cattle-prod,' Platt said. He turned something in the handle. 'Enough, I want, to kill you. Knock you down is easy.'

'If you land one,' Caz said. Above her something moved, wings high in a circle. Platt raised his arm.

'Your *alimoché*,' Caz said. 'Who'd've thought, eh?' Then she saw the hide, and someone moving, coming out. She grinned unkindly. 'Well, hey, what d'yer know? It looks like the cavalry are here!'

One hundred and thirty-two

Platt only glanced for two half-seconds, first up at the disturbed bird, then at the hide's emerging man. But in that second, Caz was on him, crashing into him, knocking him down, taking the cattle-prod from him as he fell, feeling its weight in her hand and holding it triumphantly.

She could feel the sun high above them both. She glanced at the odd weapon in her hand.

Platt looked up and began to get up, hate in his face but resigned.

'Damn!' Caz said. 'You're going to attack me!'

She put her arm out, touched him with the stick. Pressed a button.

Platt fell down.

Then she sat beside him, looked at her bloody feet, leaned out and zapped him again. This time she saw his body jerk. She was thinking about Kevin King when she shocked him the third time.

One hundred and thirty-three

Hank Carry drove Caz back to la Santa. They took the route towards Tinajo looking for the others and found two of them, cruising on their bikes, still searching for the Belgian. Caz put the pair of them straight and they went off to round up the rest of the gang.

It was very late in the afternoon. Earlier, Hank and a quiet islander called Pepe had taken Edward Platt's body as far as the road, then Hank and Caz had waited for the first police cars and an ambulance to turn up. They knew it already, but Edward Platt had been confirmed dead five minutes before DI MacInnes arrived.

A sullen police motor-cyclist had waited with Caz, she under a loose arrest while they waited for senior officers to arrive, someone who could speak decent English. The DI arrived with these. He was flushed, suddenly old, and terribly disappointed in his detective.

Pepe had gone back to the hide, then returned with a first-aid kit. Silent, he had washed Caz's bloody feet, sterilized them, then bandaged them. They had shared a deep, deep-brown-eyed understanding and the man had nodded to her in wordless respect as he finished. She too had been quiet, deep in thought, primitively satisfied, but dark and empty, as time and again behind her eyes she saw Edward Platt's body jerk under her touch.

Eventually, Tom MacInnes had gone to sit with Caz. Hank Carry had walked quietly off. The two detectives had spoken together in a formal way, slowly, deliberately, the older man offering routes for the woman to take, decisions that only she could make. After a while he stood up, content, walked to where the other policemen waited and addressed them. Minutes later, the most senior man came over to her squatting figure, took her arm at the elbow and helped her up. Then the other policemen came to her, nodding, smiling. One said '*Valiente,*' another, '*Denodado*' and then the first policeman said, 'They love you, Caz Flude. They are saying how brave you have been.'

Hank knew better than to stay, but he walked with Caz into reception, held her close for a while and then said his goodbye. Before he left, he asked at the counter for Blodwen and someone said they thought she was round the other side, in one of the bars. He grinned vaguely at Caz and disappeared to find her. Caz went to her room to shower.

When she was dressed, she came down to find the others. She found them all, still there in the Pool Bar. They had taken over the covered part and a dozen white plastic tables had been pushed together into a huge rectangle. It was surrounded by bronzed faces, mostly blonde hair, the bikers, and a subdued Otto.

Blodwen was there and Hank was still there, and Ute, but very quiet. Ina and Eric were there too, very together. She went first to them, took Ina's hand and squeezed it into a fist which she kissed. Then, still holding Ina's hand, she kissed Eric on his cheek.

The tables were covered with drinks, bottles of *El Grifo*, tall glasses, various boozes, Coke and ice. Someone had ordered pizzas and they began arriving, the waiters grinning caught up in the party spirit as they tip-toed round everyone in their light green shirts. Caz decided she was hungry and ordered a *Timanfaya* special.

While she waited for her food, Caz went to Ute. She crouched down beside her and promised her that she would do what she could about Marco. It wasn't impossible that they could get the two Brits off if they were prepared to leave the island.

Then she went to Otto and whispered. He grinned and made to speak but she put two fingers to his lips. She whispered a last time, making his face drop slightly. Then she went to the bar and paid for four bottles of wine.

After eating her pizza, she went to her room, poured a glass of wine and sat down with the telephone. When Moira answered her first call she asked about the baby. Everything was fine.

'Then tell your bloody Sergeant, Moira,' Caz said, 'anything happens to that kid now, I'm first in the queue with a baseball bat.'

'Already done,' Moira said. 'You home soon?'

'Coupla days,' Caz said. 'Soon as I can get a flight.'

'I had a scan,' Moira said quickly. 'Guess what?'

'It's a boy,' Caz said. 'You're going to call him Timothy.'

'How d'you know that?'

Moira couldn't see Caz's smile.

'You wouldn't understand, Mo'. Best not to ask.'

'Oh,' Moira said.

They said their goodbyes.

Valerie wasn't at home. She tried him on his direct line at American Express and found him.

'It's me,' she said.

'Caz.'

'I wanted to tell you some things.'

'OK,' he said. 'Are we still getting married?'

'I'm easy,' she said. 'But I wanted to tell you something.'

'I'm listening.'

She took a swig of her wine.

'I killed a bloke this afternoon, Val.'

There was silence at the other end.

'Valerie? Did you hear me?'

He spoke a little slower. The line crackled.

'I thought you said you'd killed someone.'

'I did, Val. I chased a bloke who'd killed four people. I chased him in my bare feet for about three miles. When I caught up with him, I killed him. Then I came back here and had a pizza.'

'Are you all right?'

'I feel great, actually, Val. I feel like celebrating. And Moira's fine. Did you know Moira's going to be all right?'

'What!'

'Moira, the baby's fine. It's a boy.'

'Caz . . .'

'What's up, Val?'

'Caz . . .'

'Are you gonna ask me again about getting married?'

'Caz . . .'

'Only I think it's a great idea. Y'see if I ever kill anyone else, I'd like someone I could tell . . .'

'You're drunk, aren't you?'

'I've had two glasses of wine.'

'Well, what's all this about then? You know I want to marry you.'

'I want you to wonder how I am, Val. I killed someone today. I want you to be worried.'

'I am worried.'

'Then why don't I feel it?'

'I can't answer that, Caz.'

'So when are we getting married?'

'We'll talk about it when you get back.'
'And no kids.'
'When you get back, Caz.'
'Say you love me, then.'
Silence.
'Say you love me, then.'
'When you get back.'
She put down the phone.

One hundred and thirty-four

Caz dabbed a touch of 'Paris' behind each ear.

She got up, looked at her room, then left and walked round to Tom MacInnes' apartment. Before she knocked, she took a deep breath. He didn't answer. She knocked again.

'It's not locked, Flood,' he said. She could hear the drink.

She opened the door and went in. There were two glasses out and Tom's bed was turned down. She closed the door behind her.

'So,' she said. 'You're going to tell me what I did wrong?'

He half-filled her glass and passed her a bottle of Canadian Dry.

Caz smiled. Most people would have thought it a nice smile. 'OK if I sit on the bed?' she said.

Epilogue, Gatwick Airport

Valerie was the other side of customs waiting for her. This time he had made sure. Caz came out with Hank Carry, laughing like a drain at his latest, utterly filthy joke.

This was swapped roles. Caz remembered a rush of her own jealousy once when Val had wandered out just like this, pushing a trolley for some too-smart lady called Mariella. That had been innocent too.

'Who's this?' Val said as he leaned to peck her.

'Name's Harry,' Hank said, the voice deeper than Val's.

'And?'

'And what?' Hank said.

Caz's eyes said the rest.

They walked across the marbled concourse, through the crowds and into space.

'My lift's late,' Hank said, looking into the distance.

'We'll wait with you,' Caz said. 'Fancy a drink?'

'Why not?' Hank said. Then he said, 'Ah, Peter!'

A man came over. Tall as Hank but slight, with blond, light hair, a pink face, and as he came close, ice-blue poet's eyes.

'Cheese!' he said and kissed Hank lightly, very briefly. Valerie was almost leaning backwards. 'And?' he added.

Hank introduced them to Peter. He shook Caz's hand, touched Val's.

'So,' Hank said, 'we can have that drink now, yeah?'

Valerie made a negative mumble.

'Too right!' Caz said.

They went home easily in Val's Daimler 250. He struggled to speak but managed to ask after her DI. Caz stuttered then said, 'An earlier plane. He came on an earlier plane.'

'And everything's OK. You solved the case?'

'Tom did, yeah.'

It was dark now. England. Lights.

'Can we stop for a drink?' Caz said. 'Take a walk or something?'

'You don't want to go straight home?' Val said.

'No,' she said. She wasn't ready to go home. She was remembering.

Tom had shaved, showered. Caz had drunk a strong Whyte & MacKay, sitting on his bed. He was so thin. She wondered what it would be like. When she spoke, she was quieter than she'd expected. Tom had sighed. He had said he would tell her where she went wrong. He said, as well, that the young man, Matthew Black was no better, no worse, and that Veronica Goddard could come out of hospital as soon as she had found somewhere to stay.

As he'd spoken, Caz had tried to imagine him twenty-five years ago.

'Platt sold farming equipment, Flood. Here, in Spain, other parts of the continent. There were a couple of suspicious deaths at a sports place in Portugal. He had stayed there.

'We checked the airlines, straightforward but not instant, and yes, he was on the island for every accident. And we

404

checked, he had fluent Spanish, knew the dialect here, spoke Portuguese and French.

'And we searched Giuseppe Castellano's farm. We went back because there had to be something there.'

'Was there?'

'Yes, but it was well-hidden. First time it wasn't found.'

There was paper on the table. 'Take a look for yourself.'

Caz picked it up. Handwriting, childish, Spanish.

'I can't read it.'

'But you know what it says.'

'I do?'

'You do.'

'That Giuseppe helped Edward Platt, what, for money?'

'And fear. Platt frightened him.'

'So what did I do wrong?' Caz said.

'What? Everything! You let your personal beliefs cloud your judgement, kept secrets from me, your DI, your friend, and then, this last afternoon, you went off playing Cowboys and Indians like some divvy from the Sweeney. It wasn't necessary.'

'I'd just . . . well, I'd been in the wrong, and . . .'

'You jumped the gun, Caz. You took risks. Not just for yourself but with some of the people who helped you. It wasn't impossible that Platt might have got away. He has a boat on the south coast.'

'I felt bad, Tom. And I was angry at you. You don't have to tell me I was stupid.'

'I do, Caz. I do. I have to tell you *how* stupid. The job . . .'

Caz was pouring a thick drink, her hands shook.

'DC Flood. You have let me down. I am disappointed in you.'

It felt like a knife going in.

He reached into his shirt pocket and pulled out paper sheets.

'Ah've two copies o' this,' he said, separating them. 'You can have one.'

'What is it?' she said.

'It's Giuseppe Castellano's goodbye, Caz. A translation.' He paused. 'With the money, it would have been more than enough, to convict Edward Platt.'

He turned his whisky glass in his fingers. Then he said slowly, 'What you did, Caz, you didn't need to do. It was a mistake.'

There was nothing in his voice. She looked down, something close to panic rising in her chest. For a second she thought she might be sick. Then she heard him again, more deliberate this time.

'It was a mistake. A man died. A very unfortunate accident.'

She could feel her throat pulsing. His voice was far off.

'Tell me it was an accident,' he said.

She was staring at the floor. To answer, she had to look up. Her head felt heavy. She looked coldly at him. When she saw his eyes they were empty, dark with disappointment.

He said it again. 'Tell me it was an accident, detective.'

There was only flatness in his voice but it sounded distant like the echo of a lover walking away. Caz felt like crying but then, when she made herself look at him, into his face, he wavered, another look there. The feeling went. For a second she thought she was stronger than him.

'Of course, sir,' she said. 'It was an accident. A tragedy.'

'Aye,' he said. 'A terrible tragedy.'

'Is that it?' she said.

He poured himself another whisky, looked at it, at her. Still the eyes were empty.

'I'm sorry, Tom, I was . . .'

'Stupid, Caz, ah know. But we all have t'do stupid sometimes. Like ah've bin stupid tonight, lettin' you come here t'see me.'